The Other Bennet Sister

'[A] novel that will delight *Pride and Prejudice* fans'
Independent

'Janice Hadlow has dusted down Mary, the ugly Bennet sister, and fashioned her into a heroine that even Miss Austen would approve of. A treat'
Daisy Goodwin, author of *Victoria* and *The Fortune Hunter*

'Immersive and engaging'
Guardian

'It's difficult not to race through those final pages'
Jo Baker, author of *Longbourn* and *The Body Lies*

'This gorgeous book pays homage to *Pride and Prejudice* – and follows Mary Bennet, the overlooked middle Bennet sister. It's a wonderfully warm, comforting read – perfect on a winter's night'
Sun

'I absolutely love this novel – as will any young woman who has felt herself plain, shy, bookish and crushed'
Amanda Craig, author of *The Lie of the Land* and *The Golden Rule*

Janice Hadlow was born in London and studied history at university. After a few years working for the House of Commons, she joined the BBC and became a television producer. She was the recipient of a number of awards, and is a Fellow of the Royal Television Society, as well as of King's College, University of London.

The Other Bennet Sister is her first novel. She currently lives in Edinburgh with her husband and has two sons.

Janice Hadlow

The Other Bennet Sister

PAN BOOKS

First published 2020 by Mantle

This paperback edition first published 2020 by Pan Books
an imprint of Pan Macmillan
The Smithson, 6 Briset Street, London EC1M 5NR
Associated companies throughout the world
www.panmacmillan.com

ISBN 978-1-5098-4204-9

1 3 5 7 9 8 6 4 2

A CIP catalogue record for this book is available from the British Library.

Typeset in Sabon by Jouve (UK), Milton Keynes
Printed and bound by CPI Group (UK) Ltd, Croydon, CR0 4YY

Visit www.panmacmillan.com to read more about all our books
and to buy them. You will also find features, author interviews and
news of any author events, and you can sign up for e-newsletters
so that you're always first to hear about our new releases.

For Martin, Alexander and Louis,
My three bright shining stars

PART ONE

CHAPTER ONE

It is a sad fact of life that if a young woman is unlucky enough to come into the world without expectations, she had better do all she can to ensure she is born beautiful. To be poor and handsome is misfortune enough; but to be penniless and plain is a hard fate indeed.

Four of the five Bennet sisters of Meryton in Hertfordshire had sensibly provided themselves with good looks enough to be accounted beauties in the limited circles in which they moved. Jane, the eldest, was the most striking, the charms of her face and figure enhanced by the unassuming modesty of her character. Elizabeth, the second sister, made up in wit and liveliness for any small deficiencies in her appearance; while Catherine and Lydia, the two youngest, exhibited all the freshness of youth, accompanied by a taste for laughter and flirtation, which recommended them greatly to young men of equally loud and undiscriminating inclinations. Only Mary, the middle daughter, possessed neither beauty, wit, nor charm; but her sisters shone so brightly that they seemed to cancel out her failure and, indeed, eclipse her presence altogether, so that by the time they were grown, the Bennet family was as regarded as one of the most pleasing in the neighbourhood.

It was common knowledge, however, that the Bennet girls' prospects were to be envied a great deal less than their beauty. At first sight, the family appeared prosperous enough. They were the principal inhabitants of the village of Longbourn; and their house, solid and unremarkable as it was, made up in comfort what it lacked in pretension. There were servants to wait at table, a cook in the kitchen, and a man to tend the gardens; and though Mr Bennet's possessions were not extensive, they were quite enough to sustain his credit as a private gentleman. Few of the families with whom they were intimate were sufficiently rich or genteel to condescend to them with confidence, and the Bennets were regarded, in public at least, as eminently respectable ornaments to Hertfordshire society.

But in the country, no family's business is ever truly its own, and everyone knew that the outward prosperity of the Bennets rested on very uncertain foundations. Their property was subject to an entail which restricted inheritance to male heirs; if no Bennet son was produced, the estate would pass eventually into the hands of Mr Bennet's cousin. At first, this had seemed of little significance. As baby after baby arrived at Longbourn with promising regularity, surely, it was only a matter of time before the much-anticipated Bennet boy put in his overdue appearance. But when the tally of girls reached five, and it was clear no more children could be expected, the entail cast a deepening shadow over the family's happiness. On Mr Bennet's death, his widow and daughters would be left with nothing but five thousand pounds in the four per cents, and a humiliating reliance on the uncertain charity of a distant and unknown relative. Their friends were not without sympathy for the Bennets' plight, but that did nothing to dampen their curiosity about what was to come, for what could be more compelling than to watch at first hand the probable wreck and dissolution of an entire family's fortune?

Mr Bennet refused to gratify his neighbours by displaying

any obvious disappointment at the cruel trick of fate which had deprived his dependants of the security he had once so confidently expected them to enjoy. To the world at large, he remained what he had always been: detached, amused, and apparently resigned to an outcome it was not in his power to change. To his family themselves, he seemed barely more concerned. Perhaps in the long hours he spent in his library, he wrestled with himself to find an answer to their plight. If so, he shared neither his anxieties nor his conclusions with them.

His wife, however, had none of his restraint. Mrs Bennet thought of little else but the hardships which lay in store for herself and her daughters when Mr Bennet was dead, and she was often to be heard lamenting the wickedness of the entail, both at home and abroad. Her nerves, she declared, were not equal to the strain placed upon them by such an unfortunate business. How anyone could have had the conscience to entail away an estate from their daughters she did not profess to understand; but unless something was done about it, ruin must engulf them all. She was a woman of no great intelligence and small imagination, but she possessed considerable powers of energy and application, which she devoted with all the tenacity at her command to finding a solution to their predicament. She was soon persuaded that there was only one answer to the miserable situation in which her girls were placed: they must marry, as quickly and as advantageously as possible. If their father could not secure his daughters' futures, they must look to a husband to do so.

To have seen her daughters married to men of merely respectable means would have soothed away many of Mrs Bennet's fears; but to imagine them united to husbands of ample income and substantial property was for her a joy undimmed by frequent contemplation. Nothing made her happier than to think of them in possession of elegant houses and rolling parkland, certain of never hearing the dreaded word *entail* again. She was aware, of course, that wealthy men in want of wives were not easy to find and harder still to catch, especially by girls without large dowries. But she was undaunted. Her daughters, she believed, possessed an advantage that would enable them to triumph over all difficulties: other girls might be rich, but her daughters were beautiful. This, she was sure, was the blessing that would deliver them into wealth. Their looks would attract men of the first eligibility, dazzling their eyes, winning their hearts, and persuading them to ignore the promptings of cold, mercenary common sense. It was for Mrs Bennet an article of faith that, in the absence of ten thousand pounds in the hand, a pretty face was the single most valuable asset a young woman could possess.

Her own experience confirmed her opinion, for, some twenty-five years before, it had been Mrs Bennet's youthful beauty which had swept a besotted Mr Bennet to the altar, overcoming all obstacles that appeared to stand in the way of their union. As he gazed on her handsome face, it had meant nothing to him that her father was merely a country attorney who kept an office in Meryton, or that her brother lived within sight of his own warehouses in Cheapside. He had been determined to marry her, and against all advice to the contrary, he had done so. On the whole, Mrs Bennet considered herself well satisfied with the outcome. It was true that Mr Bennet was a whimsical man who teased her more than she thought proper. But as mistress of Longbourn, she presided over a property large enough to gratify her vanity, while her husband's rank assured her the pleasure of patronising her less-fortunate acquaintances on every possible occasion. For Mr Bennet, however, the benefits of his marriage were far less apparent. His failure to consider whether his spouse's character was likely to bring him as much pleasure as her appearance had more serious and lasting consequences. The shallowness of Mrs Bennet's mind, and the limited nature of her interests, meant theirs could never be a partnership of equals. She could be neither his companion nor his friend. Her beauty had been enough to win him, but, as Mr Bennet soon understood, it was not enough to make him happy.

Fortunately for Mrs Bennet, she was not a reflective woman, and if her husband now regretted the principles on which he had made his choice of a wife, she remained oblivious of this fact. As a result, her prejudices survived unchallenged. She esteemed no qualities of female character other than beauty. Wit and intellect, kindness and good humour mattered not at all to her. Good looks trumped every other attribute. In her daughters, she valued nothing so much as their power to please.

With four of her girls, Mrs Bennet had, in this respect, every reason to be satisfied. Of Jane she entertained the highest possible hopes, for, as she frequently observed to Mr Bennet, she could not have been born so beautiful for nothing. Three further sisters, if not quite as generously blessed as Jane, were still, in Mrs Bennet's opinion, sufficiently distinguished to attract notice wherever they went. Only one of her daughters had failed her. Mary had made the mistake of inheriting neither the looks nor the charm shared by all other female members of the Bennet family. This was a sin for which, in Mrs Bennet's eyes, there could be no forgiveness, as Mary herself had quickly discovered.

CHAPTER TWO

Mary could not remember exactly when she had discovered she was plain. She did not think she had known it when, as a very little girl, she had played happily with Jane and Elizabeth, running round the garden with grass stains on her dress; or when they had huddled together before the nursery fire, warming their feet on the fender. She did not think she had known it when Mrs Hill, her mother's housekeeper, had washed her face every morning and tied a clean pinafore over her dress. She had certainly not known it when she and her elder sisters had rushed into the kitchen on baking days, begging for a crust of warm bread which they would carry away and eat together behind the shrubbery, laughing as if they would never stop. Then, she thought, she had been happy. But by the time she was seven or eight years old, she had begun to suspect something was not quite right. She saw that her mother often looked at her with an expression she did not direct at Jane or Lizzy. It was something between irritation and puzzlement, Mary was not quite sure which, but she came to recognise it very well. A summons always followed.

'Come here, child, and let me look at you.'

Mary would get down from her chair and walk across the drawing room to where Mrs Bennet sat, uneasy under her mother's scrutiny. Her hair ribbons would be tweaked, her sash re-tied, her dress pulled this way and that. But whatever it was that bothered Mrs Bennet, none of her attempts to correct it ever satisfied. She pursed her lips and looked away, frustrated, speechlessly waving her daughter back to her place. Mary knew she had disappointed her mother, even if she did not yet know in what way she had fallen short.

But she was a clever girl, and she soon understood what the sighs and frowns and dismissals meant. She could not help but notice that Mrs Bennet never talked about her appearance with the pleasure with which she described her elder sisters.

'Jane is as lovely as an angel,' her mother often declared, regarding her eldest daughter with transparent pride. 'It is a pleasure just to gaze at her.'

Jane would hang her head, for she was a modest girl, and compliments made her blush. She would not look at Elizabeth, who, when Mrs Bennet's preening grew excessive, would catch her sister's eye and try to make her laugh. Elizabeth's own appearance was not quite so much to her mother's taste as Jane's. Her dark eyes and sparkling smile were too suggestive of her lively character to win Mrs Bennet's wholehearted approval. She was too amused with the world to qualify as a true beauty; but for all her misgivings, Mrs Bennet's appraising eye acknowledged there was something about Lizzy that appealed. While she often scolded her second daughter for the pertness of her remarks and the independence of her spirit, she did not complain of her looks.

As she grew older, Mary waited hopefully for Mrs Bennet to bestow similar words of appreciation upon her. At first, she imagined her mother's approval would come naturally with time, that she would reach an age when she too would bask in her admiration. But even when she paid extra attention to herself, making sure that her stockings were straight, her face was clean, and her hair well brushed, still her mother had no kind word to offer her. Month after month, she waited, anxiously anticipating the moment when Mrs Bennet would find something about her to praise. Perhaps her eyes might be considered fine, or her figure graceful. Perhaps her hair might be her best feature. She did not mind which part of her Mrs Bennet thought worthy of notice; anything would do, as long as it allowed her the chance to take her place amongst her sisters in the glow of their mother's approval.

Mary was ten when she understood this would never happen. It was a warm afternoon. Mrs Bennet was taking tea with her sister, Mrs Phillips. Jane and Lizzy had vanished at the sound of their aunt's arrival, leaving Mary alone, perched on the sofa, twisting the ends of her hair in her hands, wishing desperately to be somewhere else. Neither her mother nor her aunt paid her any attention. Their conversation rambled on, ranging from the likelihood of Lady Lucas's cook leaving her – 'and just before the bottling season too' – to the probability of the vicar's wife being brought to bed this very week; but when Mrs Phillips dropped her voice to a whisper and leaned forward to impart a particularly choice piece of gossip, Mrs Bennet was suddenly alert to her daughter's presence.

'Mary, go down to the kitchen and bring up some more sugar. Take the bowl. Now, please.'

Delighted to be released, Mary lingered as long as she could on her errand, dawdling back along the hall, kicking her shoes against the flagstones to see how much dust she could raise. At the door to the morning room, she stopped to smooth down her dress when, emerging from the low murmur of conversation, she heard her own name pronounced. She knew she should declare herself – Mrs Hill had often told her that listeners never heard good about themselves – but she found it impossible to draw away.

'I think Mary is in better looks today,' remarked Mrs Phillips. 'A little less pale than usual.'

Mrs Bennet sniffed. 'It's kind of you to say so, sister, but I'm afraid I can't agree. For so young a girl, she has no bloom at all. Not like Jane and Lizzy. Their bloom is always very much remarked upon.'

'Indeed, they are very pleasing,' agreed Mrs Phillips obligingly. 'And I doubt that Mary will ever be admired as they are. But, sister, I wonder if you aren't rather harsh in judging her as you do? Perhaps she suffers by comparisons. If Jane and Lizzy were a little less handsome, then she might seem prettier in your eyes?'

'I wish with all my heart you were right, but I'm afraid comparisons don't come into it. Mary is simply very plain, and that's that. I blame Mr Bennet's side of the family. We Gardiners have always been remarkable for our appearance.'

Mrs Phillips topped up her tea and looked for the sugar bowl.

'Well, I'm very sorry for the girl. It cannot be easy to be the only ugly duckling amongst so many swans.'

'Yes, it is a great disappointment to me, and excessively bad for my nerves. But I find that once I look at my other daughters, I soon feel better. Where has she got to with the sugar?'

Mary edged into the room, her eyes on the floor. Her fingers were clenched very tightly round the sugar bowl as she placed it on the table. Her aunt smiled at her, but Mrs Bennet paid no attention as she slipped away. In the hall, her heart beat hard in her chest. She felt her mother's words with as much force as if they had been a blow. So now she knew, she thought, as she walked upstairs. Now she understood. She was plain – like a boiled potato, a length of unbleached calico, a flat white dinner plate. She walked into her bedroom, pulled the chair towards her dressing table and placed her face as close as she could to the little mirror. The glass was old and tarnished but provided enough reflection for Mary to see herself clearly within it. A small face looked back at her, round and pale. Yes, she thought, a dinner plate. Her grey eyes, under light eyebrows, were neither large and blue like Jane's nor dark and clever like Lizzy's. Her features were regular enough, but they were not distinguished. Her mouth was narrow, her lips thin. There was an anxious look about her, she decided. Her face did not suggest, as Lizzy's did, that she might break into laughter at any time. Her hair was a light brown. It was not gold and shining, as Jane's was. There was nothing about her, she concluded, that demanded attention or that would make anyone look upon her with pleasure. Her mother was right; she neither glowed nor bloomed. For a while she stared at the mirror, still hoping to find some bright feature, some hidden asset that might redeem her. When she found nothing, she picked up the shawl that lay hanging on the back of her chair and draped it carefully over the mirror. A single tear trickled down her face which she did not trouble to wipe away.

Mary said nothing to Jane or Lizzy about what she had heard. She supposed they knew already; her plainness now seemed so obvious that she did not know how she had not seen it herself. She did not expect them to show her any sympathy. They would never understand how she felt. How could they? Their beauty was as much a part of them as an arm or a leg – it was impossible for them to imagine life without it. Under its protection, they would leap and spring and dance into their futures; she, on the other hand, would trudge stolidly forward, placing one foot in front of the other without joy or grace. She had learned from Mrs Bennet that without beauty no real and lasting happiness was attainable. It never occurred to her to question what she'd been taught.

She had always been a cautious, watchful girl; now she thought of little else but the poor impression she must make upon those around her. The high spirits that had once inspired her to play and run about with her sisters ebbed away. She no longer had the heart for it. When Jane and Lizzy romped together or raced about the garden, everyone smiled and said they looked charming; but Mary told herself that if she were to do the same, she would appear ridiculous. It did not seem fitting for her to be light-hearted. Seriousness seemed the only quality a plain girl might adopt without exposing herself to the scorn or pity of others. Gradually she became used to it, until she came to believe that it was her nature, that this solemn, solitary, awkward creature was really who she was.

She watched with sadness as Jane and Lizzy drifted steadily away from her. They gave up their attempts to include her, rebuffed by her unhappiness. Mary was not surprised. Of course they preferred each other. How could they not? It was not long before they formed a tight, impregnable partnership, shored up by shared confidences and whispered asides. Mary could hardly believe there had ever been room for another sister in their affections, let alone herself. She bore the loss of Jane philosophically. For all Jane's sweetness, Mary had always found her a remote presence, unknowable behind her perfect face; but the gulf that had opened up between herself and Elizabeth caused her real pain. It was only as they drew apart that Mary realised how much she loved her, how much she had revelled in her lively presence. No one could make you laugh as Lizzy could, tease you into happiness, coax you into smiling at yourself with such easy charm. For a while, Mary clung on to a hope that Lizzy would be the one to save her – that she would recognise her sadness and extend her hand to help her, pulling her out of the pit of misery into which she felt she was slowly sinking. But although Lizzy sometimes looked at Mary with puzzlement, sometimes almost with regret, she neither spoke nor acted to keep her near; and soon their old closeness was nothing more than a memory.

As her elder sisters retreated from her, Mary had wondered whether she might not find a friend in one of the younger girls. When they were small, she watched them keenly, trying to see if they had inherited Jane's and Lizzy's beauty. She did not like to admit what it was that she hoped for. It seemed a cruel thing to wish that a chubby toddler might not grow into a fine young girl; but Mary could not help it. If either Kitty or Lydia turned out to be plain, then she might not feel so alone. Two plain sisters would understand each other. They would make common cause together, and surely, grow to be friends. It was not long before it became obvious this would not happen. By the time they were in their first proper frocks, even Mary could see that they followed not in her footsteps, but in those of Jane and Elizabeth.

'They are handsome little things,' declared their mother, with satisfaction. 'Not quite the equal of Jane, but very pleasing nonetheless. Four beauties out of five is a very respectable number. I'm sure no one could have done better.'

As Kitty and Lydia grew older, Mary quickly understood

that her younger sisters had as little need of her as the elder two had. Left to herself, Kitty might have weakened. She was a mild, pliable girl, eager to please. She might have been persuaded to be Mary's friend. But the youngest Bennet daughter was determined that would not happen. Even as a child, Lydia was headstrong, bold, and wilful; and once she decided she wanted Kitty for herself, Mary was no match for her. It did not take long before Kitty was entirely in thrall to Lydia, dominated by her iron whim, obediently echoing all her opinions. Soon, Kitty had as little time for Mary as did anyone else. By the time she was fourteen, Mary knew she came first with none of her sisters. She was no one's special friend or confidante. Neither her mother nor her father looked on her with any particular affection. In the midst of so large a family, she was utterly alone.

CHAPTER THREE

Mrs Bennet's behaviour only deepened Mary's unhappiness, for the pleasure she took in her four handsome daughters could not, it seemed, entirely make up for the shortcomings of the fifth; and with every year that passed, Mary's appearance irritated her mother more and more. Mrs Bennet had neither the patience nor the inclination to hide her vexation, which was provoked by a host of small failings; but few frustrated her more than Mary's hair. Each night, at her insistence, it was tied into curl papers; and each morning, as Mrs Hill brushed it out, it emerged as straight and as fine as before. Mrs Bennet could not help but regard this daily disappointment as a personal affront.

'Mary, I believe you do this on purpose to annoy me.'

'Indeed, I don't, Mama. I would make it curl if I could. Perhaps it could be swept back off my face? Then it might not be noticed that it doesn't curl?'

Mrs Bennet frowned.

'Perhaps you would rather wear a cap like an old married woman? That would cover up a multitude of sins!'

With this, her mother would march indignantly away, leaving Mrs Hill to pick up her combs and brushes again, ready to make another hopeless attempt to achieve the impossible.

Soon Mary longed for invisibility. It was better to attract no attention at all than to find herself the object of her mother's peevish displeasure. She did all she could to disappear, choosing dresses in the most anonymous colours, made up in the most unexceptionable styles. When Mrs Hill, whom she knew felt sorry for her, urged her to consider brighter shades and more flattering shapes, she refused – unremarkable greys and beiges were all she deserved. Convinced that nothing could improve the figure she presented to the world, she took no part in the conversations about hats and shoes and muslins which, as they grew older, occupied so much of Kitty's and Lydia's time. Lydia was sharp-tongued, as merciless in her judgements as their mother, and Mary feared the teasing she was sure would greet her awkward attempts to join in. It was easier to stay silent. When her sisters walked into Meryton to spend their allowances in the village's small millinery shop, she hovered outside, alone in the street. There was no point in going in. What would she do with a new lace collar, with coloured ribbons or a straw hat? Fripperies of that sort were not for girls like her.

Restless and isolated, she sought other ways to occupy her time, but her choices were few. She had no talent for drawing, and needlework bored her. She could not paint, and she disliked cards. Music, however, was a different matter. Seated at the piano, Mary felt almost happy, forgetting for a moment her deficiencies and failures. All the Bennet sisters had been taught to play. Mrs Bennet considered it a charming skill for a girl to possess, and had insisted that all her daughters acquire it, even providing a teacher for them. The genteel and put-upon Miss Allen arrived every Wednesday afternoon and taught each Bennet daughter, one after the other. Mary remembered awaiting her turn, counting the minutes till Lizzy was finished, breathlessly eager to take her place at the keyboard. At first, she had been so small that she had required a cushion in order to reach the keys. There she had sat, precariously perched, her child's tiny fingers stretching to perform her scales and arpeggios. She had loved it from the beginning, thrilled by the sounds she produced, excited as, week by week, they came gradually to resemble tunes and melodies. This was when she was still young, before she had learned to be ashamed of herself. As she absorbed the painful knowledge of her plainness, she had turned her face away from many pursuits she had once enjoyed; but her love for music was one of the few passions Mary did not renounce as she grew older. She continued to play, even as sister after sister gave up, abandoning their piano lessons as quickly as Mrs Bennet permitted. Soon only Mary and Lizzy troubled the battered family instrument with any regularity.

Something, however, had changed. When she began, music was a treat for Mary, an escape from a daily life in which there was precious little to enjoy; but by the time she entered her teens, she no longer looked upon it as merely a diverting pastime. It had slowly dawned on her that once she was seated behind the keyboard, good looks counted for nothing. At the piano, the plainest woman might outshine the prettiest if she had the ambition and single-mindedness required to do so. Although conscious of her shortcomings in so many areas of life, Mary did not doubt her powers of stamina and application; and it struck her, they could be harnessed to deliver a sense of purpose and achievement sadly lacking elsewhere in her drab existence. Why should she not direct them towards mastering the piano? She was already competent – with effort, she might become even more accomplished. The prospect of possessing a talent of her own, some mark of distinction, was thrilling to her, and she did not for a moment begrudge the work involved in acquiring it. She willingly exiled herself to the drawing room, where none but she ventured until teatime, rehearsing her exercises again and again. She was dogged in her pursuit of perfection, and eventually, she was rewarded for it. In all aspects of technique and proficiency, she was soon much improved. Miss Allen declared herself very satisfied with her progress, and assured her that if she maintained the habit of regular and rigorous practice, she could expect to get better still.

Mary was unused to praise, and this small crumb of encouragement was enough to harden her resolve and tie her to the keyboard for many solitary hours. Mostly, she did not resent the time she spent alone with her exercises; but occasionally, in the midst of her practice, she would find herself overtaken by a sadness she did not understand. It took her a while to grasp that the sensation she felt was one of regret for the pleasure and excitement that had once overwhelmed her when she played. The relentless discipline she had imposed on herself had slowly extinguished much of the delight with which she used to approach the piano. Now it was a task like any other. Her hard work and effort had brought her the expertise she longed for; but it had been achieved at the cost of a simple enjoyment she had loved more than any other.

Usually, Mary was able to convince herself this had been a price worth paying, that indulging her happiness mattered less than honing her skills. But there were times when she was assailed by doubts about what she had given up, when longing for the fulfilment and release which music had delivered broke through, despite all her attempts to repress it. One morning, as she walked towards the drawing room to begin her daily practice, music tucked under her arm, she heard the unmistakeable sound of Lizzy at the piano. She would have known her style anywhere – fast, full of bravado, so appealing that it was impossible not to turn your head and listen. The few mistakes she made did nothing to mar the pleasure of hearing her. Mary slipped silently into the room and watched her sister as she finished the piece, head tilted back, concluding with a flourish all her own, added for no other reason than her own satisfaction. Mary sat down, a little stunned by the energy and attack of Elizabeth's treatment of the song. It was nothing like her own precise and exact style, but no one could hear it and not admire it.

'That was very good, Lizzy,' she exclaimed. 'There were hardly any false notes. If you were to practise properly, you might really master it.'

Her face slightly flushed from the exertion of performing the piece, Elizabeth pushed the stool away from the keyboard, as if to signal she had done what she wished to do, and would play no more.

'That wouldn't suit me at all. I'm not sure I have the patience to master anything. The minute it began to be troublesome, I'd find something else to do.'

'But don't you want to cultivate your gift? It seems a great shame to waste it.'

'I'm not sure it is wasted if it pleases me.' Lizzy allowed her fingers to trace a simple scale. 'I sometimes wonder if you might enjoy yourself more if you applied yourself a little less.'

'But if I don't apply myself, how will I play anything correctly?'

'Perhaps,' remarked Lizzy, 'correctness and application are not the only measures of success.'

This was exactly the suspicion that sometimes disturbed Mary's own thoughts; but she pushed the idea away, for it was impossible for her to admit to it.

'I cannot believe anything worth having is to be achieved without effort and sacrifice.'

'That may be so,' replied Lizzy, 'and yet I know I'd rather listen to a piece played with happiness and a spring in its step than to all the well-drilled perfection in the world.'

'I doubt you'd care to hear a succession of mistakes,' replied Mary, 'however cheerful the person was who played them.'

Elizabeth gathered up her music and rose from the piano.

'Possibly. But really, it seems a great shame to wring all the pleasure out of music. A few false notes seem a small price to pay in exchange.'

She touched Mary's shoulder lightly as she left the room. Mary sat down and assembled her music but could not settle. Elizabeth's words had agitated her. It was not surprising to hear Lizzy speak slightingly of hard work and effort; everything came easily to her. She did not need to exert herself; charm would always see her through, even at the piano. Mary thrust her book of music onto the stand. For her, things were different. She flexed her fingers and began to practise her scales.

CHAPTER FOUR

When she felt too tired to sit any longer at the keyboard, it was Mary's custom to retreat to her bedroom and read. There she had a small bookcase in which stood the dozen or so books which belonged to her. They were so familiar that she could recite whole passages from them by heart; nevertheless, it pleased her to open them and look again at the well-remembered words. She could not recall a time when reading had not been both a comfort and a refuge. Indeed, she sometimes thought she remembered the moment when the great joy of literacy had come upon her. She was huddled in front of the fire in the nursery when the black lines on the paper that Lizzy had so patiently traced for her ceased to be random shapes and suddenly assembled themselves into letters – *A* is for *Apple*, *C* is for *Cat*.

Once she grasped this, there was no holding her back. She raced on, advancing from picture books to rhymes and fairy stories. She made short work of *The History of Little Goody Two-Shoes*, and *The Story of the Robins* did not detain her long. In those days, she read in the company of Jane or Elizabeth, the three of them sitting together up in the nursery, each occupied with her own book in companionable quiet. But as she became older and more unhappy and her sisters grew away from her, books became less a link between them than a solace for their loss. When Jane and Elizabeth whispered together without including her, when they shut the door to their room and did not ask her to join them – then it was to her books that Mary fled, finding in them a distraction from the loneliness that depressed her spirits.

She read so much that she quickly exhausted not just her own shelves, but also the scanty resources of the Longbourn schoolroom. Soon she had finished everything it contained, from the atlases of the world to hints on housekeeping; but the more she consumed, the sharper her desire for new reading matter grew. She picked up anything she found about the house, bearing it away to study at her leisure. The novels Mrs Bennet borrowed from the circulating library occupied her for a while; but their beautiful imperilled heroines, their handsome upright heroes and the complications of the plot that brought them step by convoluted step to the most improbable happy endings did not please her. She condemned them as silly, and longed for more demanding fare. Thinking she might prefer fact to fiction, she picked up Mr Bennet's newspapers, squinting at their tiny black print, spelling out to herself the unfamiliar names and places they described, until her eyes hurt and she laid them aside. She read the agricultural magazines to which he subscribed, puzzling at the images of threshing machines and diagrams of crop rotations. She spirited away the pamphlets brought into the house by the servants, with their lurid accounts of horrible crimes and dying confessions, studying the crude black line drawings of hanged men and murdered women, until Mrs Hill discovered them and carried them angrily off to the kitchen. Sometimes she happened upon more substantial volumes left about by Mr Bennet, and these she would regard with great curiosity;

but she did not dare to open them. Her father's books were sacrosanct and not to be meddled with by anyone but himself.

Mary was eighteen when she understood she could not go on in this haphazard way. She longed to develop her intellectual understanding, just as she had done her musical proficiency; but she understood that to do so, two things were necessary. First, she needed to consult a far greater range of reading material; and second, she required the assistance of a teacher. She had Miss Allen for the piano. Why should she not have similar support in pursuing her intellectual interests? Surely some steady, learned person could be found to direct her reading and give a shape to her studies. If she had been a boy, a tutor would have been provided for her; but such a thing was unthinkable for a girl. Nor was there any chance of her being sent away to school, as it was an article of faith with Mrs Bennet that the food served to boarders was stodgy and damaged the complexion. There was only one possible answer to Mary's dilemma, and that was the appointment of a governess – but it was many months before she summoned up the courage to ask her mother if this might be permitted.

She approached the subject gingerly, as she knew Mrs Bennet did not look kindly upon governesses. Indeed, it was a matter of pride to her mother that she had never employed such a person. A succession of masters had, over the years, marched up the drive to Longbourn, to instruct her daughters in those subjects she thought would add a final polish to their education. From them, she and her sisters had gleaned a smattering of French, a little drawing, and a great deal of dancing. But in matters of general education, Mrs Bennet considered her own example, supplemented by a respectable number of textbooks, as enough to equip them with all they needed to know. She had taught her girls how to cast up accounts, manage a household, and sew a good, straight seam. They all read well enough and knew enough history and geography not to look absolutely foolish in company. Anything more was not only unnecessary, but probably unwise. Mrs Bennet had not observed that learning was a quality most men sought in a wife, and she had no desire to add to her daughters' disadvantages by burdening them with a reputation for cleverness. All this Mary knew; but the desire to exercise her mind overcame her apprehension, and one afternoon, as she sat with her mother and sisters at tea, she made her request as boldly and as calmly as she could. Mrs Bennet was nonplussed, as Mary had expected she would be.

'A governess? Whatever can you mean? What could you possibly want with one at your age?'

'I should like to improve my education, Mama, to read more widely and cultivate my mind.'

'I cannot imagine what else you think you need to learn,' cried Mrs Bennet. 'Your head is stuffed full of useless facts already. I doubt there's a country in the world whose capital you don't know or whose principal rivers you couldn't name. What more could a governess teach you?'

'She could help me study in a more rational way, direct me towards books that would stretch my intellect.' Mary felt enthusiasm quicken within her. 'And she need not work only with me. She could be of service to all us younger girls. I'm sure we would all benefit from improving our habits of industry.'

Lydia, who usually paid no attention to anything Mary said, started up, horrified.

'Heaven preserve me from habits of industry! And my

mind is stretched quite enough, thank you. The last thing we
need is a governess sitting in the morning room sniffing and
looking miserable, some poor spinster with a book of sermons in one hand and a twist of snuff in the other.'

She turned to Kitty, held an imaginary pinch of snuff
under her nose, snorted, turned up her eyes, and groaned.
Kitty burst out laughing, scattering crumbs from her cake
across the table.

'I can't imagine anything more awful,' declared Lydia,
'and Kitty thinks the same, I'm sure.'

'It would be dreadful, especially the sniffing,' added Kitty
obediently. 'Please, Mama, don't do it. We're happy as we are.'

'I'm sure we could find someone we all liked,' persisted
Mary. 'Some well-bred woman with no annoying habits. And
she need come only a few times a week.'

'That's still far too often for me,' said Lydia. 'Suppose she
doesn't come at all?'

Mary ignored her, fixing her mother with a supplicant's
stare.

'Really, Mama, when you consider the benefits to our
minds—'

But it was no use. Mrs Bennet had already made her decision.

'That's enough, Mary. No one else wants a governess; and
I refuse to entertain the expense of one solely for your benefit. If you wish to learn more, that is your affair. There are
books enough in Mr Bennet's library. You may take yourself
off there, as Lizzy does, and read to your heart's content.
That is all I have to say upon the matter. I don't wish to hear
it mentioned again.'

Lydia, much relieved, helped herself to another slice of

cake. Mary knew it was pointless to say more. But as she sat there, watching her tea grow cold, the significance of her mother's words slowly dawned upon her. It had never before occurred to her that she might be allowed to enter her father's library. She often looked into it as she passed, a light and airy room, with bay windows that opened directly onto the garden, a vision of scholarly calm. Its real attractions, however, were the books which lined its walls, shelf after shelf of them, a tantalising vision for a hungry reader desperate for something new to engage her. Mr Bennet spent most of every day there, closeted in a most forbidding silence. Interlopers, as he liked to remind his family, were not encouraged to join him.

'As I do not quarrel with the general air of silliness that pervades every other part of this house, I do not think it unreasonable that there should be one room from which it is excluded.'

Neither Kitty nor Lydia, for whom the bookshelves offered no temptation, were troubled by this pronouncement. Nor was Mrs Bennet. She had no curiosity about how her husband spent his time in his library and it would not have occurred to her to try to find out. Only Elizabeth slipped in now and then to borrow a book with the same easy confidence which characterised everything she did. But Lizzy was Mr Bennet's favourite, and his usually sardonic gaze often rested upon her with a warmth and admiration he did not extend to his younger daughters. Mary had never supposed a similar welcome would ever be offered to her. Mr Bennet rarely looked at her at all, and seemed quite indifferent to her presence. She would never have considered the possibility of entering the library if her mother had not suggested it; but now the prospect of roaming freely amongst so many books overcame her fear of a refusal. She plucked up her courage and waited until she judged her father was in his least capricious frame of mind before stopping him in the hallway and asking – very tentatively – if she might be granted admission on the same terms as Lizzy. He considered for a moment before replying.

'You may come and take refuge in my library if you feel you will benefit from it. But you are to remember it is not a place for conversation. I will not be teased with idle questions. A rational calm is to prevail at all times. And every book taken down from a shelf is to be returned to the exact place from which it was removed. These rules are inflexible. Do you think you can obey them?'

'Yes, sir, I do.'

'Then I have no objection to your coming. You may begin tomorrow.'

CHAPTER FIVE

Next morning, Mary hurried through her usual tasks, desperate to be released from her mother's watchful eye. Her plain sewing seemed to take even longer than usual, her needle losing its thread countless times, while Mrs Bennet insisted two uneven hems were to be unpicked and done again. But finally she found herself standing outside the library door, daring herself to enter. Once inside, she held her breath, amazed to be within at last. Mr Bennet was at his accustomed place behind his desk. He acknowledged her curtly and returned to his work. As she looked about, Mary was both thrilled and apprehensive. She had imagined that she would have no difficulty in finding what she wanted; but standing in a shaft of sunlight in which dust motes shimmered, she realised she did not know what she was looking for or where to begin. She moved to a shelf and leaned towards the books, peering to make out their titles. Carefully, she pulled one out. Immediately, two volumes at the end of the row clattered onto the floor. The noise seemed huge, shattering the quiet. Mr Bennet looked up. Panicked, Mary grasped the two books nearest to her and hurried away. In the hall, she stood clasping them tightly to her chest. This was not how she had imagined her first visit ending.

When she felt more composed, she bore her prizes off to her bedroom and sat down to examine them. Opening the first volume, she saw it was a history of England. She was not sure whether this pleased her or not. But when she looked more closely, she discovered it was written by a woman. This surprised her. She knew that women produced books for children and that they also wrote novels; but she had not supposed they were ever the authors of serious works of history. She was intrigued and walked over to her little writing desk, where she cleared a space and propped up the book in front of her. She would give Mrs Catharine Macaulay a chance to engage her.

Mary was still in her room when Mrs Hill came in to find her and send her down for dinner.

'Your mother has been calling for you for ten minutes. She is not best pleased.'

Mary looked up absently, laid down her book, and then walked slowly downstairs. She hardly spoke during the meal, her thoughts entirely occupied by what she had read. It was not as easy to follow as the simpler works she was used to; but that did not discourage her. On the contrary, she felt the unused muscles of her mind flex and curiosity stir within her.

It took her a fortnight to finish Mrs Macaulay's first volume. When she returned to Mr Bennet's library, she looked to see if there were any other history books written by women. When she found none, she was absurdly disappointed. Her searching hand hesitated for a moment over Mr Hume's historical works, but she did not pick one of them off the shelf. No, she would continue with Mrs Macaulay before venturing upon anyone else. She took away two more volumes of hers, excited to think that a woman had acquired enough knowledge and scholarship to produce them. Over the next few weeks she devoured them avidly, waking early to study them in the morning before breakfast and returning to them late at night when the rest of the house slept. She begrudged every minute she was forced out of their company and into those activities her mother thought necessary, fidgeting through the hours spent at the tea table or wasted in useful needlework. Mrs Bennet noticed her distraction and did not approve.

'You are never to be found when wanted. And when you are about, you don't attend to anything said to you.'

Mary apologised and vowed to do better in future; but she knew her promise was a hollow one. Her life, such as it was, now took place almost entirely between the pages of her books. The events of the Civil Wars, as Mrs Macaulay explained them, the stories of Charles I and Oliver Cromwell had become more real to her than the days which passed so unchangingly at Longbourn. Her books were her mainstay, and nothing, not even her mother's loudly expressed displeasure, could make her give them up. On the contrary, her intellectual appetite grew more intense with each volume she finished; and, as a consequence, her visits to her father's library grew ever more frequent and of longer and longer duration.

She explored Mr Bennet's bookshelves with greater confidence now, venturing to look beyond the historical titles that were increasingly familiar to her, gazing curiously towards works of philosophy and theology. Dare she take one of those? She was not sure. They seemed more forbidding than the histories. And with which author should she begin? She was desperate for guidance, and often looked longingly towards her father, hoping he might notice, and offer to advise her. But he showed no interest in the books she chose, never asking what she was reading or how she had enjoyed it. For a while, she watched him from beneath lowered eyes, trying to assess how he would respond if she were to approach him; but in the end, her spirits failed her. She could not imagine how she would begin or, once he turned his cool, satirical stare upon her, how she would continue. So she went on as she had begun, with nothing but her own judgement to rely upon.

The weeks turned into months, and Mary read on and on. Jane and Lizzy watched her with bemused indulgence, glad to see her occupied, though unsure what to make of her new passion; but for her younger sisters, Mary's devotion to her books lowered her even further in their estimation. There was much whispering and laughter amongst them whenever they found her at her studies, and Lydia had soon perfected an imitation of her at work, her shoulders hunched, her nose plunged deep into some heavy volume; but Mary was not deterred. She felt herself to be making progress and refused to be either teased or shamed into giving up. She had at last plucked up the courage to begin upon some of the shorter philosophical books and was intrigued by what she discovered within them. She found the great moral questions with which they dealt intensely absorbing, enjoying the abstract arguments. In contrast to their lofty concerns, her private unhappiness seemed of very little account, and this offered her a rather chilly sense of comfort. She was both stimulated and consoled by what she read – and this encouraged her to persevere. Learning, it seemed, was not so different to playing the piano. The mind could be trained to do one's bidding, just as one's fingers could be exercised and one's technique improved. All it took was self-discipline and a willingness to work hard. But Mary soon discovered, to her cost, that there were some circumstances which even her formidable determination could not overcome; and that not all aspects of her being could be coerced into doing exactly what she wished.

She had suspected for some time that her sight was not all it should be; but had refused to acknowledge the evidence that pressed itself upon her with increasing urgency. Small print had always taxed her abilities, but now, perhaps as a result of her many hours in the library, almost any book had become impossible to read. The text swam before her, the words blurred. She tried screwing her eyes tight to focus as best she could, but it made little difference. She tried moving around the room, tilting the book towards the light or holding it as close as she could to her face, but nothing answered. In the glare of a summer's garden, she might manage a page or two, if the sun was behind her and the letters not too small; but indoors, and as the darker nights came on, she struggled to make out anything at all.

One evening, as she sat at her desk, she realised she could barely see a single line of her book. She lit one candle, and then another, placing them as close as she dared to the pages; but it made no difference. She was so angry that she felt she might scream. It seemed monstrously unfair that just as she had discovered an interest that gave her life meaning, it should be taken away from her. If she could not read, what was left to her? She closed the book carefully, with a calm she did not feel, and lay on her bed, trying to decide what she must do.

For two days, Mary attempted to live without books. She played the piano, walked in the garden, picked flowers for the drawing room, and pretended to sew. By the afternoon of the second day, she knew that, for her, such an existence was unendurable. If she was not to go mad, she must ask her mother if she might consult an oculist. This was not a request to be undertaken lightly. Mary knew it was likely to provoke Mrs Bennet to even greater heights of indignation than her attempts to secure a governess, for what could be more destructive of her meagre attractions than the wearing of heavy metal spectacles? But Mary had no choice. If the alternative was impossible, the question must be asked. All she could do was to approach her mother when she was at her least peevish, throwing herself, as boldly as she could, upon Mrs Bennet's uncertain sympathies.

Mary finally approached her mother one afternoon when she was occupied in the pantry, checking the bottled fruit that had been put up last autumn, peering into the jars to see if the plums, apricots, and greengages were still sound. As this was a task she enjoyed, Mrs Bennet was tolerably cheerful until Mary explained why she had come to see her. Then her good mood evaporated, and she professed not to credit what she was being asked.

'I cannot believe you are serious. If this is a joke, Mary, it is in very poor taste.'

'It is no joke, Mama, I promise you. I can hardly see to read. I do beg I might be allowed to have my eyes examined.'

'To what end? How do you think that will help?'

'If the oculist thinks I would benefit from it, he could prescribe spectacles. Then I should be able to read again.'

'Spectacles, indeed! And you would really be prepared to wear them? To humiliate yourself in such a way?'

'If they allowed me to read as I wish, then yes, I would be happy to wear them.'

Mrs Bennet, who had just lifted a large jar of apricots down from the shelf, deposited it onto the table with a little too much vigour. Fortunately, it did not break; but the noise made Mary jump.

'No man will look at you,' she declared, 'and every woman will pity you.'

'I hope I will be equal to bearing that, if I must.'

For a moment, Mrs Bennet was speechless, unable to conceive of such a crime against everything she held dear. But Mary steeled herself to continue.

'If you don't feel able to help me, then I will pay for it myself. I have a little money saved from my allowance. I will write to the oculist myself and ask him to call.'

Her mother wiped her hands on her apron.

'Then it seems I have no choice in the matter. Let the oculist come if he must. But I am very displeased with you, Mary. I am sadly vexed and agitated now, and it is all your fault.'

She strode towards the door, so angry that she left the jars still on the table, untouched and unexamined.

'Don't think I will attend you when he comes. Mrs Hill will take care of it. I would not be equal to the strain of it all.'

Left alone in the room, Mary's hands shook as picked up the jar of apricots and placed it carefully back on the shelf. She did not think she had ever defied her mother so openly before. She sat down heavily. But she had achieved her object. She would see an oculist. She only hoped it would be soon.

CHAPTER SIX

A week later, Mr Sparrow, a large man in a snuff-coloured coat, presented himself at Longbourn. He brought with him a large portfolio containing a number of printed cards, a large, stiff leather case, and his son, John, a tall, silent boy of eighteen.

'I hope you won't object to his presence, miss. He is learning the business, and I try to take him with me to see as much of it as he can at first hand.'

Mary looked uncertain. She had not imagined their proceedings would involve a spectator; however, young Mr Sparrow looked polite and respectful, so she nodded a silent assent. Mrs Hill ushered them into the chilly morning room, where no welcoming fire was lit in the grate, and stood against the wall to watch what happened next.

'If you please to sit in this chair, miss, as straight as you can, head upright and eyes ahead. Yes, that will do very well.'

He beckoned to his son, who brought the case to his father's side and opened it with a slow, reverential gesture. Inside were row after row of spectacles, neatly labelled and in perfect order.

'Now, miss,' explained Mr Sparrow, 'each of these pairs contains a different lens. I shall ask you to put them on, one by one. John will give you a card to look at, and you will tell me what you see. Then I shall try another, and you will look again and say if the characters on the cards appear more or less clearly as a result. Thus, we will go on until we find the right spectacles for you.'

Mary's apprehension grew as she felt the cold metal frame slide onto her nose, but Mr Sparrow's low, confident tones calmed her, and she began to feel a flicker of interest in his careful, practised methods. When she looked at the card through the first spectacles, she was so astonished to see how it distorted the letters that surprise broke through her shyness and she cried out loud.

'Sir, I can't make out anything at all! Just shapes and blurs! What does it mean?'

'It means it is not the answer we are looking for, although it points us towards where we need to go.'

He gave her another pair, and this time Mary thought the letters were a little clearer. Again and again they tried, with results that were sometimes a little better and sometimes a little worse. Despite herself, she grew so absorbed in the process that her self-consciousness melted away. She began to think of herself less as Mr Sparrow's patient and more as his ally, helping him as he tried to find the answer to her problem. At last, he placed a pair upon her nose that made her gasp in amazement. Suddenly every letter on the card appeared bright and sharp.

'Oh, Mr Sparrow, I can see every character on the cards as clear as anything! Every letter, every number! I can see it all!'

'Ah, so that's the one then,' Mr Sparrow said with a laugh. 'It is always pleasing to see so very definite a reaction. I think we may be confident that we have found the answer. This small object,' he said, leaning over and removing the lens from the frame, 'when properly prepared, will, I am certain, make the most extraordinary difference to your life.'

'It really is the most remarkable thing, sir. Can you tell me how it works?'

'Perhaps I may ask John to explain to you? Then I can see how much of what I have been teaching him has taken firm root in his mind. John, if you please?'

The young man was shy and hesitant at first, but he knew his business, and gained steadily in confidence as he described the delicate curvature of the lens, its transforming impact upon an individual eye, and the care and precision with which it must be ground, if it was to correct defective sight.

'I am learning to do that myself and should be very pleased – honoured – to have a hand in making a lens for you.'

He caught her eye as he finished, then stared at his feet, as if he had said too much. His father patted his arm, proud of his boy.

'We shall do it together and make an excellent job of it. I venture to suggest, miss, that you will be extremely pleased with the result.'

Mary looked away, unused to finding herself the object of so much attention. It was, however, not unpleasing. It was impossible to be offended by these quiet, exacting men, their minds fixed so intently upon the challenges of their profession. As she handed back the little frame, she turned towards them and smiled. Mrs Hill walked over to join them, and for a moment, they all stood together, happy with what they had achieved. Then Mary heard her mother's footstep in the hall, and her face fell.

'So, Mr Sparrow,' cried Mrs Bennet, as she strode into the room, 'what have you to tell me?'

The oculist attempted to explain his findings and his opinion of Mary's sight; but Mrs Bennet waved him away, impatient.

'That is all very well sir, but may we come to the point? Are you telling me that my daughter will have to wear spectacles?'

'Why, yes, ma'am, I believe so. I do not think she can with ease perform any close work without them. For all occupations where acute sight is needed, they will be essential.'

'But she need not wear them outside the house? They could be dispensed with in public, or in any place where people might see her?'

'That must be for the young lady herself to judge, but I am sure she would derive great benefit from being able to see properly in any situation, public or private.'

Mrs Bennet frowned. 'Thank you, Mr Sparrow. You may write to Mr Bennet, who will inform you of what we decide to do. Good morning to you.'

She gestured to Mrs Hill to show the Sparrows out. Mary watched as they were ushered away, regretting she had not been able to thank them as they deserved. Once they had gone, her mother turned towards her, indignant.

'This is very disappointing news, Mary. It is not at all what I had hoped for.'

Mary said nothing. She had no wish to anger her mother further.

'We shall go and speak to your father about it directly. Let us hear what he has to say.'

They walked to the drawing room in silence. When they arrived, Mrs Bennet threw open the door and Mary was sorry to see that the whole family were gathered there. She had hoped to avoid the embarrassment of hearing her situation discussed in front of everyone; but that was evidently impossible. With a loud sigh, Mrs Bennet sat down. Jane and Lizzy looked up from their reading; Kitty and Lydia turned away from the gloves they were examining. Only their father did not respond, determinedly studying his newspaper. Finally, Mrs Bennet could remain silent no longer.

'Mr Bennet, I have something to tell you. I'm afraid it's very provoking news. Would you like to know what it is?'

Mr Bennet lowered his paper and looked over it evenly at his wife.

'Whatever my wishes in the matter, I am sure you intend to tell me.'

'Mary needs spectacles. The oculist says she cannot see without them. There, Mr Bennet!'

She looked about her with the consciousness of having delivered a very significant and troubling piece of information. It was Elizabeth who spoke first.

'Surely, Mama, it is good to know what can be done to help Mary. If she needs spectacles, ought she not have them? It must be very hard for her to struggle on without them if she cannot see as well as she should.'

Mrs Bennet uttered a stricken little cry.

'Really, Lizzy, what can you mean? It is a dreadful misfortune for her! Spectacles are for doddering old men, not for young girls of eighteen! I refuse to believe that she really needs them. No one in my family has ever been so afflicted before. We Gardiners all have perfect sight.'

'But, Mama,' continued Elizabeth, 'you do so little close work and read so rarely that you may not know whether you need them or not.'

'How can you say such a thing! No one enjoys a book more than I do. "Read so rarely", indeed!'

'You are forgetting, my dear, that I myself wear glasses,' added Mr Bennet. 'I should not like to think of myself as an old man, doddering or otherwise, but I admit I should be quite incapable of study without them.'

'You are teasing me, Mr Bennet, but you know the truth of what I say. A man may wear spectacles, I suppose, even a young man, especially if he is a lawyer or a clergyman or such-like, and no one will speak ill of him. For a young woman it is quite a different thing. What do you think people will say when they see Mary in them? Who will want to marry her then?'

Mr Bennet looked thoughtful. 'Perhaps one of those very men you have just described will offer for her, a wearer of spectacles himself, boldly indifferent to the scorn of all the neighbourhood. Indeed, it may be the very thing that brings them together.'

'You are pleased to make a joke of it, but it is no laughing matter. The oculist says she needs spectacles to read, but why, I might ask, does she need to read so many books?'

At this, Elizabeth tried to interrupt, but her father held up his hand.

'If Mary is not to read, what other occupations are open to her? She has no taste for drawing, and, as you have so often informed me, her sewing is a great disappointment to you. I am no expert, but it seems to me that her skills with a needle are unlikely to improve if she cannot see to thread it. I suppose she might help dig the garden when the winter cabbages come in.'

Back and forth the conversation went, over Mary's silent

head. No one expected her to say anything. Instead, she allowed herself to concentrate on Elizabeth's kind words. It had been a long time since she had heard Lizzy speak about her with such concern. She knew better, however, than to expect any sympathy from her youngest sister.

'I think I should rather be blind than put such ugly things onto my face,' exclaimed Lydia. 'Giving up books would be a small price to pay to avoid that dreadful fate. What is there to be learned from reading anyway?'

Mr Bennet looked at Lydia with an expression of steady disapproval.

'It is remarks of that sort which have won you the reputation of being one of the vainest, and, I might add, one of the most foolish and empty-headed girls in the neighbourhood.'

'As long as I am not also one of the ugliest, I really do not care, Papa.'

Mrs Hill arrived bearing a fresh pot of coffee, just in time to hear Lydia's disobliging remark. When Lydia saw her, she held up her cup hopefully; but Mrs Hill seemed not to notice and carried the pot as far away from her as possible, at the far end of the table, where she offered it to Mr Bennet.

'Thank you, Lydia,' he declared, as Mrs Hill filled his cup. 'Nothing could have made clearer for me the right choice in this matter. I will not stand in the way of any member of this family who seeks to diminish the amount of stupidity in this house. Mary, if you wish to read, you shall have the where-withal to do so. You shall have your spectacles.'

Mrs Bennet looked as though she was about to argue, but her husband had heard enough.

'No, my dear, there's an end to it. I will not be plagued on the subject any longer. I shall be in the library until dinner time, and I do not expect to be disturbed.'

Mary sat for a moment, trying not to let her relief and satisfaction show. She could not remember when she had felt more pleased. Her mother would not look at her as she stood up, but Mary did not mind it. There was almost a spring in her step as she walked out of the drawing room.

It was some weeks before Mr Sparrow wrote to say that the spectacles were ready and that he would be pleased to wait upon Mrs Bennet at her convenience. Mary's mother, who considered she had done all in her power to prevent this great embarrassment, declined to be present and again sent Mrs Hill in her stead, with instructions to ensure no sharp practice was attempted at the final moment. Once the little group was reassembled, and Mary was seated, straight-backed in her chair, Mr Sparrow directed his son to open the leather bag he carried. The young man pulled from within a pair of spectacles, wrapped in a soft cloth, which he presented to Mary with a dignified flourish. Mary put them on, picked up a book from the table, opened it, and exclaimed with pleasure as the print lept into sharp focus.

'Look, Mrs Hill! I can read perfectly now!'

Mrs Hill crossed her arms over her chest and stared at her assessingly.

'I'm very glad of it, but I'm not sure what your mother will say.'

In an instant, Mary's pleasure vanished. She took off the spectacles and placed them in her lap. She had forgotten for a moment the price she must pay for her newly acquired vision of the world. Lydia's scorn rang in her ears. She might see things more clearly now, but she would appear even plainer as a result.

'Oh, no, please don't do that, miss.' She was astonished to see John Sparrow cross the room and take the spectacles from her. 'Don't allow yourself to be cast down. It's a wonderful thing to see properly, not to have to peer about and screw up one's face.' He polished the lenses with the little cloth, intent on his task. 'And really, you look very well in them. When you smile ... you look very well.' He handed them back to her with a small bob of his head before hurrying back to stand alongside his father again.

'John is quite right,' agreed Mr Sparrow, 'on both points. And once you have worn them often enough, neither you nor anyone else will take any notice of them. Of that you can be quite sure.'

Mary doubted her mother would agree, but she could not bring herself to contradict this kindly, well-meaning man.

'Thank you, Mr Sparrow. I am sure you are right. I think they will suit me excellently, and I shall take the greatest pleasure in wearing them.'

She took the spectacles in her hand and went out into the hall. As she closed the door, it seemed as though John Sparrow's gaze followed her across the room; but when she thought about it, she knew she must be mistaken. She stood for a moment, listening to Mrs Hill discussing how and when the Sparrows should be paid. Then she collected her thoughts and walked quickly away. She should go and try out her spectacles on the last volume of Mrs Macaulay.

CHAPTER SEVEN

A public ball was held at the Meryton assembly rooms several times a year. Anyone with any pretensions to taste affected to despise these simple entertainments – the rooms were too small, the music too loud, the refreshments scarcely to be borne – but there was never any question of not attending. The first ball of the season was anticipated with the greatest excitement, the more so because, although it always took place in the autumn, the exact date of the event was rarely decided upon until almost the very last moment. As the leaves fell from the trees and the evenings grew darker, expectation mounted, especially amongst the younger people who longed for an opportunity for dancing; but for many weeks, no definite information could be obtained of when it might be held. Inevitably, it was Lydia, on one of her dallying, gossiping trips to the village, who was the first to hear incontrovertible evidence of the day at last being fixed, which she bore back to Longbourn in triumph. Tearing into the hall, with Kitty hurrying in her wake, she ran straight to Mrs Bennet.

'The ball is to be held on the first Saturday of next month! I had it from Mr Thompson himself. I was passing the rooms and there he was, so I asked him, and he told me he had just this minute contracted the musicians, so I am the very first to know.'

She perched on a chair, still wearing her hat, desperate to impart all she had discovered.

'The supper is ordered, the rooms are to be swept, and the floor newly sanded to save the dancers' feet. The notice is to go into the paper tomorrow.'

Mrs Bennet, almost as excited as her daughter, clapped her hands.

'Well done, Lydia, how clever of you to have found that out. Did you hear that, Mr Bennet? The Meryton ball is settled for three weeks this Saturday.'

'Is it indeed? As I shall not be attending myself, my joy cannot be as unconfined as your own. But I am no enemy to harmless pleasure. Shall you go, Lizzy?'

'I may do,' replied Elizabeth, 'if Jane will come with me. I am not yet sure.'

Lydia looked at her with frank astonishment. '"Not yet sure"? Lizzy, how can you be so annoying? I'm sure I should die if I wasn't there. I should do away with myself from mere frustration.'

'You must endeavour to compose yourself, then,' said Mr Bennet calmly, 'for I have not yet decided if you are to go. Jane and Lizzy may attend, they have been before, and I have no fears for their good behaviour. Mary too may go if she wishes – she is old enough and steady enough to be trusted. But you and Kitty are another matter.'

Mary, who sat in the corner with her book on her knees, had never expected her name to be mentioned in the context of a ball. She could not quite believe that her father had praised her – faint praise, it was true, but she felt herself warm with pride.

Meanwhile, Kitty and Lydia set up a great wail of protest.

'You can't mean that, Papa,' cried Lydia. 'You wouldn't really prevent me from going?'

'Really, Mr Bennet,' declared his wife, 'I am sure neither Lydia nor Kitty would do anything to make us ashamed.'

'I wish I shared your confidence,' he replied. 'Neither could possibly be described as discreet or modest. And Lydia is especially headstrong.'

Lydia stood up, tears springing into her eyes. 'Papa, you are very unkind. You must let me go! You must!'

Mary usually knew better than to tangle with her youngest sister when she had been denied something she wanted, but, emboldened by her father's approving remark, she ventured to speak in his support.

'A young woman's first venture into society cannot be attended with too much care. There are many snares and temptations to overwhelm her, if she has not the judgement or experience to resist them.'

Lydia removed her hat, untying the ribbon deliberately and slowly pulling out the pins.

'Is that so?' she replied coldly. 'Well, you may be the right age to go into society, but you need not worry about snares and temptations. Just put on those spectacles and you will be quite safe, I assure you.'

With that, she flung down her hat and fled the room, pursued by Kitty and their mother, who said all she could to calm her – her father was only joking – she knew it was his way – he would change his mind, she was sure of it.

'That's what happens when you poke an angry beehive with a stick,' Mr Bennet observed to Mary dryly. 'You must expect to get stung.'

Mary rose with as much dignity as she could muster and

went upstairs to her bedroom. There she sat in front of her dressing table and pulled her spectacles out of her pocket. Carefully, she placed them on her nose and stared intently at her reflection in the mirror. She turned from side to side, scrutinising herself from every angle, making no attempt to compose her features into a smile. Her eyes filled with tears. It was just as Lydia said. The dark metal frames looked heavy on her small face, and the lenses gave her an owlish, blinking look. No one could say she was improved by them.

She was still seated there when Mrs Hill knocked at her door some twenty minutes later. She came in with an armful of clean bedclothes, but Mary knew that was not the real reason for her visit.

'I heard what passed between you and Miss Lydia.'

Mary, silent, did not look away from the mirror.

'She has a sharp tongue on her when she's thwarted,' said Mrs Hill, 'but you know that already.'

She put down the bedclothes, pulled up a chair and sat as close to Mary as she could.

'I hope you won't take it too much to heart,' she said in a low voice. 'That was anger and wilfulness speaking. It doesn't make it true.'

'Really?' replied Mary. 'I have been looking at myself this half hour, and I cannot find it in my heart to disagree with her.'

'I cannot in all honesty tell you that the spectacles do you many favours,' confessed Mrs Hill, 'but you aren't obliged to wear them all the time. And without them, you look as well as most women.'

Mary turned towards her with a sceptical frown.

'I know you don't believe me, but it's true. Your skin is clear, your figure is decent, neither too thin nor too fat. When you can see them, your eyes are tolerable and your hair is a pleasant-enough light brown, for all it won't take a curl.'

'You are very kind, Mrs Hill, but you don't need to indulge me. The mirror cannot lie.'

'Perhaps. But in truth, I don't think you see yourself at all clearly, miss. Your sisters get in the way. A daffodil seems quite ordinary when planted between lilies. But looked at without them, it has its own kind of beauty.'

'Yes, I suppose I may be said to be tall, thin, and yellow-looking.' Mary smiled bleakly. 'But if you're saying I don't bear comparison with my sisters, I have known that for years.'

'I wonder whether you would be happier if you spent less time with them, if you were to find friends who were remarkable for things other than their looks.'

'Lizzy is as much admired for her wit as for her beauty.'

'Yes,' admitted Mrs Hill, 'she is very lucky to be both clever and handsome. But I think if you went into the world a little more, you would see how very unusual it is to be blessed as she has been. Most people are far more ordinary, you know, as you would discover if you met some new company and went out now and again.'

'I don't think I have much inclination for either. I have my piano and my books.'

'I'm not sure that's enough for a girl of your age. Come now, what about the Meryton ball? I hope you'll be going along to it. If Miss Lydia is to go, I can't see why you should not.'

'Our father has not yet pronounced upon that question,' began Mary; but Mrs Hill's expression suggested she thought Mr Bennet's objections would not long withstand the determined assault mounted against them by his youngest daughter and his wife. 'I haven't made up my mind either,' she continued. 'I'm not sure I should enjoy it.'

'Why ever not? It may not be the grandest affair, but there'll music and dancing, lots of laughter and high spirits. You've never been to a ball. Wouldn't you like to see what one's like?'

'I don't know. I should have to consider it.'

'You could have a new dress if you decide quickly. I could come with you to pick out a nice muslin, and we could get it made up in a pretty style, nothing too bright or gaudy. I could do your hair for you too – not as your mother likes it, but in a way that might suit your taste. What do you say?'

'I don't know. I should be afraid ... What if no one danced with me?'

'Then you'll eat lots of ices and laugh at them for their silliness! Why don't you think about it overnight? It's a hard thing to see a girl as young as you set her face against pleasure and good fellowship. There'll be time enough for that in the future, believe me.'

When Mrs Hill had gone, Mary lay on her bed, looking at the ceiling and brooding on what she had heard. Mrs Hill's enthusiasm had piqued her curiosity, and she began to question her resolution not to attend the dance. Perhaps she was wrong to stay at home. It might be exciting to go out into the cold autumnal darkness, squeezed into the hired carriage with her sisters, bumping along the road to Meryton. She had never seen the assembly rooms at night, lit up and garlanded with paper flowers and the first of the winter holly. She thought she might like to hear the orchestra scrape out the old familiar airs and jigs and watch people enjoying themselves. Really, why should she not go? It was only a country dance. Other girls of her age had been and lived to tell the tale, and not all of them were beauties. And was it not said – although she could not, at this precise moment, recollect by whom – that, to the thinking mind, no experience was wasted? In half an hour, she had almost persuaded herself it was her duty to attend. And if she did go, then surely she was obliged to have a dress suitable for the occasion? If one went into society, it was only proper to abide by its rules. For the first time she could remember, she allowed her imagination to run away with thoughts of beautiful fabrics and elegant clothes, of colours, styles, and trimmings. Just before she fell asleep, she finally concluded that Mrs Hill was quite right. It made no sense to deny herself this opportunity. She would see a little of life, and moreover, she would make an effort to present herself as neatly, as smartly, and as becomingly as she could. She would go to the dance and and have a new dress for it too. For once, she would try to enjoy herself, as she had seen others do.

At breakfast the next day, it was clear to everyone that Mr Bennet had delivered his judgement; and Lydia's triumphant bearing made it plain that he had decided in her favour. She could barely contain her excitement, which interrupted but did not entirely prevent her rapid consumption of hot rolls and butter.

'Thank you, Papa, thank you, thank you. I swear I shall love you forever now.'

Mrs Bennet, entirely satisfied, smiled broadly at her favourite daughter; but her husband looked grave.

'Your gratitude gives me more pause for thought than your

petulance ever did. I am not at all sure I was wise to give in to you.'

Mr Bennet was a man of considerable natural perception, and there were few situations in which he did not understand what was required of him; but exertion bored him, and he could rarely be bothered to act, even upon what he knew to be right. He found it far easier to mock his daughters than to take the trouble to correct them. Only for Lizzy did he feel any real respect, which was perhaps why she alone felt able to challenge him.

'Then, Papa, why do you do so?' she asked. 'A little firmness on this occasion might impress upon Lydia that not everything is to be had by making a fuss.'

'Really, Lizzy,' cried Mrs Bennet, 'you sound just like Mary! And what, pray, has it to do you with you anyway? I shall be there to look after Lydia and Kitty and make sure they behave exactly as they should.'

Mr Bennet laid down his knife and regarded the table with bitter satisfaction.

'You see, my dears, there is no need for concern. Your mother, with her usual decorum, will ensure that neither silliness nor self-indulgence will prevail.'

Mary saw Elizabeth catch Jane's eye and watched a glance pass between them – of anxiety, regret, pain – a whole host of emotions in one brief look. Her younger sisters were oblivious. Lydia had quite recovered her usual confidence and was blithely helping herself to more tea and more jam.

'Kitty must come as well,' demanded Lydia. 'If I am to go, it would be monstrously unfair if she did not.'

Kitty nodded furiously, her mouth full of roll. But before

she could utter a plea in support of her case, Mary decided to make her own announcement.

'I think I should like to go too, Papa, if there is no objection to my doing so.'

'You want to go?' exclaimed Lydia, genuinely surprised. 'Whatever for?'

'I think it is time I saw something of the world.'

Mary had resolved to say no more than this. She had no intention of being teased by Lydia into offering a fuller explanation of her decision. Nothing on earth would have forced her to admit that she had actually begun to look forward to the ball.

'Of course you may go,' replied Mr Bennet testily. 'Everyone may go who wishes to go, providing I am obliged to hear no more about it. But, Mrs Bennet, you are to understand there is no point in applying to me for funds to buy new outfits. I will underwrite a few fripperies, ribbons and feathers, I suppose, but that is the limit of my generosity. There will be no incontinent purchasing of gowns, shawls, shoes, and the like.'

Lydia, Kitty, and their mother were equally distraught to hear this; but Mr Bennet was implacable.

'No, no, not another word. I have already been persuaded once to act against my inclination. On this subject, I am immoveable.'

'I have some little money saved,' said Mary thoughtfully. 'I never spend my allowance, so I think I shall have enough for a dress, if it can be made in time.'

Lydia glared from across the table. 'Lord, you really are the most annoying prig!'

'That may be true,' said Mary, quite calm now. 'But at

least I shall have the satisfaction of being a prig in a new dress.'

Later that morning Mary and Mrs Hill walked into the draper's shop at Meryton, and there they found a figured muslin of the palest cream – white would be too harsh for Mary's complexion, insisted Mrs Hill – shot through with a faint gold thread. Mary thought it the most beautiful stuff she had ever seen, fingering its delicate weave with a respectful touch. Once wrapped up, she refused to hand over the bulky parcel to Mrs Hill, but carried it home herself, both proud and a little fearful that she had taken such a huge step.

In her bedroom, she discussed with Mrs Hill how it was to be made up. It was impossible to ask advice from her sisters. With Jane or Elizabeth, she would have been too self-conscious; and it was far too late to attempt such a conversation with Kitty or Lydia. They would have laughed at her uncertain attempts to find a style that suited her. Besides, her taste did not run towards the flounces and ruffles that delighted Lydia. On her they would look false and wrong. She would be most at ease in a simple dress that did not announce itself too loudly. Perhaps, she thought, a plain dress was the best ornament for a plain woman?

In ten days, it was ready. The dressmaker brought it at dusk, delivering it as she had been asked directly into Mrs Hill's hands – Mary had no wish for her sisters to see the gown before she did. Hurrying up the stairs to her room, with Mrs Hill following in her wake, she was breathless with excitement. Once inside, she lit a candle while Mrs Hill locked the door. Her hands fumbled with the string of the parcel, but she soon had it open. When she held up the dress, it tumbled over her arms, the gold thread catching the gleam from the candlelight. It was as airy and delicate as a cloud, utterly unlike the well-scrubbed grey and beige cottons which she usually wore. Yes, it was plain, with no decoration to distract the eye; but there was a purity in its plainness, an elegance in its simplicity.

'It has turned out very well,' said Mrs Hill. 'Very well indeed.'

Mary held the dress up in front of herself, and peered into her mirror.

'Is it too fine for me, do you think? Shall I look ridiculous?'

'No, you will not. I believe you'll look very handsome in it.'

Mary looked shyly at her reflection. She would not go as far as handsome, but she thought she would not stand out as awkward or strange; and that was enough for her.

CHAPTER EIGHT

On the night of the ball, Mrs Hill was in great demand, hurrying from room to room, helping each of the sisters with the final adjustments to her dress, pinning and tucking, snipping and trimming. But it was Mary to whom she devoted most of her time, arranging her hair in a style as smooth and simple as her dress, with no attempt at imposing short-lived curls. When she had finished, she drew a twist of paper from her apron pocket, undid it carefully and placed it on the dressing table, revealing a small pinch of pale pink powder.

'Is that rouge?' asked Mary uncertainly.

'It is indeed, borrowed from Miss Lydia's drawer. She has enough of it not to notice the loss of such a little amount.'

'You're not suggesting I should wear it, are you?'

'Only the very smallest touch, that's all you need. Put your finger into it, as lightly as you can, and rub it very gently into your cheek.'

Mary took the little package and stared into it curiously.

'Go on,' insisted Mrs Hill. 'The very tiniest quantity. No one will know, I promise you.'

Her mind suddenly made up, Mary dabbed her finger into the powder as delicately as she could and applied it to her face.

'Just a little at first,' advised Mrs Hill. 'It's a bit like cooking –

you can always add more salt, but you can't take it out. There, that's perfect. You have a bit of colour, but you don't look painted. Time to put the gown on now, if you're not to be late.'

The dress slid over Mary's head with a confident, slippery ease; and suddenly, there she was, ready. She was almost afraid to look at herself, but plucked up the courage to stare at her reflection in the pier glass. She saw a tall young woman with a neat figure, sleek brown hair, and mild, regular features, clad in a light and pretty dress. Relief flooded over her. She knew she would never turn heads when she walked into a room, as she had so often seen her sisters do; but, as she surveyed herself with her usual critical eye, she thought she looked as well as she had ever done. She would do.

'Very pleasing,' said Mrs Hill. 'Just what we'd hoped for. But there's still one thing left to do.'

With that, she reached across Mary's face, took off her spectacles and laid them on the dressing table.

'Now you're ready. And Miss Lydia has been calling this last ten minutes.'

Left alone in her room, Mary looked at her discarded spectacles, uncertain what to do; then, after a moment's hesitation, she picked them up, stuffed them into her little evening bag, and made her way downstairs to meet her sisters.

Unusually for her, Mary was the last to come down, and when she arrived in the hall, everyone was already there, waiting and chatting. Her appearance silenced them all, as they took her in. Elizabeth spoke first, looking her up and down with appreciative surprise.

'That is a very handsome dress. You look very well in it, Mary.'

'Indeed, you do,' agreed Jane. 'The colour is just right. It suits you perfectly.'

Mrs Bennet drew herself away from the hallway mirror, where she had been making all those vital last-minute adjustments to her outfit and person, without which she would not have considered leaving the house. She examined Mary coolly. She had long hoped to see an improvement in Mary's appearance, but, as she had had no hand in her transformation, she was not inclined to be generous.

'So, miss, it seems you can make an effort when you choose. What a pity you can't be troubled to do so more often.'

'It is amazing what new clothes will do,' observed Lydia tartly. 'Anyone is improved by them. If I had a new dress to wear, I'm sure I should astonish you all!'

'I have no doubt you will do that,' remarked Elizabeth, 'new dress or not.'

Mary drew her cloak carefully over herself, pleased that her outfit had provoked nothing worse than she had expected, and followed her sisters out into the cold night air. She was silent as their coach pulled away from the house, and no one spoke to her. Jane and Elizabeth chatted in low whispers, while Lydia addressed them all in loud declarations which did not require a reply.

'Just think, Mama, I saw Dick Smythson in Meryton yesterday, and he positively insisted I should keep the second dance for him. He's engaged to that annoying Miss Denny for the first, but she's his cousin, so I suppose he was obliged. And Captain Carter has bespoke me for the third. I do hope he'll wear his regimentals; you can't believe how much he is improved by them.'

'Oh, but I can,' answered Mrs Bennet. 'I liked an officer

well enough myself once. I hope for your sake he will wear them tonight.'

'And for the fourth,' Lydia continued, having hardly noticed her mother's intervention, 'I am in hopes of William Digby. I told him he would have to find ices for me afterwards, for I'm sure to be sweating all over by then.'

Elizabeth raised her eyes in exasperation as Kitty gave way to a wail of outrage.

'Lydia, you know Mr Digby asked me for the fourth dance, you are not to steal him away. Really, Mama, tell her she musn't, it isn't fair . . .'

Huddled in the corner, Mary began to consider her own chances of finding a partner. She knew so few young men. Lydia's and Kitty's daily walks into Meryton had introduced them to numerous masculine acquaintances, especially since the arrival some months ago of a militia regiment. They met officers sauntering about the streets, bantered with them outside the milliner's shop, and counted many amongst them as their intimate friends. Jane and Elizabeth were more aloof, but even they had been sometimes known to acknowledge the salutes of the more gentlemanly of the soldiers with a polite inclination of their heads. Mary had no such small introductions to smooth over her way into the ballroom. She rarely accompanied her sisters on their trips into Meryton; and when she did, she had nothing to say to any officer whose path they happened to cross. She had no talent for charming small talk or provoking chit-chat.

As the carriage rolled into Meryton, her anxiety grew. All the excitement she had felt when she left the house began to drain away as she thought about what lay ahead. While the ball had remained safely in the future, she had been able to think of it almost with excitement. But now it was about to become reality, it felt very different. As they pulled up before the assembly rooms, her courage began to fail her. What would she do if no one asked her to dance? She had heard Jane and Lizzy laughingly lament occasions when they had found themselves with no one to stand up with; but they did so with the cheerful self-mockery of those for whom this was a rare event. They could be sure they would not linger like that for long; another partner would inevitably appear at any moment. Mary knew she could summon up neither their poise nor their confidence. As the Longbourn party gathered their cloaks and bags, eager to be out of the carriage, Mary followed her mother and sisters towards the light and noise of the ball, her heart in her mouth.

CHAPTER NINE

The crowd of people gathered at the entrance to the rooms seemed immense, as forbidding and impenetrable as she had feared. Mary was buffeted from side to side, almost deafened by the shouted greetings that echoed over her head as she struggled to make her way through the knots of excited guests huddled in the hallway. Desperate not to lose sight of her sisters – whose progress through the scrum was, she noted, followed by a number of appreciative male gazes – she pushed onwards with all the courage she could muster until, at last, she emerged into the open space of the ballroom. For a moment, she stood quite still, amazed at what she saw. The old rooms, as she knew them, were unrecognisable. There were candles everywhere, not, it was true, of the most expensive kind, and a distinct smell of tallow hung in the air; but their flickering light transformed the scuffed walls and lit up the boughs of autumn leaves hung upon them as decoration. In the distance, through a pair of double doors, she could see the inn servants laying out the supper table, the footmen polishing the serving spoons on their aprons. Upstairs, perched on the balcony, the musicians were tuning their instruments and drinking a last glass of beer before beginning their work. On the floor itself, impatient couples had already begun to gather, pacing up and down, keen for the dancing to begin.

Kitty and Lydia were quickly swallowed by the throng. Mary looked about but could see no one she knew. For a moment, she considered putting on her glasses. She scrabbled in her little bag, and her fingers clasped round them, but then she imagined Lydia's expression if she were to see her wearing them, triumphant, as if the sight of Mary's spectacles more than compensated for the insult of her new dress. Mary hastily withdrew her hand from her bag and was just beginning to panic when she felt Elizabeth's touch on her shoulder.

'Over here, Mary, we've found a place to sit where we shall be quite comfortable.'

Lizzy led her deftly through the press of people, towards a row of chairs, arranged so that their occupants could comfortably survey the dancing without being obliged to join in themselves. Their mother had already found a place there, alongside Lady Lucas, her particular friend. They spent much of their time together, for each found in the other exactly what they sought in a companion. Mrs Bennet required an acolyte; and Lady Lucas, timid and deferential, was happy to play the role of obedient disciple. Only once had the natural order of their intimacy been disturbed. When Mr Lucas, a wealthy Meryton merchant, had been honoured with a baronetcy, it seemed as though all must change, for how could a mere Mrs Bennet continue to patronise the newly minted Lady Lucas? But to her immense relief, Mrs Bennet soon discovered that her friend's title had done nothing to alter her docile temper; and that she was as prepared as ever to submit without complaint to the condescension that was an inescapable ingredient of Mrs Bennet's fond and unalterable regard.

Behind Lady Lucas's chair stood Charlotte, her eldest daughter. She was an open-faced young woman of medium height with no great claims to beauty. Her unremarkable appearance was a source of great satisfaction to Mrs Bennet, who frequently drew to Lady Lucas's attention the contrast between Charlotte's scanty attractions and those of her own daughters. Nor did she hesitate to dwell, with all the sympathy at her command, upon the disappointment her friend must feel at Charlotte's still remaining unmarried at the age of twenty-six, especially as there seemed so little chance of her changing her situation.

Lady Lucas was too fainthearted to contradict Mrs Bennet, nodding resignedly on such occasions; but her pliant nature was not without benefits for her otherwise unfortunate child. Lady Lucas possessed neither the energy nor the frustration which came so readily to Mrs Bennet; and Charlotte had been subjected to none of the recrimination and complaint which had been Mary's lot. Perhaps for that reason, Charlotte did not hang her head, ashamed at her failure to become a beauty, but greeted the world with a clear-eyed, watchful gaze. She had no illusions about her looks, but her bearing suggested she had no intention of apologising for them. Instead, she acknowledged her situation with a wry amusement; and those who did not know her well were often surprised by the acuteness of her perceptions and the sharpness of her wit. These were the qualities that had recommended her strongly to Elizabeth, who had for some years counted her as her closest friend. It was towards Charlotte's welcoming presence that Lizzy now steered Mary, before seizing for herself the last remaining empty seat.

'What a rout! I swear the crowd gets bigger every season! Soon we'll have to take turns on the dance floor. The managers will issue everyone with a number, and call us out, couple by couple.'

'Or perhaps,' replied Charlotte, 'they could limit admittance only to those young ladies fortunate enough to have secured partners for more than half the dances. The rest of us could be left in the hall, like so much unwanted baggage, to be called for when required.'

'Oh,' declared Elizabeth, 'I won't listen to that kind of talk. I don't believe you have no partners. And if you don't, it's because you greet everyone with such a baleful stare that no man would dare approach you.'

'You're quite right,' agreed Charlotte. 'I have partners aplenty lined up for me – two cousins, home from school, just old enough to be here, and an ancient friend of my father's, who will squire me onto the floor with the greatest courtesy, all the time wondering with ill-disguised anxiety when supper will be served!'

Elizabeth reached out and took Charlotte by the hand.

'I think you've been sitting far too long amongst the matrons. That's enough to dampen anyone's spirits. Now you have put the thought of eating into my head, I can't dislodge it! Shall we go and look at the food and see if we can persuade them to give us a little something in advance of the crowd? Mary, why don't you stay here? We shan't be long and we might even bring back a morsel or two for you!'

Mary watched as her sister carried her friend away, their arms entwined, heads bent towards each other, sharing a joke. Her courage had been shaken even further by Charlotte's words. If she could not secure proper partners, what hope was there for Mary? Just at that moment, the little orchestra finally struck up, and with a thunder of feet, the dancers rushed onto the floor. The noise was quite extraordinary – the music, the laughter, the acclamations – and for an instant, Mary could barely hear herself think. Couples marched, strolled, and trotted up and down the line, some with more enthusiasm than skill, but all with the greatest determination to enjoy themselves. In their midst Mary soon spotted Lydia, flushed, loud, excited, arm in arm with an officer whose regimentals were all she could have desired. Mary felt a sudden pang. Why could she not be there too, lost in the shared delight of it all? Instead, she stood amongst the seated circles of mothers, aunts, married sisters, whose dancing days were over.

At first, she had thought them a cheerful group, happy to watch the proceedings and chat between themselves; but as a second dance began and she remained unclaimed, she thought she felt their eyes directed towards her. She was sure they were discussing her, some with pity, some with scorn; she imagined them weighing up the likelihood of anyone presenting himself to ask her, and deciding the odds were low. Where were Lizzy and Charlotte? Were they never coming back? Mary looked about her with mounting unease. Her mother, she was thankful to see, was engrossed in conversation with Lady Lucas and seemed not yet to have noticed her lonely state, but she doubted this could continue for very long. She knew Mrs Bennet would not be pleased to see a daughter of hers so shamefully circumstanced. Growing increasingly self-conscious, she did all she could to seem unconcerned, to convey a nonchalance she was very far from feeling.

Then just as the music struck up for the next dance, a hand was extended to her.

'I would be grateful, miss, to have the pleasure of dancing with you.'

She looked up, surprised. She did not recognise either the voice or the face of her rescuer.

'I am William Lucas, Miss Mary, cousin of Miss Charlotte, your sister's friend.'

So this was one of the youthful relations whom even Charlotte had not considered a creditable partner. It was true he was young, perhaps not even sixteen. But that was not so far off her own age. Why should she not accept him? She smiled at him with genuine gratitude and allowed herself to be led onto the floor.

Neither Mary nor her partner embarrassed themselves. They did not trip or stumble over the other's feet. He asked her if she was enjoying her evening; she said that she was, and there the conversation closed. At the dance's conclusion, he led her back to her place, bowed politely, and moved away. It was an entirely unexceptional encounter. It was unlikely he would ask her again; and yet Mary's sprits leapt. A man – or, as honesty compelled her to admit, a boy – had danced with her. To be asked was all she had wished for. She should not have to go home from her first ball and say no one had chosen her. She almost hugged herself as she looked around for Lizzy and Charlotte. She could see no sign of Charlotte but thought she could just make out Elizabeth's familiar form, on the other side of the room, talking with her usual animation to an attentive young man. Was it her or not? Mary narrowed her eyes and peered into the distance. So intent was she in looking for her sister, that she did not hear the quiet voice at her side the first time it addressed her.

'Excuse me, Miss Mary, I do not mean to intrude, but it is very bad for your eyes to screw them up in that way.'

She turned to find a young man standing before her, respectful but concerned, clearly dressed in his newest and smartest clothes. At first, she did not know him.

'Perhaps I may be permitted to help you find whatever or whomever you are looking for?'

'Mr Sparrow? Mr John Sparrow?'

He bowed and looked down, a little self-conscious.

'I am sorry, Miss Bennet. I should not have presumed – but I did not want you to strain your eyes. I should not have spoken.'

'No, Mr Sparrow, I am very grateful to you. After all, you know better than anyone what my difficulties are. May I take advantage of you, sir? I am looking for my sister Elizabeth. I thought I saw her towards that corner. Am I mistaken?'

'No, miss, you're quite right. She was talking to a gentleman with whom she has just stood up.' He pointed towards the set of dancers readying themselves to begin. 'I believe it is Captain Carter. Of the Herts Militia.'

That would not please Lydia, thought Mary to herself, and the ghost of smile crossed her face. This seemed to encourage Mr Sparrow, who shifted somewhat nervously in his place before speaking again.

'I wonder, Miss Mary, if you would do me the honour of standing up with me for the next dance?'

For the very briefest of moments, Mary hesitated; then, impelled by the surprising rush of pleasure his invitation had provoked, she accepted.

'I should be delighted to do so, Mr Sparrow.'

He smiled back, relieved.

'Well, then, I thank you – that is to say, I'm very grateful. Very much so. Shall we remain here until the next set is called?'

While they waited together at the edge of the dance floor, he asked how her spectacles had answered – had they made it easier for her to read and to sew?

'To tell the truth, Mr Sparrow, I am no great hand with a needle, with spectacles or without. But I can't thank you and your father enough for the improvement they have brought about in my reading. I can study for hours now, and even the smallest print holds no terrors for me.'

He was delighted to hear it. Might she tell him what she read with such enjoyment? Mary looked at him warily. Was he teasing her? But his sincere expression convinced her he really wished to know, and soon she found herself telling him about Mrs Macaulay. He nodded thoughtfully. His own preference, he explained, was for works of science, but on her recommendation, he should seek out that lady's works and do his best to appreciate them.

'Are you a scholar, then, sir?'

He looked embarrassed.

'Not yet,' he admitted. 'But I very much hope to become one. My interest is in optics and the mechanics of the eye. I suppose you might say that the apple has not fallen far from the tree in that respect.'

'But that's an admirable thing,' replied Mary. 'It is only natural you should wish to increase your knowledge of a subject already familiar to you.'

'I'm very glad you think so.' He leaned a little towards her and continued in a low, confidential tone. 'My father has it in mind to send me to study medicine. He says I have it within me to become a doctor.'

'You'll go to the university, then?'

'No, my father says the best place for me is one of the London medical schools. He thinks Barts Hospital; or maybe Moorfields. Both are counted the very best in their field.'

For a moment, all his diffidence melted away; his face lit up with excitement at the thought of such a future. Then, just as suddenly, he remembered himself.

'But it is not a thing generally known. I have not mentioned it before to anyone but you.'

'It is a noble ambition, sir. I honour you for it. And I shall speak of it to no one else.'

Then the music struck up, Mr Sparrow held out his hand, and they made their way onto the floor. This time, she enjoyed every moment of the dance. The music was exhilarating; the push and pull of the other dancers as they changed partners and handed each other down the line made her feel joyfully connected, as though she was at the centre of an excited, happy band of friends. For once she was part of the pleasure, not watching it from afar. When reunited with Mr Sparrow, they both beamed at each other, delighted to be together again. When the music stopped, she was more sorry than she could say that the dance was over.

'Thank you, Mr Sparrow,' she exclaimed as he showed her to a chair. 'I liked that of all things!'

'So did I, so did I! It was the best dance I have had in a very long time. I suppose I could not persuade you to stand up with me again, if you are free?'

This time, Mary did not hesitate.

'I have no engagement for the next dance, sir, and would be delighted to be your partner again.'

CHAPTER TEN

Neither Mary nor Mr Sparrow spoke very much while they waited for the next dance. They sat quietly, recovering their breath until the set was called and the dancers lined up again. This time Lydia was nearby, a few couples behind in the line, victoriously handed onto the floor by Captain Carter. Her face registered astonishment as she saw Mary take her place. She turned her head as far as she could to see who her partner might be, and shot her sister a questioning stare; but Mary made no response and allowed herself again to be carried away by the music and movement.

When the dance finished, Lydia looked as though she might walk over and begin an interrogation directly. But Mary was relieved to see another officer approach her, and she was soon too distracted to tear herself away.

'Should you like a cold drink now, Miss Bennet? I would be glad to go and find one for you.'

Mary thought this an excellent idea and watched as Mr Sparrow marched quickly away to the supper room. She could not remember when she had last been so happy; a man had danced with her, not once but twice! She had never imagined such a thing might happen to her. She looked down at the floor to hide the pleasure she felt she could hold within herself no longer; and for that reason, she did not see

Charlotte Lucas approaching her until she was almost at her side.

'It looks as though you're enjoying yourself, Mary.'

'Why, Charlotte, you came upon me very quietly! Yes, I am indeed! The evening has been very kind to me so far.'

'You have been dancing a great deal. Your partner is the young Sparrow boy, I believe?'

'Yes, he has been very attentive.'

'You have stood up with him twice? And he has gone to find refreshments for you, I imagine?'

She nodded again, a little puzzled by Charlotte's tone.

'Mary, you are very young, and do not perhaps fully appreciate how these things are understood. If you dance with him again, it will be remarked upon. Two dances in succession suggests a liking. Three might imply something more.'

'He hasn't asked me to dance again.'

'Oh, but I think he will, if he has taken the trouble to find you a drink. That shows great consideration on his part. It is a positive battleground in the supper room.'

Although she knew she should not do so, Mary smiled again. Charlotte looked at her gravely.

'If he does, I would advise you most strongly to refuse him. Say you are tired or too much heated. That you intend to dance no more for a while.'

'But he's been so kind to me! And I have loved dancing with him!'

Charlotte regarded her with a faintly pitying look.

'I am afraid I shall have to speak more plainly. No matter how kind he is, he is not a suitable partner for you. His father visits people's houses and fits them for spectacles. Think what Mr Bennet would say.'

Overcome with shame, Mary could not at first compose herself to reply. *My father barely notices if I am in the room or not*, she thought; *he hardly speaks to me. Why should he care if I have some conversation with a polite, respectable young man?*

'For myself,' said Charlotte, staring calmly out at the dance floor, 'I do not mind at all. I am arrived at a time when I think I might look kindly on the man who runs the circulating library if he were to speak nicely to me and offer to keep new books aside on my behalf, for all he is over fifty and blind in one eye. But,' she declared, turning to look at Mary directly, 'I am not your mother. And I can promise you that if I have noticed those two dances and the refreshments Mr Sparrow expects to share with you, she will have done so too.'

She touched Mary's shoulder very lightly with her fan.

'I mention it only as a friend who understands better than most in your family how rare and how pleasing it is for women like us to be singled out in this way. But, whatever his charms, I am afraid you will find your mother has an altogether different sense of his worth.'

With that, she tipped her head in polite acknowledgement and moved away. Astonished, Mary stood rooted to the spot. *Charlotte is jealous*, she told herself. *No one wants to dance with her. Because she is miserable, she cannot bear that anyone else should be happy. She seeks to spoil for others what she cannot have for herself.* But much as she tried to resist them, disturbing thoughts began to take shape in her mind. It was only too easy to imagine how Mrs Bennet would respond to the idea of her dancing with Mr Sparrow. She pictured her mother rising up from her little gold chair, marching across the floor, declaring to a horrified Mr Sparrow that her daughter would not be standing up with him in the next set, nor in any other. She saw him humbled and humiliated as Mrs Bennet carried her away, saw him standing solitary and ashamed in their wake. She understood in an instant that this would happen. How could she have been so stupid? Lydia had seen her; she would make sure their mother knew, would laugh and crow and joke about it. She swallowed hard. She could not allow it. She could not watch while such a good man was made to look a fool, only for paying her some small attentions. By the time she caught sight of Mr Sparrow's tall figure striding back to her with two glasses in his hand, she knew what she had to do.

'I am sorry to have been so long away, but the crowd fighting for its supper was immense! I never knew Meryton was home to so many hungry people.'

'Thank you, sir,' said Mary, taking her drink, unable to meet his smile. 'It is most welcome, for I am very thirsty.'

She looked away, and from the corner of her eye, she caught an unwelcome glimpse of her mother and Lady Lucas, still seated in their sanctuary, with their heads close together in talk. Were they staring in her direction as they did so? Mary could not tell. Her stomach lurched with fear. She peered into the flickering candlelight but could not make out their faces.

'Shall we stand up once more?' John Sparrow extended his hand with the clear expectation she would accept.

'Thank you, sir, but I cannot – that is, I am afraid I must decline.'

He paused and lowered his arm.

'But why not? I thought – I thought . . .'

She could not bear to see his expression, confused and disappointed.

'I know, I know, and so did I – but – my mother – I fear –'
At last she got possession of herself enough to speak sensibly.
'I am very sorry, but I cannot dance with you again. I have
very much enjoyed it – really, I have – but cannot do so any
more. I am persuaded I have danced enough for one night. I
am sorry, but now I must take my leave.'

She handed her drink back to him, and he stood there,
two glasses in hand, as she walked blindly towards where
Mrs Bennet and Lady Lucas sat. A few hot tears sprang into
her eyes, but she wiped them away harshly. No one – and
least of all her mother – should see she was upset.

When she arrived at Mrs Bennet's side, Mary saw immediately that she was extremely displeased. 'Where have you
been?' she demanded as Mary approached. 'I haven't seen you
these two hours. Lydia told me you have been dancing – with
the oculist's son! With the boy who made your glasses! I said
it couldn't be true – that even you, Mary, would have more
consideration than to subject me to such an embarrassment.
His father keeps a shop, you know. With a bell on the door!'

Mary thought it best to say nothing. An argument would
only draw attention to her shame. Instead she took up a position behind her mother, where she could not be seen by the
revellers. She hung her head and smoothed her cream and
gold dress. She would not dance again, no matter who asked
her. The time dragged heavily after that. Occasionally, her
sisters returned to speak to their mother, or to dab scent
behind their ears. Only Elizabeth noticed Mary's sad, extinguished presence.

'Are you quite well, Mary? I saw you standing up earlier.
You looked in fine spirits. Has something happened?'

'No, Lizzy, nothing at all. I am content where I am.'

'You do not look content. I am going back for a last jog about. Won't you come with me?'

'Thank you, but no. I shan't dance again.'

At last, when all the food was eaten and all the decent wine drunk, the ball drew to a close. The musicians played 'God Save the King,' and the servants began snuffing out the candles.

Mary followed her sisters into the hall, where the guests rummaged furiously through a mountain of cloaks and coats. At the front of the scrum, Kitty was bravely plucking out any garment she recognised.

'Mary! Are you there? Here's your cloak!'

She threw it over the heads of those behind her, but Mary was too slow to catch it. Another arm reached out and rescued it. As she looked up, Mary saw it was John Sparrow. He handed it to her wordlessly. She accepted it in equal silence. Then he nodded at her blankly and was gone.

CHAPTER ELEVEN

In the carriage going home, Lydia was in the highest possible spirits. She had been forced to sit out only two dances the whole evening, and had made the acquaintance of three new officers, hitherto unthought of. She regaled her sisters with a detailed account of her successes, but they were not a very receptive audience. Jane and Kitty were both soon asleep. Elizabeth gazed out the window, and Mary played with her gloves, plaiting the fingers together and then untwisting them again, her mind far away. Finally, piqued beyond endurance by the lack of interest in her conquests, Lydia looked about her, searching for a suitable subject to tease and annoy.

'And what about you, Mary? I saw you standing up with two beaux, though it must be said, one was a schoolboy and the other a shopkeeper. What a triumph for your first outing!'

Mary threw her gloves into her lap, as angered as her sister had hoped she would be.

'At least they were both gentlemen, which is more than can be said for some of the partners you were so desperate to be seen with!'

Lydia, who much preferred an argument to silence, laughed out loud.

'You don't really mean to say that Mr Sparrow is a gentleman. Even you can't really believe that. His father has a shop in Hertford. I suppose we may look forward to seeing you serving there, wearing a green apron in daytime and drawing up the accounts by night.'

'You seem to have forgotten,' retorted Mary, 'that our grandfather had an office in Meryton, and our uncle keeps one there still. Are they not to be considered gentlemen?'

'Really, Mary, for shame!' cried Mrs Bennet. 'Your grandfather was an attorney, as is your uncle. That is a profession, not a trade.'

'But what of my uncle Gardiner? He is a merchant, is he not?' countered Mary, as furious now as her mother.

'He has his own warehouses!' exclaimed Mrs Bennet. 'And a large house in Gracechurch Street. There is every difference in the world.'

'Anyway,' concluded Lydia, happy now that everyone was cross, 'if I ever find myself in want of spectacles – which I devoutly hope will never be the case – I shall be sure to obtain them from your little business. I hope that for such a near relation, you will offer a decent discount.'

Mrs Bennet, still smarting from the insults she believed had been offered to her family, tossed her head in disdain. Nothing mattered more to her than seeing her daughters safely married; but it was inconceivable that one of her girls should unite herself to a man who had sent in his bill for Mr Bennet to pay.

'I only danced with him twice,' said Mary in a small, defeated voice.

'That is twice more than I should have permitted if I had seen you do so,' declared Mrs Bennet. 'I want to hear no more of this Sparrow. In truth, I am surprised at his presumption.'

Mary said no more. When the carriage arrived back at

Longbourn, she hurried up to her room and closed the door. She did not answer Mrs Hill's knocks. For a while she stared dry-eyed into the darkness. Then she lit a candle and undressed. She hung up the new dress, and its gold threads continued to catch the light for a while, until she finally blew out the flame.

CHAPTER TWELVE

Mary avoided all Mrs Hill's attempts to discover how she had enjoyed the ball. She hid in her bedroom, pleading a headache, or retreated to the garden, walking alone amongst the shrubs. What could she say that did not reflect badly on herself? She had insulted a man who had done nothing but treat her kindly. He had sought out her company when no one else wished for it, and she had rewarded him with a most odious dismissal. She was ashamed of herself. Why had she capitulated so quickly to Charlotte Lucas's warnings? Why had she retreated so tamely when threatened with her mother's disapproval? It was not as though that was an unfamiliar experience. She was sure neither Elizabeth nor Lydia would have been so easily cowed. Whereas she – Mary shook her head, contemptuous at her own weakness.

In the days that followed, there was not a moment when she was not tormented by guilt, or ferociously angry with herself. On the third night after the ball, once she had prepared herself for bed, she pulled up a chair to the bedroom window, opened it, and stared out into the dark, silent garden. Was this who she was? A coward, who lacked the courage to follow her own inclinations? A silly girl, too timid to trust her own judgement, who submitted dumbly to what others told her?

She breathed in the cool night air and hugged her shawl more tightly around her. That was not how she had felt when John Sparrow asked her to dance. Then she had been fearless, had she not? Then she had known her own mind. She bit her lip, forcing herself to think more clearly. In truth, she was compelled to admit that her mind had played no part at all in what happened. When he invited her that second time, when he held out his hand to lead her to the dance floor, she had not consulted her intellect, of which she was so proud. She had weighed nothing up. She had not debated whether she should say yes or no. She had not considered how it would look, or what her mother might say. She had not thought at all; she had been governed entirely by her feelings, by the pleasure she felt as he asked and the excitement that mounted in her as she followed him into the crowd.

While it lasted, it had been wonderful. A shiver of delight ran through her as she remembered how she had felt as he smiled at her. But then Charlotte had spoken and she had given in, and the result had been humiliation for both of them. For herself, she thought she could bear it. But it was inexpressibly painful to think she had inflicted hurt upon John Sparrow, whose only sin was to have been attentive to her.

She rose and paced about her bedroom. Such a dreadful thing must never be allowed to happen again. It was all her fault. Her emotions had betrayed her. Her stupid, unruly feelings had led her into error, causing misery to a man who did not deserve it. They could not be trusted and must be tamed, subdued. She must find some other guide upon which to depend.

She sat down at her desk, and her eye fell upon the many volumes piled up there. She ran her hand gently across their spines; and as she did so, an idea struck her, a thought so obvious she could not believe it had not occurred to her before. Her books would save her. Within their pages, she would find everything she needed to keep her safe from further error. Writers whose capacities far exceeded her own would tell her how to behave. Their conclusions would direct her, show her what she must do to act rightly. In an instant, she understood that the books she devoured so avidly were not merely intellectual abstractions. A thoughtful reader like herself might treat them as handbooks, as manuals of instruction, from which rules might be extracted that explained how to live a calm and rational existence.

Mary was alert now, her thoughts racing. Yes, yes, that made sense. Study would show her the way, if she allowed it to do so. The wisdom of the ages was surely more to be relied upon than her own ridiculous sentiments. But if she was to absorb and understand what she read, her mind must be clear and receptive, unclouded by strong emotions. If she wished to act rightly, she must conquer her passions. Her heart had failed her, and now her intellect must take its place. Her reason, and not her feelings, must in future be relied upon to tell her what to do. She must think more and feel less. That way she should do no more damage, either to herself or others.

She moved back to her place by the window. Low voices rose up from the kitchen, as Mrs Hill and the servants cleared the last of the supper things. Mary closed her eyes and sat quite still, willing herself to accept the decision she had made. But for all her efforts, a wave of resentment rose up unbidden from within her, protesting at the course she meant to adopt. Did she appreciate what she was about to renounce? Was she really prepared never again to experience that glorious rush of excitement that had overwhelmed her when she had danced with John Sparrow? Never again to feel so exuberantly, unthinkingly immersed in the pleasure of the moment? As she recalled that fleeting happiness, part of her flinched at the severity of the measures she had imposed upon herself. But then she thought of John Sparrow's face as he had looked when she rejected him. His remembered expression cut her to the quick. No, she had made her choice. She closed the window and made her way over to her bed. She would begin upon it the very next day. She lay there, eyes open, staring at the ceiling. There was nothing to be gained by delay.

CHAPTER THIRTEEN

The next morning, once breakfast was over, Mary made her way to the library. She was glad to find Mr Bennet was not there; it would be easier to search for what she wanted without his sceptical eye upon her. She passed over the volumes of philosophy and history which usually detained her, consigning Locke, Hobbes, and Rousseau to some future period. She had decided to begin with more practical and direct works of instruction. It took a while before she found them. But eventually, tucked into a corner, she discovered a collection of little books whose titles suggested they were exactly what she sought. She picked up *A Letter of Genteel and Moral Advice to a Young Lady* and *An Enquiry into the Duties of the Female Sex* and laid them on the table where she usually read and worked. Both were very dusty; it was a long time since anyone had taken them from their shelf. She took out her handkerchief, wiped off the worst of the dirt, and smiled as she imagined what Lydia would say if presented with them. But what was that to her? They might not please her sister, but they would do very well for her purposes. She added a few more similar works to her pile and took them away to examine them in private.

Most did not detain her for long. Even in her present low-spirited state, Mary was not much enamoured of writers who insisted that a woman unfortunate enough to be in possession of any learning had better do all she could to conceal it. That savoured too much of her mother's opinion to please her. Perhaps, wondered Mary, it was Mrs Bennet who had acquired the books in the first place? That thought did nothing further to recommend them, and she began to feel impatient with her haul. Finally, just as she was about to give up, she came upon a small book of sermons. Mary had never heard of its author, a Dr Fordyce; but as she turned its pages, she quickly discovered that his ideas were far more to her taste.

Unlike his fellow authors, he thought it a sad thing for a woman to remain in ignorance, her intellect neglected and unformed. For him, an inclination towards serious reading was an excellent quality in a female, a habit to be cultivated rather than concealed. It was much to be regretted, he added, that so many ladies read only novels. Such works could not add to the stock of their knowledge and offered instead a false and misleading picture of the world. Mary paused at this. Mrs Bennet was a great reader of novels. Dr Fordyce made some excellent points. She decided she would read on.

As she did so, she discovered that Dr Fordyce took a dim view of many of her mother's ruling passions. In his opinion, the hours spent on female fripperies such as dress, hair, and other adornments was time thrown away; these were empty distractions with which no sensible woman should concern herself. True beauty, he declared, had nothing to do with outward appearance. It came from within, the product of a well-regulated mind and a properly formed understanding. These qualities, and not a pretty face, are the real measure of a woman's worth. Mary took her pencil and carefully underlined this sentence. It was so much the opposite of everything her mother believed that it could not help but please her.

However, continued Dr Fordyce, it was regrettably the case that for some foolish people, good looks remained the only standard by which a woman is judged; but those of more discernment understand that a steady, informed character is a prize of incalculably more value. Theirs is the only good opinion worth having. Those who value more superficial qualities need not be attended to. The woman who grasps this important point will not bother herself with the pursuit of the empty trappings of fashion. She will use her time more sensibly, seeking to absorb any knowledge that will help her make the correct choices in her journey through life.

Mary closed the book, elated. She had found what she wanted. In Dr Fordyce's words, she heard Mrs Bennet's vision of the world entirely rejected, while her own passions were thoroughly and completely vindicated. For the first time since the ball, her despondency lifted a little. Through her bedroom window, the garden sparkled with the first frost of winter. A pale sun shone in a sharp blue sky. Mary saw none of this, indifferent to everything but her new sense of purpose. She pulled a sheet of paper from her drawer and began to transcribe those passages from Dr Fordyce which she had found particularly satisfying. She had been right to think that study was the answer. Study, hard work, and Dr Fordyce would keep her from going wrong again.

For weeks, Mary worked tirelessly in the library, making notes on everything she read, covering page after page in her neat handwriting. Once she had exhausted Dr Fordyce, she moved on to other writers of whom he approved; and from them, she was handed on, via footnote and reference, to yet more of similar inclination. There was rarely anyone in the library except herself and her father; but he never enquired what she was doing. His indifference was nothing new; but now that she felt herself embarked on something of real importance, it began to provoke her. She longed to know what he would think of the task she had set herself. He was a reading man, the only Bennet, besides herself, with an appetite for scholarly works. If anyone was to understand the urgency of her desire to find a rational way to live, surely it would be him.

She put down her pen and stared into the still library air, imagining how it would be if that were to happen. She saw herself explaining her plans to him, calmly and steadily, with none of the flustered self-consciousness that usually afflicted her in his presence. He listened, neither mocking nor belittling her. And as she spoke, she grew more confident, blooming in the warmth of his approval. A bridge had been crossed, a bond formed between them – they had become partners in a shared endeavour. From then on, the library was no longer silent, but was full of lively conversation, as father and daughter shared their ideas. Mr Bennet asked for her opinions of writers she had read, and suggested names of those she had not. Slowly but steadily, Mary saw herself invited, not only into her father's intellectual domain, but also into his affections, both of them places where, until now, only Lizzy had been admitted.

Far away in the depths of the house, a door slammed, a servant called out, and Mary was shaken abruptly from her daydream. Back in the real world, her father's expression, as he turned a page of his book, was as sardonic as ever, and just as unreachable. Only in her dream would Mary have the courage to approach him directly. Attempting it here – in the library, face-to-face – no, she could not do it. She would not know how to begin. She saw herself retreating in confusion under the power of his merciless smile. And yet, she could not resign herself to giving up. The dream in which he became her intellectual confidante was too seductive to abandon. If she could not trust herself to speak to her father, she must find some other way of making her ambitions known to him.

The answer finally occurred to her one morning as she walked into Meryton. She had not wanted to leave the library, but Mrs Hill had harried her until she agreed to put on her coat and go out into the fresh air. She went alone, dawdling along the quiet lanes, her thoughts directionless. It was not until she was at the outskirts of the village that she was struck by a thought that was both exciting and terrible – what if she were to see John Sparrow there? She stopped and stood motionless amongst the nettles, considering. If their paths crossed – if her saw her – perhaps he would ask how she did – she would reply – he would speak again – and somehow, perhaps, she might get out an apology, an explanation for what had happened – and then he would – But no, she told herself, this was foolish. This was precisely the kind of silliness in which she had resolved not to indulge. It would not do. If they were to meet, all she could expect was a curt raising of his hat as he walked on. He would not stop to talk.

Her eyes filled with tears. Perhaps she should turn back? But that would prove she was even more fainthearted than she had already shown herself to be. She wiped her face and pulled up her collar against the cold. She would go into Meryton – but not for one moment while she was there would she allow herself to think of John Sparrow.

She walked bravely down the single street, looking neither to the left nor the right; but when she came to its end, she had no further idea what she was to do there, for she had left Longbourn without any object in mind beyond her arrival. She supposed she might look at the shops; that was what her sisters would do, but the haberdashers where Kitty and Lydia spent their allowances was of no interest to her. Instead, she headed to the stationers.

Staring through the shop window, she looked longingly at the thick cream paper, fine sharp pencils, and perfumed sealing waxes. Beautiful writing things always made her mouth water, and these were particularly attractive. How satisfying it would be to have some useful occupation on hand for which they could be used. They would be the perfect materials to use in composing a little book, for example; the different coloured inks could be used very prettily to illustrate favourite sayings. As she regarded them hungrily, it occurred to her that such a book would be the perfect gift for her father, demonstrating to him not only the strength of her affection, but also the extent of her reading. She could choose extracts from her favourite authors, copying them onto its pages and presenting them in a way that was sure to intrigue and impress him. It would say what she could not, displaying the range and depth of her interests. Her work was sure to be a better advocate for her ambitions than anything she could say to him.

She grew more and more excited as she thought about it. The intellectual challenge, deciding which passages to include, came first of course. But there would be a great deal of pleasure in making the little book as pleasing to the eye as it would be to the mind. She would buy the best volume she could afford, with a soft leather cover and good quality paper for its blank pages. She would need a new set of pens, some coloured inks, and perhaps an ebony ruler; she had always wanted one of those. Her manner was positively jaunty as she entered the stationer's shop to make her purchases; and her cheerfulness lasted all the way home, as she began to plan how the title page might look. It was only when she sat down at her desk that she realised she had left Meryton with no sighting at all of John Sparrow. She felt a sharp pang of regret; but before it could take hold, she stiffened her resolve. She opened the new book, took out her ruler, gathered her pens together, and began to write.

CHAPTER FOURTEEN

Mary worked slowly, taking care to ensure everything was done to the very best of her abilities. There were times when she was impatient to know what Mr Bennet would think of the little book; but she curbed her desire to make haste, for she had gradually understood the true significance of her task. She had long since ceased to think of it as a simple work of compilation. She knew now it was far more than that. It was nothing less than a calling card inviting her father to recognise her for who she really was – a like-minded spirit, a daughter it would be easy to love, if only he could be persuaded to notice her. It was this conviction that kept her hard at work, day after day, hour after hour, decorating the margins and ornamenting each page number with coloured flourishes. She would spare nothing to make her book of extracts the most accomplished of its kind.

One cold day, when unseasonal showers kept all but the bravest indoors, for once, Mary was not alone in the library. While she sat at her table, her papers spread out around her, Elizabeth was perched in the window seat, knees drawn up before her, a book in her hand. She knew the rules that governed visitors to Mr Bennet's library as well as anyone; and for much of the time, she was obediently silent. But every so often, a little chuckle of amusement escaped her – until finally, she could not help herself and laughed out loud. Mary looked up, shocked at such a breach of discipline, but Lizzy merely smiled, offering her father an apology that was anything but abject.

'I'm sorry, Papa. I didn't mean to disturb you.'

Mr Bennet took off his spectacles and gazed at Elizabeth with such warmth that Mary's heart contracted. Perhaps, once he had read her extracts, he might look at her in the same way.

'What are you reading, my dear, that pleases you so much?'

'It's Miss Burney's *Evelina*. I've read it so often and yet it never fails to make me laugh.'

Mr Bennet put down his book.

'And which parts of it do you find most amusing?'

'The comic characters are very well done, but I think I enjoy those moments most where the humour is entirely unintended. Who wouldn't smile at a hero who is not only single and strikingly handsome, but is also conveniently possessed of ten thousand pounds a year? And who could fail to be amused by a heroine wise enough to unite in her person outstanding beauty and a mind so superior that the hero is quite prepared to overlook the vulgarity of her birth?'

She closed the book, her expression alive with pleasure.

'I am only surprised it took them so long to realise they were destined for one another. I should have thought such a remarkable pair would have recognised their fate in ten pages at most. So yes, I laugh – but I must confess, I envy them their cheerful conclusion. If only real life were like that!'

'That is just the kind of happy ending I should wish for you, Lizzy,' declared her father softly. 'I would arrange it myself if it lay within my power.'

'You need not fear for me, Papa,' she replied. 'I am much

more sensible than I look. I am quite prepared, I promise you, to settle for something – or perhaps I should say, someone – far more ordinary than Miss Burney's hero.'

It was painful for Mary to watch the intimacy between Elizabeth and their father, and know she was excluded from it. The affection that flowed so easily between them was exactly what she yearned to experience for herself. She stared down at the notes laid out in careful order on her table, at the books marked with slips of paper to remind her of passages she had enjoyed. That was the purpose of all this work. That was why she applied herself so tirelessly, day after day. All she wanted was to see Mr Bennet look at her with even a hint of the tenderness which he now directed at Lizzy.

But she must not let her mind run in that direction; it would only upset and distract her. She must concentrate on something less distressing. She watched as Lizzy took up her book again. It was a long time since Mary had read a novel. It did not surprise her that Mrs Bennet enjoyed them; but she found it hard to believe that Elizabeth, with her quick under-standing, regarded such works so indulgently.

'But, Lizzy,' she ventured, 'if you think so little of these books, why do you continue to read them?'

'You quite mistake my meaning,' replied Elizabeth. 'These are loving criticisms on my part. For all the little faults in *Evelina*, I shall always be its firm friend.'

'But aren't you wasting time that might be better employed elsewhere? Dr Fordyce says novels are very unsuitable for women to read; their morals often leave much to be desired, they have nothing of worth to tell us and they convey no proper instruction.'

Elizabeth sat up straight, serious now.

'For me, that is one of their chief recommendations. I do not care to be told what to think at every turn of a page. And I do not agree that they have nothing to tell us. These are works in which the most thorough knowledge of human nature is displayed, the greatest powers of the mind described. No, I cannot sit by and leave the novel undefended.'

Mary searched through her notes, hunting for a favourite quotation. 'Dr Fordyce says books of history and philosophy are more useful for a female mind. They enhance our understanding, while novels only arouse our passions.'

'I cannot see why a woman of sense shouldn't enjoy both. I should consider it an insult to be denied the pleasures afforded me by Miss Burney because it might make me less receptive to those of Mr Hume. Dr Fordyce, however, I leave to you. I shall not compete for his company.'

Mr Bennet, who had been watching the conversation with interest, laughed out loud at this.

'Well said, Lizzy! Well said, indeed! And you are quite right about Fordyce. Milk-and-water stuff. All cant and obsequiousness, not worthy of serious notice.'

Mary looked down, unable to bear the affectionate smiles that passed between her father and sister. She knew Lizzy had routed her. But the humiliation of her defeat was as nothing to the pain she felt in hearing her favourite Dr Fordyce spoken of by Mr Bennet with such disdain. It had never occurred to her that her father would not share her appreciation for Dr Fordyce's ideas.

Elizabeth slipped off the window seat, readying herself to leave. Generous in victory, she held out her book to her sister.

'Shall I leave you my copy of *Evelina*, Mary? I think you might enjoy it if you would allow yourself to do so.'

'I shall try it if you wish,' replied Mary in a low voice. When she did not reach up to take the book from her sister's hand, Elizabeth laid it amongst the other volumes on the table, where Mary noticed it quite obscured her well-thumbed copy of Dr Fordyce.

Once Elizabeth had gone, Mr Bennet turned back to his own reading, a very faint expression of pleasure just visible on his face. Mary sat thinking for a few minutes. When she spoke, her voice semed very loud in the silent room.

'Papa,' she ventured. 'May I ask you a question?'

Her father started up, as if surprised to find her still there.

'Do you really think so meanly of Dr Fordyce? I have been studying him for some time.'

'I'm afraid those are unlikely to have been hours well spent. I consider him a tedious, unprofitable read; but you may have reached other conclusions.'

'Can I ask your opinion of other books I have been look-ing into? Blair's *Sermons*? Paley's *Evidences of Christianity*? Hannah More on female education?'

'Well, Paley is at least a proper thinker. I suppose you may derive some benefit from what he has to say. The others are quite worthless, unless you have a taste for arid morality and pompous sentiment of the most obvious kind.'

Mary closed her eyes for a moment, trying to gather her thoughts. She had clearly made a great error in judgement. How could she have been so foolish as to imagine Mr Bennet would approve of the authors whose words she had been copying out so carefully and with such keen expectation?

'If you don't approve of the writers I have chosen, can you suggest any whom you value that you think I might enjoy?'

'I'm not sure I should venture to do so. Your tastes seem very ... *strenuous* for so young a girl. They don't seem to tend much towards the light, bright, or cheerful.'

'No, Papa, I don't think they do. I wish to be informed, not entertained.'

'Indeed? Well, the best advice I can give you is to follow your own instincts. They will be a far better guide than anything I can suggest. One way or another, they will direct you towards what you require.'

He picked up his book again, and Mary knew she was dismissed. She gathered together her papers, closed the door of the library, and walked to her bedroom. She understood now that the book of extracts over which she had laboured with such care was quite useless. Mr Bennet would find nothing in it to admire. Every writer she had included was regarded by him with contempt. Sitting at her writing desk, she turned the pages of the little book, looking at the entries she had made with such hope, that had cost her so many hours ungrudged effort. A loving father would have been pleased with the gift regardless of its contents, because his child had taken the trouble to make it, but Mary knew Mr Bennet would not be so indulgent. It would do nothing to raise her in his estimation. On the contrary, it would confirm his opinion of her silliness, of her unworthiness to be noticed, valued, or loved. It would certainly not persuade him to look at her as he did at Lizzy. Stone-faced, she opened the drawer of the dressing table, placed the book of extracts within it, and slammed it shut.

CHAPTER FIFTEEN

With no task to work upon, Mary found it difficult to fill the long hours that stretched before her each day. She read until her eyes ached, but she struggled to summon the enthusiasm that had once driven her excitedly onwards. She practised at the piano until her fingers grew stiff, and when they would no longer obey her, she went out, walking along the familiar path into Meryton. No one offered to accompany her, and she did not seek out a companion. On her return, she was not asked where she had been or what she had done. At mealtimes, the conversation ebbed and flowed around the table, rarely requiring a response from her. She had nothing to add to Lydia's and Kitty's breathless reports of the comings and goings of their favourite officers, or to her mother's confidential account of her sister Phillips's new housemaid. She never again attempted to join in any of the conversations between Mr Bennet and Elizabeth. Mostly she sat silent, paying little attention to what was being said. So at first, she barely noticed her mother's announcement that the neighbouring house of Netherfield had been let at last. But Mrs Bennet was so excited by the news, and returned to it so often that soon even Mary was aware that a young man of large fortune had arrived from the north of England in a chaise, taken one look at Netherfield, and agreed terms on the spot. It appeared the new tenant's name was Mr Bingley and that he was single – although her mother was determined he should not remain in that state for long.

'You must know,' Mrs Bennet informed her husband one morning at the breakfast table, 'that I am thinking of his marrying one of our girls.'

'Do you really imagine,' he replied evenly, 'that his principal intention in settling here was to choose a wife from amongst our daughters? It seems an unlikely inducement for signing a year's lease, even on the most advantageous terms, especially as he has yet to set eyes upon any of them.'

'That will be quickly remedied if you'll go and call upon him. Once you have introduced yourself, there's nothing to stop us making a visit. But we can't do that until you've seen him. It wouldn't be polite.'

'I'm not sure I agree. Why should we make ourselves the prisoners of custom? I see no reason why you and the girls shouldn't call whenever you choose. Or perhaps they should go alone? You're still as handsome as any of them, and Mr Bingley might like you the best of the party.'

Mrs Bennet was not to be deflected by compliments, however justified she felt them to be.

'Come, Mr Bennet. You know we can't go unless you do. It would seem very odd indeed.'

'You may have a point. Perhaps it would be simpler if I wrote to Mr Bingley, giving my consent in advance to his marrying whichever of our daughters he preferred. That might save a great deal of time and trouble.'

'I'm sure it's very unkind of you to tease me in this way. If you won't call, others will not be so delicate. What if Sir

William Lucas gets there before you? Will it make you happy to see Charlotte Lucas established at Netherfield? Every moment you delay might be of consequence.'

Mr Bennet leaned back in his chair, satisfied now that his wife was thoroughly agitated.

'I admit you are faced with a dilemma. What is to take precedence, the claims of proper behaviour or the prospect of losing so promising a son-in-law? I'm not sure I can advise you. What say you, Mary? You are a young lady of deep reflection, I know, and read great books and make extracts.'

Mary looked up, astonished. Surprise forced every intelligent response from her mind, and she could think of nothing to say. Her father stared at her for a moment, deeply amused, before turning his attention back towards his wife.

'While Mary is adjusting her ideas, let us return to Mr Bingley.'

As her parents resumed their bickering, Mary sat stupefied. It was surely not possible Mr Bennet had been aware of the little book she had intended to present to him? No, she had shown it to no one, and it still lay safe in her drawer, his name on the front page, accompanied by a dedication he would never now see. He had perhaps noticed the hours she spent in his library copying out quotations, but he could know nothing of the purpose towards which her work had been directed. It was painfully evident from his arch expression that she had been right not to show it to him. He would not have valued it. Her scholarly ambitions were as ridiculous to him as the hours Kitty and Lydia spent decorating hats or discussing the merits of shoe buckles.

Mary's spirits were lower than usual at supper and at

breakfast the next day. Her father's disdain weighed heavily on her, and for as long as Mr Bingley remained the principal subject of conversation, she had nothing to say. Then, on the third evening, the mood around the table suddenly lifted. Her mother beamed; Lydia and Kitty laughed and poked each other. Even Mr Bennet looked pleased, content with a tease which had delivered everything he could have wished.

It was soon apparent that while strenuously maintaining to his family that he would not call upon Mr Bingley, Mr Bennet had in fact made his way to Netherfield that very morning and paid his respects. He had always intended to go; but he had resolved not to deny himself the pleasure of provoking his wife by telling her so. Mrs Bennet did not care. She was delighted that the first obstacle to the marriage of one of her daughters to Mr Bingley had been surmounted; and she did not doubt any further difficulties would be conquered with equal ease.

A few days later, Mr Bingley himself arrived at Longbourn to return Mr Bennet's visit; but to Mrs Bennet's extreme frustration, no one except her husband was admitted to his presence. He remained closeted in the library, and the only glimpse to be had of him by the female part of the family was from a first-floor window as he rode away, from which all that could be discerned was that he wore a blue jacket and rode a black horse.

When taxed by his wife with inhuman disregard for her feelings in not introducing Mr Bingley to her, Mr Bennet replied that the young man had business in London and had not the time for the pleasure of a meeting.

'But he was most insistent I should pass on his apologies to you and all the young ladies of the household. He added that he hopes to have the pleasure of seeing us all at the next Meryton assembly, which he is determined to attend. And, as two of his sisters will accompany him, alongside some other friends and relations, he looks forward to introducing them into your company, as well as himself. A rather exhaustingly polite young man, in my opinion.'

Kitty and Lydia cheered out loud at this news. Once they had satisfied themselves that Mr Bingley was not in the militia and did not wear a uniform, their interest in him had waned somewhat; but the arrival of other young men was a prospect that could only be greeted with enthusiasm, for it was entirely possible that some amongst them might be officers.

CHAPTER SIXTEEN

As the assembly was only a few weeks away, Mrs Hill was soon hard at work, cleaning, repairing, taking in and letting out, doing all she could to ensure that the Longbourn outfits were fit to be seen alongside the metropolitan fashions that were sure to be worn by Mr Bingley's female guests. One evening, as she came into her bedroom, Mary found Mrs Hill examining the new dress she had bought for the last ball, brushing down its neat bodice and shaking out its cream and gold skirts.

'Shall you wear it, do you think? This would be very much the right occasion to show it off again.'

'It didn't bring me much luck on its last outing.'

Mrs Hill put down the dress and sat on the bed.

'I saw Mr Sparrow in Meryton last week. He told me John is gone off, headed for London to become a doctor. He stopped me in the street as pleased as anything. He's sure the boy will end up with a practice in town, appointments at a guinea a time and his own carriage waiting at the door.'

Mary walked to the window. She did not want Mrs Hill to see the regret she suspected must be only too plainly written on her face. There was no chance now of apologising for her behaviour. She would never be able to make amends for the way she had treated him.

'What I mean by telling you,' continued Mrs Hill, 'is that

you don't need to fret about seeing him again at the assembly.' She picked up the dress and placed it carefully on a hanger. 'He is a sweet-tempered lad, but not right for you.'

'He was kind and generous and seemed to enjoy my company. That was pleasure enough for me.'

'Your parents would never have stood for it.'

Mary considered this. Her father, she thought, with his contrary spirit, might have enjoyed watching such an unlikely connection unfold, relishing the opportunities it offered to exercise his wit at the expense of all concerned. Her mother, however, would never have appreciated the joke. She would have opposed it with all the considerable reserves of outrage at her command; and hers would have been the last word on the matter, at least until young Mr Sparrow, the oculist's assistant, had transformed himself into Dr Sparrow the wealthy physician.

'Perhaps I was simply unfortunate in my timing. If Mr Sparrow had been already in possession of that carriage you mentioned, then things might have been very different.'

Mrs Hill shrugged.

'That's the way of the world, I'm afraid.'

'All we did was dance together. I didn't want to *marry* him. How could I, when I hardly know him? I merely liked talking to him. No one has ever sought me out before or listened with interest to anything I say. He noticed me and made me laugh; and for that, he earned the contempt of everyone around me. And I was so swayed by their prejudice that I crumpled up and ran away. That was a fine return for his kindness.'

'Well, what's done is done.'

Mrs Hill stood up; she had work to do and they could hear Lydia's impatient voice in the hall.

'Far worse things have happened, and men and women have lived to tell the tale. But I hope you'll go to the assembly, and not stay at home brooding over what can't be altered. And I think you should wear the new dress. It suits you, and it's wasted hanging in the wardrobe.'

Over the next few days, Mary's thoughts blew this way and that, uncertain whether she would follow Mrs Hill's advice or not. Sometimes, she quailed at the prospect of another ball, having experienced at first hand the dangers and humiliations that lay in wait for the unwary. But another part of her bridled at the idea of hiding herself away. She suspected if she did not go, it would become easier to refuse the next time and the next, until she turned herself into a complete recluse. No, however reluctant she was, she must go.

But although she eventually persuaded herself it was right to attend, nothing could convince Mary to wear the gold and cream gown. Its delicate prettiness did not suit her mood. Instead, ignoring Mrs Hill's pleas, she put on a plain dress and twisted her hair into an unbecoming knot at the back of her head. When she glanced in the mirror, she saw a colourless figure, her face pale, her clothes drab. There was nothing about her to attract anyone's attention; even to herself she seemed almost invisible. For a few moments, she looked at her reflection without expression. Then she slipped her spectacles into a little bag. There was no reason not to take them.

She said little on the journey into Meryton, but her mother and sisters more than made up for her silence. Kitty and Lydia, determined not to sit out a single dance, were already arguing about whom they should dance with, and in what order. Mrs Bennet was vocal in her eagerness to set eyes at last upon Mr Bingley, and declared herself almost as keen to meet the rest of his party, for who knew if it might not contain another eligible young man? Jane and Elizabeth refused to speculate about what the ball might promise, but Mary thought she caught even in them a sense of excitement. Only she felt nothing at all as the carriage pulled into the village.

CHAPTER SEVENTEEN

The Meryton rooms were as hot and as crowded as she remembered them. The green boughs on the walls were just as charming, the candles just as numerous and, as the strong smell of tallow suggested, bought just as cheaply as before. Through the great double doors she saw, as she had done before, a generous supper being laid out; and in the centre of the ballroom, couples were beginning to take their places for the next dance. It was all as it had been when she was last there; but this time, she knew better where she belonged. She walked decidedly towards the chairs where the mothers, aunts, and grandmothers had established themselves and looked for a place to sit amongst them. Her sisters claimed seats here too, but Mary knew they would use them only as perches to rest upon between dances, poised to be seen to most advantage before another partner presented himself and whisked them away. Mary, who suspected her stay would be of longer duration, settled on a chair set a little away from the front, where she hoped to feel less exposed.

Here for some thirty minutes she remained, uninvited to join the lively throng on the dance floor. As she sat, her eyes strayed upwards to the musicians on the balcony, playing with such energy that she could almost feel the heat of their efforts. Perhaps, she thought, that was where she should be – occupied in a task she enjoyed, safely removed from the probability of failure below. As she brooded, however, she became conscious of a ripple of interest in the conversations around her, a twitter of activity amongst the seated mothers. Following their glances, nods, and gestures, peering across the room she saw that a small party of people had arrived and stood surveying the scene. She did not recognise any amongst them, but their clothes and bearing suggested there could be no doubt who they were – Mr Bingley and his friends had arrived at last.

Mr Bingley – for, as he stood at the front of the little group, urging them forward, there could be little doubt of his identity – was a good-looking young man, with a cheerful, engaging expression. Behind him stood two women dressed in the first fashion whom Mary concluded must be his sisters. They looked less eager than their brother to plunge into the crowded room. Neither smiled. Two further gentlemen accompanied them. One, who was later discovered to be the husband of the eldest sister, was not much noticed; but the other quickly drew the attention of everyone in the room. He was tall, he was handsome, and he was known to be the possessor of a fine estate in Derbyshire. For a while, his appearance and his history attracted the approval of the men and alerted the interest of the women; but Mr Darcy's manners quickly doused the warmth of everyone's approval. His expression was grave and severe. He made no effort to conciliate the assembly and, unlike his friend, seemed to take no pleasure in his situation. Mr Bingley's willingness to please and be pleased was much to be preferred. He allowed himself to be introduced to as many people as wished to meet him, praised the look of the rooms, the liveliness of the music, and the prospect of supper; and when he made known his intention to dance every dance, his ascendancy over his remote and silent friend was complete.

It did not escape notice that Mr Darcy took to the floor only with the women of his own party, while Mr Bingley chose his partners from amongst the Meryton ladies. Mary watched as he led Charlotte Lucas onto the floor. This was an unexpected gesture; his choice of her sister Jane for the next dance seemed far more in keeping with the natural order of things. Jane, she thought, looked particularly handsome, her cool, unruffled beauty appearing to great advantage amidst the noise and heat of the ball. Bingley danced with her with obvious enjoyment and seemed reluctant to let her go, claiming her company after the set was over and talking to her with great animation, as Jane modestly looked away from his appraising smiles. *He will ask her again*, thought Mary, *if not now, then later. This will be a triumphant night for Jane.*

She was surprised when Charlotte Lucas sat down next to her. Mary had avoided her since the last ball. She did not doubt that the fault for what had happened then was in most respects her own; but she thought Charlotte a little guilty too. Had there been a hint of relish in the way she had delivered her warning about John Sparrow? A touch of jealousy in her insistence that Mary abandon him? These were unworthy thoughts, which Mary was ashamed to entertain; but as she had been unable yet to drive them from her mind, she had chosen not to put herself in Charlotte's company until she could get the better of them. However, as Charlotte greeted her with every appearance of friendship, Mary resolved to do all she could to return it in good faith.

'You have tucked yourself away in a very secluded place

here,' she began. 'Is this a wise decision? No one will ask you to dance if you are invisible to the human eye!'

She smiled as she spoke, but behind her good humour, her face was taut.

'Oh, I'm quite well where I am. I can see everything here. I don't miss a thing.'

'I'm not sure that's quite true. Watching what happens isn't the same as being part of it. You are missing something, of that you can be sure.'

'This feels like the best place for me.'

'Perhaps, if you have already decided to withdraw from the fray.'

Unsettled by the turn of the conversation, Mary tried a lighter tone.

'Well, your own good fortune won't have gone unnoticed tonight. You were the first woman Mr Bingley stood up with – what an honour, to be marked out in such a way!'

She tried to sound as sincere and as playful as she could. She did not much care for Charlotte, but she did not like to see her in so bleak a mood.

Charlotte looked towards the dance floor, where Mr Bingley was leading Jane out again for a second dance.

'Yes,' she replied thoughtfully. 'I was the polite choice, the evidence, if you like, of his good manners and willingness to charm us all. But he didn't look at me as he already looks at Jane.'

Mary followed Charlotte's glance. It was true, Mr Bingley was now utterly absorbed with her sister, his eyes following her as she moved up the line of dancers.

'I know very well what I must do and say next,' continued Charlotte. 'I must smile and nod and look unconcerned at my

dismissal, while laughing and teasing Jane about her new con-
quest. And that is what I will do. I'm used to it. But I tell you
what it is, Mary – I'm not sure if I can do it for much longer.'

Mary shifted uneasily in her seat. Charlotte's sudden candour disturbed her, and she was uncertain how to respond.

'I am nearly twenty-seven years old. I have been coming
to balls like this for ten years. And not once has anyone
looked at me with the admiration Mr Bingley is now directing at Jane. Not once have I been the one around whom
other women gather, congratulating, and exclaiming. No – it
is always my lot to cheer on the triumphs of my friends.' She
pulled at her gloves distractedly. 'Lord knows, I don't expect
much. But I should like to have something of my own before
it is too late. Some mark of affection, some sign I have been
wanted and preferred.'

'You have parents who love you,' ventured Mary, 'and
brothers and sisters to care for.'

'Yes,' replied Charlotte, 'and I know that should be enough,
but with every day that goes past, I find that it isn't, quite.'

Mary moved her hand uncertainly towards Charlotte's
arm. She did not trust herself to speak, recognising in Charlotte's words the same fears that had begun to loom large in
her own darker moments. What if no one ever wanted her?
Her spirits fell as she looked around the room; none of the
men she saw there seemed likely to prefer her to the prettier,
louder, livelier women who paraded and coquetted about the
floor with so much confidence. This was only her second ball,
and she already felt she had failed. Could she endure a decade
of humiliation and rejection with the fortitude Charlotte had
shown? Mary withdrew her hand, afraid her touch might provoke in Charlotte an outpouring of emotion to which Mary

would not know how to respond. She felt the power of Charlotte's despair, and it saddened her. But then Charlotte looked up and arranged her features into her usual expression of pleasant expectation.

'But here comes Lizzy! And at just the right moment to dispel this gloom.'

Mary screwed up her eyes, just as John Sparrow had told her not to, and spotted Elizabeth winding her way through the stragglers at the edge of the dance floor, striding towards them. With the briefest of acknowledgements, she pulled a chair towards them.

'I have such a tale to relate that it really wouldn't wait, so I came straight to find you. It can't be said to reflect particularly well on me, but it is so good a joke that I have decided to purchase your laughter at the expense of my dignity – such as it is!'

Before Mary or Charlotte could reply, she raced on with her account. It appeared that as the previous dance began, she had had no partner – 'that may be said to have been the first of my misfortunes' – and was compelled to sit and watch the proceedings from a seat some rows back from the dance floor. She had been there only a few minutes when she noticed Mr Bingley and his tall friend approach and stand before her. She had not meant to listen to their conversation, 'but really, they spoke so decidedly that it was impossible to ignore.' Thus, willingly or not, she had heard Mr Bingley berating Mr Darcy for his reluctance to dance. The room, he insisted, was full of charming women, any one of whom would be delighted to stand up with him. Why did he not ask some fortunate girl to be his partner? It did not reflect well on him to hold himself so aloof; it made no sense to march about the room with such an obvious determination not to be pleased.

'I could not wait to hear how he would answer such a very justified rebuke,' continued Elizabeth. 'But he was not in the least mortified, replying with some warmth that Mr Bingley had danced with the only handsome girl in the room, by which he meant Jane, of course. But his friend was not prepared to surrender his point so easily. While he agreed that Jane was indeed "the most beautiful creature he ever beheld" – and please note, those were his actual words – he persevered, with perhaps more gallantry than tact. What about her sister, he asked? She is pretty enough and not engaged. Should he like to be introduced to me?'

Lizzy paused for a moment to take a breath.

'And then this proud man – I think we all now know his name is Darcy – turns and looks me straight in the eye and says – and I will do him the justice to believe he didn't think I could hear him – "She is tolerable, but not handsome enough to tempt me"!'

She turned from Mary to Charlotte, laughing. 'What do you think? Is that not the most extraordinary thing you have heard?'

'Well, it is justly said that listeners never hear good of themselves,' said Mary.

'If that is the case, then I have certainly been properly punished,' declared Elizabeth. '"Tolerable", indeed! Was there ever such a milk-and-water insult as that! "Not handsome enough to tempt me" – as though we women have no other occupation than to lay ourselves out to be agreeable to him!'

'It does suggest a good deal of presumption on his part,' mused Charlotte.

'Yes, but I am glad of it, for it has enabled me to decide my opinion of him. I was not sure what to think at first when I heard him so complained of for his coldness and his want of common courtesy, for by then I had only *seen* his bad behaviour; but now that I have *heard* for myself that he is just as disagreeable as he appears to be, I shall have no hesitation in condemning him out of hand!'

Charlotte smiled consolingly.

'I am sorry you have been so disappointed in your new acquaintance, Lizzy. But it does not look as though his indifference has pierced your heart very deeply.'

'No, I dare say I shall survive it.' Lizzy stood up and surveyed the room. 'I only regret that I'm unlikely to have the opportunity of paying him back in kind. I really would delight in seeing his pride somewhat humbled – but I don't think our paths will cross again. And, as I'm sure Mary would agree, there is little point in hankering after what we cannot have, so I shan't brood on the wrong done to me. I will go instead in search of something to drink and a partner whom I hope will have the good taste to find me more than merely "tolerable" – or will at least refrain from expressing any contrary opinion until he is well out of earshot.'

'Lizzy will never be short of admirers,' observed Charlotte, as they watched her walk away. 'She will always attract notice wherever she goes.'

'It is impossible to be indifferent to her,' agreed Mary. 'When she's in a room, you always know she's there. Even when she says nothing at all, she looks as though she might, and that it is bound to be something witty.'

'Whereas you and I . . . Please do not take it ill of me if I say that I don't think people wait with the same eagerness to hear what we say next. We do not sparkle as she does.'

Mary looked gloomily at the skirts of her colourless dress.

Perhaps she should have worn the gold gown? If no one else had noticed it, it might nevertheless have made her feel less insipid.

'No, I don't suppose they do.'

They sat quietly, each contemplating the gulf of pleasure and possibility that lay between themselves and Elizabeth. Finally, Charlotte spoke, in a voice of quiet determination that Mary had not heard her use before.

'I'll tell you a secret, Mary. I've made a promise to myself that I will not come to another of these balls as an unmarried woman. If I'm still single by this time next year, I intend to put on a cap and declare myself an old maid.'

'Really, Charlotte, what can you mean? I see that you're in low spirits tonight, but that's far too significant a step to be taken without very serious consideration. Have you discussed it with Lizzy?'

'Of course not, she would never understand. But I think you might. And I hope you will allow me to explain myself a little.'

'I am happy to listen if you wish me to do so.'

Charlotte stared into the distance, her expression unreadable.

'When I was about your age, I imagined marriage was a reward for good behaviour and patience. I thought that if I was obliging and did as I was told, it was inevitable that I should end up as someone's wife. If it didn't happen this year, then surely it would in the next. But I waited and waited and smiled and smiled, and yet here I am – a single woman still.'

'And is that so terrible a fate?' ventured Mary. 'When one

looks at how some husbands and wives live together, it doesn't seem as though marriage always brings happiness.'

'You cannot seriously think that the life of an old maid is to be preferred?' cried Charlotte with some vehemence. 'Think of the unmarried women of your acquaintance, living on whatever their families allow them, eking out their subsistence with a few piano lessons or a little discreet dressmaking, mocked and disdained by all. No, for an educated woman, brought up to be genteel as we have been, the future holds no prospect but marriage or misery, depend upon it.'

'But if that's your opinion, why are you so willing to embrace a life you despise? To put on your cap, as you say, and abandon yourself to an existence you believe intolerable?'

'I suppose I dangle such a dreadful prospect before myself to concentrate my mind on the alternative. I know I am approaching the years of danger; I must act soon or not at all.'

'I'm not sure I understand you,' said Mary. 'In what possible way can you act? Do you mean to go around asking men to marry you?'

'No,' replied Charlotte ruefully. 'I haven't arrived at that degree of boldness quite yet. But I won't disguise from you that I'm prepared to do everything I can – within the bounds of propriety, of course – to find a respectable man to be my husband. If such a one were to cross my path tomorrow, I should not answer for his chances of escaping me.'

Her tone was light-hearted, but Mary did not doubt for a moment that she meant all she said.

'I sometimes think,' Charlotte continued, 'that for some men, especially those without much experience of society, it must be a great relief when a woman throws off discretion and doesn't hesitate to convey how readily she would agree to become his wife. It must be a terrible thing not to know before you ask what the answer to a proposal of marriage is likely to be. The certainty of acceptance must be a tremendous encouragement to the making of an offer.'

'You say nothing at all of love. Do you really think it a good idea to marry where there is no affection?'

'Well, I am not romantic, you know. The last ten years have cured me of that. I am not Lizzy, who will always be sought after. Women like me who aren't overburdened with a choice of suitors must learn to discipline their feelings. I'm sure I would settle now for anyone with a little money of his own who wasn't positively unkind. I no longer look for a great love. A comfortable home and the security of a proper settlement is all I ask.'

She turned to look directly at Mary.

'I hope I haven't shocked you. I've been brooding on these things for so long that it is a great relief to open my mind and speak about them to someone; and for all kinds of reasons, I thought you might understand how I have come to think as I do.'

'You are certainly very frank.'

'Yes, I have spoken very plainly, and not only because it was a pleasure to talk honestly for once of matters which are not usually discussed.'

Charlotte's usual half smile had disappeared. She was entirely serious now.

'I suppose I also thought you might learn something from my experience and apply it to your own future prospects. I'm offering you advice, if you wish to take it. So – don't waste time as I have done waiting for something to happen. Fortune really does favour the brave, you know. Don't believe you can find happiness celebrating the good fortune of others. An eternity spent smiling and cooing over the good luck of your friends makes the heart sick in the end. And above all, don't long for what you cannot have, but learn to recognise what is possible, and when it presents itself, seize upon it with both hands. It seems to me this is the only route to happiness for those of us born with neither beauty, riches, nor charm.'

Charlotte reached for the little bag at her feet.

'There! What a collection of portentous observations! I don't imagine your favourite Dr Fordyce would approve, but then he has not the knowledge of the world that I have.' She stood up, all briskness now, and readied herself to leave. 'I am not at all surprised after such a lengthy confession to find myself extremely hungry. I shall go and see if I can hunt down Lizzy and compel her to the supper table.'

She did not ask Mary to accompany her; nor did she look back as she made her way towards the dining room.

For the rest of the evening, Charlotte's unexpected declaration occupied Mary's mind. She thought about it as she sat eating an ice with her mother. When she picked up the printed programme for the evening, put on her glasses and appeared to be studying it, Charlotte's words rang in her ears. She was still considering them when, to her surprise, she heard her own name mentioned. When she turned to see who had spoken, she saw Lady Lucas a few footsteps away, eagerly pointing out to Mr Bingley's sisters those of the Bennet family to whom they had not yet been introduced.

'And lastly, of course,' declared Lady Lucas, 'there is Miss Mary Bennet, the most accomplished girl in the neighbourhood.'

Before she knew it, Mary's eyes met those of the younger

Bingley sister, who bobbed the smallest possible curtsey in acknowledgement.

'That is a great achievement, to be sure,' she said, 'and one which, judging by appearances, is very much deserved.'

Flustered, Mary curtsied back.

'I honour your commitment to learning,' Miss Bingley continued smoothly. 'Study clearly trumps all other considerations in your mind. You are an example to us all.'

Lady Lucas smiled, and the Bingley sisters swept away. It was only once they had gone that Mary realised she was still wearing her spectacles.

CHAPTER EIGHTEEN

No ball can be properly considered over until every detail of the evening has been thoroughly examined, weighed, and dissected the day after the event; and it was a sign of how much there was to discuss that breakfast was barely cleared away at Longbourn when a party of Lucases arrived to begin the discussions.

'You began the evening well, Charlotte,' said Mrs Bennet. 'You were Mr Bingley's first choice.'

'Yes – but he seemed to like his second better.'

'Oh,' declared Mrs Bennet, with an unconvincing attempt at surprise. 'You mean Jane, I suppose? To be sure, it did seem as if he admired her.'

'Indeed he did,' continued Charlotte. 'I heard him mention that he thought her quite the prettiest woman in the room.'

'You may have said so,' agreed Mrs Bennet, 'but I am glad to hear you confirm it.'

Charlotte agreed those had indeed been Mr Bingley's words. Mrs Bennet did not attempt to disguise her satisfaction that her eldest daughter had been so publicly preferred to Charlotte; she looked from her to Lady Lucas with unconcealed joy. Although she watched her carefully, Mary could not detect any waver in Charlotte's fixed smile, no crack in her expression of mild, good-natured resignation.

'My overhearings were more to the purpose than yours,

Lizzy,' Charlotte continued playfully. 'Poor Eliza! To be considered "only *tolerable*"!'

'It is a great snub,' agreed Elizabeth with mock gravity. 'But I must endeavour to bear it.'

Mrs Bennet was not so easily placated. She could not regard the disparagement of her daughters as anything other than a grievous insult; but what was to be expected of a man whose behaviour had attracted such universal disapproval? Mr Darcy had shown himself to be disagreeable, everyone had said so. It was obvious to all that he was an unpleasant man, haughty, cold, reserved, and eaten up with pride. Mrs Bennet declared Lizzy was to take no notice of him.

'If you were to meet again and he asked you to stand up with him, I hope you would say no.'

Elizabeth agreed such a thing was quite impossible, and the conversation ran back and forth, with Mr Darcy's person, manners, and character all weighed up and found wanting. It was some time before Mrs Bennet was ready to return to the more gratifying topic of Jane's success with Mr Bingley, but before she could do so, Mary spoke.

'I wonder if we are quite fair to condemn Mr Darcy as quickly as we do. There is a difference, you know, between pride and vanity. One is much more to be condemned than the other. The vain man wants others to think well of himself, regardless of his virtues. Pride relates more to our honest opinion of ourselves.'

She looked around searchingly at her listeners, hoping for a reply; but no one, it seemed, had anything to add to her remark.

'Is it not possible,' she persisted, 'that Mr Darcy has some justification for his self-belief? Perhaps he has a right to be proud.'

Mrs Bennet threw up her hands in exasperation.

'Really, Mary, none of us needs a lecture on what to think of that man. We have all made up our minds, and don't require any further direction from you.'

Mary blushed, realising she had once again struck the wrong note. There was silence, until a young Lucas brother, who had reluctantly accompanied his sister and mother to Longbourn on the promise of cake, which had not yet been forthcoming, piped up.

'If I were as rich as Mr Darcy, I should not care how proud I was! I should keep a pack of foxhounds and drink a bottle of wine every day.'

Mrs Bennet assured him that if she were to see him at it, she would take away his bottle directly – he said she should not – she insisted that she would – and soon the level of talk was as loud and as lively as it had been before Mary had spoken. When the Lucases finally took their leave, Charlotte stopped for a moment by her side.

'Our interventions are only welcome if they are agreeable,' she murmured, 'and by that, I mean that they reflect what everyone else thinks and are delivered with a most submissive smile.'

CHAPTER NINETEEN

When Sir William Lucas announced his plan to give a sociable little dinner, it came as an unwelcome surprise to Mrs Bennet. She had not anticipated that the Lucases would seize the opportunity to invite Mr Bingley, along with his friends, to meet the families of the neighbourhood in which he had chosen to make his home. It was extremely aggravating not to have thought of this idea herself; and she received news of it with considerable indignation.

'I consider it great presumption in them to hold such a dinner,' she declared, 'and very much intended to serve their own interests. They mean to have Mr Bingley for Charlotte, Mr Bennet, I'm sure of it. I've rarely seen such behaviour. I wonder they are not ashamed.'

'Then I shall write and explain we cannot attend,' replied her husband. 'It would obviously be painful for you to witness their machinations at first hand.'

'Whatever are you thinking?' cried his wife, exasperated. 'Of course we must go. I won't see Jane cut out by that contriving Charlotte Lucas. I shan't take my eyes off her for a minute.'

'In that case, I shall convey our acceptance and look forward to what promises to be a most pleasant evening spent amongst out oldest and dearest friends.'

Thus it was that Mary found herself, when the appointed evening rolled around, in an undistinguished seat at the least favoured end of Sir William's dining table, playing with her food and wishing the dinner over. From a rather better situation nearer Mr Bingley and his friends, Charlotte occasionally caught her eye, her cheerfulness no longer seeming as natural as Mary had once assumed it to be. Her bleak confession at the ball echoed in Mary's mind as she surveyed the guests, all of whom appeared to be enjoying themselves with a gusto that grated on Mary's sombre frame of mind. Her mood darkened further as she watched the men gathered round the table, and it struck her very forcibly that not one of them would consider her as a potential wife. There was Mr Bingley, working as hard to please as he had at the Meryton ball, all smiles and jollity and good nature. But for all his easygoing charm, Mary sensed he would never notice any woman who was not a beauty; and having Jane before his eyes, why would he look for anyone else? Mary rarely thought as one with Mrs Bennet, but as she watched Mr Bingley and Jane together, there seemed little doubt he was smitten with her.

As her gaze moved on towards the grand and severe Mr Darcy, Mary almost laughed at the sheer impossibility of his thinking of her in any way at all. He had not even registered the fact of her existence. She thought she saw him look sometimes in Elizabeth's direction, but Lizzy resolutely ignored him, his use of the fatal word 'tolerable' woundingly fresh in her memory. At the other end of the table were a noisy group of young men in uniform, rather red in the face from too much wine, flirting with Kitty and Lydia. Mary found it impossible to tell them apart. She thought they were unlikely to be as particular as Mr Bingley or his friend; but where good looks were not to be found, they required jolliness and tearingly high spirits, and Mary had neither.

The truth was, she thought bitterly, that there was no one in her immediate society who considered her worthy of attention; and if this was so when she was still young, why should it improve as she grew older? In all likelihood, her next ten years would be spent very much like Charlotte's lost decade, with little to hope for and not much to make her happy. As the evening went on, Mary felt herself steadily diminished by this knowledge, imagining herself fading from view, minute by minute, hour by hour, until she felt as though she had disappeared altogether, leaving nothing behind to remind anyone that she had ever been there at all.

It was only when dinner was over and the cloth cleared that she rallied somewhat. Dancing was called for; and, seeing an opportunity to break out of her unhappiness, Mary volunteered to oblige the company at the piano. For the rest of the evening, she hammered out Scottish and Irish airs while her sisters and the Lucases took to the floor with the keenest of the officers. When she could play no more, she received the thanks of the dancers with mixed emotions. She was glad to have done something other than sit in silence but felt she had purchased the gratitude of the party by absenting herself from their number. She thought she heard Charlotte reminding her how unprofitable it was to be content with warming your hands at the happiness of others, and it saddened her to think this might be her destiny, enabling pleasure for those around her while never enjoying it herself.

CHAPTER TWENTY

It came as no surprise to Mary when a letter arrived for Jane at Longbourn from Miss Bingley, begging her to come to Netherfield to join the party there. They were sadly bored and longed for company; perhaps she would drink tea with them? Could she also be persuaded to dine? Jane read the invitation to the family in her usual measured tones, but Mary saw that, beneath her shyness, she was pleased. Her mother, however, was almost beside herself with excitement.

'So much for Lady Lucas's plans! I knew he had no interest in Charlotte, and I was right. You must go on horseback, Jane, you shan't have the carriage. It looks as if it will rain later, and if it does, they will be compelled to offer you a bed. The longer you stay there, the better. What an opportunity for you!'

The protests of Jane and Elizabeth on this point went unheard. Jane was to ride and that was that. The risk of a soaking was well worth the chance of securing another day as Mr Bingley's guest. So Jane was dispatched, wearing only a cloak and light shoes. When the anticipated downpour arrived rather earlier than had been expected, there could be no doubt that Jane must have been caught in the deluge; but Mrs Bennet was not in the least concerned.

'A little rain never hurt anyone, you know, and they will be obliged to keep her now.'

Elizabeth, however, was far from being so sanguine. She was not at all confident her sister would survive her drenching unscathed, and when news reached Longbourn the next day that Jane was confined to bed with a chill, Elizabeth was consumed with anxiety. She begged for the use of the carriage to go immediately to attend her sister; but her mother was implacable.

'I'm not at all afraid of her dying. She will be taken good care of. As long as she stays there, all will be well.'

Elizabeth submitted uneasily to Mrs Bennet's will for most of the following day; but when no letter arrived announcing Jane's full recovery, she could stand it no more and declared her intention to walk the few miles to Netherfield to see for herself how Jane fared. She paid no attention to her mother's insistence that Lizzy was not wanted there, that she would merely get in the way, scuppering her carefully contrived plan. Mary listened as the arguments went back and forth, round and round. She could not see that Elizabeth's presence was as necessary as she thought. If Jane were really ill, surely a message would have been sent to that effect from Netherfield. And if Jane was indeed so unfortunate as to be seriously unwell, Lizzy's walking so far through muddy fields and wet roads to reach her did not make sense. She might become ill herself, and then what help could she be to Jane?

'I admire the activity of your benevolence,' she ventured quietly to Elizabeth, in as dispassionate a tone as she could muster. 'But every impulse of feeling should be guided by reason; and surely, exertion should always be in proportion to what is required.'

Elizabeth turned towards her, more angry than Mary could remember seeing her.

'That is a calculation I am happy I have made correctly,' she said coldly, 'so you need not trouble yourself further on my behalf. And I must disagree with you on the competing claims of reason and feeling. When not warmed up by feeling, reason is a very chilly, uncomfortable discipline by which to live your life. I am surprised to hear you speak in this way, Mary. It is most unappealing. I will leave as soon as I have put on my boots. I hope to be back for dinner.'

In fact, Elizabeth's return was by no means so immediate. She found Jane in a condition which convinced her she could not be left until her recovery was more certain; and in this unintended manner, Lizzy found herself quite by chance a guest of the Netherfield house party, where she stayed for the better part of a week.

When Jane was well enough to receive them, Mr Bingley invited Mrs Bennet and her younger daughters to come to Netherfield and visit Jane themselves, and all but Mary eagerly accepted.

She was still smarting from Elizabeth's rebuke and preferred to hide away at home. It had been painful enough to feel herself the object of her favourite sister's scorn. It was worse to realise that Elizabeth had been quite right to scold her, for Jane had indeed been as ill as she feared. Lizzy's heart had been a better guide to what was best for Jane than Mary's cool reasoning. Mary was ashamed of what she had said, and did not feel ready yet to find herself in Lizzy's company. Instead, she stayed behind at Longbourn, walking alone in the garden and blaming herself for having made yet another wrong judgement, for having spoken when she had far better have said nothing at all.

It was here Charlotte Lucas found her when she called to find out how Jane did.

'I hope,' she said, 'that Jane has not allowed her illness to prevent her making the most of her time at Netherfield. It would be a pity if it has distracted her from achieving the main purpose of her visit.'

'I believe Miss Bingley asked her principally as company for herself and her sister. I think they felt the need of a new face at the card table.'

'That may have been how the invitation was worded,' replied Charlotte knowingly, 'but depend upon it, that was not their only motive in summoning Jane to them. They would never have asked her if they were not convinced of their brother's partiality for her.'

They had arrived at a little bench situated under a quince tree. Charlotte sat down and motioned for Mary to join her.

'So you believe it was Jane's task to do all she could to win his sisters' friendship and seek their approval?'

'Undoubtedly, that can do no harm and may indeed do a great deal of good.' Charlotte loosened the ribbon on her hat and let it rest on the back of her head. 'But,' she continued, 'Jane has been given an extraordinary opportunity to make Mr Bingley aware of the strength of her regard. I do hope for her sake that she has taken full advantage of it.'

'I know your opinions in these matters,' said Mary. 'But I'm not sure Jane's attachment is strong enough to justify such bravery. I could not say what she truly feels for Mr Bingley. If she is not yet sure that she loves him, she can hardly be expected to persuade him that is the case.'

'On the contrary, I should say that is exactly when such a declaration is most required. Delay may be fatal to her chances. It's plain to everyone that she likes him and enjoys his company. What else can she require? If it's love that she wants, well, she stands as good a chance of finding it with him as with anyone else.'

'Do you really think so little of the tender emotions, Charlotte? She hardly knows him – how can she possibly be certain he would make her happy?'

Charlotte bent down and plucked several long blades of grass.

'I sometimes wonder whether you have truly absorbed any of the ideas contained in those books you read with such enthusiasm. As I recall, most of their authors insist it is companionship that forms the basis of a truly happy marriage. Passion, they tell us, is very soon spent, and is anyway a most uncertain foundation for domestic felicity.'

She began to plait the grass together, fixing all her attention upon her task as she spoke.

'You may talk like a rational creature, but beneath that disciplined exterior hides a true romantic nature. You keep it well concealed, but it makes an appearance every now and then, before you rush to snuff it out!'

Mary blushed. 'No, not at all – I merely wondered whether a marriage can be embarked upon with any real possibility of happiness if the husband and wife know so little of each other when they begin. And if one or both of them pretends to feelings they do not yet possess, then surely that cannot promise well for their future.'

'I see we will never agree, but I do assure you that happiness in marriage is entirely a matter of chance. If Jane were to be studying Mr Bingley's character for another year, it would make no difference. She has as good an opportunity of being happy with him as with any other man she might meet. I wish her success with all my heart, but if she has failed to build on her advantage, well, she has no one to blame but herself. In her position, I would not let such a chance slip through my fingers.'

'Tell me, Charlotte, are you really so unhappy, situated as you are?'

Charlotte threw her grass plait upon the ground and stood up.

'I cannot pretend my feelings have altered since we last spoke. Come, shall we find Mrs Hill and see if she can be persuaded to offer us tea?'

CHAPTER TWENTY-ONE

It was another week until Jane was well enough to return home, and some days after that before she was allowed downstairs. Mrs Bennet showed no remorse for what had happened, meeting Elizabeth's reproachful looks with an indignant assertion that Jane would thank her once she was married. She was sure it could not be long before Mr Bingley made his declaration. It was therefore not surprising that, when one morning at breakfast, Mr Bennet announced that he hoped she had ordered a good dinner for that night, since he expected the arrival of a guest, Mrs Bennet's mind leapt immediately to the possibility – the very exciting possibility – of its being Mr Bingley; but her husband immediately corrected her.

'I am sorry to disappoint you, my dear. It is not he, but another young man who will grace us with his presence later today. I speak of my cousin Mr Collins, who, when I am dead, may turn you all out of this house as soon as he pleases.'

As Mr Bennet had intended, his words provoked general astonishment and surprise. Everyone spoke at once, deluging him with questions until he was obliged to hold up his hand and ask for quiet. Only then, and at a pace of his own choosing, did he reveal the story behind their unexpected visitor's impending arrival. It appeared that a month earlier,

Mr Bennet had received a letter from his cousin proposing himself as a guest.

'About a fortnight ago, I answered it, for I thought that it required early attention. Should you like to hear what it says?'

He put on his glasses and with a flourish extracted the letter from a pocket of his coat. It covered many pages, and Mr Bennet read it in a manner as slow and pompous as the language in which it was written. Mr Collins began by regretting the breach which had for so long subsisted between Mr Bennet and his father. However, now that his revered parent was no more, he thought it incumbent upon him, if it lay within his poor powers, to heal the hurt inflicted by this quarrel. His recent ordination had made him feel the desirability of a reconciliation even more strongly.

'He observes,' continued Mr Bennet, 'that "as a clergyman I feel it my duty to promote the blessings of peace in all families within my influence". He goes on – and I think this will be of particular interest to you, my dear – "that on these grounds I flatter myself that my present overtures of goodwill are highly commendable, and the circumstances of my being next in the entail of the Longbourn estate will be kindly overlooked on your part, and not lead you to reject the offered olive branch".'

Mrs Bennet threw down her napkin, scattering breadcrumbs from her plate.

'I think it very impertinent of him to write to you at all, and very hypocritical.'

'I fear you are too unkind to him. He acknowledges his sin just as fully as you could wish. He says he is "concerned at being the means of injuring your amiable daughters" and indeed "begs leave to apologise for it". Indeed, he professes his "readiness to make them every possible amends – but of this hereafter".

'What can he mean by that?' asked Mrs Bennet, a little mollified now. 'I shall not discourage him if he means to do something material for the girls.'

'There is more – much more, as it happens, but nothing further on that point. He tells us a great deal about his good fortune in securing a valuable living in Kent, and of his indebtedness to "the bounty and beneficence" of his worthy patroness, "the Right Honourable Lady Catherine de Bourgh, widow of Sir Lewis de Bourgh". Towards this lady, he informs us, it will always be his endeavour "to demean myself with grateful respect".'

He folded up the letter and tapped it on the table.

'We may expect this peacemaking gentleman at four o'clock today. I very much look forward to making his acquaintance.'

'He must be an oddity, I think,' declared Elizabeth. 'I cannot make him out. Can he be a sensible man, sir?'

'No, my dear, I do not think he can. There is a mixture of servility and self-importance in his letter which promises very well. I am impatient to see him.'

Mr Bennet looked around the table with genuine anticipation, and Mary felt a twinge of sympathy for the hapless Mr Collins. His intentions seemed to her honourable, if perhaps not very happily conveyed.

'In point of composition,' she suggested, 'his letter does not seem entirely defective. The idea of the olive branch, perhaps, is not wholly new, yet I think it is well expressed.'

Her words made no impact at all. The conversation had

grown loud again, as the probable motives for Mr Collins's visit were enthusiastically debated, not, on the whole, much to his credit.

'He appears to mean nothing but good in coming here,' she continued, raising her voice against the hubbub. 'Is it right to condemn him before we have even met him?'

No one listened. After a while, Mary stood up, pushed her chair back neatly into place, made a respectful nod to her parents, and left the table. As she walked down the hall, she could still hear the family talking. She thought it probable that no one had even noticed her absence.

Later that afternoon, the object of all this discussion arrived, exactly on time. He was a tall, heavy-looking young man in his mid-twenties, with a solemn and stately air. His voice was rather louder and his manners stiffer and more formal than a family drawing room required. But the more he spoke, the more he pleased his hosts. Mrs Bennet was delighted to be addressed with all the respectful consideration she felt was her due; while her husband was equally gratified to find their visitor in every way as ridiculous as he had hoped.

Mr Collins's compliments to his fair cousins – his pleasure at discovering their good looks far exceeded even the most enthusiastic reports, his conviction they must expect to be very quickly and advantageously disposed of in marriage – were not much to the taste of those to whom they were addressed. They were, however, music to their mother's ears, though she could not resist observing it was very unfortunate they should have no proper portions to bring with them to their husbands, 'things being settled so oddly'.

'You allude, perhaps,' murmured Mr Collins, 'to the entail of this estate?'

'Yes, sir. It is a very vexing situation.'

'I could say much on the subject,' he observed, grinning at his cousins with a particularly arch and irritating smirk, 'but I am cautious of appearing forward and precipitate. But I can assure the young ladies I come prepared to admire them! At present, I will not say any more, but perhaps when we are better acquainted . . .'

Jane and Elizabeth looked sternly away, while Kitty and Lydia did not try to hide their boredom. Only Mary looked at him with curiosity. It could not be denied that he did not make a very impressive figure. He had none of the swagger of the officers Kitty and Lydia so admired, nor the cheerful warmth of Mr Bingley. And he certainly possessed nothing of Mr Darcy's natural gravity, the authority and assurance that commanded deference wherever he appeared. As she watched him talking to her mother, admiring the disposition of the rooms, the elegance of the furniture, and the colour of the curtains, it was hard not to find him foolish. Everything delighted him; he seemed not to understand where appreciation ended and flattery began. Yet, for all his obsequiousness, he frequently failed to please. He seemed not to notice that Mrs Bennet did not like to hear her sofas compared to those which his esteemed patroness, Lady Catherine de Bourgh, had placed in her second-best morning room. He would do better, Mary thought, to say less and think more; but as he rambled on, she understood that would never happen. He would always condemn himself out of his own mouth, and would do so in complete ignorance of the poor impression he made. She began to feel apprehensive on his behalf about how he would fare at dinner. Mr Collins offered her father such a tempting opportunity for exercising his wit that she could not imagine any circumstances in which he would forgo it.

CHAPTER TWENTY-TWO

In the event, Mr Bennet hardly spoke at all during dinner. He allowed himself the merest ghost of a smile when Mr Collins, praising the food with the same extravagance with which he had admired all the other distinguishing marks of the house, asked to which of his fair cousins he was indebted to for its cookery. Mrs Bennet replied with some asperity, observing they were very well able to keep a cook and none of her daughters had anything to do in the kitchen. Chastened, Mr Collins rushed to make amends, and continued to do so long after Mrs Bennet considered herself appeased. It seemed to Mary as if he spent quite fifteen minutes apologising, while everyone else stared, embarassed, at their plates. But it was only when all was cleared away and the servants had withdrawn that she saw her father compose his features into an expression of polite enquiry and devote himself to the agreeable task of exposing as many of his guest's failings as was possible before the coffee was brought in. He began by declaring that Mr Collins seemed very fortunate in his patroness; could he enlighten them any further about Lady Catherine de Bourgh, who seemed so solicitous of his comfort and well-being?

He could not have chosen a better subject. Mr Collins was eloquent in her praise, extolling her affability and condescension, her graciousness in approving his sermons, her generosity in inviting him to dinner, her extraordinary civility in some-times asking him on a Saturday night to make up her pool of quadrille when another gentleman had disappointed her. For a lady of her rank, such behaviour was as exceptional as it was pleasing. She had even seen fit to distinguish his humble parsonage with a visit and had approved all the alterations he had made there, although she had been kind enough to inform him the upstairs closets required more shelves.

As he blundered on, the pity Mary had begun to feel for him grew. Her sisters, she knew, had already dismissed him. She could not say that she herself found him an admirable character; but she knew how it felt to hear one's words greeted with puzzlement, scorn, or indifference, and her sympathy for him increased, even as he seemed determined to make his situation worse.

'Lady Catherine seems far more agreeable than many great ladies,' observed Mrs Bennet. 'I believe, sir, that she is a widow, and that she has a daughter?'

Mr Collins agreed this was so.

'What kind of young lady is she? Is she considered very handsome?'

It was unfortunate, replied Mr Collins, that Miss de Bourgh did not enjoy the good health usually considered essential to beauty; but, as he frequently assured Lady Catherine, her looks were of the refined kind which marks the young woman of distinguished birth.

'Has she been presented at court, sir?'

'Her indifferent health unhappily prevents her being in town,' Mr Collins explained. 'As I told Lady Catherine, this misfortune has deprived the British court of its brightest ornament.'

He looked around, as pleased with himself as he was with his remark.

'I am happy on every occasion to offer those little delicate compliments which are always agreeable to ladies.'

Mary closed her eyes for a moment. He had surely sealed his fate now. She saw her father sit up.

'I have more than once observed to Lady Catherine that her daughter was born to be a duchess,' continued Mr Collins. 'These are the little things which please her ladyship.'

'You judge very properly,' said Mr Bennet. 'May I ask whether these pleasing attentions proceed from the impulse of the moment, or are they the result of previous study?'

'They arise chiefly from what is passing at the time,' replied Mr Collins, 'and though I sometimes amuse myself with composing such elegant little compliments, I always wish to give them as unstudied an air as possible.'

Mr Bennet nodded, delighted to discover that his cousin was quite as absurd a figure as he could possibly have wished. Nothing in his features betrayed his pleasure; apart from a glance or two at Elizabeth, he gave no sign of it. Mr Collins himself was quite unconscious of the judgement that had been passed upon him, raising his glass in happy ignorance of his condemnation. But Mary was ashamed. It seemed a dishonourable thing to treat a guest in such a manner, even when he was as foolish and silly as Mr Collins.

When they rose from the table and made their way to the drawing room to take more coffee, Mary attempted to speak a few kind words to her cousin in recompense. She trusted his journey had gone well, and that he was not too tired? Was this the first time he had been in Hertfordshire? He answered perfunctorily, his eyes searching for a seat which would place him as close as possible to Jane. Throughout dinner, he had smiled at the eldest Bennet sister with a warmth which was not returned; but he appeared not to notice her coolness. When the general conversation petered out, everyone having exhausted their stock of empty politeness, Mr Bennet suggested that their guest might entertain them by reading aloud. Mr Collins eagerly assented, and after a brief scouring of shelves and side tables, a book was produced. But when handed to Mr Collins, he looked at it with disdain. It was, Mary saw, her mother's latest volume borrowed from the circulating library.

'I beg your pardon, but I am afraid I must disoblige you. I never read novels. Perhaps you have something else?'

Mary considered him hopefully. Perhaps his literary tastes were closer to her own than to her mother's? In the ensuing bustle, while new books were searched for, it occurred to Mary that he might enjoy one of her own favourite titles. Rushing to fetch it from its accustomed place, she handed it to him quickly, before any alternative could be offered.

'Perhaps this might be more to your liking, sir?'

'Ah, yes, Fordyce's *Sermons*!' he replied approvingly. 'We shall not go wrong with this!'

Mary dropped her eyes and smiled with secret pride as he opened the familiar pages and began. He read exactly as might have been expected, slowly, portentously, and with exaggerated solemnity. But Mary was thrilled to hear the well-known phrases spoken aloud, without irony or disdain. As his voice rolled on, she began to consider whether there might be other interests she and her cousin shared – had he read Blair's *Sermons*, she wondered, or perhaps even something by Bishop Berkeley? How exciting it would be to discuss them with a like-minded reader. Her thoughts dwelt so keenly upon such rich possibilities that she did not see Lydia fidgeting with boredom on the other side of the room; and her sister's sudden exclamation was almost as great a surprise to Mary as it was to Mr Collins.

'Do you know, Mama, that my uncle Phillips talks of turning away Richard, and that if he does, Colonel Forster will hire him? I shall walk into Meryton tomorrow to hear more about it.'

Lydia was immediately bid by her two eldest sisters to hold her tongue, while Mrs Bennet apologised profusely. In truth, only Mary genuinely regretted that they should hear no more, for Mr Collins was seriously offended and had closed the book with an aggrieved frown.

'I have often observed how little young ladies are interested by books of a serious stamp, though written solely for their benefit. It amazes me, I confess.'

Just at that moment, coffee finally arrived; and in the distraction created by its being laid out, Mary leaned across to Mr Collins and sought to soothe his ruffled dignity.

'I am very sorry you did not continue, sir. I am a great admirer of Dr Fordyce and have read the sermons through on many occasions. This is my copy, you know.'

'I am glad to hear that one amongst you is interested in advantageous instruction. It is true nothing is so beneficial to young ladies as well-directed reading, though not all are disposed to appreciate its importance.'

He shot an affronted glance at Lydia, who, absorbed in a low, confidential conversation with Kitty, did not notice at all. Mary persevered.

'As you think so highly of Dr Fordyce, I should very much

like to hear what other authors you enjoy. Not all young women are indifferent to works of a serious nature. I myself am very keen to discover other books that may be of benefit to me.'

'That is very commendable in you, and I am glad to hear it. But I hope you will forgive me if our conversation is postponed for another time. If you will excuse me, I intend to propose myself to your excellent father for a game of backgammon. I feel I can be of no further use amongst the ladies.'

With the smallest of ingratiating bows, he was gone.

As she lay in bed that night, Mary turned the events of the day over in her mind. There was no doubt Mr Collins could not be considered an amiable man. His manner was pompous, he was puffed up with self-regard, and during the short time he had spent in their company, he had done everything in his power to make himself look ridiculous. And yet, for all his failings – or perhaps even because of them – the flicker of sympathy she had felt for him, as her father encouraged him to display ever more incriminating evidence of his foolishness, had not been entirely extinguished. Beneath his stiff and artificial manner, she thought she had caught a glimpse of something uncertain, a nervousness hidden behind his smirk. He was not at ease with himself, and she could not help feeling a little sorry for him. She knew what it was to believe herself out of place and always in the wrong, and thought that he might too.

His choosing to read from Dr Fordyce had only increased her sense of fellow feeling. It was true he had not seized the opportunity to discuss with her other works of a similar nature; and she had to admit that his conversation did not suggest his intellect was of the most acute and brilliant kind.

But perhaps during his stay, she could learn more about his tastes. They might read together, discussing their opinions at the end of a morning of quiet study. She saw herself, little by little, winning his confidence, encouraging him to think of her as a partner in serious pursuits.

Suddenly she was startlingly aware of the direction her thoughts were taking. Was it possible she was considering Mr Collins as a possible suitor? She was shocked and a little ashamed. She had not consciously intended to think of him in such a light, and yet she could not deny the possibility had begun to take shape in her mind. What was she thinking? She had met him only for a few hours, and his character had hardly been such as to captivate or amuse. It was true she had felt sorry for the treatment he had received at her family's hands; and of course, there was Fordyce. But a shared taste for improving literature was surely not enough to begin thinking of him as a potential husband?

Charlotte of course would have laughed at her misgivings, arguing that a couple brought together by a common interest stood as good a chance as any of finding happiness; and that an appreciation for the works of Dr Fordyce might be a firmer foundation for marriage than the turbulent emotions of love. Mary's rational mind saw the sense of such arguments; but when she applied them to herself and Mr Collins, her spirit faltered. She thought she might in time learn to live with a man whom she did not love, if that was her destiny. Perhaps she would become as adept as Charlotte in fixing her eyes on the practical benefits of a loveless union. But she was not sure she could endure to be tied forever to a husband she could not respect. The marriage of her parents, always before her eyes, demonstrated only too clearly the miserable consequences of such a choice. Where there was no real esteem, contempt and bitterness soon followed. If she was seriously to consider Mr Collins as her partner in life, she must find something worthwhile in him, or she really should not continue to think of him at all.

At first this did not seem an easy task. When she recalled the many ways in which he had exposed himself during the evening, her heart sank. But she urged herself to think more coolly, to try to rise above the first impressions he had made; and with a little effort, her determination eventually proved almost equal to the challenge.

Looked at with dispassion, it might be argued that none of his sins were of the very worst kind. Yes, he was foolish and silly; but he did not seem vicious or degraded. No scandal attached to his name, he was neither a drunkard nor a debtor, and his temper gave no suggestion of violence. Most of his faults, thought Mary, lay in the way he presented himself to the world, and that perhaps was not so grievous a crime? He was still a young man, and his errors need not be fixed and unalterable. Some of the worst might be corrected in time, especially if he were to fall under the influence of a sensible woman. Under her gentle discipline, he might learn a little restraint; encouraged by her delicacy, he might acquire some dignity; and directed by her taste, he could perhaps become the kind of man for whom a wife could eventually come to feel, if not love, then at least some mild regard.

And if Mr Collins was capable of becoming a better man, why should she not be the one who effected his transformation? None of her sisters would be prepared to take on such a task, nor equal to achieving it. She was the one Bennet daughter who, by accepting Mr Collins, might make it possible for him to grow into a more sensible being. Mary shifted in her bed, aware of where her thoughts were leading her. Perhaps it was her duty to marry Mr Collins, to save him from himself?

Of course, in becoming his wife, she would secure her own future as well as his. As Mrs Collins, she would be both comfortable and secure. At the same time, she would deliver the greatest prize of all, for marriage to him would keep the Bennet property in the Bennet family line and remove forever the looming shadow of the entail. She smiled bitterly to herself in the darkness as she imagined her mother's response when she understood it was the least loved and most disregarded of her daughters to whom she owed the prospect of a happy old age. It was a triumph that would offend Mrs Bennet very deeply. That alone rendered the prospect of marriage to Mr Collins almost worthwhile.

She turned over, unable to settle, and vigorously shook out her pillow. All this was very well, but what chance did she have of securing him? There was little doubt he was ready to marry. He had hinted to Mrs Bennet this was his intention, and his very presence at Longbourn suggested he was disposed to make a choice from one of his five cousins, although Mary was candid enough to admit there was no reason to suppose Mr Collins had any preference for her. It had been Jane's lovely face which had attracted his attention. But then she remembered Charlotte's insistence that a man's preference might be turned around by a woman truly determined to win him. Charlotte would have told Mary her task was clear – she must communicate her readiness for matrimony by any means necessary, flattering Mr Collins's pride, and pumping up his self-regard, guiding him step by careful step towards the realisation that she and she alone was the only sensible choice for him to make.

As she turned it over in her mind, it seemed to Mary that dispassionate reasoning – of the kind advocated so forcefully by Charlotte and, indeed, by all her favourite authors – admitted no doubt in the matter. Marrying Mr Collins was the rational thing to do. Both of them would benefit from such a union. He offered her escape from an uncertain destiny, the possibility of a comfortable home, and the salvation of her family's finances. She promised him a sympathetic temper, an interest in serious subjects, and the prospect that, by managing his worst excesses, she might enable him to present a more pleasing figure to the world.

But even as Mary congratulated herself on the clarity of her thinking, something within her resisted, her heart rejecting the conclusions her head had so easily arrived at. Could she really imagine herself as Mr Collins's wife? What if she were wrong, and there was no better Mr Collins for her to discover? Could she bear to be yoked to man who could not open his mouth without provoking derision? Even if it proved possible to cajole him into making her an offer, was there really any possibility of their making each other even tolerably happy? Pity and self-interest on her part, coupled with ignorance and naivety on his, seemed very fragile foundations on which to build a life together, whatever Charlotte might say. Unbidden, an image sprang into her mind of John Sparrow at the Meryton assembly, holding out his hand to invite her to dance. She remembered them smiling together, their shyness dissolving under the pleasure they discovered in each other's company. He had held her little bag and offered to take her spectacles out and clean them with the cuff of his shirt when no one was looking. They had both laughed, and then they had danced again.

Life with Mr Collins would never be like that, she thought; but then she could hardly expect to meet a John Sparrow again, a man who had, for the first time in her life, made her feel carefree and at ease. Those few happy hours with him had been but a little thing, she told herself, quickly snuffed out by the sneers of those around her and by her own timidity. But it had given her a glimpse of what happiness felt like; and that was hard to erase from her mind. Now it was over, dead and buried, never to be repeated. John Sparrow was many, many miles away and would not return. It did no good to repine. It was not long since she had assured Lizzy every impulse of feeling should be guided by reason. Now she must apply that lesson to herself. Her choices were few and of too much importance to be influenced by unruly emotions. Sense and not sensibility must be her guide.

CHAPTER TWENTY-THREE

In the morning, as Mary was pushing extra pins into her hair in an attempt to secure it, Mrs Hill came quietly into her room.

'So your cousin is arrived, miss.'

'He is indeed.'

'And what do you think of him? What kind of man is he?'

'I'm afraid he hasn't won many friends in the house. My sisters think him dull and my father has decided he is a fool – but you are not to repeat that, I beg.'

'But what about you, miss? I asked your opinion of him.'

Mary peered into the mirror. Her hair was not a success. Without a word, Mrs Hill picked up a brush, took out the pins and let it down. As she worked, Mary decided to speak as candidly as she could. She trusted Mrs Hill, and thought it would help to express her thoughts aloud.

'He does seem absurd at times,' she began, 'but I don't believe there is anything really wicked about him. I think he is unsure and uncertain and that makes him inclined to talk too much to no good purpose. He believes his flattery will please those to whom he speaks, but the result is often the exact reverse.'

'You feel sorry for him, then?'

'A little. He is such a tempting target for my father's

teasing that it is impossible not to feel some sympathy for him, although I admit no one else seems to think as I do.'

Mrs Hill was now twisting Mary's hair in a smooth knot with practised skill, anchoring it securely at the nape of her neck.

'Does that mean you might look at him ... in a friendly manner?'

'That's a very direct question.'

'I'm sure you know what I mean,' replied Mrs Hill, unperturbed. 'I wondered whether you have thought about him ... in a marital way. He talks like a reading man, and he's already asked to use the library – your mother wants me to make sure it's dusted this morning. You'd have your books in common. He isn't a showy sort of gentleman ... not someone to value a pretty face above all other considerations.'

Mary took a green and gold ribbon from her dressing table and began to run it absently through her fingers.

'You say that, but he hasn't taken his eyes off Jane since he arrived.'

'Well, we know her thoughts are elsewhere, and likely to stay that way, I should think.'

'If Jane refused him, I'm sure he'd think of Elizabeth next. I should be a very poor third choice.'

'I shan't reply to that – you know it makes me sad to hear you so hard upon yourself. But I doubt Miss Elizabeth would have him. You might still have a chance. Would you like me to put that ribbon in your hair?'

Mary looked at it, surprised, as if she had not known it was in her hand.

'Oh, no, I don't think so. It's too bright for me.' She placed it hurriedly back on the dressing table. 'But even if he could be persuaded to make me an offer – what kind of happiness do you think I could look forward to with him?'

Mrs Hill considered her handiwork, pushing a last pin into Mary's hair.

'They say marriage is a lottery and none of us knows if we've drawn a winning ticket until it's too late.' She passed Mary a small mirror, so that she could see her head from the back. 'But whatever you think of him, as his wife you'd be mistress of Longbourn – and that's something to consider, is it not?'

Mary stared into the mirror, contemplating her neatly dressed hair.

'In my opinion,' concluded Mrs Hill, 'you have as good a chance of catching him as anyone. You should think very hard about it before letting someone else steal him from under your nose. A man like him, whatever his little annoyances, won't be around forever.'

She laid down the combs, and having delivered herself of the point she had always intended to make, left the room. For a few seconds Mary did not move, sitting and thinking before she rose and pulled on her shawl. As she did so, she felt a strand of her hair slip down. Angry, she thrust in a pin with too much force, making her head throb as she walked downstairs to breakfast. She arrived in the hall just in time to see Mrs Bennet follow Mr Collins out of the drawing room. He looked self-conscious but pleased with himself; her mother seemed excited, as though she could scarcely contain what she had just been told.

Throughout the meal, she beamed at Mr Collins, handing him the hottest rolls and helping him to the butter and jam. Mary watched him closely; she thought she could guess at the contents of a conversation that had left both him and her mother so ebullient. He must have spoken to her about his intentions. A shiver of apprehension passed through her, as she contemplated what this meant. She must decide now if she intended to follow her head or her heart – whether she would listen to the promptings of duty and self-interest, or cover her ears and hope against hope for something better. Her mind was soon made up. She said nothing until everyone else had gone and only she and her mother remained. As Mrs Bennet played idly with the remains of a slice of toast, Mary got up and carefully closed the door.

'Excuse me, ma'am, but I wonder if I might ask you something?'

Mrs Bennet nodded absently.

'Is it your belief that Mr Collins has come here to ask for one of us in marriage?'

Her mother looked up, surprised.

'What do you mean by asking me that? Have you been listening at doors?'

'Indeed, I have not. He has dropped several hints that suggest that might be his intention.'

'And if it is, what has it to do with you? I'm not sure what you mean by questioning me.'

Mary struggled on, trying to suggest a confidence she did not feel.

'I have been thinking very hard about it, and it seems to me that of all my sisters, I might be the most sensible choice for him. I think our interests coincide; we are both of a serious turn of mind and might grow to suit each other well enough. I'm sorry to speak so boldly, but I've tried to consider the situation as rationally as I could before raising it with you.'

Her voice shook a little at the end, but she did not waver.

Mrs Bennet looked at her daughter, speechless; words seemed briefly to have failed her.

'Well, you are full of surprises, to be sure. But you are right, Mr Collins does intend to ask for one of you girls in marriage. He told me so this morning. Of course, his first thought was Jane; but as I've explained, I have every reason to expect she will shortly be engaged to a gentleman of rank and fortune.'

She smiled into the middle distance, the mere thought of such a happy event enough to please her.

'I suggested he transfer his hopes to Lizzy, and he seemed pleased enough to do so.'

'Was that entirely wise? I don't think there's any chance of Lizzy accepting him; their dispositions are so very different. She's in no hurry to marry and can expect many other offers.'

Mrs Bennet began to grow annoyed.

'If he couldn't have Jane, it was Lizzy he wanted, and it was hardly the moment to suggest alternatives. What am I to do, offer him around the family like a parcel? I'm sure he would never have thought of you – your name wasn't mentioned at all.'

Mary flinched. The pin she had pushed so clumsily into her head was hurting her, but this was not the moment to adjust it.

'I'm sorry if I've angered you,' she continued. 'I didn't intend to make any claims for myself. I know I don't possess the attractions of Jane or Lizzy. But I thought as I am the only sister likely to look favourably upon him, it would be sensible to direct his attentions towards me. If he made an offer, I should feel obliged to accept him. It would keep Longbourn for us, besides taking your least marriageable daughter off your hands. Those and those alone have been my motives in speaking.'

Mrs Bennet was not mollified.

'That's finely said, but I don't think Lizzy will refuse him. I intend to make sure she does not. There will be no need for anyone in reserve. You are not to meddle in things that don't concern you, and you are expressly forbidden to mention any of this to Elizabeth. To be frank, Mary, I'm amazed at your presumption.'

She stood up, indignantly gathering her skirt before her.

'I don't want to hear another word from you on the subject. And your hair has come down at the back. Please attend to it.'

When her mother had gone, Mary poured herself some tea. At first, her hand shook slightly, but by the time she raised the cup to her mouth, she was calmer. Mrs Bennet's words shocked her very much. She knew her mother had no hopes she would make a marriage of the kind she dreamed of for her other daughters; but Mary had not realised until now how little she featured in her mother's plans at all. Nothing, it seemed, was to be done for her. She was unworthy of any consideration, not fit even to serve as a consolation prize to a disappointed man. If proof had been needed that Charlotte was right when she insisted a young woman must unflinchingly pursue her own best interests, she had surely received it this morning. She could hear the servants outside, waiting to come and clear the table, and knew it was time to leave. For the merest instant, as she got up from her chair, she wondered if her mother's rejection was in fact a blessing in disguise, that she was being offered a chance to think again, that she was not required to lay herself out to please a man she hardly knew and wondered if she could ever love. But it was a thought she quickly buried. There was no alternative to Mr Collins. Even Mrs Hill had urged him upon her. She was foolish to imagine she deserved anything else. If her mother would not help her secure him, then she must do so alone.

CHAPTER TWENTY-FOUR

As Mary walked into the hall, she had already begun to turn over in her mind how she might proceed. She knew she had no talent for the playfulness which Elizabeth deployed so easily. She could see only one way of attracting Mr Collins's attention: she must do everything possible to alert him to the interests they shared, demonstrate to him by every means in her power that in terms of tastes and disposition, she was the only Bennet sister who might offer him a reasonable chance of happiness. So absorbed was she in these thoughts that she hardly noticed her two younger sisters heading towards her along the passage with their usual air of barely suppressed excitement. Lydia seized her arm, and spoke in a whisper loud enough to be heard in every adjacent room.

'Unless you wish to be teased and annoyed by the dullest man in the neighbourhood, go as fast as you can past the library. *He* is in there, wandering about and pretending to look at books.'

Kitty looked over her shoulder, as if she feared they might have been followed.

'I think he saw us, for he called out as we went past, but we pretended not to hear.'

She caught Lydia's eye, and they both laughed.

'That was unkind and disrespectful,' declared Mary. 'Mr

Collins is a guest in our house and deserves proper consideration from us all.'

Lydia rolled her eyes and pulled a face. 'You are very welcome to offer him all the consideration you want, proper or otherwise, but we intend walking into Meryton to escape him. Come with us if you wish – unless you'd rather stay and listen to another of his lectures.'

'I would rather spend the morning hearing Mr Collins read an interesting book than wander about Meryton mooning after officers.'

'Just as you like,' replied Lydia nonchalantly. 'We obviously have very different ideas about what is interesting. Kitty and I will go and put on our boots and leave you to be improved.'

They bustled away, and Mary, conscious she had yet again been made to look a prig, continued on her way to the library. There she found Mr Collins, a large folio open on the table before him. He looked up as she entered, his expression registering neither pleasure nor surprise at her arrival. He wished her good morning and returned to his book. Mary took up her usual position at her little table, and opened a volume of her own; but it was soon evident, from his sighs and fidgets, that he was not engaged by his reading. Mary plucked up her courage. This was exactly the kind of opportunity she must learn to seize.

'Excuse me, sir, but it doesn't appear you're quite satisfied with the book you have chosen. I know my father's library very well and would be happy to help you find something more to your liking.'

'That is very polite, but I assure you, I am happy with what I have.'

'My father's system of cataloguing is of his own devising,

and the logic is not always apparent to those who do not know it. I could point out where he keeps works of moral and philosophical interest.'

'Thank you, but I will content myself with this for the time being.'

He turned the pages one after the other, his attention clearly elsewhere. Mary made herself try again.

'I was very sorry you weren't able to finish your reading from Dr Fordyce yesterday. I found it most instructive.'

Mr Collins inclined his head very slightly in acknowledgement.

'I should be very glad to hear more, if you ever felt moved . . .'

Before she could finish her sentence, Mr Bennet came into the room. Mr Collins stood up, all attention, and made a formal bow.

'I hope, sir, you will excuse my intruding into your place of study. I took the liberty of acceding to the invitation extended by you with such generosity last night, to think of your library as my own.'

Mr Bennet murmured the briefest acknowledgement, and seated himself at his desk.

'Anyone is welcome here, provided they abide by the rules of the house. As Mary may have told you, I encourage the preservation of a companionable silence, as being most conducive to civilised reflection.'

Mr Collins expressed his eager willingness to comply; and for a few minutes, nothing was heard but his page-turning. But Mary saw he was still unsettled, and it was not long before he addressed Mr Bennet directly.

'Your library, sir, is blessed with very elegant proportions and a quantity of natural light.'

Mr Bennet looked up, a hint of irritation discernible in his expression.

'It has neither the size nor the scale of Lady Catherine's library at Rosings Park,' continued Mr Collins blithely, 'but it is of very respectable proportions for a gentleman's residence such as your own.'

'I am glad it meets with your approval.'

'Indeed it does, sir. And your gardens, too, are admirable. Although their size must limit their ambitions, they are extremely well-kept and make a very pleasurable sight.'

'Again, I am indebted to you. I imagine, however, that the grounds at Rosings are of a different degree of excellence?'

'Yes, Lady Catherine always says the long walk and the parterre exceed in perfection anything to be found in the county. I have often agreed with her that this is so. Nothing is as noble as the view from the north terrace towards the ha-ha.'

Mr Bennet closed his book.

'Your thoughts seem more directed towards the pleasures of the outdoors than to study this morning. It seems most unfair that you should confine yourself inside. Lydia and Kitty are, I believe, readying themselves to walk into Meryton.'

Mr Collins looked uncertain.

'Elizabeth and Jane intend to accompany them. I suggest you join them. It will be a very cheerful party for you all.'

At the mention of Lizzy's name, Mr Collins hastily stood up.

'I should be delighted to attend them. I shall go and find them directly.'

He did not look at Mary as he hurried from the room. Should she follow him? She was not certain whether it would be fitting to rush after him. She laid down her book and tried to make up her mind. But before she could do so, Mr Collins was heard in the hallway begging his fair cousins to wait for him. There was a clatter of boots, a flurry of voices, the front door was heard to shut, and then all was again silent.

'You did not wish to go with them, Mary?' enquired Mr Bennet.

'I don't think my presence was required.'

'At least you have the consolation of being spared your cousin's company for an hour.'

'I think he means well, Papa. His manner I agree is unfortunate, but I believe his intentions are sincere.'

'Do you think so? If that is indeed the case, then I think I would prefer the company of an insincere man of sense to . . . well, I shall not say fool, because he is such a close relation.'

He returned to his book in a manner intended to suggest that further conversation was at an end. Mary picked up her own volume, but now it was she who was distracted.

For the rest of the morning, she brooded on what she should do next. Her thoughts went this way and that, but finally she stirred herself to action. She went to her bedroom, fetched her copy of Fordyce, and carried it to the drawing room, where she stood looking about for a few minutes before putting it on a small table, where she thought it most likely to catch Mr Collins's eye. Beneath it, she placed Mrs Macaulay, in case his tastes ran towards history. Satisfied, she walked to the piano and searched through her music, choosing pieces she thought he might enjoy, nothing too frivolous, and arranged them next to the keyboard. If an opportunity to play for him offered itself, she would be ready to grasp it. Then she sat down and waited for the walking party to return. After a while, she heard her mother's voice directing the laying of the table for luncheon; and a moment later, Mrs Bennet slipped silently into the drawing room, closing the door firmly behind her.

'When the others are back, and we sit down at table, I do not want there to be any confusion about where each of us will be placed.'

'I am sorry, Mama, but I'm not sure I understand you.'

'Really, Mary, I think you do. Lord knows your conversation this morning was forward enough. It does you no favours to be so missish now.'

Ashamed, Mary hung her head.

'Well, let me make myself understood. Mr Collins will be seated next to Lizzy. There will be no attempt to swap seats.'

'Of course. I would never put myself forward in that way . . .'

'I am very pleased to hear it. I will have no interference with my plans.'

When the family assembled, Mary found herself at the furthest possible distance from Mr Collins. It was impossible for them to have any conversation together. From her end of the table, she watched Elizabeth do all she could to deflect his attentions while remaining within the bounds of politeness. Mary looked on with frustrated incomprehension. How could Mrs Bennet refuse to understand that Elizabeth would never have him? Why, indeed, did Mr Collins not see that himself? Instead, he battled on, quite blind to Lizzy's ill-concealed distaste. It was many minutes before he drew himself reluctantly away from Elizabeth and addressed her mother instead.

'I was delighted to be introduced to some gentlemen of my fair cousins' acquaintance this morning.'

'Indeed, sir?' replied Mrs Bennet, signalling to the servant to offer Mr Collins another leg of chicken. 'Whom did you meet?'

'We came upon two of the officers,' interrupted Lydia,

delighted at the opportunity to talk upon her favourite topic. 'Mr Denny and another quite new one, just this minute arrived. He was not even in his red coat yet, although he said he has his commission.'

'His name is Mr Wickham,' added Kitty, helping herself to more peas. 'And while we were talking to them, Mr Bingley arrived, together with his friend, the tall, proud man who never speaks.'

'That would be Mr Darcy,' explained Mrs Bennet to Mr Collins, 'a very disagreeable man.'

'Really, ma'am!' exclaimed Elizabeth. 'It cannot be fair to prejudice Mr Collins against him to such a degree. We barely know the gentleman.'

Mrs Bennet was unmoved.

'What we have seen of him is hardly to his credit. His haughtiness gave universal offence at the last assembly. I am sure no one has a good word to say for him.'

'"Judge not lest ye be judged in your turn,"' ventured Mary. 'That is what Scripture enjoins upon us.' She looked towards Mr Collins to see if he would approve.

'My cousin is right, of course,' he replied, favouring her with a bland smile. 'But society, as well as Scripture, has its claims upon us all. No one of us can afford to ignore what is owed to politeness.'

He tried to catch Elizabeth's eye, but she occupied herself resolutely with her chicken.

'I thought Mr Wickham seemed rather taken by Lizzy,' suggested Lydia with a grin. Elizabeth turned back to the table, her expression outraged.

'What *can* you mean, Lydia! Really, you are quite ridiculous!'

'He spoke to you far more than to any of us. And you didn't appear to mind it.'

'That is quite enough,' declared Mrs Bennet sharply, with a sideways glance at Mr Collins. 'Lydia always takes these little jokes too far.'

The rest of the meal proceeded in a distinctly subdued fashion. Lizzy was embarrassed, Mr Collins piqued, and Mrs Bennet angry. As soon as the table was cleared. Elizabeth escaped to her room while Mrs Bennet pursued Lydia into the garden, where she could be scolded away from view. Mary wandered aimlessly towards the drawing room, where she sat at the piano and began to play. Soon she was quite lost in the music. A few minutes later, she saw Mr Collins come in, but she continued with her playing until all the piece's loose ends had been satisfactorily tied up and its complexities resolved.

When she turned to face him, he was smiling with what looked like genuine pleasure. 'My congratulations, cousin. You play with great exactness. I imagine you practise a great deal to achieve such precision?'

Mary admitted this was so.

'I commend you for it. It is only through hard work that anything of value is to be achieved.'

'I am very pleased you enjoyed it.'

'I have often remarked to Lady Catherine that her daughter, Miss de Bourgh, would no doubt have been an excellent musician if her health had permitted her to learn an instrument. The weakness of her constitution unquestionably deprived us of a musician of the very greatest accomplishment.'

'I'm sorry to hear that, sir. I would be happy to play for you again, if you wish.'

'Sadly, I must deny myself that pleasure, as I am engaged to your mother, who is to show me the disposition of her back-stairs linen cupboards. Lady Catherine has condescended to suggest some improvements in that line might not go amiss in my humble parsonage, so I am keen to avail myself of Mrs Bennet's expert knowledge while I may.'

He stood up, making his accustomed bow.

'But I must thank you for allowing me to listen to you. It filled an empty moment most pleasurably.'

After his departure, Mary sat at the keyboard, reflecting. Although he had refused her offer to continue, Mr Collins seemed to have enjoyed hearing her play. Indeed, he had never before appeared so animated in her presence. She stroked the keys noiselessly as she considered the implications of this. Perhaps it was music and not reading that would best attract his attention? She struck a single chord which echoed round the empty room. If that was so – and the more she considered it, the more she was persuaded she was right – then she must do all in her power to show off her skills at the piano to their very best advantage, so that he could not help but notice both them and herself.

She was still wondering how this might be achieved when the door burst open and Kitty rushed in. 'We've just heard the best possible news,' she gasped, her hat awry. 'We've run in to tell everyone.'

'Yes, yes,' cried Lydia, following fast behind her. 'There's going to be a ball! At Netherfield! And it's fixed for a week today.' She paused to catch her breath. 'Mr Bingley came in person to invite us. He met Lizzy and Jane in the garden. We saw him just before he went away. What news, eh?'

'He's asked us all,' cried Kitty. 'Even Mr Collins. Mama will be so excited.'

'Did Mr Bingley not think it proper to come in and ask our mother himself?' asked Mary.

'He was with his sisters, and they had not the time,' said Kitty.

'That doesn't seem very polite.'

'Really, Mary!' Lydia exclaimed. 'What does it matter who asked whom? Anyway, I'm sure it was his dreadful sisters who declined to come in. They make it quite clear they think we're beneath them – all those simpering smiles to Jane and nasty little sniggers to each other – don't imagine I haven't seen them – but I don't care! *He* has behaved admirably. He said he should hold a ball and he has been true to his word.'

'Shall you go, Mary?' asked Kitty.

Mary picked up her music, turning the question over in her mind. If Mr Collins was to be there, and if she was serious in her attempts to arouse his interest, she was clearly obliged to attend. The dance could be as much an opportunity for her as it was for any of her sisters.

'I think I might. I can work in the morning, and I think it right occasionally to join in evening entertainments. Society has its claims upon us all, and I think some moments of recreation and amusement are desirable for everyone.'

Lydia burst into laughter.

'You sound *exactly* like Mr Collins! You were clearly meant for each other. What a pity it is that he has eyes only for Lizzy!'

At dinner that night, all conversation was directed to the coming ball. Mrs Bennet was consumed with anticipation. She had convinced herself the ball was intended entirely as a compliment to Jane and, brushing away her daughter's embarrassment, began to debate how quickly it would be followed by an offer from Mr Bingley. Her husband paid no attention to his wife's speculations, but to the surprise of his family, announced that he too would attend. Since Bingley had done him the honour to ask him, he should go and drink his wine and eat his supper and be as content as a sensible man could be in such a situation.

Elizabeth did not usually address Mr Collins more than was required by the demands of politeness; but now, allowing goodwill to triumph over dislike, she unbent sufficiently to ask her cousin if, as a clergyman, he thought it proper to accept his invitation and join in the evening's amusements. He gave his answer very determinedly.

'I am by no means of the opinion, I assure you, that a ball of this kind, given by a young man of character, to respectable people, can have any evil tendency; and I am so far from objecting to dancing myself that I shall hope to be honoured with the hands of all my fair cousins in the course of the evening.'

Lydia suppressed a giggle. Mrs Bennet glared at her, as Kitty, Jane, and Lizzy stared away, in any direction but his. Only Mary steeled herself to gaze at him expectantly. But Mr Collins turned, as she had suspected he would, towards Lizzy.

'I take this opportunity of soliciting yours, Miss Elizabeth, for the first dance especially.'

Elizabeth looked stricken, but was forced to agree. Mr Collins made no similar offer to Mary, which merely confirmed the conclusion she had arrived at earlier. If she was to make any impression at all upon him, it must be through her skill at the piano. Her looks could not help her, and he had barely acknowledged her studiousness, although she done her utmost to parade it before him. Music was the last remaining lure by which he might be persuaded to notice her; and the Netherfield ball offered the perfect opportunity to display the full extent of her talent. There she would perform with such brilliance that neither he nor anyone else would be able to ignore her. She sat back in her chair, pleased to have a plan. She would arrange to have extra instruction from her music teacher to ensure her playing was at its very best. This was too important a moment to leave anything to chance.

CHAPTER TWENTY-FIVE

Miss Allen, Mary's piano instructress, was thin, grave, and silent, a woman who had perfected the art of self-effacement to such a degree that when she was not at Longbourn, Mary found it hard to recall exactly what she looked like or how old she might be. She was the unmarried daughter of a curate, living in lodgings above the milliner's shop, from which cramped and dingy rooms she strove night and day to preserve her precarious hold on gentility. It was Miss Allen's fate that haunted Mary's darkest hours, her sad and anxious face which sprang into her mind when she imagined what the future held if she did not marry. For that reason, Mary had called upon Miss Allen's services rather less in recent months than before. But today, here she was, toiling up the Longbourn drive, her shabby cloth bag heavy with sheets of new music for Mary to consider. Together, they spent the morning studying them; and by midday, they had decided on three pieces. Mary would begin with a sonata by Haydn, intended to display her hard-won proficiency at the keyboard; go on with a few Scottish airs designed to make her listeners smile; and finish with a selection from *The Harmonious Blacksmith*.

'Your choices feel entirely right,' concluded Miss Allen, as she packed up her things and readied herself to walk the two miles to her next lesson. 'The Haydn will impress everyone who hears it, and the airs will be very cheerful. Everyone will have the words to "Robin Adair" in their heads.'

Mary closed the piano lid. An idea had occurred to her earlier in the morning, and she wished to find out Miss Allen's opinion of it.

'I have been asking myself if I'm offering enough to the company by merely playing the song. I thought I might venture to sing it too. The effect would be very fine if I could manage both. What do you think?'

Miss Allen buckled her bag and fussed with her gloves.

'I'm not sure your vocal talents are as strong as your playing. If you wish to show yourself to the greatest advantage, I suggest you concentrate on what you do best and confine yourself to the keyboard.'

Usually this would have been enough to quash Mary's ambitions; but not today. She had set her mind on achieving something spectacular, and was not to be easily deterred.

'Other ladies will play and sing.'

'We cannot all excel equally at everything we do.' Miss Allen looked tired as she stood up to leave. 'Miss Elizabeth's abilities might be said to be the exact opposite of your own. Her voice is strong, but her playing lacks discipline. You, on the other hand, are an extremely competent player, but your voice is not your greatest asset.'

'You are very candid, to be sure.'

Miss Allen sighed.

'I don't think I would be serving you by telling you only what you wish to hear. Your playing will please everyone, but your singing is perhaps best enjoyed by your family alone. I mean it kindly and have no wish to offend you.'

Mary assured Miss Allen that she did not take her words

ill; but as she stood at the window, watching the music teacher make her way down the drive, Mary knew she would not follow her advice. She went back to the piano and placed a new sheet of music on the stand with a most determined air. For once she would not be told what to do, would not meekly accept that Elizabeth must always surpass her in everything she undertook. She would practise for three hours every morning until the day of the ball, exercising her voice until it matched the proficiency of her fingers. Hard work and dedication should supply what nature had not, making it impossible that Mr Collins, and indeed everyone else, should not be amazed by the virtuosity of her performance.

CHAPTER TWENTY-SIX

Mrs Hill was delighted when Mary asked her to iron the gold and cream dress as she intended to wear it to the Netherfield ball.

'I was afraid you were going to be stubborn and refuse it. This is exactly the right occasion to show yourself off.'

The next few days passed in a flurry of practice and preparation. When the night of the ball finally arrived, Mary felt she was as ready as she would ever be. She had devoted every spare hour to the piano, rehearsing her pieces until she knew them so well that she could have played them in her sleep. She had been more circumspect with her singing, partly as she was afraid of tiring her voice; but also because she did not wish to reveal to her family her intention to sing as well as play. Miss Allen's response to her suggestion had not been what she hoped to hear. She would not risk any further discouragement by announcing it to anyone else. The surprise would be all the greater when they heard her perform.

The knowledge that she had made every possible effort, that no one could have worked harder, soothed her nerves somewhat as Mrs Hill helped her get ready. When she put on the dress, it too felt right. Turning this way and that in front of her mirror, she saw that its bright airiness still flattered her, that its simplicity worked well alongside the plain style in which Mrs Hill had arranged her hair. Mary was satisfied.

She would not provoke gasps of admiration, but she looked neatly put together. She took a final glance at her reflection – and as she did so, all unbidden, a memory flashed ino her mind of John Sparrow smiling at her. It was a pang to the heart – but with a great strength of will, she suppressed it. It would not do. She breathed a little faster as she left her room and walked down the stairs, but she forced herself not to dwell upon it. She could not allow herself to become agitated. Nothing was to interfere with the serene state of mind her performance would require.

When she arrived in the hall, she found her parents, Kitty, and Lydia waiting there, ready to leave. Mrs Bennet's temper had not been improved by standing about, and she relieved some of her anger by scolding Mary vigorously for her tardiness; but when, a few minutes later, neither Jane, Elizabeth, nor Mr Collins had appeared, her patience was exhausted.

'I shall be extremely vexed if Lady Lucas arrives before we do. Lydia, go up and ask them what they are about!'

'I'm sure they are busy beautifying themselves,' declared Mr Bennet, 'eager to look their best for any marriageable young men who might be found at tonight's entertainment. I should have thought such close attention to their interests would have merited your entire approval, my dear.'

'That might be pardonable in Jane,' replied Mrs Bennet, 'for she has Mr Bingley to consider, but who has Lizzy to please?'

'Perhaps Mr Wickham?' suggested Lydia, with a look of mock innocence which provoked her mother still further.

'If you knew how my nerves are troubling me at this very minute, Lydia, you would not say such things. And where, pray, is Mr Collins?' she wailed. 'I thought he, at least, had more consideration!'

'He is no doubt hard pressed to choose an outfit that will suggest both his high opinion of himself and his readiness to flatter his superiors at every possible opportunity,' observed Mr Bennet smoothly. 'It is a considerable requirement to ask of a coat and shirt. We may be here for quite some time.'

Mrs Bennet had no opportunity to reply, as, at that very moment, the three latecomers arrived together in the hall. Indeed, neither she nor any of the other Bennets were required to speak for quite some time, as Mr Collins at once began upon a profuse apology and a lengthy account of a lost cravat, a soliloquy which, being so often repeated, occupied most of the journey to Netherfield.

When their carriage pulled up outside Netherfield, the house seemed to Mary more imposing than she remembered. The entrance was lit with several flaming torches, upon which Mr Bennet directed his most amused smile; but Mary privately thought them rather fine. The interior was even more grand, with some very imposing furniture and pictures. Mary stood before one, trying to identify the artist, when Mr Bingley advanced to welcome them, radiating his usual good humour to all, although his greeting for Jane was particularly heartfelt. Mary wished Mrs Bennet had not chosen to remark on the fact by nudging Mr Bennet quite so noticeably; but she did not think of it any further once they were in the public rooms, which were packed full of people and alive with the noise of excited conversation.

'A positive rout,' murmured Elizabeth, as they looked around for someone they knew. Across the room stood Mr Bingley's sisters, imperious, heads held high; and by their side was his reserved and haughty friend, who, catching sight of Elizabeth, made her an unexpectedly gracious bow.

'Look, Lizzy,' whispered Jane, 'I believe Mr Darcy is greeting you. Look, he is bowing directly towards you.'

Elizabeth made the briefest of acknowledgements, and turned abruptly away.

'He really is insupportable, teasing me in this way! Let us ignore him. I think I see Charlotte over there beside the fireplace.'

It was a fortnight since Charlotte had been at Longbourn, and there was much news to impart. Having pointed out Mr Collins to her friend, Elizabeth enjoyed describing his oddities and quirks, retelling all his silliest speeches to so much effect that Charlotte could not help but laugh.

'Is he really so ridiculous a figure? Come, Mary, you shall tell me the truth.'

'He doesn't always present himself to his best advantage, but I don't think there is any real harm in him.'

'That is very lukewarm praise!'

'Well, you may judge for yourself,' observed Elizabeth, 'for he is approaching us this very moment.'

The musicians had struck up; and Mr Collins had come to claim Elizabeth for the dance. With many professions of regret for removing her from the company of her charming companions, he led his cousin towards the floor. Charlotte surveyed them keenly as they went.

'He is a clergyman, then. Does he have a decent living?'

Mary explained as fully as possible everything she could recall about Lady Catherine, the generosity of her patronage, her marked condescension, and Mr Collins's humble parsonage in Kent.

'I suppose in the fullness of time he will also inherit Long-bourn.'

'As my father likes to say, once he is dead, Mr Collins may turn us all out, whenever he wishes.'

To Mary's surprise, Charlotte took her hand, holding it for a few moments, then just as briskly removed it. Her gesture conveyed her sympathy more powerfully than anything she might have said. Both were silent for a moment, until Charlotte spoke again.

'So for all the frailties which amuse Lizzy,' she observed quietly, 'Mr Collins is in many ways a very eligible young man.'

'That's certainly how my mother sees it,' replied Mary. 'She is determined he'll marry one of us. At the moment, her preference – and it would seem, his own – is for Lizzy.'

Charlotte drew back, astonished.

'I should have thought that most unlikely.'

'That is my opinion exactly,' declared Mary, relieved to be able to discuss Mr Collins with a disinterested listener. 'Everything he says annoys her, and she does all she can to avoid him.'

'Poor man,' observed Charlotte wryly. 'I would not wish your sister's disdain upon anyone. But although he has not been so fortunate as to please Lizzy, it is not impossible that another woman might accept him.'

'I'm sure you're right,' said Mary. 'No one could call him sensible, but he has qualities which might be cultivated by a wife with the right turn of mind. Indeed, if he were to come under the influence of a steady, thoughtful woman, he could be much improved; and she might stand as good a chance as most of ending up tolerably content with her lot.'

'Good Lord, Mary,' declared Charlotte with a laugh, 'the conversations we had about marriage have made a great impression upon you! When you talk in this way, I might almost be listening to myself!'

Mary was about to reply, for there was much more she would have liked to say on the subject of marriage and Mr Collins; but she saw Elizabeth approaching them and knew it could not be pursued in her presence.

Charlotte understood this too; and when Lizzy arrived, she greeted her in a very different tone, light, bright and unconcerned.

'So you are released from your purgatory, I see. Do tell us how it was – we were too absorbed in our conversation to pay much attention to you and Mr Collins.'

Elizabeth groaned and held out her foot.

'Every step in the wrong place, his shoe always ending up upon mine. If he had concentrated more and apologised less, it might not have been so trying, but as it was – well, let us just say I am finished with dancing for a while.'

Charlotte, who had been peering into the far side of the room, suddenly bent her head towards Elizabeth.

'You may be compelled back onto the floor more quickly than you think. Mr Darcy is coming towards us with such cold determination that it can only mean he is about to ask you to stand up with him.'

Elizabeth protested that such a thing was impossible, objected that it could not be so. But just as she had finished declaring its utter improbability, the gentleman himself arrived and stood before her. In the most formal manner, he begged the pleasure of her hand when the dancing began again; and she was so taken by surprise that she accepted.

Immediately, he turned on his heel and walked away, leaving Elizabeth dumbstruck at her own decision.

'Whatever possessed me to agree? I can't imagine what I was thinking.'

'I dare say,' said Charlotte consolingly, 'that once on the floor, you will find him very agreeable.'

'Heaven forbid! That would be the greatest misfortune of all! To find agreeable a man whom one is determined to hate!'

'I imagine you will bear it. I do beg you, Elizabeth, do not make yourself unpleasant in the eyes of a man of such consequence.'

Elizabeth argued the contrary for a while, reminding Charlotte of the many objections to Mr Darcy's character, temper, and demeanour; but when the music began, not having contrived a valid excuse to snub him, as she thought he deserved, she went reluctantly to join him in the dance. Mary and Charlotte watched with curiosity to see how she would manage it. At first, she was silent and aloof, but soon she and Mr Darcy were talking to each other with every appearance of lively animation.

'Your sister has a great deal to say to a man she insists she does not like,' remarked Charlotte.

'Yes,' agreed Mary. 'It's very surprising.'

'Perhaps she doesn't know her own feelings as well as she thinks. She may not be as accustomed as we are to subjecting them to minute examination. When everything comes to you so easily, there must be little reason to ask yourself why that's so.'

Together Charlotte and Mary walked towards the supper table and watched the dancing draw to a close.

'I hear you are to play for us later tonight,' observed Charlotte politely.

'I think so, if the company is happy to hear me. I've chosen a few pieces I hope will please.'

For a moment, she was tempted to tell Charlotte everything – how, inspired by her words, she had begun to think of Mr Collins as a potential husband, how impossible it had proved to attract his attention, and how, this very evening, she hoped to conquer his indifference with a remarkable performance at the keyboard. It would have been a relief to speak plainly to someone who would understand, who might have sensible advice to offer – but before she could do so, Elizabeth hurried over to them, eager to share her impressions of her dancing partner. She had only just begun to catalogue his shortcomings when they were interrupted again, this time by Mr Collins, who bustled into their presence with news he thought they would be as keen to hear as he was to impart.

'Excuse my interrupting you, ladies, but I thought it right you should know I have made a most significant discovery.'

He bent towards them with an air of the greatest solemnity.

'I have found out, by a singular accident, that there is, in this room, a distinguished relation of my patroness.'

'Really, sir?' asked Charlotte. 'May we know who it is?'

'You will be surprised to hear,' he announced, 'that it is the gentleman fortunate enough to have danced the last set with you, Miss Elizabeth. Mr Darcy, it appears, is a nephew of Lady Catherine de Bourgh. What have you to say to that?'

'I suppose,' began Mary, when no one else volunteered a

reply, 'it may be said to show how very small are the circles in which we all move – how close are the ties that bind us.'

'Yes,' agreed Charlotte, 'it is remarkable how –'

She did not finish her sentence. Elizabeth broke in, her voice full of the urgency of one to whom a dreadful idea has just occurred.

'Sir, please tell me you do not plan to introduce yourself to Mr Darcy?'

Mr Collins looked a little affronted.

'Of course I shall. Indeed, I feel I must apologise for not having done so earlier.'

In vain did Elizabeth attempt to dissuade him. Mr Darcy was of a proud disposition, she explained, and would not welcome uninvited familiarity. If the connection was to be acknowledged, then it fell to Mr Darcy, as the superior in consequence, to make the first approach. But Mr Collins was not to be swayed. Adopting an expression which seemed to Lizzy to combine supplication and presumption in equally shameful measure, he made his way to the group amongst whom Mr Darcy stood and began to speak.

It was perhaps fortunate that they were too far away to hear exactly what was said; but Mr Collins's voice was strong and carrying, and the words 'apology' and 'Lady Catherine de Bourgh' were frequently repeated and impossible to ignore.

Elizabeth closed her eyes in horror.

'How could he expose himself in this way?'

Charlotte watched with amusement.

'I think a snub has very definitely been administered. It appears that poor Mr Collins has been soundly dismissed.'

'I'm afraid you're right,' agreed Mary. 'Mr Darcy has not deigned to notice him. Poor man, I'm sorry for him.'

'How can you say that,' cried Elizabeth, smarting with humiliation, 'when his behaviour reflects so badly upon us all? Look at Miss Bingley, smirking at her sister! Nothing could have pleased them more than to see one of our family show themselves to be so ill-bred!'

Charlotte took Elizabeth's arm. 'Come, Lizzy, there is no need to be so cross. I'm not sure why you set such store by the opinions of those you do not respect.'

Elizabeth was silent with anger; but she allowed herself to be gently led away from the scene of Mr Collins's embarrassment.

'Let us find somewhere a little quieter to sit,' murmured Charlotte soothingly. 'We shall have a glass of wine and put it out of our minds.'

By now, most of the chairs were full, and the only vacant seats were closer to Mrs Bennet than either Charlotte, Elizabeth, or Mary would have preferred. From their places, they could not help but overhear everything she said; and Elizabeth's temper did not improve as her mother loudly informed Lady Lucas of her confident expectation that Jane and Mr Bingley would very soon be married. When Mr Darcy and the Bingley sisters, also in search of refreshment, happened to station themselves close by, Elizabeth's misery was almost complete. Mary watched her grow more and more agitated as Mrs Bennet's conversation went on and on, audible to anyone around them. The music could not silence her. Instead, she simply raised her voice, all the better to assure her friend that, in her view, not the least advantage of Jane's marrying so well was the likelihood of it throwing her younger daughters in the way of other rich men. At this, Elizabeth could bear no more and stood up. Mary saw her dart a glance towards Mr Darcy, who stared back, grave and disapproving.

'Please, ma'am, I do beseech you to speak less audibly. Mr Darcy is quite close by and cannot help but hear you.'

'And what is Mr Darcy to me, pray, that I should be afraid of him?'

Elizabeth stood up abruptly, and walked away.

'I'm not sure why Elizabeth is so angry,' whispered Mary to Charlotte, as she watched her sister force her way through the crowd. 'Our mother's behaviour does not usually affect her so powerfully.'

'I think she is ashamed,' replied Charlotte. 'That is a new sensation for her, because I do not believe she has ever felt such a strong desire to make a good impression on those around her. Her own talents and vivacity have always been sufficient recommendation. But now I think she feels she is being judged by the actions of her relations. A most uncomfortable idea.'

They watched as Elizabeth reappeared from the throng on the far side of the room, where she caught sight of her father, for whom she had clearly been searching. She approached him very decisively, and addressed him with great feeling. He looked towards Mrs Bennet, still gossiping with Lady Lucas; and then at Mr Collins, who was now seen attempting to converse with a freezingly aloof Miss Bingley. To his daughter's imploring expression, he returned only his usual detached smile. Even from a distance, it was plain to Mary that he had declined to act upon Elizabeth's appeal to rein in the behaviour of his family. His laughed and touched her shoulder; but Elizabeth was not to be placated. She left him without a word. Her face was stony as she returned to her seat. She sat a little apart from Charlotte and Mary, making it clear she did not wish to talk.

'There is nothing to be done but humour her as best we can,' whispered Charlotte. 'While this mood is upon her, I think it essential not to provoke her further.'

CHAPTER TWENTY-SEVEN

Mary sat quietly through the next few sets, waiting with increasing apprehension, for her moment to arrive. Finally, it was time. The dancers left the floor and the musicians, released from their labours, went in search of their supper. Now was the moment when the musical ladies stepped forward. Miss Bingley claimed the first place, striding confidently towards the piano, head in the air, to the general approbation of the room. She had chosen a very lively piece, which she attacked with great verve. She finished with a flourish, and turned beaming towards her audience, almost daring them not to applaud. When they did so, she basked in their praise for some minutes, before sweeping back to her seat, her pride evident in every haughty step she took. Mary swallowed hard. It was now or never. She stood up, her music in her hand. As she passed Elizabeth, to her amazement, she felt Lizzy grasp her arm. Her sister looked intently into her face, her hand tight on Mary's sleeve.

'Give us something *simple* we can admire, and, I beg you, do not make it too long.'

Mary shook herself free, and walked towards the piano. The vehemence of Lizzy's words unsettled her. She began to feel nervous – anxiety welled up within her – but she rallied her courage and told herself she must be calm. Once seated, she put on her glasses, placed her music on the stand, raised her hands, and began.

It was easier once she had started. She knew the piece so well that she hardly needed to think about it; and her disciplined fingers flew about the keys just as she wished. Her spirits rose. Surely she was acquitting herself exactly as she had hoped? She had made no mistakes – her timing was perfect – then, almost before she knew it, the sonata was at an end. She lifted her hands from the keyboard, her heart fluttering. It was over. Relief flooded through her. She looked up to face the company and was delighted to see signs of appreciation, a scattering of nods and smiles. A few listeners even offered up a little polite applause. She could not see Mr Collins – but she knew he must be somewhere in the audience. He must have witnessed her success. An unaccustomed euphoria flooded through her. She would attempt her second piece with new confidence – and she would definitely accompany herself with a song.

She began again with her cheerful Scotch air. But by the time she reached the second verse, she knew she had made a terrible mistake. Miss Allen had been right. Her skill was as a player, not a singer. Her voice was weak, her manner tentative. She simply could not do it. Fear made her even worse, and she quickly sensed that she had lost her audience. At the far end of the table, a murmured conversation had begun. When she looked up from her music, she thought she saw the eldest Bingley sister make a mocking face to the younger. She began to panic – but what was she to do? To stop would be fatal – there was nothing for it but to press on as best she could. As she did so, she was certain she caught a meaningful look from Elizabeth directed towards their father – she thought she saw him respond – but she flicked her eyes downwards, determined to think of nothing but the music. When she finally stopped singing, there was some sympathetic clapping, for which she was profoundly grateful. Perhaps it had not been as bad as she imagined? But it quickly died away, and she could not deceive herself she had been well received. When she lifted her hands from the keyboard, they were trembling. For a moment, she could not compose herself; then she heard her father's voice, low and clear above the general chatter. When she looked up, he was standing beside her, his arm held out towards her.

'That will do extremely well, child. You have delighted us long enough. Let the other young ladies have time to exhibit.'

She was so astonished – so taken aback – that at first she did not know what to do. It took a moment before she understood. Mr Bennet was there to stop her playing again, to lead her away from the piano. He held out his hand and beckoned her gently towards him. She blinked in confusion. He beckoned again, this time more insistently. She thought she might faint – but instead she gathered up her music and followed him blindly as they wove their way through the guests, trying her utmost not to catch anyone's glance.

Immediately, Miss Bingley was on her feet, striding forward to reach the piano. Soon the room rang once again with her playing, as polished and as glittering as the lady herself. Mr Bennet led Mary back to her seat. She sat down heavily. She could not meet his eye. He stood beside her for a minute or so, but when it was clear she did not intend to speak, he sighed and walked briskly away. Her face burned with shame. Everyone had seen. Her mother, Kitty, and Lydia. The horrible Bingley sisters. And of course, Mr Collins. They had all watched as she had been so brutally and so publicly shamed. They had all seen. When, a little while later, Elizabeth arrived and sat next to her, Mary did not acknowledge her presence.

'Come, Mary, don't be angry. You cannot expect to be the only one to play tonight.'

Her voice was consoling, and she reached for her hand; but Mary, furious now, shook her off.

'This was your doing! You made our father stop me!'

Now it was Elizabeth's turn to look away. When she finally met Mary's angry, wounded stare, it was plain she had decided to admit the truth of the accusation. She had the good grace to look a little abashed as she conceded Mary was right.

'I am sorry it was done so bluntly. Our father might have acted with more tact.'

She put out her hand again.

'It was for your own good. I did not want to see you mocked. It really wasn't my intention to hurt you.'

Overwhelmed with indignation, Mary threw her music off her lap. The pages floated slowly to the floor and landed at her feet.

'How could I not be hurt? Everyone saw. Everyone. And don't you dare tell yourself you did it for me. That's a lie. You did it for yourself – to spare *you* embarrassment in front of people you want to impress.' Tears began to prick her eyes. 'I did not think you could be so cruel, Lizzy.'

Elizabeth sat very still; for once, it seemed she had nothing to say. Then Charlotte arrived and placed a comforting arm round Mary's shoulders, urging her not to cry and offering her a handkerchief to wipe her face.

'Let us go and take a breath of air,' she said softly, 'just the two of us.'

Elizabeth did not attempt to stop them or accompany them but remained where she was. No one spoke to Mary or Charlotte as they made their way through the crowd. As they reached the door they passed Mr Collins, talking at the top of his voice to anyone who would listen. If he had been so fortunate as to be able to sing, he assured his audience, he would have had great pleasure in obliging the company with an air. 'For music is a very innocent diversion, perfectly compatible with the profession of a clergyman.' He was in excellent spirits and paid no attention at all as Mary passed him, leaning on Charlotte's arm. His indifference was for Mary the final blow. She supposed it was a proper reward for her presumption. She did not know why she had allowed herself to imagine she was worthy of any man's attention, that there was anything she could do to please. Well, she had been properly punished for her foolishness, slighted and humiliated by those who were supposed to love her. And despite all she had endured, she loomed no larger in Mr Collins's thoughts now than when he had first arrived at Longbourn.

When they reached the garden terrace, Charlotte sat Mary down and spoke with the firm kindness with which one might address an unhappy child, urging her to consider that few people but herself would have noticed what happened, and none would have thought Mr Bennet's intervention arose from anything but fatherly concern that she should not over-exert herself. As for Lizzy, it was impossible she had meant Mary any real harm. They had both noticed her agitation earlier in the evening; she was not herself and had acted in the heat of the moment.

But Mary was not to be consoled.

'I think you know that isn't true,' she replied. 'She felt I had shamed her, and that if I went on, I should do so even more. That was her only consideration.' She breathed in more deeply, trying to control her agitation. 'She thought only of herself. I have always loved her the best of my sisters. I knew she didn't care for me as she used to – but until tonight I never realised she was so bitterly ashamed of me.'

Charlotte squeezed her arm.

'She was ashamed of everyone tonight, and if I know her at all, which I believe I do, she will now be more than a little ashamed of herself as well. Don't take things too much to heart. You look a little calmer now. Shall we go back in and see whether Lydia and Kitty have left us any ices?'

Mary wiped her eyes one last time, and they drifted back into the house. But although persuaded to go back inside, she refused to return to her old place near her mother. She could not bear the prospect of Mrs Bennet's curiosity, and instead retreated to a chair at the very back of the room, where there was no danger of her being noticed by anyone. At first, Charlotte stayed loyally by her side; but eventually, she agreed to rejoin the party, promising she would return regularly to see how Mary did. Once alone, it was a little easier for Mary to compose herself, and gradually she grew calmer. To keep her thoughts from returning to the moment of her humiliation, she forced herself to survey the company from her seat in the shadows. If she could not enjoy the ball herself, she might at least observe what others were doing. She began to find this strangely comforting. It soothed her mind to fancy herself above and beyond the emotions that governed everyone else at Netherfield. In this detached mood, she watched as Jane danced again and again with Mr Bingley, her eyes cast modestly away from his admiring smiles. She stared at Miss

Bingley, standing as close as she dared to Mr Darcy, her sharp features consumed with longing when she thought he could not see. So that was how it was? Mary turned away. Elsewhere amongst the dancers, she could just make out Lydia and Kitty in the midst of the line, their dresses pale against their partners' brilliant uniforms, Lydia's face ecstatic as she whirled round.

Emboldened by the sensation that she was not really there at all, Mary rose from her seat and walked a little further round the dark hinterland of the room. From there, she saw her mother, talking, talking, talking, holding forth to Lady Lucas, while her friend, head bowed, listened obediently. She caught sight of Mr Collins, bobbing hopelessly around Elizabeth, his persistence defeating all her attempts to shake him off. Only when Charlotte appeared at her side did Lizzy finally escape. Mary's heart softened as she watched Charlotte bear Mr Collins away, selflessly conducting him towards supper, chatting as she went. There was nothing Charlotte would not do to help her friends, even when, like Lizzy, they did not really deserve such consideration.

When she was satisfied there was no more to see, Mary returned slowly to her chair. There she was surprised to find a small glass of strawberries placed on it, a silver spoon balanced on the rim. Puzzled, she looked about to see who might have left it there, suspecting it must have been Charlotte; but instead, it was Mr Bennet's broad back that she glimpsed, hurrying away into the crowd. She picked up the glass and turned it round in her hand. She understood this was her father's way of making amends, the closest he would come to an acknowledgement that he had hurt her.

She knew he would never willingly speak to her of what he

had done. But if she had pressed him to tell her why he had left the strawberries without staying to present them himself, she could easily imagine his answer. *'It has all the virtues of an apology with none of the embarrassment of an explanation.'*

Despite herself, she almost smiled. He would never feel for her what he did for Lizzy; but he had thought about her enough to bring her some strawberries. He knew he had hurt her and was sorry. She supposed that was something. She pulled the glass towards her and plucked one out, biting into it as tears again came into her eyes.

Soon after, the ball drew to a close. It was late, past two o'clock, when the Bennets stood in the hall, waiting for their carriage. Once they were settled inside, even Lydia's chatter soon subsided, her head leaning on Kitty's shoulder as she fell asleep. Everyone was silent, some from happiness, some from exhaustion, others from a consciousness that the evening had not turned out as they had hoped. Only Mr Collins kept up a steady stream of conversation all the way back to Longbourn, quite untroubled by the fact that he received no reply.

CHAPTER TWENTY-EIGHT

Mary stayed late in bed the following morning. She did not feel ready to join the others. She knew the conversation would be all about the ball and was certain her humiliation at the piano would be too compelling a subject to be tactfully ignored. She could imagine only too well the opportunities that topic would offer Lydia to tease her and resolved to stay where she was until breakfast was over. Mrs Hill brought her a dish of tea and offered to comb out her hair, but she would not be persuaded to leave her room.

So it was that she missed the dramatic events that unfolded after the table was cleared. Even upstairs, she was aware something had happened. She heard the hurry of footsteps in the hall and her mother's voice raised in angry exclamation; but these were not unusual occurrences, and it was only when Kitty and Lydia burst into her room that she understood what had caused them.

'Mary, you *must* get dressed and come downstairs,' exclaimed Lydia. 'There's been such an upset, you won't believe it!'

'You can't imagine what's happened!' cried Kitty. 'You'll never guess in a million years!'

Mary sighed. 'That's probably true. But I really don't care.'

'Oh, I think you will,' said Lydia. 'Even you will enjoy this.'

'Are you going to tell me or not?'

'Mr Collins has made Lizzy an offer!' exclaimed Kitty. 'And she has refused him!'

Mary sat up, her heart beating fast. She was not suprised Mr Collins had declared himself; she had always thought he would do so. But she had not expected him to move so quickly.

'Mama is furious,' said Lydia, throwing herself down on Mary's bed, 'and says Lizzy will have him, if she has anything to do with it. She carried her off to Papa, so that he could make her see sense. But he told Lizzy her choice was a sad one, for her mother would never see her again if she refused to marry Mr Collins, and he would never see her again if she did!'

Kitty clapped her hands. 'Isn't it killing?'

'And now everyone is cross.' Lydia leapt off the bed and seated herself at Mary's dressing table, turning her face from one direction to another, entirely pleased with what she saw. 'Mr Collins has stormed off. Papa has shut himself in the library. Lizzy won't say anything at all, while Mama is beside herself, and says no one takes any account of her feelings.'

'It's quite the best thing that's happened this age,' said Kitty, with deep satisfaction. 'What do you think, Mary?'

Mary lay back in bed. It was a good question, and one to which she did not have a ready answer. Her sisters ignored her silence for a while, chattering away between themselves about what might happen next. But when they saw that Mary did not find the business as amusing as they did, they went away and left her alone. She got up and began to brush her hair. She did not pose before the mirror as Lydia had done, but looked directly into her reflection, as if asking herself what she should do now.

She washed quickly. Mrs Hill had brought up the water some time ago, and now it was barely warm; but she did not notice. She laid out a dress on her bed, and sat down beside it blankly, as if she had forgotten what it was there for. Her mind was elsewhere. She had never imagined she would be the first sister to whom Mr Collins proposed; but she had persuaded herself she might merit consideration as his second choice. If her efforts had succeeded, this should have been her moment. Once he had been refused by a woman who would never accept him, he might have been ready to listen to one prepared to say yes. It was now, when he was still smarting from Lizzy's rejection, that Mary had hoped to turn his thoughts to her, soothing his wounded pride and reminding him of the interests they shared, showing by her every word and gesture that she was the only Bennet sister he should seriously think of as his wife.

But as she pulled her dress over her head, she realised none of these things would happen now. She would always be invisible to him. Even the public humiliation she had suffered at the piano had not been enough to capture his attention. She supposed she should be grateful her shame had passed him by – but, oh, to be ignored and dismissed by a man like Mr Collins! That was a harsh corrective to any ideas she might cherish about her own worth. As she struggled to tie her sash, she told herself she really had no right to be bitter. Her pursuit of him had been prompted solely by rational considerations; she could not claim her heart had been broken. And yet something within her cried out that it was not fair. She was the only one who had tried to see the good in him, who thought he had the potential to become a happier, better man, but it had not been enough to win him. Nobody wanted her, it seemed, not even a man she did not love.

When finally she made her way down to the drawing room, the first wave of the storm had passed; but anger and resentment hung heavy in the air. Mrs Bennet lay on the sofa, lamenting her woes to anyone who would listen. Lizzy stared out of the bay window that faced onto the orchard, her expression set and determined, refusing to respond to her mother's complaints. Mary did not know whom to approach, and stood uncertainly in the middle of the drawing room, afraid to speak lest she draw their frustration upon herself.

She could not have been more relieved when she heard the bell and Charlotte Lucas was announced. Charlotte had been invited to spend the day at Longbourn, but in the drama of that morning's events, this had been quite forgotten. Before she had taken off her hat and coat, Lydia and Kitty had gleefully imparted to her every detail of what had occurred, but to their disappointment, Charlotte had betrayed neither shock or surprise. Instead, she had acted with characteristic calm self-command. Once in the drawing room, she had laid a soothing arm on Lizzy's tense and angry shoulders; and had then approached the prone Mrs Bennet, asking in a low concerned voice if there was anything she could do to assist her.

'It is kind of you to think of me, my dear Miss Lucas, for no one is on my side, nobody takes my part.'

Charlotte offered to call for tea, a glass of water, perhaps; but Mrs Bennet brushed away her suggestions.

'If you really wish to help me, you would talk some sense into your friend over there, insist she run after Mr Collins as quickly as she can and tell him, with all the charm she can muster, that she has changed her mind.'

Charlotte looked towards Lizzy, who firmly shook her head, which provoked her mother to berate her even more.

'I tell you what, Miss Lizzy, if you take it into your head to go on refusing every offer of marriage, you will never get a husband at all – and I am sure I don't know who is to maintain you when your father is gone – I shall not be able to keep you.'

Mrs Bennet continued in this vein for some time, dwelling at length on Lizzy's inability to see a good thing when it was staring her in the face, until she was interrupted by the arrival of the gentleman himself. Mr Collins had returned from his exile in the garden and stood at the drawing room door, the very picture of injured dignity, declaring that he should like to speak to Mrs Bennet, if it was at all convenient. Mrs Bennet roused herself reluctantly from her couch, declaring she was at his disposal for anything he wished to ask of her.

Elizabeth immediately left her seat at the window and sailed past Mr Collins without a word. Mary and Kitty dutifully followed her; but once she was on the other side of the drawing room door, Mary was surprised to find that both Charlotte and Lydia were still within. She could only suppose they had contrived to make themselves as inconspicuous as possible and, for that reason, had not been ejected. It did not surprise her that Lydia should behave in such a manner; but that Charlotte should do so was most unexpected.

It was not long before Mr Collins emerged, with the self-conscious air of a man who has just delivered himself of a weighty decision. He nodded towards his waiting cousins with a superior smile, and walked swiftly away. Once he had disappeared, they crowded into the room, eager to find out what had been said.

Mrs Bennet had returned to her sofa, her eyes closed, her handkerchief placed over her face.

'I am not equal to describing what has befallen us,' she announced in a low, disappointed moan. 'Go away, all of you, and leave me alone. Charlotte and Lydia can tell you what he said.'

Once the door had been closed on Mrs Bennet's grief, Charlotte leaned heavily against it. Mary noticed that even she was now a little excited, her eyes brighter than usual.

'He has "withdrawn his pretensions to Lizzy's favour",' she declared.

'Yes,' cried Lydia. 'He's pulled out! You've lost your chance, Lizzy! It's all over for you!'

'His manner was more resentful than his words,' Charlotte continued. 'But he says he is resigned, and I think he means it. You need not fear he will renew his pursuit.'

Elizabeth fanned her face with an exaggerated gesture of relief.

'I'm very glad to hear it. I don't think I could have borne much more of his good opinion.'

'But some other poor girl may not be so lucky,' added Lydia, 'for he told Mama he still hopes to find himself "an amiable companion". I very much hope it won't be me.'

'You are rather young for that,' said Charlotte. 'I think you are safe enough. But it is clear he does still hope to discover some fortunate woman to preside over his parsonage.'

'Well, whoever she is, she must form her own conclusions as to the desirability of an offer from Mr Collins,' Lizzy said with a laugh, her good humour quite restored. 'I am only relieved to be free of him myself!'

With that, she took Charlotte's arm, and they walked into the garden to continue their conversation in the open air. With nowhere else to go, Mary made her way to the library, but once there, found she could not settle to her work. She wandered to the window, where she watched Elizabeth and Charlotte walking on the grass. Elizabeth was chatting to her friend with all the ease in the world. It was as if the painful events of last night had not taken place. She had said nothing to Mary about their bitter exchange, But then, thought Mary, as this morning demonstrated, Lizzy's life was so full of incident that perhaps she had already forgotten it. Mary's own humiliation must seem a small thing, easily blotted from Lizzy's mind when she had so many more extraordinary matters to think about.

Or, Mary considered, perhaps it was she herself who was the small thing, and thus easily disregarded. No matter how distracted she might be, Elizabeth always had sympathy and consideration enough to lavish upon Jane. When a letter had arrived that morning from Miss Bingley, regretting that she, Mr Bingley, and indeed all their party had been urgently called away to London, no one could have been more attentive to her bereft sister than Lizzy was to Jane.

Mary blew on the window and wrote her initials in the little patch of condensation. As she did so, she saw Mr Collins appear in the garden, cross the lawn, and approach Charlotte and Lizzy. He bowed stiffly. Even from a distance, his discomfort at meeting Elizabeth was clear. But in an instant, with the smallest dip of a curtsy, Lizzy excused herself and walked away, quite slowly at first, her steps growing faster and faster, until she was running towards the gate, flying out onto the path into Meryton. Once she had gone, Mary watched as Mr Collins offered Charlotte his arm. Charlotte graciously accepted, and at a steady, unhurried pace, they made their way into the beech grove until they were quite out of Mary's sight.

CHAPTER TWENTY-NINE

The following night, the Bennets were engaged to dine with the Lucases. There had been some debate whether Mr Collins would attend; but when applied to, he very pointedly declared himself more than willing to spend an evening where he was so sure of being pleased.

When the family arrived that evening at Lucas Lodge, Mary was struck by how smart the rooms appeared. They were not lit and decorated with such attention when it was only the Bennets for supper; and Charlotte herself had taken equal trouble, dressed in an elegant white gown with green ornaments.

'Is that a new dress, Charlotte?' asked Mary. 'It looks very smart.'

'Yes, I decided a while ago to lay waste to my allowance and spend it entirely on fripperies. I don't suppose Dr Fordyce would approve, but it does raise the spirits not to be the worst-dressed woman in the room for once.'

'That's most unfair. You are always very well turned out.'

'Thank you. But for once, I feel rather better than that – and I must admit, it's a very pleasing sensation.'

As Mary surveyed her, she thought there was indeed something different about Charlotte tonight. It was not only her new gown; there was an animation about her, a suggestion of excitement in her features which Mary had not seen before.

When they went in to dine, Mary saw she was placed at the end of the table with Elizabeth and Lydia. Mr Collins occupied the place of honour, and Charlotte was situated close by him. Mrs Bennet was seated as far away from the two of them as politeness allowed.

'Charlotte could not have been more obliging,' whispered Lizzy, as the first course was served. 'There is almost no chance of our being required to talk to Mr Collins from here, unless he were to spend the evening shouting at us, which I think even he would hesitate to do.'

Mary nodded, but as the meal went on, she watched Charlotte with increasing curiosity. Her attentiveness to Mr Collins was really very marked. She helped him to the best dishes, made sure his glass was filled, listened to his conversation with every appearance of interest, and laughed winningly when some active sign of amusement was called for.

'Lizzy,' Mary asked, as the dessert was brought in, two delicate tarts and an ice decorated with spun sugar, quite unlike the homely puddings usually to be found on the Lucases' table. 'Do you think it possible that Charlotte is fond of Mr Collins?'

Elizabeth looked at her, amazed.

'Of course not! She's far too sensible for that! She is all generosity, and I am more grateful to her than I can possibly express.'

But whenever Mary looked up, there was Charlotte, deferential and smiling; and there was Mr Collins, his self-possession restored, looking as pleased and as satisfied as she had ever seen him.

Mr Collins was not at breakfast the following morning. He left word he should be out and that he was not sure when he should have the pleasure of seeing them again. As she buttered her bread, Mrs Bennet looked uneasy. His absence unsettled her and made her cross; and soon, the lengthy reiteration of her familiar grievances drove everyone from the table except Mary.

'I am glad to have the opportunity to talk to you alone,' began her mother. 'Please attend, as I have something important to say to you.'

Mary put down her cup.

'I have been thinking about Mr Collins. Since Lizzy was so selfish as to refuse him, it has not been easy to know what to do next. Jane we may consider as already spoken for. Kitty and Lydia are very young to be thinking of marriage and are far too lively for him. So I have turned my mind towards you.'

'Towards me?'

'Yes, I think you understand me. Do not trifle with me this morning, Mary, my nerves are not equal to the strain.'

'I am sorry, Mama. But when I asked you, only a week ago, to consider if I was not perhaps best placed of all my sisters to suit him, you were adamant I was not.'

'Please don't be more vexing than you need to be. A great deal has changed since then, as even you must see.'

'Yes, indeed. But I'm afraid we may have left it too late. I might have stood a chance at the beginning, especially if you had worked as hard on my behalf as you did for Lizzy. But I don't think he would have me now.'

'Don't be ridiculous! Why on earth not? Who else can he ask? Let us hear no more of *he will not*. But I need to be sure that you will accept him when he does offer. We cannot have a second refusal on our hands.'

Mary looked down at the table, as she felt herself flush with shame.

'It really doesn't matter whether I will or will not take him. I promise you it is too late now. He won't choose me.'

Mrs Bennet flung down her napkin and stood up, infuriated.

'You are a very silly, ungrateful girl, and there is no talking to you. But I am not finished with you yet. We will speak about this again when I am feeling better.'

She slammed the door as she left the room. Mary sighed and stared out of the window. She was surprised to see Charlotte Lucas walking down the drive to the house. She had not been expected this morning, but Mary thought her presence would be very welcome. Her steady manner was always beneficial when feelings ran high in the Bennet household. And if Mary was able to speak to her alone, she might discover more about her inclinations towards Mr Collins. Perhaps her mother was right and Mary had been mistaken? She supposed it would be useful to know.

But although Mary waited for Charlotte to arrive, she did not appear. When Kitty passed the door, Mary asked if she had seen her, and was told Charlotte had gone straight to find Lizzy. It seemed they had been closeted together in the drawing room ever since. It was nearly half an hour before Mary heard the door open and close. Still there was no sign of Charlotte. It was only when Mary looked out of the window that she saw her, walking briskly down the drive, clearly eager to be gone.

Mary ran to the hallway, seized her coat, and ran after her. She was sure something was amiss and was determined to discover what it was. She caught up with Charlotte just as the drive opened up onto the lane. Out of view of the house, there she stood, breathing hard and flinging her gloves from hand to hand. Mary rushed towards her.

'Didn't you hear me calling you, Charlotte? Why didn't you stop?'

Charlotte looked up. Mary had never seen her so distressed.

'I'm so sorry,' she said, trying to smile and failing. 'I was so taken up in my own thoughts that I didn't hear you.'

'Something has happened, I can see that it has. Won't you tell me what it is?'

Charlotte seemed unsure how to reply. She paced up and down the dusty path, kicking at the stones with her boots. Finally, she made her way to a low wall and settled herself upon it. She seemed a little calmer now.

'I suppose I may as well explain. Everyone will know about it soon enough. And you might understand better than most people why I have acted as I have.'

She pulled a few weeds from the wall and began to twist them in her hands.

'Mr Collins made me an offer of marriage earlier this morning, and I have accepted him. The wedding is to take place within the month.'

Mary sat down heavily beside her. So her suspicions had been right.

'I felt it my duty to tell Lizzy before it was generally announced. I didn't think my decision would please her – we have always had such very different ideas on the subject of matrimony – but I did not expect . . .'

Her voice trembled for a moment, and Mary saw her hands

were shaking. 'I confess, Mary, I did not expect her to greet my news with such horror and contempt!'

'Those are very harsh words, Charlotte.'

'She cried out when I told her. She declared the engagement "impossible"! I tried to explain my motives – that I asked only a comfortable home – that, given his character and connections, I was as likely to achieve that with Mr Collins as with any other man of my acquaintance – I reminded her I was not romantic – but she was not to be moved. The look on her face as I tried to justify myself was very painful to me.'

'It must have been a great shock to her. Once she is used to the idea, I'm sure all will be well again.'

'She soon recollected herself, and then she was polite enough, offering congratulations and wishing me all possible joy. But, oh, Mary, I can tell I have fallen very far in her estimation!'

She covered her face with her hands, and a sob escaped her. Mary knew only too well how it felt to have Lizzy's goodwill withdrawn from you. She searched for some words of comfort or reassurance, but found none. She took Charlotte's arm in hers and they sat in silence until Charlotte cried no more.

'I'm glad you followed me,' she said haltingly. 'I was afraid I might have forfeited your friendship, as it seems I have Lizzy's. I thought you might feel that I have, as they say, cut you out. That in securing my own future, I have denied you a similar chance of escape.'

A strong breeze blew, and Mary realised she had rushed out without her hat. If anyone were to see them, it would seem a very strange situation, two young women perched on a wall, the wind whipping at their skirts, one of them hatless. But, thought Mary, if that person had heard their conversation, they would have found it even more extraordinary. She hesitated before replying, unsure how candid she should be. But she had nothing to lose now – why should she not tell Charlotte the truth?

'It is true I wondered whether it was not my duty – to my family as well as to myself – to try to persuade Mr Collins to marry me. But I couldn't manage it. No matter what I did, he was quite indifferent.'

'You're very hard on yourself. You might have done better, given more time,' Charlotte said, almost herself once more. 'But I couldn't afford to be overnice on this occasion. An opportunity of this kind might never offer itself to me again. I am too old to be generous, even to you.'

Charlotte slid off the wall, and resumed her pacing, crossing and recrossing the path as she spoke.

'I cannot pretend I love him. As you have said yourself, he can hardly be considered a sensible man. But if I had any doubts I had done the right thing, they vanished when I told my family about his offer. I've never seen my parents more overjoyed; and my brothers were almost speechless with relief. I won't be a dead weight on their hands now. They all thought I was destined to be an old maid; but now I will have a husband and can look forward to a home of my own.'

'One day, of course, that home will be Longbourn.'

Charlotte had the grace to look self-conscious.

'But not for many years, I hope.'

In the wood just beyond the path, a great crowd of rooks flew into the air, shouting and cawing angrily as they rose above the trees. *Longbourn will belong to Charlotte*, thought Mary. *It might have been mine if I had succeeded with Mr Collins. But I failed and instead, he has chosen Charlotte.* She stared at the birds as they wheeled in the sky, quite indifferent to her pain. That Mr Collins should want to marry Jane or Elizabeth was only to be expected; one only had to look at them to understand. But what had Charlotte to recommend her? *Why*, Mary asked herself, *was she his choice and not me?*

'You have been so honest with me, Charlotte, that I hope you won't object to my being equally direct with you. Please do not spare my feelings in your answer. I should like to know why you believe Mr Collins preferred you to me?'

Charlotte stopped her pacing, and joined Mary once more on the wall. She was not at all offended at the question.

'I suppose you could say that my flattery was more determined, my eagerness to please more insistent. I'm sure Lizzy would argue I was readier than you to surrender my pride and conquer my feelings in pursuit of worldly advantage.'

She picked up a stone from the path, and threw as it far as she could into the field beyond, as if dismissing Lizzy's opinion with the same vehemence.

'But I think there is another difference between you and me. I have never hidden from you that I am unhappy in my circumstances and planned to do all I could to change them. But it is my situation I dislike, not myself. I'm not sure the same is true of you. It's hard to persuade anyone, especially a man, that your regard is worth having if you have none for yourself.'

The breeze was a proper wind now, and Charlotte shivered. She pulled her coat tighter around her and stood up, ready to go.

'And that, I promise, is the last piece of advice I shall ever offer you. Please try to think of me as generously as you can. I should warn you that my father intends to call upon your family later today and inform them of the coming happy event. I don't imagine what he has to say will be much to Mrs Bennet's taste.'

CHAPTER THIRTY

When Sir William Lucas appeared at Longbourn that afternoon, his announcement that his eldest daughter was shortly to be united with Mr Collins was met at first with astonished disbelief. As Mr Collins himself had taken pains to ensure, with a combination of tact and apprehension, that he was away from home, he could not be applied to, either to confirm or contradict the report; but at first it seemed impossible to credit.

'Good Lord, Sir William, how can you tell such a story!' exclaimed Lydia. 'Do not you know that Mr Collins wants to marry Lizzy?'

Sir William admitted he understood this had indeed been so – but he assured his listeners that was no longer the case. Mr Collins's affections were now fixed upon a different object, and there could be no doubt of his intending to marry his daughter as soon as was convenient. Elizabeth, who could no longer bear to see him so obviously disbelieved, raised her voice above the confusion to agree that all Sir William said was true, for she had heard it from Charlotte's own mouth just a few hours before. At the same time, she sought to put a stop to the exclamations of incredulity of her mother and her sisters by offering Sir William congratulations as fulsome as could be justified on such an occasion. Jane joined in with great good nature, and even Mary managed to wish them well. But Mrs Bennet said almost nothing at all until Sir William took his leave.

Then her anger was quite as terrible as Mary had feared. At first, she refused to believe the story at all; then gradually, her mood shifted from doubting its veracity to abusing those at its heart. Mr Collins had been taken in, and by what means she did not like to consider. Who knew what methods Charlotte Lucas might have employed to ensnare him? She had always thought her a sly, untrustworthy girl. She hoped the match might still be broken off, and if it was not, then she wished they might never be happy. If Elizabeth had done as she ought and accepted him, now it would be she and not Lady Lucas who was planning a daughter's wedding. But no one attended to a word she said; her wishes were always disregarded.

When Mr Collins eventually returned, an atmosphere of superficial politeness was, for a few painful hours, restored. Over the dinner table, Mrs Bennet even managed to offer him a few chilly congratulations; but it could not be said to have been an enjoyable evening. Everyone except the future bridegroom was subdued. Only he seemed unconcerned, referring with no discernible embarrassment to his dearest Charlotte, and observing how often it was that an initial setback was eventually revealed to be a blessing in disguise, heralding as it did a prize of even greater value.

'In your case,' observed Mr Bennet, 'the time between the two events was mercifully short, was it not?'

Mr Collins agreed, quite unembarrassed, that this was indeed so, and he did not count it as the least of his blessings that he had not been obliged to wait too long for his good fortune. Perhaps more to his listeners' liking was the information that he did not intend to trouble them much longer with his presence at Longbourn, but would return as soon as possible to Kent and arrange his affairs there. He hoped, however, that they would not object to his visiting them again in a few weeks' time? As he and his amiable Charlotte were to be joined in matrimony at Meryton, it would be of incalculable convenience if he could persuade them to accept him once more as their guest.

It was impossible to say whether gratitude at his going so quickly or disappointment at the speediness of his return was uppermost in the minds of those around the table; but when the meal was over, only Mr Collins seemed entirely happy with the way events had unfolded, laying down his napkin with every appearance of complete satisfaction.

His departure did nothing to improve Mrs Bennet's temper. She was teased, as it was intended she should be, by frequent visits from Lady Lucas, who, in the first flush of her surprise at Charlotte's news, seemed to have briefly thrown off her usual deference, missing no opportunity to confide to her friend how delightful was the prospect of having her eldest daughter so respectably and imminently married. This could not help but remind Mrs Bennet of the continued and inexplicable absence of Mr Bingley, who appeared to be in no hurry to return to Netherfield and make Jane the offer which she had so publicly anticipated. She had even begun to weary of scolding Elizabeth, who could never be brought to show a proper sense of guilt for what had happened, no matter how frequently it was pointed out to her. Humiliated and resentful, Mrs Bennet sought a new target with which to occupy herself, and soon it was Mary who felt the lash of her displeasure.

Turning over in her mind every detail of what had taken place in the days before Mr Collins's proposal, it did not take

Mrs Bennet long to convince herself that Mary knew more than she had hitherto disclosed about Charlotte's intentions towards Mr Collins; and during many an otherwise aimless hour, she sought to extract from her daughter any information that might rebound to Charlotte's discredit.

'When I told you I was ready to think of you as a possibility for Mr Collins, I recall you saying it was too late. I wonder, Mary, what you meant by that. Did you know that Charlotte was already scheming to catch him?'

'I really couldn't say, Mama. I merely observed that she was often in his company and that she paid him a lot of attention. I believe we all thought it was a kindness on her part, to distract him away from Lizzy.'

'She was certainly very successful at that,' declared Mrs Bennet. 'She distracted him into making her the offer that should have been ours! I can't imagine why you didn't mention it to me. I should have put a stop to it very sharply, I can tell you.'

'I think Mr Collins had already decided that if he couldn't have Lizzy or Jane, he would look elsewhere. I don't think it was entirely Charlotte's doing. It seems very unfair to blame her for her own good fortune.'

'How can you be so foolish! One of you should have snapped him up, as I said on numerous occasions. Lizzy was wilful and wicked and would not have him, and you would not exert yourself enough to try. To have been outmanoeuvred by that cunning little minx Charlotte Lucas is unbearable. You and Lizzy are both to blame, and I cannot forgive either of you for it.'

There seemed no point in reminding Mrs Bennet of the conversation in which Mary had offered herself up as a prospect for Mr Collins's hand, and of her peremptory rejection of it. Mary knew it would only fan the flames of her mother's indignation. As it was, her presence, which had always irritated Mrs Bennet, now provoked her almost beyond endurance. Her daily practice at the piano was painful to her mother's ears; her books cluttered up the drawing room. There was ink on her fingers, had she not noticed it? She was to scrub it off this minute. This was not a counting house and she was not a clerk. Was there nothing she could do about her hair? It made her mother itch to find her scissors. Could she not put on a more becoming dress? The colours she wore were as dull as ditchwater. But nothing roused Mrs Bennet to anger so much as Mary's spectacles. 'I warned you that no man would marry you if you wore them, and I'm afraid to say I have been proved right. If I had had my way, perhaps things now would be very different, but that we shall never know.'

On and on her mother went, the waves of her displeasure breaking over Mary like a rough and unrelenting sea. There was nothing to be said and nowhere to hide. When Mr Collins returned at the end of a fortnight, Mary was almost relieved, for his presence required Mrs Bennet to rein in her complaints, in public at least.

Mary hoped his arrival might encourage Charlotte to visit Longbourn again. Once so regular a guest, she had not been seen there since the announcement of her engagement. Mary believed she absented herself, knowing that her presence was offensive to Mrs Bennet; but she suspected that she was also avoiding Elizabeth. Their last interview had been painful for them both; and their attachment had cooled as a result. Sometimes, Mary thought she missed her more than Lizzy. She had come to think of Charlotte as her friend and felt the loss of her company very keenly. But with circumstances as they were, she had not thought it wise to risk her mother's disapproval by calling at Lucas Lodge herself; and it was some time before they met again, when Mr Collins brought her on his arm one afternoon to tea.

Mary had looked forward to seeing her again; but when Charlotte sat down at the tea table, it was soon apparent this was not to be the cheerful encounter she had hoped for. Charlotte came very much in the character of Mr Collins's fiancée, rather than an old friend of the family; and Mary was given no time at all to talk to her in private. Instead, the little party sat in formal state, making conversation that would never have suggested to a stranger that, with the exception of Mr Collins, these people had known each other all their lives. Their frosty reception did not encourage Charlotte and Mr Collins to stay very long. Once they were gone, Jane and Lizzy soon stole away; and Lydia and Kitty quickly followed. As dusk fell, Mary found herself alone in the drawing room with her parents. She picked up her book and tried to lose herself in its arguments, but her mother's voice, angry and querulous, and her father's replies, designed to tease and annoy, made it impossible to concentrate.

'It was inexpressibly distasteful for me to have to receive them and worse still to be obliged to be civil to that odious Charlotte.'

'As you didn't seem to exert yourself overmuch in the direction of civility, it is to be hoped you will recover very quickly.'

'Did you see her looking about the place as if she already owned it? They were speaking very low together in the hall, and I couldn't hear what they said, but I'm sure they were discussing what they should do with Longbourn when it is theirs. Did you not observe it, Mr Bennet?'

Mary's father replied that he had not; but Mrs Bennet took no notice, and the recital of her grievances went on. As she sat silently in the corner, it struck Mary with painful force that this was how she would spend the rest of her life. Her sisters would marry, and she would be the only daughter left at home. With no one to talk to and nothing to do, she would be obliged to listen to her mother's complaints day after day, month after month, year after year.

'Indeed, Mr Bennet, it is very hard to think that Charlotte Lucas should ever be mistress of this house, that I should be forced to make way for *her* and live to see her take my place in it!'

'My dear, do not give way to such gloomy thoughts. Let us hope for better things. Let us flatter ourselves that I may be the survivor.'

It was as if a great abyss had opened up before Mary, and in it, she saw nothing before her but loneliness. In the space of a moment she understood how fervently she longed for affection. She would not say love, for that seemed too much to ask. A spark of fellow feeling would be enough, a little warmth to make the time pass more pleasurably. Her books alone, she realised, would never entirely suffice. Even her music seemed pointless. No one cared what she played as long as it drew no adverse attention from others. Her chief purpose in life appeared to be the avoidance of notice. Her heart contracted with pain; it was almost too much to bear.

'I cannot stand to think that *they* should have all this estate. If it was not for the entail I should not mind it.'

'What should not you mind?'

'I should not mind anything at all.'

'Let us be grateful, then, that you are preserved from such a state of insensibility.'

Perhaps Charlotte had made the right choice. Now she could look forward to a husband and a home, with children perhaps to come. She would have a position in the world and a purpose in life. It was true she had paid for her better prospects by marrying a man she did not love, but she did not seem to regret the bargain she had made. Mary had watched her closely today, observing her already managing Mr Collins with a smiling deftness, never giving any hint she found his behaviour ridiculous or his presence annoying. Charlotte was all deference to her husband-to-be; though Mary saw too that she revealed nothing of her real self in his company. She would never be truly natural with him; she would never pay him the compliment of letting him know what she really thought or felt. Was that the kind of companionship Mary wanted? A union based on a lie?

She looked around the room, taking in every familiar detail – the curtains faded at the edges by the sun, the stain on the carpet where her father had once spilt a glass of red wine and which no amount of scrubbing could remove – and it seemed as though the walls closed in around her. She might never escape their confines now. She had done all she could to act as reason dictated and find a way out – but it had not answered. It was Charlotte who carried off the prize; it was she and not Mary who had sat beside Mr Collins all afternoon, with her mild, guarded smile and air of defiant satisfaction, avoiding the touch of his hand as they discussed the arrangements for their wedding.

Charlotte had found her release – and Mary could not blame her for it – but she knew she wanted something more. She had done all she could to suppress it, but she longed to feel emotions that were honest and true, that were not intended to flatter and deceive. Yes, she could not deny it – she yearned to meet a man who would put an end to her loneliness, who would not think her awkward and plain, who liked the things she liked and did not think them foolish, a man whom she could love and who would love her back in his turn.

She felt almost light-headed as she admitted the truth of it to herself. But almost as soon as the thought took shape, doubts and fears crowded in upon her. Where would she meet such a man? Not in Longbourn, that was certain. And even supposing she did, why would he look at her? What had she to offer? It was weakness to entertain such imaginings. Allowing yourself to think them only made their absence harder to bear.

'How anyone can have the conscience to entail away an estate from one's daughters, I cannot understand. And all for the sake of Mr Collins too! Why should *he* have it more than anyone else?'

'I leave it to yourself to determine.'

Mrs Bennet was finally silenced. The clock ticked and the fire crackled. Mary closed the book which sat unread before her. She must resign herself to circumstances that were unlikely to change. She rose from her seat, picked up the poker, and began to stir the coals.

PART TWO

CHAPTER THIRTY-ONE

Two Years Later

Mary had brought a book with her, but the jolting of the carriage made it impossible to read. For a while she tried her best, anxious to have something to occupy her mind; but after an hour or so, she gave up and threw the book aside. She wiped the corner of the dirty window with her handkerchief and watched the countryside pass by. They were not far from Longbourn now. Every house, every cottage, every hedgerow was familiar. There was the orchard where the best plums were to be had. There was the field where the bull had charged the cowman's son who had distracted it with his hat. And there was the path to Meryton, down which she had so often walked, trailing behind Kitty and Lydia, wondering what she should do with herself while they rushed into the milliner's shop to spend their allowance. The landscape looked as it had always done. But for the family who had once lived so quietly in this damp green corner, everything was different. Mary stared at the trees, her inward eye recalling the events which, one after another, had shaken them up and turned them inside out.

Lydia's elopement with Mr Wickham had been the first of the dramas. Lydia had always been wild and impulsive; but no one had imagined her thoughtlessness would have quite such far-reaching consequences. When news of her flight first broke upon them, there had seemed nothing to be done. Mary still recalled her father's defeated look as he trudged into the hall at Longbourn, returning empty-handed from a fruitless search for the couple in London, his eyes bleak, his face grey, his habitual expression of ironic detachment quite extinguished.

Then, against all expectations, a marriage ceremony had been somehow arranged, the slippery Mr Wickham bribed or threatened into walking an eager Lydia up the aisle. At first, it was not known how it had been contrived. The revelation that it was Mr Darcy to whom the Bennets owed their youngest daughter's hurried nuptials was received with as much, if not perhaps more astonishment than Lydia's actual running away. It was hardly to be wondered at that the family prejudice against him ebbed away somewhat as a result; but, with the possible exception of Jane, none of the Bennets foresaw what was to happen next. No one could quite believe it when Elizabeth confessed that Mr Darcy had made her a proposal of marriage; and they were even more astounded when she announced she had accepted him. Mary was incredulous. How could she marry a man she had always declared to be proud, cold, and disdainful? Lizzy insisted he was not like that at all – she had misjudged him – pride had blinded her to his true nature. She argued the case for his virtues with all the warmth with which she had once denounced his vices, and gradually her passion turned the tide of family opinion. Once the fact of Lizzy and Mr Darcy's love for each other had been acknowledged – for no one who saw them together could believe it was not so – their union seemed as inevitable and as right as that of Jane and Mr Bingley, which took place with similar haste, none of those involved seeing any reason for delay.

The weddings had rendered Mrs Bennet almost speechless with joy. Three daughters married in the course of a year, the two eldest to men of consequence and standing. It was everything she had always hoped for. Neither she nor her remaining daughters would starve or be thrown upon the parish; she could hold up her head once more amongst her friends and enjoy the superiority she felt was her due. In no time at all, her manner toward Lady Lucas was again one of condescension, for the mother of the mistress of Pemberley had nothing to fear from the parent of a mere Mrs Collins. When Kitty was claimed the following year, by a respectable clergyman with a handsome living, her satisfaction was complete. The triumph of her eldest daughters' marriages enabled her to turn her head away from the irregularities of that of her youngest. Mrs Bennet never spoke of the way Lydia's marriage had been brought about, nor of the rackety existence which Mr and Mrs Wickham subsequently led, moving from place to place, never settling and always in need of funds. Sometimes she sent Lydia small gifts of money to help her in any immediate difficulty, but she always made sure Mr Bennet knew nothing of it. His sympathy for the misfortunes of their youngest daughter was never as extensive as her own, especially when he was called upon to express it in pecuniary form.

With her sisters gone, Mary soon felt herself sinking into the existence she had so long dreaded. Her days went by with little variety. She studied, and she practised at the piano, her music echoing through the empty house. But she quickly discovered she had less time for her pursuits than before, for Mrs Bennet could not bear to sit alone for long and found even Mary's company preferable to her own. These were the hours Mary found hardest, for her mother had nothing to say to her, and in the absence of any affectionate kindness, readily fell back into querulous complaint. It was a relief to them both when Mrs Phillips called, for then Mary was permitted to retreat to the library. Her aunt's voice, however, was loud and carried far beyond the drawing room; and it was by this means Mary discovered how her situation was viewed by those who considered it at all.

'What a blessing it is for you to have Mary still at home,' observed Mrs Phillips one airless afternoon. 'I'm sure you would be quite solitary without her.'

'Perhaps,' replied Mrs Bennet, unconvinced. 'Although she has no conversation of the kind I enjoy.'

'But it must be easier for her now that she's no longer mortified by comparisons between her sisters' looks and her own. That cannot have been easy for a young girl. Now she will be judged on her own terms. And who knows where that might lead?'

'You have always spoken in her favour, sister, and I thank you for it. But I see no likelihood she will change her situation anytime soon. She and I must rub on together for a few years yet. It is a burden I must learn to bear. Will you have a little more tea?'

Mary tried not to brood too much on what the future held. She was more of her mother's opinion than her aunt's; and considered it a day well spent if she got through it without falling into despair. But then, when it was least expected, an event took place which overturned forever the fragile certainties on which Longbourn had been balanced for so long, shattering the expectations of both mother and daughter. The existence of the entail had made Mr Bennet's death the subject of much conversation over the years, but it had been so often talked about that no one had supposed it would actually occur, or not, at least, for many years. When he died in his sleep, with no warning of his impending end, the shock to his family was as dreadful and as surprising as if its possibility had never been mentioned before.

The distress of his wife and daughters was severe and sincerely felt. None of them could imagine life without him; but all the sisters except Mary had husbands to comfort them, and new obligations to fill the place he left in their hearts. On the day of his funeral, Mary took from her drawer the little book of extracts she had composed for him with such hopeful affection, held it in her arms, and cried without restraint. She would never now enjoy the satisfaction of having pleased him, of seeing his eyes light up in pride at something she had done. It was true such a possibility had appeared increasingly remote as the years went by; but she had never quite given up the hope that one day it would happen. The certain knowledge that now it could never do so was perhaps the sharpest pain that grieved her.

CHAPTER THIRTY-TWO

When all the formalities had been observed, Mary accompanied her mother to the north of England, where they were to stay with Mr and Mrs Bingley until a more permanent arrangement could be made for them. However, Mrs Bennet had not been long in their house before it was apparent she would never willingly leave it. The loss of Mr Bennet seemed to weigh less heavily on her nerves with Jane to look after her, and Mr Bingley to ask how she did with such regularly solicitous attention.

Mary, however, did not find her sister's home so comfortable. She was grateful for the invitation to stay; but somehow, she could not settle. Jane was never less than gracious, but her kindness did not put Mary at her ease. There was something distancing in Jane's benevolence, bestowed as it was equally upon both those who deserved it and those who did not. It was an admirable quality, but spread so generally that Mary knew it implied no special warmth for her. Jane's deepest affections were reserved for Mr Bingley and Lizzy; only they were granted access to her private heart, and Mary knew she would never be invited to join them. This knowledge made Mary's dependency upon her sister harder to bear than if there had been stronger feelings between them.

However, she thought she could have borne this if it had not been for the presence of Caroline Bingley in the household. This lady had none of her brother's charm and affability; she had always been of a proud, resentful disposition, but disappointment had soured her still further. As Mary had seen at the Netherfield ball, her feelings for Mr Darcy had been strong, and she had hoped one day to secure him for herself. It had been a cruel humiliation to see another woman preferred; but to have lost him to Elizabeth Bennet, who had neither fortune, family, nor long acquaintance to recommend her, was all but intolerable. In consequence, Caroline Bingley was unhappy and angry in equal measure but, it being impossible to vent her frustration on Mrs Darcy, she decided to console herself by abusing her sister in her place.

She did not open her campaign until she considered sufficient time had passed since Mr Bennet's death, for there were niceties to be observed, even in spite. But once she was satisfied that brief amnesty had expired, Miss Bingley was relentless. She was an accomplished practitioner in the art of insult and knew exactly how to deliver pain in a few well-chosen words, always pronounced with a smile. She began with Mary's clothes, which presented her with a very obvious target but one she did not disdain to seize.

'How refreshing it is,' she remarked one afternoon at tea, 'to see a young woman with the courage to defy the dictates of fashion, or indeed, those of human nature itself, for most of us are foolish enough to want to look as well as we possibly can. I salute you, Miss Bennet, as an example to us all.'

Mary could think of no reply, and hung her head, unable to meet Miss Bingley's hard, unflinching simper. She was equally lost for words when, a few days later, Miss Bingley begged, with a very arch expression, for the honour of her advice. She had been asked by a friend who had recently engaged a governess to suggest a suitable dressmaker for her – 'one whose fees recommend her more than her taste' – and she felt sure Mary would know just such a person. When she had exhausted the subject of her appearance, Miss Bingley turned to Mary's books, picking them up and reading out their titles in tones so pompous that both they and their reader were made to look ridiculous.

'Only a very superior understanding could rise to the challenge of such works. Or one which had no other distractions with which to occupy itself. Scholarship is a fine thing, no doubt, but I am not sure I should wish to acquire it at the cost of every social grace.'

On and on it went. Mary bore it with all the resignation she could muster. Sometimes, she looked around to see if anyone else had observed Miss Bingley's jibes, but they were spoken in such low, confiding tones that no one seemed to notice them. Mrs Bennet rarely concerned herself with Mary at all; and Jane seemed so cocooned in happiness that it was impossible anything unpleasant could penetrate her contentment. Only once did Mary catch a disapproving glance directed by Mr Bingley towards his sister after she had made a particularly disobliging remark in his hearing; but far from correcting her behaviour, his mute rebuke merely encouraged her to take more trouble in concealing it.

For a while, Mary hoped Miss Bingley would grow tired of attacking her; but the weeks went past, with no slackening in either her tormentor's energy or ingenuity, and Mary began to wonder for how much longer she could bear it. She did her best to ignore her, attempting neither to acknowledge nor respond to any hurtful words. But her courage wavered as she understood Miss Bingley's desire to wound was far greater than her ability to withstand it.

One night, as she sat alone in the drawing room, waiting for the rest of the company to arrive, Mary found herself looking with interest at the piano which occupied pride of place there. It was polished and gleaming but very seldom used; she did not think she had heard anyone attempt it since she arrived. She walked across to it and raised the lid, wondering how it would sound, how the keys would feel under her fingers. It was only when she was seated at the keyboard that it struck her that this must be the very instrument on which she had been playing when her father had so humiliatingly put an end to her performance at Mr Bingley's ball. A shiver ran through her as she recalled the shame she had felt, the frantic desire to vanish into thin air. She had not performed in company since, and thought she would never do so again. She trailed her fingers lightly over the keys and struck a single note. The piano was in tune. For a moment she hesitated, the horror of that evening fresh again in her mind. But it had been so long since she had played, especially on an instrument as fine as this. The keyboard was so inviting – the keys so smooth and well-balanced – the urge to play overwhelmed her, and before she knew it, she was tearing into a Scottish air with a tremendous attack, quite unlike her usual precise style. It was the very piece which had sealed her fate on that dreadful night, Mr Bennet extinguishing so many of her hopes. She had not consciously chosen it; but once she knew what it was, she could not let it go, but drove it passionately towards its conclusion. She was breathless when she finished, lost in the powerful emotions the music had awakened in her. It was only when she felt more composed that she looked up from the keyboard; and saw Caroline Bingley standing by the door. It was impossible to say how long she had been there. She smiled her icy, ingratiating smile.

'Please don't say I have left it too late to hear more.'

Miss Bingley walked towards the piano, her fan in her hand, her expression demure.

'Or perhaps you fear you have delighted us enough already?'

Mary's eyes filled with tears. She could not speak but stood up and hurried to the door. She caught a glimpse of Miss Bingley's face as she passed, alive with pleasure at having finally found the tenderest place on which to land her blow.

As Mary ran upstairs to her bedroom, she knew she could stay with Jane no longer. Her spirits were not robust enough to repel Caroline Bingley's spite, and she saw that if she remained, she would soon become accustomed to her attacks, shrinking a little more each day under her blows until she thought she deserved no better. No, she would not allow herself to become Miss Bingley's cowed and willing victim. If she was not prepared to fight, then she must retreat, and do so quickly. Pemberley was not far away. Why should she not write to Elizabeth, asking if she might spend a little time with her there? The more she thought about it, the more the idea pleased her. Pemberley would offer her a refuge from Miss Bingley's bullying, a haven of peace and quiet where she could lick her wounds and recover. But perhaps, she thought, it might do more than that. There she might also find the courage to confront at last the fears that troubled her more with every passing day. What would become of her now that Mr Bennet was gone? Where would she live? What could she do? These were questions so painful and so disturbing that she had not allowed herself to reflect upon them since his death, banishing them to the far corners of her mind, from whence they sometimes emerged to taunt her – at night, when she could not sleep, after a particularly painful encounter with Miss Bingley or an afternoon with her mother. At Pemberley, freed from these provocations, she might become calm and rational enough to face the question of her future directly. And perhaps Elizabeth would help her. She was happy now – blissfully so, from all Mary had seen and heard. Surely Lizzy would not grudge a little time to assist and advise a sister who was so very far from enjoying that joyful state herself? Soon Mary had convinced herself this was the best course of action; and as she could think of no other, she decided not to go down to supper but picked up her pen and began to write to Elizabeth straight away.

She did not have to wait long for an answer, and a few days later, her scanty belongings secured on its roof, she clambered into the coach that was to take her to Pemberley. Mrs Bennet did not come out to say goodbye; early morning departures jangled her nerves. It was Jane who saw her off, standing on the steps alongside Miss Bingley, who waved her away with every appearance of regret at poor dear Mary's wholly unexpected departure.

CHAPTER THIRTY-THREE

When she arrived at Pemberley, Mary's first feeling was one of relief. Here there was no one to insult her or make her miserable; instead, Elizabeth greeted her with a most welcoming smile and took her arm as they made their way through the hallway. She asked no questions about her sudden departure, for which Mary was grateful. She did not feel ready yet to talk about Caroline Bingley.

'Should you like to see over the house? I thought we might take the grand tour after you've had tea. I don't think you saw much of it when you were here before.'

Mary had rarely seen Elizabeth as proud as when they walked together through the huge rooms, her pace quick and eager, her voice lively as she described and pointed and informed, her pleasure in her new establishment apparent in every tireless step. They viewed the sculpture gallery and the most notable family portraits; they stood at the door of the library, which was the largest Mary had ever seen and to which Lizzy was sure Mr Darcy would be pleased to grant her access when he returned home in a week or so. In the meantime, the sisters established a very comfortable routine. They drank their coffee in the yellow morning room and took tea in Lizzy's boudoir. They ate alone in the dining room with the Chinese wallpaper, a servant standing behind their chairs.

When they needed fresh air, they strolled together through the grounds, Lizzy drawing Mary's attention to every remarkable feature, to every wood, pond, or possible improvement. Here she thought she might plant a flower garden. In this quiet corner, she had an idea of establishing a school.

But nothing delighted them both as much as the hours they spent in the nursery with young Fitzwilliam Darcy. He sat on Mary's lap, a sturdy toddler in a white frock, his direct, assessing stare suggesting he was already in possession of his father's determined will. It was not until their third or perhaps even their fourth encounter that he showed he had also inherited his mother's charm. He took Mary by surprise, reaching out his hands towards her with a broad, enticing grin, his fingers sticky and warm as they clasped hers, before turning back to his mother and holding up his face for a kiss. It was impossible not to laugh and smile, and Mary did both very readily.

'You seem very happy, Lizzy.'

'Indeed I am. I'm not sure I deserve it; but I intend to behave as if I do. I won't apologise for the great good luck I've been granted. But in truth, Mary, I am really very grateful. I never imagined I would be so admirably suited. And although I don't choose to let everyone know it, there isn't a day when I don't give thanks that things turned out as they did. Not a single day.'

Very moved, Mary reached over and touched Lizzy's hand. For an instant, Mary felt nothing for her but a rush of affection and a desire it might be returned. She knew she would never forget Lizzy's betrayal on the night of Mr Bingley's ball – for all her attempts to excuse her sister's behaviour, she could not give it any other name – but had begun to hope that in the future, relations between them might be warmer once more. Lizzy was secure and content, no longer teased and annoyed by her family, desperate to distance herself from the embarrassments they caused her. Perhaps, thought Mary, this serenity would encourage Lizzy to look more kindly upon her, to think more generously of her and her situation. If they could recover just a fraction of the pleasure they had taken in each other's company when they were young, that would be enough. Mary would not expect more.

As the days rolled by, there were moments when Mary allowed herself to believe her hopes might be realized. It seemed to her that she and Lizzy had become great friends once more, perfectly at ease with each other. They were happy together, requiring no other company. They read, walked, chatted, and played with Fitzwilliam, who now knew Mary well enough to bestow upon her an occasional lordly smile. It was exactly what Mary had once longed for; and she began to feel the weight of the anxiety which burdened her imperceptibly lighten. She wondered if she felt bold enough yet to speak to Lizzy about her future, to confide in her that she did not know where she should go or what should become of her, that she quailed when she thought of the few choices open to her. Could she confess that the thought of living alongside her mother appalled her? Surely Lizzy would understand that particular horror. No one had more good sense or more acute penetration. When she imagined the relief of having Lizzy as her confidante, Mary felt her spirits rise. She would tell her about Caroline Bingley and her taunts. She allowed herself a little smile as she considered how, with a single tart remark, Lizzy would take the sting from Miss Bingley's insults and make Mary see her as she really was: ridiculous, petty, and eaten up with bitterness. She felt a sense of calm sweep over her; but she did not admit, even to herself, that she had begun to wonder whether she might eventually find a home at Pemberley, whether somewhere in the great house, amidst all the statues and paintings and boudoirs and drawing rooms, there might be a place for her.

Then Mr Darcy returned. He had been in London on business, and now came home, bringing with him his sister Georgiana, a fine-looking girl of nineteen. Immediately, the tenor of their little party shifted. Mr Darcy was not a demonstrative man, but his character was of such a strong and decided nature that it could not fail to impress itself very powerfully on those around him. With Lizzy and his sister, his habitual gravity was tempered by affection. To Georgiana he was a kind and indulgent brother; to Lizzy a passionately attached husband. But as the days passed, Mary saw that in her company, he was never at his ease. He was always strictly polite and gentlemanly, but around her, he could not unbend. It was not long before his air of detached correctness unsettled her, and she began to grow self-conscious around him. She did not know how best to raise herself in his opinion. Should she try to join the conversation, attempt a liveliness she did not feel in order to show herself a pleasant and amusing guest? Or was it better to say nothing at all, choosing instead to efface herself as much as possible in the hope of simply escaping his notice?

She soon discovered that neither stratagem worked. When she was silent, she merely confirmed his opinion of her dullness. When she sought to entertain, she always struck the wrong note. Then Elizabeth would intervene, smoothing everything away with a joke or a laugh. Under Lizzy's tender, amused gaze, her husband became another man, warm, smiling, taken by surprise at his own happiness. Mary once caught a look pass between them of such intimate intensity that she dropped her eyes, as flustered as if she had come upon them alone and unawares. It was this that finally led her to understand there was nothing she could ever do to win Mr Darcy's goodwill. He had no desire to bridge the distance between them. He was far too well bred to show it, but she saw with absolute clarity that he longed for her to be gone. Her presence was more than a petty irritant; it was a constraint on his desire to indulge his strongest affections as freely and as openly as he wished. Only when she had left Pemberley could he be himself again, secure amongst those he loved best, unhampered by the company of a stranger at his table, of an awkward guest in the breakfast room, on the terrace, in the nursery, anywhere in fact where he wished to be alone with his wife.

Mary felt the truth of this revelation with an almost physical pain, certain that her happy days at Pemberley were numbered. She did not think her welcome would long survive Mr Darcy's impatience with her. Indeed, it was painfully apparent that Lizzy had already drifted away from her, preferring to spend her time with her husband rather than her sister; and when he was occupied with business and unavailable to her, Georgiana was always with them. Mary rarely saw Lizzy alone now. The companionable hours they had enjoyed together when she first arrived were not repeated; now it was Georgiana who walked arm in arm with Lizzy, Mary following a few steps behind.

Georgiana Darcy was a timid, watchful girl, somewhat in awe of her brother and plainly delighted to have discovered in Elizabeth such an agreeable and sympathetic friend. Mary often caught her looking at Lizzy with frank adoration; and saw too that her feelings were returned, that Lizzy enveloped her in all the warm affection Mary had hoped might one day be directed towards herself. It was sometimes hard for Mary to watch as her sister coaxed Georgiana delicately out of her shell, encouraging her to think better of herself and not to be afraid of displaying her talents. In the afternoons, they sat in the drawing room as Georgiana practised at the piano, her slender figure shown to advantage as she leaned over the keyboard, her pale hands extended in scales and arpeggios. Mary was compelled to admit she played well, so well in fact that she did not dare approach the piano herself, unwilling to suffer by comparison. She tried to banish jealous thoughts, but it hurt to watch Lizzy offering Georgiana all the praise she had once yearned to receive herself. Lizzy never asked Mary to play. Instead, at the end of a particularly demanding piece from Georgiana, Lizzy applauded loudly and turned to Mary, her face shining.

'Wasn't that fine? Don't you think she is extraordinarily good? Have you ever heard anything better done?'

Mary shook her head.

'No, I do not think I have. Well done, Georgiana.'

Her face faintly flushed from exertion, Georgiana smiled briefly towards Mary before rushing to sit at Elizabeth's side, the better to enjoy her approbation. Georgiana did not speak to Mary, but she rarely did. Her silence was in part a product of her shyness; but Mary suspected there was more to it than that. Sometimes she caught Georgiana observing her with mild, puzzled surprise. *What exactly are* you *doing here?* she seemed to ask. *However did this happen? And how long do you mean to stay?* There was no malice in her curiosity, just a faint whiff of bemusement. As Mary watched Georgiana engage Lizzy in cheerful conversation, in which it was clear she could have no part, she began to ask herself the same questions.

Later that evening, resting on her bed before dinner, already dressed but conscious it was too early to go down, Mary heard the sound of one of her favourite sonatas coming from the piano below. She would have known Lizzy's style anywhere, bold and blithely indifferent to the odd false note. She sat up; as the sonata came to an end, she heard laughter, voices raised in pleasure. There was a pause; then a new piece began, played with a delicacy that could only be Georgiana's. Quietly, she stole downstairs and stood outside the door, listening. No one looked towards her. There was Georgiana, intent at the keyboard, her expression rapt. There was Mr Darcy standing at her side, turning the pages of the music, smiling as he never did when Mary was near. And there too was Lizzy, her hand draped over her husband's arm, looking up at him with transparent affection, while their little son played at their feet, banging his toys in a rhythm that did not entirely complement the beauty of the song. The foursome was as perfectly composed as a painting, handsome, charming, and entirely self-contained.

Georgiana finished the piece with a flourish. Mr Darcy proudly patted her shoulder while Lizzy clapped her hands. Mary closed her eyes and turned away. It was impossible for her to go in and join them. Her presence would only break the spell. In that moment, Mary understood that while she would never be treated harshly at Pemberley, there were other ways of being made to understand you were not required. Mr

Darcy would never warm to her. He might tolerate her for Elizabeth's sake, but in his eyes, she would always be the worst possible version of herself, gauche, clumsy, and dull. Georgiana's situation was very different. She would never be a guest to be endured on sufferance. She was family, loved by both her brother and Lizzy, always welcome to make her home with them. If there was a place at Pemberley for an unmarried sister, Mary knew, as she watched the little group around the piano, it was not for her. She did not belong in these elegant rooms, amongst these beautiful people. They had each other, and that was enough.

When Mary told her sister she intended to leave Pemberley, Elizabeth had not entirely understood the reasons for her decision, but did not press her too hard for an explanation. Perhaps she too had begun to sense Mr Darcy's irritation with Mary's presence; and forced to decide between preserving the comfort of a beloved husband and her duty to an awkward sister, she did not protest very convincingly when Mary announced her departure. Mary's proposed destination, however, surprised her. She found it hard to believe she intended to visit Longbourn.

'But why should you want to go there? It must be full of so many painful associations.'

Mary did not choose to explain that her present circumstances were hardly conducive to happiness, nor to confess that she could think of nowhere else to go.

'I think I should like to be somewhere familiar again, to be surrounded by places I know. I hope I might find it consoling.'

'Really? It seems a strange way of seeking solace. Won't it distress you to see the Collinses established in our old home?

I'm not sure I'd want to see Mr Collins at his ease in our father's library. Or Charlotte presiding over our mother's tea table.'

'Yes, I don't doubt that will be difficult. But I'll be able to walk in the woods and sit in the garden. I can read Papa's books. And Charlotte could not have urged me more eagerly to come.'

Lizzy said no more. Mary was too tactful to add that the prospect of seeing Charlotte had in fact been one of the principal inducements which had driven her to beg an invitation to Longbourn. She was desperate to discuss her unhappy state with someone; and she understood now that neither Jane nor Lizzy could help her. Securely settled with men they loved, they could have no understanding of her fears. Charlotte, however, was a different matter, for she knew what it was to feel hopeless and alone. Mary had not always found her advice palatable, or agreed with her conclusions, but she longed to talk to someone who had once shared her predicament. Perhaps the ideas that had so shocked her when Charlotte first confessed them might not seem so dreadful now. The experience of the last two years had certainly helped her understand why Charlotte had embraced them so determinedly. And in her secret heart, Mary hoped that her stay at Longbourn would result in something more than guidance. She longed to find out whether Charlotte had been right when she insisted a marriage founded on self-interest rather than love stood as good a chance as most unions of turning out well. Were Charlotte and Mr Collins happy? And if so, should Mary make up her mind to follow Charlotte's example? But she said none of this to Lizzy.

CHAPTER THIRTY-FOUR

As the carriage jolted along on the final approach to the house, Mary felt her whole body tense. When they cleared the trees, she would see Longbourn again. Then as the familiar outline came into view, she gasped – she could not help herself – and leaned forward keenly to take it all in. At first glance, everything seemed as it had always been, the house sitting with its usual confidence in its small park. But as she drew nearer, Mary saw that Longbourn presented a far smarter face to the world than it had done when the Bennets occupied it. The gravel drive was swept and weeded, the window frames neatly restored and the front door painted a deep and lustrous black. Yet there was no time for her to absorb these changes before the door was flung open and the lady of the house appeared. As Mary climbed down from the carriage, it rushed into her mind that she must not forget to call Charlotte 'Mrs Collins'. But before she knew it, she found herself kissing Charlotte's cheek, her arm taken firmly as she was led into the house which, until so recently, had been her home.

In the drawing room, sitting down to tea, they were formal with each other at first. Enquiries were made into the health of the Bingleys, the state of Mrs Bennet's nerves, and the well-being of the Darcy family. Mary confirmed she had left them all in good spirits.

'Elizabeth particularly asked to be remembered to you.'

Charlotte smiled politely.

'I'm very glad to hear she is happy. Though it must be difficult not to be so, established as she is.'

'Yes, she has been very fortunate. I think she knows it and is thankful.'

Charlotte inclined her head but said nothing more. The affection between Charlotte and Lizzy had never recovered from the blow dealt to it by Lizzy's horrified response to Charlotte's acceptance of Mr Collins's proposal. Charlotte was not easily disconcerted; but she had not forgotten the shame she had felt as Lizzy stared at her with frank disbelief, unable to credit that any woman of sense could consider such a man as a suitor. Charlotte had been glad when Lizzy married and moved away to Derbyshire, and had steadfastly refused Mr Collins's entreaties to solicit an invitation to Pemberley. When asked to attend the celebrations for young Fitzwilliam's christening, she had declined. She suspected Elizabeth had not changed her opinion, of either her marriage or her husband; and did not care to be reminded of either by her disapproval or pity. The friendship that had sustained them for so many years had withered, little by little, until nothing was left of it but the occasional exchange of mild civilities.

Charlotte leaned across the table and poured more tea into Mary's cup. Mary was struck by her air of prosperity and self-possession. She was carefully dressed, in clothes that bespoke quality rather than the first fashion; but their rich sobriety suited her. Along with her new wardrobe, Charlotte had acquired an air of easy authority that had not been noticeable when she was merely Miss Lucas, an unmarried woman fast approaching the perils of her thirties with no suitor in view.

'I see you have put on your cap, Charlotte. As you always said you would.'

Charlotte laughed.

'Yes, I believe I once told you I should do so, one way or another. But I must admit, it gives me far more pleasure to wear it as a wife than as an old maid.'

Mary flinched a little – these were not words she liked to hear – but Charlotte did not seem to notice.

'Mr Collins apologises that he is not here to join me in welcoming you. He has business in Hertford, but if he is not too much detained, he will join us for dinner.'

She leaned back in her chair, and fixed Mary with a steady, assessing gaze.

'And what of yourself, Mary? Tell me how things are with you. Mr Collins and I were both delighted to receive your letter. You know, I hope, that you will always be welcome at Longbourn, whenever you choose to visit us. May I offer you some sugar?'

Mary shook her head.

'But I confess I was also a little surprised. We had imagined you happily settled with Jane or Elizabeth.'

'Yes, both have been very generous. Indeed, all my sisters have been most solicitous. Jane says I may always stay with her. Kitty asked me to join her at the rectory, and even Lydia – well, that would hardly suit, but it was a kindness in her to her ask.'

'And did none of those possibilities appeal?'

Mary felt apprehension rise up within her. Part of her wanted to throw up her hands and cry, *No, no, none of them will work, they will all grow tired of me, and then what will I do? Tell me!* But she was not ready to confess her deepest fears to a young woman who seemed altogether more commanding and less vulnerable than the Charlotte she remembered. Flustered, she pulled her glasses from her pocket and began to twist them in her hands.

'I think it would be a great fault in me to make so important a decision as my place of habitation without allowing time for proper reflection. I have many important considerations to ... consider. And it is rightly said that those who make judgements in haste will repent in leisure.'

Charlotte smiled a brisk little smile.

'Indeed it is. Well, I hope you will find your stay here conducive to such serious thinking. I shall certainly do all I can to make it so. Now, if you don't think it will distress you, I wonder if you would like to see over the house before resting? We have made a number of improvements since – since we arrived. I should very much like to hear your opinion of them.'

For the first time, Mary looked properly around her. She had been so intent on mastering her own feelings that she had barely registered her surroundings. The drawing room had been quite transformed. The sofas were newly covered, the walls distempered, and the floor sanded. At the windows hung curtains of dark figured velvet. As Mary contemplated their splendour, Charlotte looked on with deep satisfaction.

'They look very well, don't they? I bought them at the sale when the Collingwoods sold up. There's a little woman in Meryton who can do anything with a needle. She cut them down for me. I was in agonies when she wielded the scissors, but I own I'm delighted with the result.'

Mary nodded obligingly, and followed Charlotte as she marched down the old, familiar passages. It was unsettling to be shown around a house where she had lived for so long as if she were a stranger; and the sight of so many well-remembered objects and places brought a lump to her throat. There on the landing stood the long clock, exiled from the drawing room after Lydia's shoe, thrown in a passion at Kitty, had cracked its glass and stopped its pendulum. There was the little table in whose drawer her mother had kept her needles, wrapped up in a silk bag that always smelled of camphor. Everywhere she looked, something recalled the past with such force that Mary was almost overpowered by sadness and regret; but she kept her polite smile in place, and did nothing to halt the flow of her guide's enthusiasm. Charlotte's initial consideration for Mary's feelings had quickly evaporated, her delicacy entirely eclipsed by her pride in her home. Mary was led into every room and urged to admire it, encouraged to inspect every new-built cupboard and every blackened fire grate. She did so without complaint, until she had exhausted every word of praise and approval at her command. Finally, she could think of nothing more to say than that the house smelled very fresh and sweet.

'I have a floor polish made to my own recipe flavoured with oil of lavender. It is these little touches that make such a difference,' Charlotte said, as she looked around her, entirely satisfied with her domain and confident it had been displayed to the very best advantage.

'But now I should like to show you my greatest achievement. I think he will be awake now.'

In the nursery, Mary's heart missed a beat as she took a seat near the fire, where she and Elizabeth had once sat, books in hand, making out her letters. Now she was introduced to the room's new owner. William Collins was a stocky, fair-haired toddler, who, when released from his mother's hugs, stared curiously at Mary from the safety of her lap.

'He is a very fine child,' declared Mary. 'You know, he looks at me in exactly the same way as Lizzy's son – the same frank and interested look! You must be very proud of him.'

'Oh, yes, in my opinion, he is a prodigy amongst boys. And of course, he is somewhat older than Fitzwilliam. I imagine my William is much further on – he must be taller, more forward? He even talks a little.'

Charlotte stroked her son's downy head, as delighted by her child as she was by her house.

'He is a very remarkable child. Everyone says so.'

It was almost dark by the time Mary was released to rest for a while before dinner.

'I'm sure I don't need to show you to your room,' declared Charlotte, as she made her way to the kitchen to ensure all was in order there. 'You will hardly have forgotten where to find it.'

As she pushed open the door, Mary saw that a few candles were already lit, and that her bag was open on the bed. At her dressing table stood Mrs Hill, who was calmly unpacking her brushes and unfolding her clothes, as if they had seen each other only yesterday.

'Mrs Hill! I am so very pleased to see you!'

'As I am to see you, Miss Mary. It has been a long time since we last spoke.'

'I hope all is well with you and Mr Hill?'

'Yes, thank you. It was a great relief to us when Mrs Collins decided to keep us on. I should have been very sad to leave Longbourn.'

'I understand that only too well.'

'Of course, it is different with all of you gone. It will never be the same without your poor father. And Mrs Collins is very exacting. But we rub along together quite happily.'

For a while, Mary answered enquiries about the health of her mother and sisters, receiving in return all the limited news that Meryton could supply. At first, Mrs Hill asked no difficult questions; it was only when she began to hang up Mary's clothes that she betrayed a curiosity about Mary's situation.

'Is this what you wore at Pemberley, miss?'

'Yes, we were just family while I was there, no formality at all.'

'But for evenings you must have had something smarter to put on. Did you not choose to bring it with you?'

'I left my better things there, so as not to give trouble. So much packing and unpacking.' She looked away, trying not to meet Mrs Hill's sceptical eye. 'And we are told not to think too much of our appearance. The sin of pride, you know.'

'What about the dress you wore to the Meryton ball? I always thought that looked very well on you. It seems a pity not to have it with you.'

'I'm afraid it is a very long time since I have had occasion to wear it. But if I had known Longbourn had become so grand, I should certainly have given it an airing.'

Mrs Hill looked about to ask more, then instead confined herself to observing that those dresses Mary had brought would be improved by a little care and attention, and that with her help, Mary would cut as credible a figure as was possible with such outfits.

CHAPTER THIRTY-FIVE

By the time Mary walked into the dining room, Charlotte was already in place, presiding at the top of the table. She seemed even smarter and more sleek than she had done in daylight, straight-backed and assured, head held high. She fitted effortlessly into her surroundings, a perfect complement to the glowing furniture and newly gilded mirrors, the last piece of a jigsaw that completed a picture of domestic order and content. To her surprise, Mary found herself faintly in awe of this new version of her old acquaintance. In a few years, Charlotte would be an imposing figure; by the time she was forty, she would be quite formidable.

'I do not know what is keeping Mr Collins,' Charlotte remarked. 'He is usually a most punctilious timekeeper.'

The two women were drinking their first glass of wine by the time Mr Collins came hurrying into the room.

'My dear Miss Bennet, how can I apologise enough? I was detained by the bishop, and it was not in my power to leave. It was most unfortunate, but as I'm sure you'll agree, our personal inclinations must always give way to the duties owed to superior rank.'

Charlotte signalled to a servant to fill Mr Collins's glass. Her husband was flustered, put at a disadvantage by his late arrival.

'I regret to say, Mrs Collins, that I might have been a little earlier had I not been incommoded by the absence of a few necessities in my dressing room. The clean neckcloths were not where I have become used to finding them.'

'I am sorry to hear it,' replied his wife evenly. 'I will speak to Mrs Hill. But I'm glad to see you are suitably attired now, and no doubt ready to greet our old friend.'

Mollified, Mr Collins turned to Mary with a broad, accommodating smile.

'You are most welcome, Miss Bennet. I will not say to *our* home, as that might seem a painful allusion to a house that was so recently your own place of residence, and might have remained so, had circumstances been different. But man proposes, God disposes, as it is most justly said. I hope that gives you some comfort.'

'Why, yes, sir,' Mary replied. 'We are all of us subject to the caprices of fortune.'

'Mary has just returned from a long visit to Pemberley,' volunteered Charlotte smoothly. 'I'm sure you will want to hear how she found everyone there.'

As Mary recounted the particulars of her stay in Derbyshire, the air of awkwardness around the table began to dissipate, helped by the excellent red wine which Charlotte ensured was in generous supply. Mr Collins listened with every appearance of interest to all Mary could tell him about the various livings held by Mr Darcy and the parsonage houses attached to them. Once he understood that few of them produced tithes equal to those he himself enjoyed, he grew increasingly affable. Charlotte said little, but Mary noticed she was assiduous in ensuring that every dish reached his end of the table before her husband asked for it. The food

was plentiful and of a far higher quality than Mary recalled
had been served at Lucas Lodge.

'May I compliment you on the dinner, Charlotte? It really
is very good.'

'Thank you, Mary. I was determined to do all I could to
maintain the reputation Longbourn had always enjoyed for
the excellence of its cooking. I'm very pleased if you think I've
succeeded.'

Warmed up and calmed down with a few grilled soles and
a leg of lamb, Mr Collins turned a benevolent face towards his
wife.

'My dear Charlotte is an excellent manager. As you will
have seen for yourself, everything at Longbourn bespeaks
taste and comfort, and always in a style appropriate to the
station in which Providence has been pleased to place us.'

Charlotte did not meet Mr Collins's fond smile but
dropped her eyes to her plate. When he reached across to pat
her hand, she did not respond. His hand lingered above hers
for only a moment before he withdrew it, busying himself
with the dessert and asking Mary whether Mr Darcy had put
up any pheasants in his park. For the rest of the meal, Charlotte was all attentiveness, helping Mr Collins to the ripest
slice of cheese or the choicest piece of fruit; but it seemed to
Mary as if there was a coolness in her solicitude. Perhaps they
were merely tired. Mary felt herself to be on the edge of
exhaustion and was relieved when Charlotte finally rose from
the table, firmly conveying that supper was over.

'Mr Collins, Mary and I will leave you to finish your wine.
She has had a long journey and I'm sure she's in great need of
sleep, although she is far too polite to show it.'

As they left, Mary glanced behind her. The room shimmered in the candlelight, glowing with warmth and prosperity. At the table, Mr Collins sat alone, cracking nuts with solitary concentration as he poured himself another glass of wine.

A little later, Mary lay in the dark of her old room, comforted to find that although the bed had new hangings, the springs of the mattress still creaked in the way she remembered. As she stared up at the freshly painted ceiling, she reflected on what had been a most extraordinary day. Revisiting the house had not proved as painful as she had expected. Although there were moments when she found herself almost unbearably moved, as some small corner or chance encounter brought back to her such a strong sense of the past that it almost overwhelmed her, this had happened less often than she had feared. Charlotte's improvements had scrubbed away so much that was familiar about Longbourn as she had known it, had so efficiently erased the life the Bennets had lived there, that little remained to prompt regret for what had gone.

Charlotte herself had proved almost as transformed as the house. It seemed to Mary as if Charlotte had grown in every way – in confidence, stature, and self-possession. The word that best described her, Mary thought, with all its connotations of order and security, was '*established*'. Watching her as she managed the little empire of her household and garden, as she hugged her child and marshalled her servants, as she transformed the appearance of Longbourn into a vision of her own imagining, it was impossible not to believe she had found the place in the world she had always longed for. Judged on those terms, it seemed impossible to argue with the bargain Charlotte had made when she married. But as Mary finally drifted off to sleep, she remembered Charlotte's refusal to meet her husband's eyes, the bleak impression of Mr Collins staring into his wine as she and Charlotte left the room. They cast a shadow over the rosy glow of her first impressions. Mary pushed them to the back of her mind. Rational observation, not the unreliable promptings of emotion, should be her guide. Reason would conclude whether Charlotte's choice had been correct, and whether it was one she might consider adopting for herself.

CHAPTER THIRTY-SIX

In the weeks that followed, Mary's days took on a pattern that suited her very well. She breakfasted in her room, staying aloof from the early morning bustle of the family, joining Charlotte only when the floors were swept, young William fed, and that night's dinner ordered. When everyone else was busy, she sat at the old familiar piano and played for as long as her fingers would allow. At Longbourn, there was neither competition for a seat at the keyboard nor any risk she would be mortified by the superior skills of another. In the afternoons, she tried to be useful, following Charlotte into the garden in a borrowed apron, pruning knife in hand; sometimes she carried a basket to the poultry yard to gather eggs. Each day was perfectly uneventful; and slowly, the despair that had come upon her in Derbyshire began to lose the sharp edge of its pain. Now it was a dull ache of sadness which she was resolved to conquer if she could. At the dinner table, she forced herself not to think of how it had looked when she and her sisters crowded round it; and when she saw Charlotte sewing in her mother's chair, sitting exactly as Mrs Bennet had done in order to catch the light, she compelled herself not to turn away. But for all her determination to accustom herself to the new order of things, she still felt a pang of grief when she walked past her father's library, which she had not yet had the courage to enter. And she declined to accompany Charlotte on social visits, knowing herself not yet ready to brave the curiosity of her old neighbours, who would demand to know, with no sense of delicacy, what she intended to do, where she planned to go. As she had no answer to give, she preferred to avoid all such encounters whenever she could. Still, in general, she found the steady routine of life at Longbourn congenial enough. No one harassed or teased her; and she never felt exposed or out of place. Charlotte was solicitous but not overbearing, and Mary began to enjoy her company. It was some time before it occurred to her just how much of Charlotte's time was available to her. One afternoon, as they were cutting the last of the tulips to take into the house, it struck Mary how rarely they encountered Mr Collins and how very little time he and his wife spent together.

'I imagine,' she asked tentatively, 'that Mr Collins is very occupied with business during the day?'

'He certainly has a great deal to do,' replied Charlotte. 'The time of a clergyman can scarcely be called his own.'

'But even when he is at leisure, he rarely joins us here or walks with us in the evenings. Does he like to be so solitary?'

'I do not think he minds it. He is at present very taken up with making a little arbour near the orchard. It was a suggestion of mine he has quite seized upon. He is doing much of the work himself, which is most beneficial for his health. I hope to have a seat placed there when it is finished.'

'Should you like to go and help him, Charlotte? I am very happy to continue here alone.'

Charlotte reached out and grasped a particularly fine bloom, snipping it briskly through the stem.

'No thank you, Mary, I am very well where I am. We shall all meet again for dinner soon enough.'

Seeing there was no more to be said, Mary put down her scissors, gathered her flowers into an orderly bunch, and began to walk back to the house. As she rounded the yew hedge, she caught sight of Mr Collins in the distance. With his coat off, and his shirtsleeves rolled up, he was digging at the ground with a furious intensity. She watched him until he threw down the spade and, wiping his brow with his sleeve, leaned disconsolately against the garden wall. He did not look happy. Mary turned away abruptly, keen he should not see her. It was an unsettling encounter; she felt almost as though she had intruded on some private grief.

Over the next few nights, she watched her hosts with a new awareness. Charlotte was as unruffled as ever, smilingly deferential to her husband. But the more Mary studied him, the more uneasy Mr Collins seemed. Mary saw how often he tried to catch Charlotte's eye, or to engage her in conversation, and how with every appearance of politeness, she always avoided him. Eventually, disheartened, he said no more, but looked away in silence. Mary had no doubt now of his state of mind. She was too familiar with the experience of misery not to recognise its familiar marks on another. But what, she asked herself, had Mr Collins to be unhappy about? He had a comfortable home, the wife he had wanted, and a healthy son in the nursery. What could have lowered his spirits to such a degree? It was true Charlotte was not the most demonstrative of spouses, and did not seem much given to public displays of affection; but she always showed the utmost consideration for his wishes, and no hint of irritation or ill-temper ever escaped her lips. Mary's own parents had not always lived well together, but the causes of their dissatisfaction had been easy to understand, and all too forcefully expressed. Whatever troubled Mr Collins was not nearly so apparent.

Perhaps it had nothing to do with his circumstances. Perhaps his character had a disposition to melancholy. Even in her limited experience of life, she had observed that some people were miserable in the midst of prosperity, while others remained cheerful in even the harshest of conditions. Lydia, for example, was never really cast down, even though her circumstances could hardly be described as easy. Whereas she herself . . . She did not like to complete that thought, preferring instead to ask herself the question in more abstract terms. How, she mused, are we to understand happiness, and the ways in which it is brought about? Is it determined by inherited temperament? Or is it all a matter of chance, a quality arbitrarily bestowed on some but not on others? Do our circumstances matter? Are beauty and wealth more likely to produce happiness than goodness and self-sacrifice? And is there anything an individual can do to improve their own sense of contentment and satisfaction?

As Mary considered these questions, it occurred to her that she might usefully pursue them further. It had been some time since she had applied her mind to a weighty intellectual question; and this one seemed especially suited to her current circumstances. Her father's library was particularly well provided with the philosophical works she would require, and there were no other calls on her time to distract her. Besides, she felt ready to exercise her reason again, to pit it against a challenge which would call on all her resources of concentration and effort. She did not deny that there was also a more personal application to such a study. An exploration of the nature of happiness could add to her understanding of her own situation, and might even counter her own strong tendency to despair.

The following afternoon, as Charlotte stood in the hall, tying on her hat in preparation for a visit to Lady Lucas, Mary asked if she might have permission to spend a few hours in the library while she was gone. Young William gambolled about their feet, banging his favourite toy on the stairs. Charlotte scooped him up, laughing.

'I cannot imagine why the peace of that comfortable room could possibly be preferred to an afternoon with my mother and this monster of a boy! But, really, there's no need to ask. Please make use of it whenever you choose.'

By the time the front door closed, Mary was already inside the library. For a moment, she stood quite still, surveying the room where she had spent so many hours. There was her father's desk, cleared now of his books and the muddle of papers that had always covered it. What had he been reading, while he sat there, inscrutable, amused by some secret joke, and unreachable to everyone but Lizzy? Mary would never understand now what this place had meant to him and how he occupied his mind within it. She walked with as much self-possession as she could muster to the bookshelves. It felt strange to search them without feeling his eyes upon her, no longer apprehensive that she would irritate him by taking too long or making too much noise. She moved amongst the shelves with a quiet, determined freedom until she finally found what she wanted. Then she sat at the table she had always used and began to turn the pages of her book.

CHAPTER THIRTY-SEVEN

At first, Mary had the library entirely to herself. She arrived in the middle of the morning, established herself in her place, and did not leave it until required to dress for dinner. Soon, she became used to her solitude, and even began to relish it. She was therefore caught completely by surprise when one afternoon Mr Collins burst in unannounced, carrying a large sheaf of papers with the evident intention of working there himself. He had thrown his bundle onto the desk and had sat down heavily in her father's old chair before he noticed Mary at the far end of the room.

'My dear Miss Bennet! I did not know you were here! I cannot apologise enough for my unmannerly intrusion. I will withdraw immediately.'

Mary stood up, embarrassed.

'No, sir, it is I who am at fault. This is your room and I am a sad trespasser in it. Mrs Collins gave me to understand it would not be required by you for some time. I should never have settled myself here if I had known you had business to attend to.'

More mutual apologies were offered and declined; and eventually it was decided that Mary should remain where she was, and that her presence should not in the least bother Mr Collins or incommode him in any way, and he would hold himself in readiness to depart at the least hint from her that she wished him gone. As Mary had no desire to expel him from his own study, soon no more was heard but the scratching of his pen and the turning of her pages, until Mr Collins excused himself and bid her a polite farewell.

When Mary herself eventually gathered up her books and left to go and dress, she met Charlotte in the hall.

'I am so sorry to hear your studies were broken in upon by Mr Collins earlier today. I know he is very sorry to have disturbed you. Shall I ask him to work elsewhere? He could use the little parlour, no one goes there in the afternoons.'

'Please do not do so on my behalf, it is his library, after all. But perhaps if my presence does not annoy him, I could continue to study at the far end of the room? I have all my books laid out and am comfortably established there. I promise I will do nothing to irritate him.'

'I doubt very much whether any irritation or annoyance would come from you,' replied Charlotte briskly. 'I'm sure that scheme will work very well. I shall suggest to Mr Collins that you become joint occupants of the library, each with your own well-defined and separate territories. It is a plan I find answers admirably in many circumstances, so I see no reason why it should not do so in this case.'

Upstairs in her room, as Mrs Hill did her hair, Mary's thoughts wandered back to Charlotte's words. The calming rhythm of the brush and the companionable silence that surrounded them encouraged her to ask a question directly which she might otherwise have hesitated to broach at all.

'Mrs Hill, do you think that Mr and Mrs Collins are well matched?'

Still brushing, Mrs Hill considered.

'As well as most, I'd say. They don't argue and there's never any trouble between them.'

'Yes, but do they like each other? Do they enjoy each other's company?'

'I can tell you've never been married, Miss Mary. They've been together for a few years. You can't expect them to behave like young lovers.'

That was not what Mary had seen at Pemberley. Lizzy and Mr Darcy's wedding had taken place not long after that of Mr and Mrs Collins, but time had done nothing to dampen the strength of the affection they felt for each other. Even Mary, with no experience of the workings of the heart, could not fail to recognise the pleasure they took in each other's company. No one's presence delighted her husband more than Lizzy's; and her face lit up with happiness every time he entered the room. But things were very different at Longbourn. Here, Mary had seen no loving glances exchanged, no cheerful contentment, no desire to spend as much time as possible with each other. On the contrary; it struck Mary that while the Darcys were rarely apart, Mr and Mrs Collins were hardly ever together. Of course, it could not be denied that Charlotte had much to occupy her. There was her boy to look after and her household to manage, with far less assistance than Lizzy could call upon. And once those duties were fulfilled, the improvements to the house absorbed what little leisure remained to her. It seemed there was always something that demanded Charlotte's attention, calling her away from her husband, preventing her from accompanying him on outings or sharing any small pleasures with him.

Then there was the little arbour, which took up so many of Mr Collins's spare hours. Mary had begun to wonder whether

Charlotte had requested its construction with the sole intention of its absorbing her husband's energies, and putting as much distance as possible between himself and her. This was an ungenerous thought, and Mary sought to repress it. But the more she saw how their lives were ordered, the harder it was to ignore the possibility that Charlotte had deliberately arranged her time so that she spent as little of it as possible in the company of her husband.

In the mirror, Mary watched as Mrs Hill secured her neat bun into place.

'They seem to be apart for much of the day.'

'Well, there are many different ways to make a marriage work. And if that's the one they've chosen, it's not up to any of us to ask why.'

'But what if one of them didn't choose it?'

Mrs Hill sighed.

'Then they won't be the first to have found matrimony not quite what they'd expected, and they'll have to make the best of it. There you are, Miss Mary, you're quite done.'

At dinner, Mary felt ashamed of herself as she watched Charlotte minister efficiently to Mr Collins's every need. Her curiosity seemed poor recompense for Charlotte's hospitality; surely it was ungrateful, distasteful even, to speculate about the private concerns of her hosts in this way. But the more she observed them together, the more she was convinced of the gulf that lay between them; and also, and perhaps more surprisingly, that for all her polite attentions, it was Charlotte who was the architect of it. Behind her mild, compliant demeanour, she was entirely self-contained. Nothing Mr Collins said or did touched her; her feelings were locked up and battened down, in every way inaccessible to her husband. As

Mary stole a glance at Mr Collins's resigned expression, she realised that he knew this; and that the unhappiness she sensed in him was the result of this knowledge.

Mary could not sleep that night, disturbed by what she had seen. When she first arrived at Longbourn, she had assumed the success of the Collins marriage could be judged by Charlotte's sentiments alone. It had not occurred to her to consider Mr Collins's feelings in the matter. He had achieved his ambition of finding a respectable woman willing to marry him – surely that was enough? What more could he have hoped for? It was not possible he had expected love? Mary had not considered him capable of deep emotion; but she saw now she had been mistaken. Charlotte had made whatever accommodations had been necessary to resign herself to a marriage of convenience and, superficially at least, was content. It was her husband who was left miserable in an arrangement of his own making.

CHAPTER THIRTY-EIGHT

Mary was working in the library one morning, enjoying her solitary state. Then, just as she had decided he did not intend to join her there, Mr Collins appeared at the door, with a self-conscious air.

'Miss Bennet, I understand from Mrs Collins that it will not inconvenience you if I work for a few hours at my desk. Please tell me if that is so – if not, I will depart at once.'

Mary assured him, as she had done before, that she would be very agreeable to their sharing the room and eventually he sat down and began to shuffle his papers. Mary applied herself to her books and was soon so thoroughly engaged with them that the next sound she heard was Charlotte calling them both to tea. As he readied himself to leave, Mr Collins beamed at Mary with relief.

'I am most grateful to you, Miss Bennet. I was not at all disturbed. You were so quiet it was as though there was no person in the room but myself.'

'I am glad to have been so . . . negligible a presence, sir.'

His face fell.

'I did not mean to sound ungracious. But very few people understand the importance of silence as an aid to concentration. It is an essential requirement for anyone wishing to undertake serious study, but seldom found, I am afraid to say, especially amongst the fairer sex. You, however, do not seem much given to idle and unreflecting chatter.'

'I am glad to hear it, sir. It is true I do not have much of a gift for polite conversation.'

Discomfited, Mr Collins gave a little laugh and hurried away. He was clearly satisfied with their arrangement, though, for the next day, and the days following, he arrived in the library every morning, saying little, working his way diligently through his correspondence. But on the fourth day, after an hour or two had passed, Mary was surprised to see him approach her little table.

'I am afraid my curiosity has triumphed over my manners. May I ask, Miss Bennet, what you are reading with such assiduity?'

Mary looked up, surprised. She had never supposed it would be he who broke the silence.

'Well, I am looking into works I enjoyed when I lived here. Books I found profitable and useful.'

'You are reminding yourself of past pleasures, then? To a thinking mind, there is no better recreation.'

'Partly, that is so. But I am also engaged in an exercise. An investigation, if you like.'

His incredulity registered plainly on his face.

'Really? Is it of a scholarly nature? If so, perhaps I may be able to assist. I am always at the disposal of any seeker after knowledge, ready to guide the uncertain tastes of those as yet unacquainted with works of a serious complexion.'

Mary was not used to discussing her intellectual pursuits with anyone, and her first instinct was to retreat. But his condescension irked her. She held up her head and looked him in the eye with more boldness than was usual.

'I am interested in human happiness, sir, in the better understanding of what it is and how it may be achieved. I wish to explore whether it is a state which arises from the chance convergence of circumstances, or whether it is a condition we may will ourselves to possess. I want to understand how we may recognise it when it is within our grasp and in what ways we can learn to live without it if we are not lucky enough to experience it.'

Mr Collins was clearly very much taken aback.

'Well! That is an extraordinary occupation for a young lady! I never suspected your interests were so philosophical. I confess I imagined you were secretly reading novels, ashamed to be seen so frivolously engaged.'

'I should not be afraid to acknowledge any book I thought worthy of my time and application, though it is true I am no great reader of fiction. I find works of fact more congenial to my mind.'

'Do you, indeed?'

Mr Collins sat down and reached towards the little hoard of books piled on the table.

'May I see in which direction your tastes incline?'

He picked them up one by one, examining their titles.

'Locke, Paley, Rousseau – even Mr Hume! You venture into some unexpected places, Miss Bennet. Did your father know you were reading such works?'

'He may have done, but I don't think he was very interested in anyone's studies other than his own.'

Mr Collins fingered his clerical collar.

'I am surprised he had such books upon his shelves at all. They suggest a mind not wholly satisfied by Christian teaching. I should be sorry to think that was the case, but even more grieved to learn that you yourself had been influenced by them.'

'Oh, no, my faith is too firmly grounded to be shaken in the way you describe. And I cannot agree that it was wrong in my father to possess such books or to allow anyone who wished to read them. Even Dr Fordyce says it is desirable for our minds to be challenged, for only thus can we learn to distinguish good arguments from bad.'

'You put your case most forcefully, Miss Bennet. And this enquiry of yours, this study in human happiness. May I ask if it is a purely intellectual pursuit? Or does it have perhaps a more personal application?'

Mary had not expected such a penetrating question.

'I suppose all enquiry is a mixture of the intellectual and the personal. How can we know where one begins and the other ends?'

This time it was Mr Collins who looked away.

'An interesting question. I shall consider of it, Miss Bennet.'

He nodded, turned on his heel, and left her alone in the library. For a while, she stared out the window, reflecting on their conversation. Then she opened the largest and most challenging volume from the books before her, put on her glasses, and began to read.

CHAPTER THIRTY-NINE

Mary was not sure whether Mr Collins would return to the library while she worked there. She was conscious of having ventured rather too closely towards a painful truth and thought he might not choose to share her company again. But the next day, he arrived at his usual hour. He did not speak, and nothing disturbed the silence of the library until he withdrew a few hours later. The day after was the same; and the one after that. It was not until the third morning that he cleared his throat and approached her table with a book in his hand.

'Miss Bennet, I have been giving some thought to our recent discussion, and after much consideration, have decided I should not be doing wrong in offering this small volume to you. I think you will find it very illuminating. It is the *Ethics* of Aristotle. Do you know it?'

Mary shook her head. He sat down and pushed the book towards her.

'I think you will find it pertinent to your study. Aristotle has a great deal to say about happiness, all of it interesting. And although he did not have the benefit of hearing the word of God himself, many Christian thinkers value him highly. For that reason, I feel quite easy presenting it to you.'

Tentatively, Mary picked it up.

'I suggest you read a little every day to accustom yourself

to his style. At the end of the week, we shall talk about what you have learned. I have a feeling you will enjoy it.'

He returned to his desk and bowed his head over his papers. Mary stayed just long enough for her departure not to appear ill-mannered, before hurrying to her bedroom, where she could examine the book in private. As she did so, she felt her heart beating fast. For as long as she could remember, she had longed for someone to interest themselves in her studies. That it should be Mr Collins, of all people, who showed the first hint of curiosity in her intellectual pursuits was astounding to her. He had been insensible to all her overtures when he first arrived at Longbourn, indifferent to every attempt of hers to engage him in her interests. But these were old wounds now, and while they sometimes throbbed a little to remind her of their existence, they had been succeeded by so much later pain that they no longer hurt as they once did. Now she felt nothing but gratitude that he should have chosen a book for her to read as she opened it eagerly and began to turn its pages.

She soon saw he had been right to warn her it would take a little while before she was comfortable in the presence of such a distinguished mind. But she persevered, and gradually began to get the measure of the great man's precise, exacting prose. It was not an easy read, but she enjoyed the challenge it posed; and by the end of the week, she hurried to the library eagerly, keen to discuss what she had read. Mr Collins was waiting for her, his papers pushed aside.

'So, Miss Bennet, I look forward to hearing what you have learned from your first encounter with one of the most profound thinkers of the ancient world.'

'I read it with much interest, sir. And I have made a few notes.'

'An excellent habit in a scholar which I hope will enable you to explain clearly to me what Aristotle has taught you about happiness.'

'You want me to describe my impressions?'

Mr Collins nodded. For a moment, Mary hesitated, but took a quick breath and began.

'Aristotle tells us we can be truly happy only when we are virtuous – and by that I think he means when we behave in a way that promotes our goodness, that brings out our best qualities.'

'Yes. Go on.'

'But it is often difficult for us to recognise what virtue looks like because we so readily confuse it with pleasure. Pleasure can deliver us enjoyment – the feelings we derive from good food, good conversation, the contemplation of beauty – but these things do not last. Enjoyments are transient, but true happiness endures. That is its distinguishing quality.'

'Indeed. And how does Aristotle suggest such happiness is to be achieved?'

'Well, it is hard to sum up his thoughts succinctly without losing the subtlety of their perceptions –'

'But if I press you to do so, Miss Bennet?'

'Then I should say he tells us it is only through self-knowledge that genuine happiness is to be had. Only when we know ourselves – when we have examined and understood our strengths and weaknesses, when we have been honest enough to admit what we really desire from life – only then do we have any chance at all of attaining it.'

Mr Collins was delighted.

'Bravo, Miss Bennet! A most convincing summary. We shall make a classical scholar of you yet!'

Mary returned his smile, a little self-conscious but eager to continue.

'Do you think we might go on, sir? To the end of the book?'

'I think we must, or we shall never know how his ideas develop. You must read a little more and then we shall talk about it again.'

The more Mary read, the more her confidence grew. In her next discussion with Mr Collins, she articulated her thoughts more readily, and with greater clarity. The silence, which had once been the library's defining quality, was replaced by animated conversation, conducted with such energy that eventually, even Charlotte noticed it. One after-noon, as she and Mary worked in the garden, she observed this was the first time they had been outside together for more than a week.

'You seemed to be having a very lively time of it today. I hope Mr Collins is not boring you. He is apt to be passionate on those subjects that interest him, and it can be very fatiguing. You must not feel obliged to keep him company, you know.'

'But I'm not in the least bored, I promise you! On the contrary, I have found it extremely interesting and am very grateful for the time and trouble Mr Collins has bestowed upon me.'

At this, Charlotte looked sharply in Mary's direction. Mary, pulling up a particularly stubborn weed, did not notice and went on.

'Should you not like to pursue some course of study yourself, Charlotte? Mr Collins makes it all so easy, I'm sure you would find it as stimulating as I do. Why don't you join us?'

'I'm afraid I have enough to occupy me already, with a house to run and a child to look after. I have no leisure to spend my mornings discussing philosophy. What, I wonder, would Aristotle have to say about that?'

Mary, attacking the unresponsive earth with a trowel, did not catch the hint of acerbity in her tone.

'Very little, I expect. You are quite right, Aristotle does not show much interest in how women achieve happiness, or indeed, in women at all. I shall ask Mr Collins about that at our next discussion.'

Charlotte stood up suddenly, dropping her scissors into her apron pocket and handing Mary her basket.

'I must go and see about dinner. I shall leave you to bring in the flowers.'

She did not say goodbye but marched briskly and unsmilingly away. Mary watched her go, puzzled, at a loss to understand how she had offended.

She was still a little nervous when she sat down to dinner, afraid of provoking Charlotte further; but Charlotte seemed herself again, presiding over the table with her usual orderly calm. Or was there perhaps the very faintest change in her manner, a new watchfulness, so subtle and so imperceptible that Mary was barely sure it was there at all? As the meal ran its course, she told herself she had been mistaken; but she could not put herself quite at ease and was glad when they rose from the table. Later, as Mrs Hill brushed out her hair, Mary did not respond to her attempts to engage her in conversation. Her thoughts returned again and again to Charlotte's state of mind until she felt she had exhausted every attempt to understand her behaviour, and resolved to consider it no longer. Once Mrs Hill had gone, she picked up her Aristotle and read a few lines before blowing out the candle and attempting to get to sleep.

CHAPTER FORTY

ary watched Mr Collins closely when he arrived in the library to see if his demeanour suggested Charlotte had confided the source of her irritation to him; but he seemed unaware of any ill feeling. On the contrary, he seemed in buoyant spirits.

'I have a proposition for you, Miss Bennet. As you have demonstrated such a taste for classical learning, I have been reflecting on whether it would be proper for me to lead you more deeply into the study of this great treasury of human knowledge.'

He sat down beside her.

'I have considered it most carefully, and taking into consideration your great steadiness of temper, have concluded no harm is likely to come of it. I am satisfied what I intend will not be productive of any adverse consequences.'

He pulled from his coat pocket a small and rather battered volume and laid it before her.

'This is a dictionary of the Greek language, together with a grammar suitable for beginners. It is old, as you can see, but in my humble opinion, remains the best of its kind. It was mine as a boy. I had an excellent tutor who taught me to love the language, and it was he who gave me this little book. It is not an easy study, but one which richly repays the efforts made to master it. And all attempts to do so must start first with the principles laid out herein.'

Mary put down her pen, astonished.

'Are you suggesting I should learn Greek, sir?'

'Indeed I am. I am aware it is not usually regarded as a suitable subject for young ladies, but, if you will forgive an observation of a personal nature, I have never met a woman with interests as scholarly as your own. I think that you are perfectly equal to it.'

He leaned over and opened the pages.

'Look, here is the alphabet in its entirety. This is alpha, and here at the end is omega. You have surely heard of them? And here are all the others in between, with the sounds they make written beside them.'

She rubbed her glasses with her sleeve and stared intently at the unfamiliar shapes.

'What do you think, Miss Bennet? If you are willing, I am prepared to make a trial of it with you.'

For a moment, she hesitated – it would be like learning to read all over again, with entirely new letters to master, and what if she should fail? – but then excitement rose up in her, and she knew she could not refuse.

'Oh, yes, Mr Collins, I should like it of all things!'

He smiled.

'So should I, Miss Bennet. So should I.'

Mary's first exercise was to memorise the Greek letters. She sat alone in the library with the little grammar and a large pile of paper, staring at them till her eyes ached, tracing their shapes with her pen while sounding out their names under her breath. Sometimes Mr Collins insisted she repeat them to him out loud. At first, she feared to appear ridiculous, but he would have none of that, and soon she had conquered her embarrassment, speaking up clearly and without shame. She made excellent progress, and one afternoon, as they all sat at tea, Mr Collins asked his wife if she would like to hear her friend recite the letters of the Greek alphabet.

'She has worked very hard and I am sure, my dear Charlotte, you will be astonished to hear how she has advanced.'

Mary looked up from her cup, a blush rising in her face. She caught Charlotte's expression as she did so, and it was suddenly very plain to her that Charlotte would take no pleasure at all in hearing her perform. She stumbled through the letters, unsettled by Charlotte's level, appraising stare, which grew tighter with every low, excited prompt with which Mr Collins helped Mary towards omega and the end. When she finished, it was he alone who clapped his hands.

'Well done, Miss Bennet! You are a tribute to the value of hard work and an ornament to your sex! What do you think, Mrs Collins? Has she not done well?'

Charlotte gazed at Mary with an expression of mild curiosity, as though she was seeing her clearly for the first time.

'I see you have been making excellent use of your time in the library. I had not understood before quite how you occupied yourself there, but I see now what you have been doing. Well done, indeed.'

'We will make a scholar of you yet, Miss Bennet,' exclaimed Mr Collins. 'I am quite sure of it. But I shall hear no more from you today. Mrs Collins, you will recall I shall not be in to dinner tonight, as I have business in Hertford. I must leave you two ladies to entertain yourselves.'

Still smiling with pleasure at the progress of his pupil, Mr Collins rose and left the table. Once he was gone, Charlotte poured the last of the tea into her cup. She did not offer any to Mary.

'As Mr Collins will not be here, I think I will go to bed early tonight. I do not feel like eating. I'm sure Mrs Hill will bring something up to you if you want it.'

'I am sorry you are so tired, Charlotte. Is there anything I can do to help? I am quite at leisure for the rest of today.'

'No, thank you, I'm sure I will manage well enough on my own. But we may not see much of each other, as I expect to be very busy.'

After that, Charlotte was silent, and soon, with a rather chilly nod, she too took her leave. Alone at the table, Mary felt a growing sense of apprehension. This time there could be no mistaking Charlotte's displeased tone – nor, Mary feared, the source of her irritation. She resented the time Mary spent in the library with Mr Collins. The word 'jealous' sought to make itself heard in Mary's mind, but she would not allow it to do so. It was such a ridiculous idea, so foolish and so fantastical that Charlotte could not seriously entertain it. It was hard to imagine two people less likely to be guilty of any impropriety than Mr Collins and herself. She was not the kind of woman to whom men made themselves agreeable; and he was hardly the man to attempt it.

Once her anger had subsided, Charlotte would surely see the truth of this. A little cool consideration must persuade her of the injustice of her suspicions. Mary had always thought of Charlotte as the calmest and least emotional of beings; and her feelings for her husband did not seem passionate enough to have overwhelmed her capacity for rational judgement. Her indignation could not last. Charlotte would soon be her usual self once more, dry, measured and collected, able to laugh at an idea that was really too preposterous to imagine. Mary would say nothing about it at all. Not a hint, not a word of anything untoward had ever passed between herself and Mr Collins. This was the truth. She would not dignify any other supposition by even attempting a denial; and indeed, resolved to think of it no further.

In search of distraction, she wandered into the library, took out pen and paper, and prepared to practise her Greek letters. She pulled out the little dictionary, and hesitated for a moment before opening its pages – what if Charlotte should see and ask her where she got it? But this was ridiculous. She had done nothing wrong and would not be made to feel a guilt she did not deserve. She leaned the book against another and began to write, speaking the names of letters very quietly under her breath.

CHAPTER FORTY-ONE

B y the end of the day, Mary had covered sheet after sheet in Greek script. Her eyes ached as she took off her glasses and rubbed them. She decided to carry her work upstairs and review what she had done. It would be interesting to see if her most recent efforts showed any improvement on her early scribbles. In her bedroom, she spread the pages over her dressing table, lit two candles, and was examining them closely when Mrs Hill came in. At first, she busied herself with a little tidying and folding; but soon she came and stood beside Mary, peering curiously at the papers.

'What is this? I haven't seen writing like this before.'

'It is Greek, Mrs Hill, as it was spoken in ancient times, the language of great philosophers and poets.'

'Is this what Mr Collins is teaching you? How to speak and write Greek?'

'Yes, he has been kind enough to instruct me when he has the time.'

Mrs Hill stood up and looked directly at Mary.

'He seems to find the time, doesn't he? You're in the library together most afternoons.'

'It is only for a few hours a day. It does not call him away from his other duties, and I have little enough else with which to occupy myself.'

'He sees more of you than he does of Mrs Collins. They don't study together, do they?'

Mary felt alarm mount in her; her mouth grew dry and her heart began to beat faster.

'That is because she has no taste for this kind of learning. It does not interest her.'

Mary sat down heavily on the bed. Mrs Hill, seeing her distress, hurried to her side.

'I did not mean to upset you. Really, I did not.'

'Has Mrs Collins spoken to you about this? Has she made any mention of it?'

'Lord, no! She is a close woman and gives little away. She would never speak to me on such a subject. And listen, Miss Mary, you mustn't imagine I believe you've done anything wrong. I know that isn't in your nature. But you don't understand yet how the world works. People put two and two together and make five. Sometimes just the look of a thing can be enough to cause trouble.'

Mary sat very still, dumbstruck with shame.

'I had to warn you,' went on Mrs Hill. 'I care for you too much to keep quiet. Something had to be said.'

Mary nodded. When it was clear she did not intend to reply, Mrs Hill left the room, closing the door quietly behind her. Once she was gone, Mary buried her face in the pillows. How could she have been so stupid? Because she knew there was nothing wrong in those scholarly afternoons, she had not considered how they might look to others. She had enjoyed them so much she had allowed her pleasure to overwhelm her judgement. Had she learned nothing at all from her experience with John Sparrow? She had sworn then she would never again allow herself to act so thoughtlessly; yet here she was, making the same mistake again. She was a fool, an ignorant, blundering fool, too heedless or too wilful to have imagined the consequences of her behaviour.

She lay back on her old bed and thought of Charlotte. If Mrs Hill had noticed the time Mr Collins spent in her company, and the pleasure he seemed to derive from it, Mary had no doubt his wife had seen it too. Charlotte's anger at the dinner table was not a sudden explosion of resentment, provoked by the pride Mr Collins had so tactlessly displayed as Mary recited the Greek alphabet. It had been simmering away for some time, stoked up by the hours Mary spent with her husband, by the satisfied expressions on their innocent, uncomprehending faces as they emerged from the library after a profitable afternoon's study. If Mary had not thought it possible to be feel jealousy over a man one did not love, she knew better now.

It took her most of the night to decide what to do. A braver woman might have gone to Charlotte and tried to explain the truth of the matter, insisting that their behaviour had been utterly misunderstood. But Mary knew she could not do this. Speaking directly of it to Charlotte gave the situation a significance it did not deserve; and Mary suspected she would not acquit herself well under Charlotte's accusing stare. She would stumble and bluster, and in her confusion, might imply a guilt she did not deserve. Charlotte would be merciless, and Mary was not equal to combatting her scorn. She was rather afraid of the person Charlotte had become and was certain such an encounter would not end well.

But something must be done; and Mary soon understood what was required. The Greek lessons must be given up, and she could spend no more time alone in Mr Collins's company.

As she lay in the darkness, she knew this was the correct decision, the only possible choice; but when she contemplated what it would mean, it was a bitter prospect. Yet again, she was to surrender her own enjoyments in order to gratify the perceptions of others. She had obediently dismissed John Sparrow when told propriety demanded it. Now she was about to relinquish all the satisfaction her new studies had begun to afford her, in order to avoid any suggestion of an intimacy she had not encouraged, did not feel, and was certain did not in fact exist.

Dutifully, she asked herself, as she had done many times during her sleepless night, if she was deceiving herself, searching her heart for the smallest hint she hoped for anything more than friendship from Mr Collins. As always, she found nothing, no evidence of any suppressed tender sentiments. No, the feelings that Longbourn had provoked in her were of a very different kind. When she walked through the well-tended rooms, when she watched Charlotte busy in the vegetable garden and, above all, when she saw her take young William in her arms and kiss his downy head – there was an emotion that coursed through her with such power that she thought everyone must notice it. But it was not love for Mr Collins. It was a sense of deep, angry longing – a longing for the life that might have been hers if things had turned out otherwise, a longing to be settled, to have a home she could call her own, a secure place in the world. But she was increasingly persuaded this would never happen now, that she would always be a guest in the lives of others, compelled to shape herself to whatever was required of her by those on whom she depended.

It was, however, true that her opinion of Mr Collins had changed during their time in the library. She had grown used to his company, and had been surprised to discover that his most irritating traits were far less in evidence when he was not seeking to impress an audience. He had been a patient instructor, and his open appreciation of her understanding had been very gratifying – no one had ever praised her before with such unfeigned enthusiasm. Mary almost laughed in the dark as she considered that she felt more warmly disposed towards him now than she had ever done when she had hoped to make herself his wife. He was an altogether more sympathetic figure than he had appeared then, not least because she knew that he was unhappy, and that aroused her pity. But that was the limit of her affections. There was nothing more between them than the friendship of like-minded scholars. What must happen next therefore seemed unfair to them both, but she knew it must be done, and quickly, before her spirits failed her.

In the event, Mr Collins was engaged with business until after tea; and it was not until late afternoon that she opened the door to the library and found him already at his desk, pen and paper in front of him.

'Come, Miss Bennet, this will not do. We have verbs to decline and cases to learn.'

She sat down, unable to meet his smile.

'I am afraid, Mr Collins, that I do not think we can continue with the lessons. I think it is no longer fitting that we spend so much time together.'

He was so surprised that it was a moment before he spoke.

'Miss Bennet, whatever can you mean? There can be no suggestion of any wrongdoing. My character as a clergyman of the Church of England should be enough to dispel any such suspicion. And I always keep the door a little ajar, as you have seen.'

'I understand that, sir. And I am hardly the kind of woman to make a man forget what he owes to himself and his family. But I am no longer comfortable to go on as we have. We know we have nothing to reproach ourselves with, but appearances, it seems, are against us.'

His face fell.

'Has there been talk? Gossip? Has it reached ... other ears?'

'No,' declared Mary, with more assurance than she felt. 'These are my concerns alone.'

She hoped this would bring the conversation to an end, and began to rise to go, but to her surprise, he stood up and spoke in an unexpectedly measured tone.

'Please stay a moment, Miss Bennet. I beg you will hear me out before you go. I will not attempt to argue with you. If it is your conviction that the lessons must end, then I cannot quarrel with you. Your delicacy does you credit. I admit I see no wrong in them myself. But I am not a courageous man, and although I might say now I wish them to continue, I know myself well enough to suspect that I would not have the resolve to maintain that opinion if I found it seriously challenged.'

Mary took her seat again. There was nothing to be heard but the steady tick of her father's clock on the mantelpiece.

'But I cannot allow our time together to end without telling you how very much I have enjoyed it. You have an excellent mind for a woman, and it has been my pleasure to instruct you.'

She tried to speak, but he held out his hand to stop her.

'More than that, your company has been enjoyable to me in every possible way. To have someone to talk to, who appears to find interest in my conversation, who does not disdain or ignore me – that has been a new sensation, one, I regret to say, which has not often been vouchsafed me.'

He walked to the window and stood staring out at the rooks in the trees.

'I have always known I did not possess a talent for making friends. My father, you know, was a bitter and disappointed man. There were many things that made him angry, but chief amongst them, I fear, was myself. He made it plain enough I was the worst of the many vicissitudes life had inflicted on him. He told me often enough I was worthless, and I soon learned to take myself at his valuation. Then he died, and I thought it within my power to change my life forever.'

Mary was astonished at the unexpected turn of his conversation. She sensed these were confessions he had not volunteered to anyone before, and did not rush away, as she had intended. He had been kind to her, and she owed him her honest attention.

'So what did you do, sir?'

'I went up to the university. I was ordained. I thought once I went into the world, I could turn myself into someone different, easy and obliging; but it did not work. Other men seemed to have the knack of it, but I could not see how it was done. I was stiff and odd and awkward. No matter how hard I tried, I always struck – and, I suspect, still continue to strike – the wrong note.'

Mary looked down, embarrassed.

'I longed to be what I saw others were, charming and always ready with a pleasing remark. For a while, I thought that I could learn what came naturally to others. I imagined that if I acquired the appearance of confidence, the reality would follow. It never did, of course. And yet I worked so hard at it! Do you remember your father asking me once at dinner if I made up in advance the compliments I then thought were so pleasing to ladies? I was such a fool that I told him the truth. Of course I did. How else would they occur to a man such as myself?'

It had begun to grow darker in the room as dusk came on. Outside, Mary heard the cattle pass down the lane to their evening milking.

'I consoled myself with imagining how different life would be when I inherited Longbourn. Then I should have a fine house and a fine wife, for I never doubted the prospect of one would produce the other. And now I have both, and I find myself no less solitary than I was when I had neither.'

He sighed but did not turn round.

'There is my William, of course. My hope is that as he grows older I may have more success with him than has been my lot with everyone else, and that he may come to like me a little. That prospect has sustained me in some of my most unhappy moments. Otherwise, I thought myself resigned. I expected nothing more.'

Suddenly, he turned away from the window and looked directly at Mary.

'But then you arrived, and we began our lessons. I did not think much of it at first. But you were clever and eager, and I liked that. I was easy in your presence; I found myself happy when we were together.'

'Oh, sir, please don't say any more, it makes me so sad.'

'Our minds are congenial, our tastes are similar. I began to

think how different my life might have been if I had been less
foolish when I first arrived here looking for a wife. I did
not understand then what makes a marriage work. I did not
see what was right before my eyes. If I had not been so
thoughtless or so hasty, I might have chosen someone who, in
time, could perhaps have learned to love me. I might have
chosen you.'

Mary could not speak. Two emotions rose up in her, with
such power that she closed her eyes, waiting for them to abate
a little so that she could control herself again. The first was
pity. It moved her very much to see Mr Collins expose his
secret self to her, to confess his loneliness and despair. She was
no stranger to such sensations, and they provoked in her the
strongest response of fellow feeling. But at the same time, she
found herself consumed with rage, with a fury so intense that
she wanted to hammer her fists at him, to shout and scream.
*Why were you so blind? Why didn't you see me, when I did
all I could to make you notice? Why did you not understand that of all of them I was the only one, the only one,
who might have suited you? Why didn't you ask me? Then I
would be here and settled and secure and content – and
we would have lived better together than you do now, because
I would have been more grateful, kinder than she is* – but she
took a few deep breaths and looked up, certain of what had to
be said.

'I am very touched, Mr Collins, by your words. You speak
so warmly that I cannot fail to be moved. Like you, I have
not been used to much affection and, for those reasons, will
always think fondly of what you have said. But I think you
understand as well as I do that nothing can come of it.'

She picked up the little Greek dictionary and held it in her hand as she spoke.

'I too have greatly enjoyed our lessons and have found much pleasure in your company. But I beg you, sir, not to let that enjoyment run away with you. I think you see me in far too rosy a light. I fear my main attraction is one of variety. I am like a twist of salt and pepper, a new flavour in a habit of life that has become very familiar to you. I'm sure that once you grew accustomed to me, my shortcomings and irritations would become only too apparent.'

Mr Collins tried to interrupt, but Mary did not allow it.

'It makes me very miserable to see you so sad. But in truth I think you have the prospect of happiness within your grasp if you choose to reach for it. I have no doubt Charlotte has the capacity to become the wife you want, the companion you say you long for. She is steady and generous and good-hearted and I'm sure she yearns for affection just as you do. May I suggest you talk to her as you have talked to me over the last few weeks? And then I am sure you will not fail in what you hope for.'

Suddenly her voice shook.

'I have said all I can say – I am sorry, but now I really must go.'

She left the room hurriedly, and Mr Collins did not attempt to stop her. Once she had gone, he sat for a while at the window, before closing the shutters against the darkening evening.

On the far side of the garden, Charlotte sat on a small bench which offered a clear view into the library. From there, she had watched her husband and Mary engage in such animated conversation that neither noticed her dim presence as dusk enveloped her. For a while, she stared at the ground, motionless, until it grew too cold to remain. Only then did she return to the house, gathering her shawl around her shoulders, her step as determined as the expression on her face.

CHAPTER FORTY-TWO

Mary took great pains to avoid Mr Collins after their conversation, hoping it would not be apparent to anyone but herself that she was doing so. She sensed he was doing the same; when they passed on the stairs, he could not meet her eye, but bowed his head and turned away. At the dinner table, he was cordial but distant, confining his conversation to polite enquiries about how Miss Bennet had spent her day. To Mary's surprise, it was Charlotte who was now most vocal, chatting away about young William's doings, filling the silences that might otherwise have loomed with embarrassing significance between them. She never referred to the sudden discontinuance of the lessons in the library; indeed, she seemed to have recovered all the affability and warmth with which she had greeted Mary at her arrival. At first, Mary was puzzled – she did not entirely understand the change in Charlotte's manner – but she decided to follow her lead and respond with equal cheerfulness. Perhaps, she thought, the storm had passed, and things could return to the way they were. She ardently wished this might be so; and sometimes, as she watched the Collinses together, she allowed herself to believe her hopes were justified. Certainly, Charlotte seemed far more engaged with her husband. She smiled at him more often, listened to his conversation with more interest, and even touched his hand occasionally as they sat at the table. From beneath lowered eyelids, Mary watched Mr Collins's expression change from surprise to gratitude, tentative feelings of pleasure visible on his face whenever Charlotte offered him some mark of affection. Some of the anxiety which had tormented Mary since Mrs Hill's warning began to disperse, and she allowed herself to hope the worst was over.

One afternoon soon after, she met Charlotte in the hall tying on her apron, a pair of gardening gloves in her basket and a large notebook in her hand.

'I'm afraid, Mary, you will be left to your own devices until supper. Mr Collins and I will be in the garden for as long as the weather holds. I have been considering the new arbour and am resolved to make it as elegant and inviting as possible. I have even drawn up some plans. What do you think?'

She opened the notebook and passed it to Mary, who turned over the pages gravely.

'I think it looks charming. It will be a great addition to Longbourn.'

'Yes, we think so. I have always felt the want of one before. Fortunately, Mr Collins finds my ideas exactly to his taste. He says they have given him a new enthusiasm for the work, which I must say does not surprise me. I never think it is a good idea to leave important matters entirely in the hands of husbands. Even the best of them can be led astray. Sometimes they need guidance to see clearly what is the best solution to any little difficulties they may have encountered.'

She put on her hat and tied it under her chin.

'But then, which of us can say we haven't sometimes lost sight of what is required of us? I'm sure I have been as guilty of it as Mr Collins.'

She pulled on the gardening gloves, brisk and workman-like.

'The arbour might be considered a standing affront in that respect, a monument to our dilatoriness, if you like. But all that's behind us now. In future, we shall combine our forces, work together to make it a thing of beauty. The fresh air will do us both good. If you choose, please feel free to spend your time in the library. I think you will have it to yourself from now on.'

With a final bright smile, Charlotte walked into the sunlit garden. Mary stood in the hall, watching her go, before making her way to the library. There, she took up her Aristotle, but could not settle. The silence, which had once seemed a natural accompaniment to study, now made her feel lonely and restless. She missed the easy exchange of opinions, the sound of another voice. With no like-minded companion to encourage her, the Greek alphabet no longer brought her the pleasure it had once done. It gave no satisfaction to pronounce it when there was no one to correct her. She struggled on for an hour or so, and then wandered over to the window. In the distance, she saw Mr and Mrs Collins at work on the arbour. He leaned on his spade, while she marked out on the ground the plans she had drawn up. They seemed happy. Mary sat there for some time, staring at them as the library clock ticked away.

CHAPTER FORTY-THREE

A few nights later at dinner, Mr Collins announced that they were soon to expect a visitor. 'We are to be honoured with the presence of my erstwhile patroness, Lady Catherine de Bourgh. She is travelling to Derbyshire next week and has expressed a desire to break her journey here for a few hours, to see for herself how my dear Charlotte and I go on in our new home.'

'We are delighted at her condescension,' murmured Charlotte, not catching her husband's eye.

'Indeed we are. The only misfortune – a very grave one, in my opinion – is that I cannot be here myself to greet her. The bishop has called a meeting of his clergy on that day, and though I have begged him to release me from the obligation, his lordship is implacable. But I have written to her ladyship, explaining the unfortunate circumstance, and she has graciously indicated her willingness to be entertained by Mrs Collins alone on this occasion.'

He smiled at Charlotte, who reached across the cloth and took his hand.

'I have no doubt that you will acquit yourself admirably, my dear. As, I am sure, will you, Miss Bennet. Lady Catherine does not stand on ceremony and you can expect the privilege of being introduced to her.'

Mary smiled politely, with a confidence she did not feel.

She had heard a great deal from Lizzy about Lady Catherine and suspected her famous condescension would not be extended to plain, unmarried girls like herself. It would be best, she thought, to attract as little attention as possible, to do or say nothing at all that might provoke either Lady Catherine's interest or disdain, for the first, she was sure, must in her case invariably lead to the latter. Next morning, as the house was readied to receive its grand visitor, Mary had ample opportunity to practise the art of disappearance. Charlotte did not invite her to assist in the preparations, and Mary did not force her presence upon her. She was uncertain what to make of Charlotte's shifting mood, sometimes cheerful, sometimes chilly and correct. It seemed easier simply to absent herself whenever she could, and she spent much of her time seeking out places where she should not be in the way. She was walking through the garden towards the orchard when she came upon Mr Collins approaching from the other direction, to the discomfiture of them both.

'Miss Bennet, I do beg your pardon. Believe me, it was not my intention to come upon you unawares.'

'Oh, no, sir, it is my fault entirely. It is your garden, after all.'

His face softened. She sought to walk on as quickly as she could, but before she could do so, he addressed her.

'I do not wish to add to your embarrassment, but please allow me to say a word to you. I am conscious my behaviour in the library last week was not as it should have been, and I have long hoped to find a moment when I might seek your forgiveness. I am sorry if I caused you pain – although I cannot apologise for telling you how much I have enjoyed your company, for that was the truth.'

'That is kind of you to say, sir, but –'

'No, please don't think I intend to repeat any other observations which escaped me that afternoon. All I wish is to
thank you for the advice you so wisely offered me as you left.
It was of inestimable benefit. I have already begun to act upon
it, with, I venture to hope, encouraging results. I will always
be grateful to you, for both your delicacy and your perception. I shall not trouble you further.'

With that, he bowed and walked quickly away. Mary did
not see him again until she watched from her bedroom
window as his horse was brought round, and he rode off to
his appointment with the bishop. Shortly afterwards, a grand
and well-appointed carriage rolled up the drive. Mary
straightened her dress and went downstairs, as prepared as
she supposed she would ever be to meet Lady Catherine de
Bourgh.

She waited in the drawing room, keen not to usurp Charlotte's privilege of standing on the steps to greet her
guest. Soon Lady Catherine swept into the room, tall, imperious, clad in the most beautiful silks Mary had ever seen. She
seated herself in the best chair, from which she surveyed
everything around her with an unblinking stare.

'I must congratulate you, Mrs Collins, on the improvements you have made to this room since I saw it last. It has
elegance without presumption, comfort without any unsuitable pretensions to fashion. You may tell Mr Collins it has my
entire approval, with the exception, I am afraid, of the curtains at those south-facing windows. The sun will fade the
chintz. You must replace them with something lighter.'

'Thank you, ma'am, for such sound advice. Before I bring
in some refreshments, may I be permitted to introduce to you

Miss Mary Bennet, who is staying with us here? She lived here at Longbourn with her family before Mr Collins and I arrived.'

Lady Catherine looked long and hard at Mary.

'You are a sister of the present Mrs Darcy? You do not much resemble her.'

'No, ma'am, I have heard that said before. I am very pleased to make your acquaintance. Elizabeth has often spoken to me of you.'

Lady Catherine frowned.

'Has she indeed! I should be glad to hear it was in polite and respectful terms. She has a most particular way of expressing herself. As you clearly do not share her looks, it is to be hoped you have also failed to inherit the pertness of her manners.'

'I have never heard Mrs Darcy speak of you with anything but the greatest consideration.'

Lady Catherine declined to say more upon the vexed subject of Mrs Darcy. Tea was brought in, and she was persuaded to accept a small slice of cake. When both had been compared to their disadvantage with what was to be had at Rosings, and Charlotte duly instructed to find both a better grocer and a more skilled cook, Lady Catherine turned her attention back to Mary.

'What is the purpose of your visit, Miss Bennet? How long do you intend to stay?'

'Miss Bennet is welcome to stay with us for as long as she wishes,' said Charlotte smoothly. 'There will always be a place for her in what was once her home.'

'And I suppose it might still be so now, if it had not been for that unfortunate entail. I wonder your father did not find a way to have it broken. A clever lawyer can manage anything, if given the right encouragement. It is a very hard fate for your mother and sisters to be left so sadly unprovided for.'

'It is not quite as bleak as that, ma'am. All my sisters are married now, and both Mrs Bingley and Mrs Darcy have offered my mother a comfortable home.'

'Yes, your two eldest sisters married very advantageously. And that despite the scandal of the youngest one's elopement. That was cleverly hushed up, was it not? Where does she live now?'

'Mrs Wickham is at Newcastle with her husband's regiment. My other sister, Catherine, married a clergyman in Derbyshire.'

'How very convenient for her to be so near the others. So that just leaves you?'

Charlotte reached out to fill Lady Catherine's teacup.

'Yes, Lady Catherine. Mary is the only Bennet daughter as yet unmarried.'

'And what do you propose to do about that, Miss Bennet? Your looks are against you, and I understand your father had almost nothing to leave you. No portion and no beauty will not make you a very enticing prospect for most young men.'

'Forgive me, ma'am, but I think you underestimate Miss Bennet,' declared Charlotte in her sweetest tone. 'She has many excellent qualities of which your ladyship may not be aware. She is too modest to say so herself, but she is without doubt the most accomplished young lady in the neighbourhood. She plays the piano very well and is an excellent scholar. She is well read in every subject, from history to philosophy and theology. She has lately begun to study Greek.'

'Greek!' exclaimed Lady Catherine. 'Surely not! That is a

most unsuitable pursuit for a young lady. Had I been consulted, I should certainly have advised against it. The classics are rightly considered the exclusive preserve of gentlemen.'

At last, Mary found her voice, and sought to rescue herself from the forbidding impression created by Charlotte's unstinting praise.

'Mrs Collins is far too generous in her estimation of my abilities. It is true I am of a bookish turn of mind, and I enjoy the time I spend at the piano, but I fear my enjoyment of both far outruns what I am capable of achieving.'

'Your lack of pride does you great credit, Miss Bennet, and marks you out as a very different character to your elder sister.'

'Indeed,' continued Charlotte, 'Mary has been a most accommodating guest, always willing to fall in with the wishes of others and never putting herself forward. It only makes it more unfortunate that she has as yet no permanent home where she could be appreciated as she deserves.'

Shocked, Mary turned towards Charlotte, who, busy with the tea things, did not return her look. Lady Catherine, taking another slice of the despised cake, noticed nothing at all.

'I cannot imagine you would be welcomed into the household at Pemberley. I doubt they have any desire to admit another into the tight little circle they have established there. And I don't imagine you wish to settle in too close a proximity to your mother. Your two younger sisters, for different reasons, offer no solution. You find yourself in difficult circumstances, Miss Bennet.'

'I am grateful to your ladyship for your consideration, but I have not decided what I will do next. I do not as yet feel as concerned for my prospects as you do.'

'You are not overburdened with choices,' continued Lady Catherine, as if Mary had not spoken, 'but there is one situation for which you seem to me admirably suited. Mrs Collins may not have told you that I am particularly interested in assisting young ladies with the talents and capacity to become governesses.'

Charlotte inclined her head slightly but said nothing. Mary felt fear rise in her.

'I always say,' continued Lady Catherine, 'that nothing is to be done in education without steady and regular instruction, and nobody but a governess can supply it. It is wonderful how many families I have been the means of supplying in that way.'

'But I don't want to become a governess,' protested Mary weakly. 'I do not think I am at all suited to it. I know I would dislike it extremely.'

'I have just placed four nieces of Mrs Jenkinson, all unmarried and likely to stay so, in the most delightful situations. Only the other day I recommended another young person, who was merely accidentally mentioned to me, and the family are quite delighted with her.'

'Really, ma'am, I do beg you not to think of me in that way. My inclination does not lie in that direction at all.'

'Mrs Collins, did I tell you of Lady Metcalfe's calling yesterday to thank me? She finds Miss Pope a treasure. "Lady Catherine," she said, "you have given me such a treasure." I think, Miss Bennet, that you have it within yourself to become exactly such a treasure as Miss Pope.'

'Forgive me for contradicting you, ma'am, but I fear that is not the case. I cannot say too often it is not a life I should want for myself.'

For a moment, Lady Catherine regarded Mary with incomprehension.

'But come, Miss Bennet, what do you propose instead? You are a plain woman with no money, inclined to be clever. We have already established marriage is unlikely for you. Do you wish to remain a burden on your friends and family for the rest of your life? No, depend upon it, governessing is the answer. Once you have considered it, you will see I am right. Mrs Collins, I am most grateful to you for introducing Miss Bennet to me. It will be my pleasure to find her a place and to do so with the utmost despatch. Once a decision has been made in these matters, it does not do to delay.'

For the rest of her stay, Lady Catherine was almost gracious, wholly satisfied by the prospect of meddling in the life of a woman powerless to resist her. She was in the highest spirits as she took her leave.

'I thank you, Mrs Collins, for a most enjoyable and, may I say, productive afternoon. Miss Bennet, I shall write to you as soon as I have news, which will not, I think, be long in coming. No, do not thank me now, wait until you are properly settled before conveying your gratitude to me.'

CHAPTER FORTY-FOUR

Mary did not accompany Charlotte to the door to see Lady Catherine depart. She crumbled the remains of a piece of cake between her fingers, growing increasingly uneasy as she waited for Charlotte to return.

'I thought that went very well,' declared Charlotte, as she bustled back into the room. 'Lady Catherine seemed very taken with you. I really do believe she will exert herself to find a suitable situation for you.'

For the first time since she had been at Longbourn, Mary raised her voice.

'But she is offering me something I do not want, which I am sure would make me unhappy! Charlotte, you cannot imagine I want to become a governess? Why ever did you put the thought into her mind?'

Charlotte felt the side of the teapot and decided it was just warm enough to risk another cup. She offered one to Mary, who shook her head.

'If I did, it was quite unintended. But once it was mentioned, I cannot deny I saw its advantages. You have always been proud of your accomplishments and worked hard to perfect them. Why should they not serve to recommend you now?'

'Because they are being used to usher me into a life I would hate! I do not wish to live in some other person's house, dependent on their goodwill and with not a moment to call my own.'

Charlotte sipped her tea.

'No, I see it is not without its difficulties. But – and I feel I must be blunt, Mary – your situation at present is in many ways not so different. You have no settled home. Neither of the possibilities offered by Jane or Lizzy is to your liking. I understand your reluctance, but it leaves you few other choices. Kitty has no room, and Lydia – well, that is plainly out of the question. So where will you go? Of course, you are welcome to stay with us as our guest – but I think we both understand that cannot be a lasting solution.'

She wiped her hands on her napkin and began to fold it neatly on the plate.

'In such circumstances, I think you must ask yourself whether it would not be desirable to have some occupation, at least until you decide on some other course of action. I must warn you that once Lady Catherine has an idea in her head, it is very difficult to resist her. So if you have some other notion in mind, I would urge you to act upon it as soon as you can.'

Mary's face was hot with humiliation. She put her head in her hands to hide her misery. To her surprise, Charlotte pulled her chair towards her, and laid her arm gently on her shoulder.

'I know it looks as though I am determined to cause you pain, but I assure you that is not the case. I tried once before to make you see the world as it is. I know it took you a while to accept my advice; and I know you felt I had betrayed you by seizing an opportunity you had just begun to appreciate, that I had opened your eyes to a possibility only to snatch it away for myself. I tried my best to explain.'

She looked into Mary's eyes with the greatest earnestness.

'I told you then that despite all the sympathy I felt for you, I had no choice but to put my own interests first, that sometimes women like us are obliged to be selfish. And now I find I am obliged to be selfish again. I see only too plainly that you are in a difficult place, and I am sorry for it; but I cannot allow you to disrupt our life here.'

She removed her arm, sat back and sighed.

'In some respects, I will admit this – interlude, shall we call it? – has actually been of service to me. It made me look again at my own behaviour. I knew when I married that I was not in love. I told you that I was never romantic. But I see now that I might have been more kind. You have shown me that I have it in my power to make our lives together more pleasant than they have been, which I think will benefit me quite as much as Mr Collins. He would like to be better friends with me if I would permit it; and I think we shall both go on more happily if I do. For this, Mary, I must thank you. It was not a consequence you intended to bring about, but I am grateful to you nonetheless.'

Charlotte picked up her teacup and sipped her tea delicately.

'But I'm afraid there is far more chance of our achieving that contentment if you are not here. There, I have done you the honour of being candid. So here is the last piece of advice I will ever offer you. Make a decision and make it a bold one. Perhaps it may be to start a new life as a governess; perhaps not. But I urge you to find some way of beginning again, to put yourself amongst fresh scenes and different people. Imagine a new future for yourself. Only then, I think, will you have any chance of escaping your past.'

Mary wiped her eyes. Charlotte's frankness had been refreshing in its way. It forced her to think rationally, to gain control of her emotions.

'Thank you, Charlotte. I will go away and consider what you've said.'

'I have probably said far too much. But I assure you it was meant kindly.'

CHAPTER FORTY-FIVE

Mary did not think she could endure dinner that night. Instead, she sat alone in her room, trying to decide what to do. It was clearly impossible for her to remain at Longbourn. Charlotte had been honest, but she was also implacable. But where was she to go? Pemberley was out of the question, and her courage failed her when she imagined returning to the Bingleys', subjected once more to the complaints of her mother, and Caroline Bingley's torments. No, she did not think she could bear it. But who else could she ask? It was not until the following morning that a new possibility occurred to her.

Perhaps the Gardiners might take her? Her uncle and aunt were without doubt the most generous of her relations. Mr Gardiner was everything his sister Mrs Bennet was not, open-hearted and cheerful, without pretense or affectation. His wife was equally kind and sensible. Their residing in London had meant Mary had not seen them herself for some years, but she had heard much from Jane and Elizabeth of the consideration which they had extended to both sisters when they had been troubled and needed to escape the confines of Longbourn. Mr and Mrs Gardiner had happily offered them refuge in their home when it had been most needed; perhaps they would be prepared to accept Mary on similar terms?

The more she considered this possibility, the more hopeful she became. After Mr Bennet's death, Mary had received from Mrs Gardiner a letter of condolence in which her sincere regret at Mary's loss and her frank appreciation of the difficulties of her situation had touched her very much. It had concluded with an invitation to visit them whenever she wished. Mrs Gardiner understood that, as Mary had not been much in London, the prospect of staying with them there might seem a very formidable step; but she was to understand that their house at Gracechurch Street was always to be thought of as a second home to her, if she wished to join them there.

It was quickly plain to Mary that the Gardiners were her best and indeed only hope. She did not find it easy to write the letter proposing herself as a guest to them; but the prospect of another encounter with Lady Catherine overcame any shrinking sense of delicacy that might once have troubled her. She knew she must get away before that lady ushered her firmly into a schoolroom, ignoring all her protests and delightedly closing the door behind her. Mary did not know what might become of her in London, but she was pleased to discover that she had courage enough to prefer an uncertain future to one she knew would make her unhappy.

By the end of the week, she had her answer, and it was just as she had hoped. Mrs Gardiner replied they would be delighted to see her and that she should come as soon as she found it convenient. They would give her a room at the back of the house, where the noise of the City was least likely to trouble her; and if she could contrive to get herself on the coach from Meryton, Mr Gardiner would be happy to meet her at Charing Cross.

Charlotte received Mary's news with equanimity. She offered no comment on her decision, other than offering to write to Lady Catherine, explaining that family circumstances had called Mary away from Hertfordshire, making it impossible for her to take up her ladyship's kind offer to find her a situation. Indeed, now she was certain Mary was leaving, much of Charlotte's old warmth returned. She made sure Mary's clothes were properly packed, helped her gather up her books, lent her the money to pay the coach fare, and even included a pot of her lavender-scented floor polish as a gift for Mrs Gardiner. Mrs Hill was far more distressed to see her go.

'I should hate to think the conversation we had a while ago was the reason for your leaving. I never intended to make trouble for you.'

'No, Mrs Hill, none of this is your fault. If it is anyone's, it is mine. There were things I did not see clearly, and your words made me more aware of the risk I ran.'

'You should not take all the blame upon yourself. Excuse me if I say I think Mr Collins might have acted more carefully.'

'I think both of us were in error,' said Mary sadly. 'I was foolish. I thought I had found a friend, someone with whom to share my interests, who seemed to enjoy instructing me. It never occurred to me that any other construction might be put upon the time we spent together. I am not the sort of woman that men fall in love with.'

'You think too little of yourself. It makes me sad to hear it.'

'Well then, I will say no more. But I am glad to see that Mr and Mrs Collins seem far more contented with each other than used to be the case.'

Through the window, the couple were just visible in the

garden, occupied as ever around the little arbour. Charlotte stood, plans in hand, while her husband positioned a sapling. William ran round them, laughing and shouting at the top of his voice.

Mrs Hill suddenly seized Mary's hands and held them tightly.

'One day I shall see you come back here as a married woman. I'm sure of it. It is what you deserve. And when it happens, I shall drink to your health, with the greatest joy.'

Mary leaned over and kissed her cheek.

'Shall we ask Mr Hill to come up and take down my bags?'

A short while later, Mary stood on the front steps, watching as her possessions were loaded onto the coach. Soon she was ready to go. All the family were assembled to see her off. William gave her a sticky kiss; Charlotte pecked her cheek and urged her to write as soon as she reached London; and Mr Collins made his usual bow. He had said very little to her since she announced her intention of leaving. She supposed he felt a little ashamed now of the intimacy they had shared in the library. But he held out his hand to help her into the carriage, and once she was settled, without a word he placed a small parcel on the seat beside her, before returning to stand alongside his wife and child.

All three waved as the carriage pulled away. Mary waved back, gazing back at the house as it receded slowly into the distance. As she watched the figures of Mr and Mrs Collins grow smaller and smaller, it struck her that Charlotte's new attitude to her husband in many ways resembled her ambitions for Longbourn itself. She had acquired both as unimproved properties. There were exterior elements that did not please, but she was astute enough to appreciate that the basic structures of both were sound. A woman of vision and patience might shape something of value from such raw materials; and although the result might never aspire to the heights of fashion, or display a thousand graceful details, it could be made solid and dependable, offering comfort and security to those satisfied with such unobtrusive virtues. Charlotte dearly loved a project, and Mary had no doubt she would succeed as admirably with Mr Collins as she had done with Longbourn.

The coach was well onto the Meryton road before Mary remembered the little package. She undid it carefully, peeling back the wrappings before revealing the little Greek dictionary. A small slip of paper poked out from between its pages. On it was a line of writing in Mr Collins's hand. She had to slip on her glasses before she saw that it was in Greek. It took a few minutes and recourse to the dictionary before she was certain she understood what it said. But she recognised the quotation. It was one they had often discussed together.

'*Our happiness depends on ourselves.*'

She took off her glasses and leaned her cheek against the cold window. She had been determined not to cry when she arrived at Longbourn, and would not give in to tears now she was leaving. She took the slip of paper, placed it carefully in the dictionary, and put both safely in her bag. The carriage rolled on through the countryside as she tried not to think of what might lie in front of her. Tomorrow she would be in London, and Longbourn would seem very far away.

PART THREE

CHAPTER FORTY-SIX

It was dark when Mary arrived at Gracechurch Street. The coach had been full, the journey long and tedious. Mary was exhausted as she was ushered into the Gardiners' dining room, convinced she could not manage supper. But the lively greetings of her four small nephews and nieces cheered her; and the genuine affection with which her uncle shook her hand and her aunt embraced her buoyed up her spirits. To her own surprise, she found herself able to consume a surprising amount of toasted cheese before gratefully climbing the stairs to bed.

Mrs Gardiner had been as good as her word and given Mary a room at the back of the house. It was indeed quieter than those at the front, but Mary's countrified ears were nevertheless aware of a distant bustle of human activity taking place just out of earshot. As she finally drifted off to sleep, she could be in no doubt that she was really in London now. She had asked for this opportunity and it had been granted her. She must do all she could to be worthy of it.

The Gardiners' house was built of yellow London bricks, and rose, tall and thin behind black railings, with a dark green door and high windows on each floor. It stood on Gracechurch Street, while a longer stroll delivered the walker into the very heart of Cheapside. Mary had long ago heard her uncle declare that these were the two finest shopping streets in

London, possibly in all of Europe; and anything that could be desired, from the homeliest necessity to the grandest indulgence, was to be had in one or the other of them, if the customer had the money to pay for it. As they sat at breakfast and Mary sipped her coffee, Mr Gardiner proudly repeated this boast. Mary suspected it was a favourite theme of his, but his wife gave no sign she had heard it before. She smiled as her husband continued, describing in ever greater detail the range of goods which could be purchased, the luxury of the establishments that sold them, and the ingenuity of the merchants who supplied them. Mr Gardiner's little quirks and habits do not vex and annoy her, observed Mary; they provoke her indulgence, not her anger.

'Well, Mary,' declared Mrs Gardiner, as she folded her napkin and placed it on her plate. 'You have heard so much talk of these wonders that you must long to see them for yourself. You were a mere child when we last took you amongst them.'

'I remember a great toy shop,' said Mary wistfully. 'A vast palace of dolls, as I recall.'

'Ah, yes, that would be Dunnett's,' replied Mr Gardiner, 'a place with which our children are very well acquainted.'

As soon as the magical name was uttered, a loud clamour arose at the younger end of the table, with four voices begging to know if they were to be taken there today, for they surely deserved it, as they had been so very good. Leaving her husband to adjudicate on the rights and wrongs of their case, Mrs Gardiner pulled her chair away from her children and towards Mary, the better to make herself heard.

'Mr Gardiner is quite right,' she said. 'The City shops truly

are one of the great sights of the town. Shall we go this morning and take a look?'

Mary readily agreed; and an hour later, she found herself
hurrying in Mrs Gardiner's wake as her aunt launched herself
into the crowds thronging Gracechurch Street. Some shoppers
marched briskly forward with a clear purpose, their minds set
on a particular purchase; but by far the greater number
seemed happy to saunter about, moving idly from one shop to
another, lingering to peer into their well-stocked windows. As
she dawdled behind her aunt, Mary found herself joining
them, transfixed by the sheer number and variety of the goods
on show. In little more than a few paces, she was enticed by
displays of stockings, hats, fur tippets, fine shoes, watches and
even ironmongery – how Charlotte Collins would have
enjoyed half an hour amongst those grates and firebacks,
thought Mary, almost fondly. At the door of every shop,
smartly dressed young men invited customers politely to step
in, it was impossible to show all they had in the window, there
were even finer things to be seen inside.

Mary thought she had never seen so many people. It was
amazing that they did not trip over each other; and yet everyone seemed to know exactly where to move so as not to
collide with each other. Gradually, she began to fall into their
pace – it was rather like a dance, which made sense once the
steps had been mastered – and the bustle and busyness, which
had at first intimidated her, began to feel invigorating. She had
just begun to enjoy herself when Mrs Gardiner came abruptly
to a halt before an especially magnificent frontage.

'There,' she declared proudly. 'What do you think of that?'

It was at least ten years since Mary had last stood before
the premises of Edward Gardiner & Sons, purveyors of fine

household linens. It had seemed imposing even then, with its many floors and grand, pillared entrance. Now it was much smarter than Mary remembered, with an elegant frontage which had not been there before, and striped awnings extended over the pavement to protect customers from the rain. Behind one of the large glass windows, plain linens in every shade, from milky cream to sturdy brown, hung in great wide lengths. A second window was full of patterned jacquards, arranged from deepest red to palest pink. A printed notice begged to inform customers that all requirements could be catered for, from the most elaborate damasks to the hardest-wearing calicos – even stuffs not presently on show might be obtained if requested. Mrs Gardiner stood, slowly contemplating the building floor by floor, from roof to basement, as if she had never seen it before. Finally, she turned to Mary with an expression in which pride and satisfaction were equally combined.

'Even though I say it myself, it does look very smart.'

Mary followed her aunt's appreciative gaze, taking in the size of the shop, the quality of the materials it sold, and its general air of prosperity. These well-appointed premises, she thought, made possible the solid, polished comfort of the Gracechurch Street house, the gilt mirrors above every fireplace, the many portraits of the Gardiners that decorated its walls, capturing them singly, together, and as a happy family group, master and mistress of their small domestic empire, their children frolicking around them. This was the business that underwrote the matching china on which breakfast, tea, and dinner were served, the cutlery with their initials engraved upon it, the rich rugs on the floors, and the Chinese wallpaper in the drawing room. The unassuming fabrics laid out before

Mary in rolls, lengths, and bales made possible the commodious beds, the best mattress Mary had ever slept upon, the heavy linen sheets, and the silk quilts. The unobtrusive well-being that marked every aspect of the Gardiners' lives had its origins here. The warehouses paid for it all.

'I've seldom seen a finer place,' Mary finally replied. 'You must be very proud.'

'I am indeed,' answered Mrs Gardiner simply. 'When we began, we lived right next to the shop, you know. It has not always been easy. But for the moment, at least, I feel our efforts have been rewarded.'

'You think of yourself and Mr Gardiner as partners in the enterprise, then?'

'Of course. We women are barred, by custom and a thousand other petty considerations, from attempting such an undertaking alone. But I flatter myself that Mr Gardiner could not have succeeded as he has without my help. He has often told me that my judgement in matters of taste, quality, and prices has been of the utmost use to him.'

The shopman standing at the door suddenly recognised Mrs Gardiner and made her a deep and very respectful bow. She acknowledged him with equal solemnity, then paused for a moment, as if considering her reply.

'So yes, like all the best businesses – and, I might say, the best marriages too – Mr Gardiner and I are indeed a partnership.'

No one, Mary reflected, could have described her own parents' union in such a way. The recollection was painful to her; and to avoid dwelling upon it further, she asked whether they might perhaps go inside the shop and look around. Mrs Gardiner thought not at present. They must make their way home, for the children's lessons must be begun before midday. But she should be very glad to take Mary on another occasion.

'And of course,' she added teasingly, 'when you have a house of your own to furnish, I shall be glad to show you the very best linens you can possibly require. We shall roam the warehouses together. It will be my pleasure.'

Mary could produce no answering smile; but Mrs Gardiner seemed not to notice.

'In the meantime, however, there are plenty of beautiful things more suited to your present circumstances. There are some lovely printed cottons to be had this year. And some of the prettiest silks I've seen in a long time, ideal for a young girl like yourself.'

Suddenly conscious of her well-worn coat and much-washed dress, Mary gathered both around her a little more tightly.

'I'm not sure I'm suited to finery. I think I'm better with something plain and unassuming.'

'Perhaps,' said Mrs Gardiner. 'But good things don't need to be showy or gaudy, you know. Sometimes the very best stuff can seem quite plain, until one examines it closely. It is only then that one sees its true quality.'

Their eyes met. Mrs Gardiner's expression gave nothing away. If she had intended a meaning deeper than what was said, she gave no hint of it. 'But just as you wish. Let's not talk of it now. Shall we fight our way back home?'

She held out her arm. Mary could not remember when anyone had sought to walk with her in such a friendly manner, and hesitated. But Mrs Gardiner did not withdraw her invitation, and Mary shyly linked her arm with her aunt's. To begin with, it seemed strange; but Mary soon grew accustomed to it and began to feel how pleasant it was to stroll along in such easy intimacy. Her opinion of Mrs Gardiner grew warmer with every step. She had often heard Jane and Lizzy sing her praises; and although she had spent only a morning with her, Mary knew for certain now that they had not exaggerated her virtues. Mrs Gardiner was lively and kind, with a quick mind, and a frank curiosity about the concerns of those for whom she cared. She was inquisitive; but she was not meddlesome. She employed her intelligence to understand what others thought and felt, the better to help them if she could. She wanted those around her to be happy; entirely satisfied with her own circumstances, it pleased her to see those she loved as contented and comfortable as she was herself. By the time they arrived back at Gracechurch Street, Mary thought she had never met anyone whom it was so easy to like. There seemed no reason not to surrender herself to the full force of her aunt's appeal; and although she was usually cautious in all matters relating to the affections, in this case she felt more confident. She was already certain that Mrs Gardiner was to be trusted, and even allowed herself to hope she might become the friend Mary so desperately yearned for.

CHAPTER FORTY-SEVEN

Family life at Gracechurch Street was very different from what Mary had known at Longbourn. She had not been there long before it was plain that Mrs Gardiner loved her husband and four children with a strong, steady devotion. Her feelings were fully returned, and neither she nor Mr Gardiner saw any reason not to express them as openly as possible. At Gracechurch Street, there was affection enough for everyone. With something of a pang, Mary saw that her aunt and uncle had no favourites amongst their children, but loved them all equally. They rarely scolded either their two lively daughters or their two cheerful sons, preferring that they should be a little more jolly and bouncing and a little less disciplined and silent than absolute correctness required. As a consequence, there was, in the Gardiner household, a great deal of capering and frisking and jumping about, which made it rather too boisterous for very refined spirits; but for anyone in need of a little tenderness, it was a singularly welcoming haven. The longer Mary spent in its soothing surroundings, the more she understood why both Jane and Elizabeth had been so restored there.

For while Mrs Gardiner cared deeply about the well-being of her nieces, she understood that when dealing with young women it was not always wise to demonstrate concern too plainly. It was nearly twenty years since she had left off being a young woman herself, but she had not forgotten how tiresome it was to be constantly poked and prodded with questions. She deduced that something had happened to upset Mary at Longbourn, but did not seek immediately to discover what it was. Instead, she fed her, encouraged her to sleep late in the morning, and generally enveloped her in all the unobtrusive attention of which she was capable. At first, Mary was too dazed to appreciate it, but gradually, she understood with what care she was being treated; and after she had been at Gracechurch Street about a week, she attempted to thank Mrs Gardiner for it.

As her gratitude was all she had to offer, Mary was keen to convey it with as much feeling as possible. She composed a little speech in her head, but it was not easy to find the right moment to deliver it. Finally, one morning after breakfast, when their nurse had taken the children away to be washed and dressed, she seized her opportunity.

'I wanted to say how very grateful I am for all the kindness you have shown me,' she began. 'I am all the more sensible of your generosity, for, although I invited myself into your house, you have welcomed me with the most open arms imaginable. It is often said that offering hospitality to strangers is one of the noblest virtues, but there are few who practise it with as much sincerity as you and Mr Gardiner.'

'Well, you can hardly be accounted a stranger,' replied Mrs Gardiner. She was somewhat distracted, occupied in gathering up her children's books from the floor, where they had been strewn by their owners before they were carried off to be made decent.

'And I shouldn't want you to feel too heavy a sense of obligation,' she continued, stacking the little volumes into a pile on the sofa. 'We are very glad to have you here. Your sisters were free to stay with us for as long as they wished, and we are happy to extend the same invitation to you.'

'I only hope there is some way in which I can repay your kindness,' Mary replied. 'I know I am not as amusing as Lizzy nor as useful as Jane, but there must be something I could do to assist you.'

Abruptly, Mrs Gardiner stopped what she was doing and looked up from her sorting.

'Mary, I do hate to hear you speak in that way. It makes me so very sad. We would not have asked you to remain here if we did not find your presence agreeable. I hope you understand that?'

'I'm sorry,' Mary faltered. 'It is only that – I did not want to presume . . .'

'You are the least presuming person I know,' declared her aunt, as she placed the books alongside the others on the sofa. 'And please, let us hear no more disobliging criticisms of your own character. The only condition I shall apply to your staying with us is that you try to speak more kindly of yourself. It that a rule you think you can obey?'

Mary bit her lip. She could not imagine anything more pleasing than to spend more time in this welcoming house where she had begun to feel herself at home.

'I – I will certainly try.'

These few hesitant words hardly did justice to the strength of her feelings, but before she could say more, the pile of books her aunt had so carefully balanced on the sofa slid slowly but unstoppably back onto the floor. Mrs Gardiner watched them fall with a resigned smile.

'Then you are welcome to stay as long as you wish – or for

as long as you can bear it. As you can see, it is a regular Liberty Hall here, and we don't stand on ceremony; but if you don't mind that, I think you'll do well enough. We shall be delighted to have you amongst us.'

Mary's heart was too full to speak. Instead, she joined her aunt on the carpet and began to pick up her nephews' and nieces' books.

CHAPTER FORTY-EIGHT

At first, Mary found it hard to accept the truth of her good fortune. She could not quite credit that she would not be obliged to take up her pen again and write to her mother or the Bingleys, cowed and defeated, asking for permission to slink back to Derbyshire. But now she knew she was to stay with the Gardiners, she was determined to do as her aunt had requested, and no longer speak so slightingly of herself. Indeed, she would attempt to go further. She would do all she could to enter into the spirit of their household, to behave with as much good humour as the Gardiners did themselves. If she had been invited to join their family, it was only right she should not dampen their pleasures with sad looks and awkward silences. She would endeavour to make herself worthy of their generosity by entering as fully as she could into the Gracechurch Street life.

She began by offering to instruct her young nieces on the piano. Mrs Gardiner hesitated, asking if she understood what this would involve. She was sad to say that neither of the girls showed any evidence of talent. Would Mary not rather spend the time playing for own amusement? But Mary would not be deterred, assuring her that she really wished to help; and in the end, her aunt capitulated.

'If you are determined to sacrifice yourself, I will not stand in your way. Both Marianne and Jane should practise far more often than they do. If you could spare a few hours to keep them at their scales, I should be very glad of it.'

The following morning, and every subsequent day at eleven o'clock, Mary found herself sitting beside her young cousins at the piano, beating time for them and correcting their finger positions. At first, both she and the little girls were shy; but they were sunny, friendly creatures, and their reserve was soon forgotten. By their third lesson, they were chattering away freely, with every appearance of pleasure. Against all her expectations, Mary too found herself enjoying the lessons, especially as her pupils began to show a marked improvement in their performance. Perhaps Lady Catherine had been right and she would have made a good governess after all?

She even began to look forward to family dinners. These were very different from the ordeals she had endured at Long-bourn; at Mr Gardiner's table, there was no teasing and no snubbing. He liked meals to be as pleasurable as everything else in life. The better she came to know him, the harder Mary found it to believe he was her mother's brother. He was so sensible, so gentlemanly and so affable that it was impossible to credit they were such near relations. He did not stand on his dignity and was often to be found on the carpet playing with his children, holding them in his arms and tousling their hair. They were not afraid of him, and chattered away in his presence without the slightest restraint. One night, as he shook his two noisy sons off his lap and attempted to finish his dinner, he caught Mary's eye.

'No one could say these children are seen and not heard.'

'All the better for them, I should say. They always look very happy.'

'I hope so. I hate to see children crushed and silenced by

too much correction. Home should be a pleasant, laughing sort of a place, I always think. What do you say, George? Edward, what is your opinion?'

The boys merely nodded their agreement, their minds already on another game. Mary glanced up to see Mrs Gardiner looking over the candles at her husband and sons; Mr Gardiner caught his wife's eye and smiled back. It was the briefest gesture, but it seemed to Mary to contain within it all the depth of their feelings for each other. It was strange, she thought, but the Gardiners' mutual affection did not make her feel more alone, as she had at Pemberley, where the intensity of the Darcys' passion had left her painfully conscious of her own exclusion. At Gracechurch Street, the pleasure her uncle and aunt took in each other was felt to advantage by all around them. Mary had no doubt her nephews and nieces felt it and benefited from it. She even began to sense its effects herself.

Little by little, her frozen feelings began to thaw, and as they did so, she raised her head and began to look around, curious to discover more of what lay beyond the Gardiners' house. At first, she contented herself with short strolls to the end of the street. But soon she craved to go further afield. The City crowds no longer intimidated her as they had once done, and she soon thought herself ready to brave longer journeys. Mrs Gardiner would not allow this until they had trod the pavements together often enough for her to be assured that Mary had mastered enough of the neighbourhood's complicated geography to be allowed out alone. Finally, she allowed it, but only when Mary swore to follow all her advice – 'do not stray too far away, speak to no one, and if you feel uneasy, find a respectable woman and ask for her protection'. With these words ringing in her ears, in a short while Mary was soon familiar with all the most interesting streets in the vicinity. Soon it was her habit to put on her hat and walk from Gracechurch Street to Cheapside and beyond, with no other object but to enjoy the atmosphere of each new place she discovered. She would never have believed she would come to take so much pleasure from losing herself in the city's crowds. There was a freedom, she concluded, in being one amongst so many, in knowing you might never again see the people who passed you so closely with such uninterested eyes. You could be anyone – no one knew who your family was, or where you came from. It could not be more different from Meryton, where your name and history were common knowledge, and your past would always define you. Here, no one cared. It was a thought that gave her a little twinge of fear, but also of excitement.

CHAPTER FORTY-NINE

One spring afternoon, when she returned from a walk, Mrs Gardiner called Mary to join her in the drawing room. When Mary entered, she found her aunt sitting on the sofa with a preoccupied air. This was unusual, for she was rarely disconcerted; and as Mary sat down opposite her, she began to fear Mrs Gardiner must have some difficult message to deliver. They chatted for a while about what Mary had seen on her outing; but eventually Mrs Gardiner began upon what was clearly the point of their conversation.

'Since you joined us, we have lived very quietly, but that is about to change. We always become more sociable as spring approaches. It's our custom to give some little dinners and other small entertainments, simple gatherings for friends and relations whose company we enjoy.'

Mary's heart began to beat faster. She was certain now that something difficult was about to be said. Perhaps if she could imagine what it might be, if she were to speak first, she could save her aunt the embarrassment of having to raise the delicate subject herself.

'Nothing extravagant, all very domestic,' continued Mrs Gardiner. 'But there will be rather more social life in the house than you've been used to.'

'I hope you will not feel any obligation to include me,' said

Mary quickly. 'I will be happy to stay upstairs with the children. I have my books – I will be quite content, I assure you.'

Mrs Gardiner looked at her with genuine surprise.

'Can you really suppose,' she asked, 'that we would arrange a pleasant dinner for family and friends, and send you off into exile upstairs?'

'I would understand if you did,' replied Mary. 'I do not sparkle much at dinners, I'm afraid.'

'Perhaps that says more about the dinners you have so far attended than it does about you,' declared Mrs Gardiner. 'And anyway, in our house, no one is obliged to sparkle. Which, I find, makes it far more likely that they might. So, you will join us, I hope?'

Mary knew this was not the moment to confess that the prospect of a London dinner filled her with apprehension, but nonetheless she hesitated.

'Come, Mary, do me this favour. You might even enjoy yourself.'

Mrs Gardiner would never have hinted that she thought her niece was obliged to accept; but Mary had no doubt that she was. When she considered all the kindnesses, great and small, which had been showered upon her since her arrival at Gracechurch Street, she knew she must welcome the invitation with the simple graciousness with which it had been made.

'Thank you,' she replied. 'I should be very glad to join you. And I will try my very best not to disappoint you.'

'I know that will not happen,' said her aunt, reaching for the bell and ringing for tea. After it had been brought in, she returned to the task at hand.

'You misunderstood my meaning earlier, but you were

right in perceiving I had something of importance to ask you.'

Mary replaced her cup in its saucer and put it carefully on the table. She had no idea what might be coming.

'If you are to become a social being,' announced Mrs Gardiner, 'we must dress you properly for the part. We must buy you some new clothes.'

'New clothes?' asked Mary. 'I don't think I understand.'

Her aunt put down her own cup and surveyed Mary with the wary patience of one who does not expect to carry her point without a great deal of effort.

'You are a sensible girl, so I will be candid with you. What you wear now might be suitable for quiet days in the country but will not do for evenings in town. We must smarten you up a little, my dear.'

Mary flushed. It appeared that even in Gracechurch Street, she was never to escape the vexed and humiliating subject of her appearance. Mrs Gardiner reached across the table, holding out her hand to reassure her.

'I know this is not an easy subject to discuss, but let me tell you how I consider such things. I see plainly enough that you don't like to make a fuss about dress – that you dislike having attention drawn to you. But there are times when the best way to ensure you are not remarkable is to conform to the expectations of those around you. You are a rational being. You must see that if we are to go into society, it makes sense to obey at least some of its rules.'

'Yes,' said Mary. 'I made such an argument to myself once, a while ago.'

'Then why, may I ask, did you abandon such excellent reasoning?'

'I lost the heart for it. I was persuaded to buy a new dress, and the first time I wore it, I behaved very badly to someone who deserved better. I decided I did not deserve to wear nice clothes if I could not trust myself to act properly in them.'

This was not the reply Mrs Gardiner had expected; and she was so surprised that she almost laughed.

'Lord, Mary, if that rule were to be applied universally, not a woman in London would be decently dressed!'

But Mary did not return her amused smile; and Mrs Gardiner, perceiving her obvious unhappiness, understood this was a hurt that ran very deep.

'I'm sorry. I did not mean to make light of whatever it was that happened. But I beg you to consider whether your response to it was justified. Because you were unhappy once when wearing a pretty dress – it was pretty, I hope?'

'Handsome rather than pretty,' murmured Mary. 'But I liked it.'

'I'm glad to hear it. But it makes no sense to assume that every time you wear something becoming, the outcome will be the same. On the contrary, as you have obviously reflected very seriously upon your actions, it seems most unlikely you will repeat them.'

Mary clasped her hands round her knees, considering. It was hard to dispute her aunt's logic. She could not deny that when spoken aloud, her reasoning did not sound very sensible. There was a knock on the door as the maid arrived to clear away the tea things; but Mrs Gardiner, clearly keen to carry on the conversation, shook her head and the maid slipped quietly away. Mrs Gardiner topped up their cups with what remained in the pot.

'It is a little stewed,' she said as she handed it to Mary. 'But I prefer it strong, myself.'

She leaned forward across the little table that sat between them and addressed her in a low but steady voice.

'I realise this is a delicate matter,' she said, 'but I am determined to persevere. I know you've always been told a woman's worth can be measured only by her beauty, by the way she presents herself to the world. But please believe me when I say there is a middle way between an obsession with one's appearance and an absolute denial of its importance. I do not consider myself a vain woman, but I admit it pleases me to be smartly turned out. And I would like you to feel the same.'

Mary surveyed her aunt, taking in the trim figure she presented as she sat on the sofa. Mrs Gardiner was not a beauty; but, as Mary was compelled to admit, this made little difference to the favourable impression she made. Her clothes became her; they were admirably chosen to suit her person and her situation, and in them, she looked exactly as she should, smart and yet completely at her ease. And her aunt achieved it with none of the fuss or effort with which it had been pursued at Longbourn. Staring down at her own familiar cotton dress, she began to feel impatient. Her resolution to stay hidden behind such dull and unremarkable garments began to waver. Perhaps Mrs Gardiner was right. Perhaps the time had come to discard them and begin again.

'I am not suggesting anything elaborate,' Mrs Gardiner went on. 'We could begin with three or four day dresses and two for evenings. A new coat, perhaps, and certainly several hats. A straw hat or two. Some silk stockings rather than cotton. And we might also visit Mr Dolland and find you a more pleasing pair of glasses.'

At a stroke, the fragile image that had begun to take shape in Mary's mind of herself transformed by a few choice garments was shattered. As Mrs Gardiner listed everything she would need to enter city life with confidence, Mary knew it could not happen. Even if she convinced herself she was worthy of buying new things, even if she accepted she was not condemned forever to hide herself beneath clothes that neither flattered nor pleased her – even then she could not do as her aunt wished. She could not possibly afford it.

'I understand what you say,' Mary began, choosing her words with care. 'And I admit my misgivings must look foolish when exposed to the scrutiny of common sense.'

'I am glad to catch a glimpse of the old, rational Mary at last,' said Mrs Gardiner. 'I confess I had begun to wonder where she had gone.'

'But even if I am persuaded by what you say,' Mary continued, 'I'm afraid it won't make any difference. I have no money, aunt, with which to pay for new things.'

'But I do,' declared Mrs Gardiner. 'And I should be delighted to buy them for you. It would be my pleasure!'

Mary shook her head.

'I cannot think of that. I am already indebted to you in so many ways and cannot bear to add to my obligations.'

'I am not sure there is such a thing as obligation between those who truly care for each other.'

'You are very kind. But I cannot accept.'

Mrs Gardiner stood up and smoothed down her dress.

'I thought you might say that; and while I don't agree it is necessary, I understand your reluctance. But there is another who would like to help you, whose assistance I feel you might accept with no such embarrassment.'

Mary was amazed. She begged her aunt to tell her who this person was and how they knew of her circumstances. But Mrs Gardiner brushed away all her enquiries and instead calmly rang the bell for the servant.

'We have sat here long enough. Sarah can come in now and clear the trays.'

She held out her hand to Mary in invitation.

'I know you have been out already, but I feel the need for some air. Have you yet discovered the pretty garden at Finsbury Circus? No? Then that is where we'll go. We can speak there quite freely.'

CHAPTER FIFTY

As Mary and Mrs Gardiner stepped out of the front door, Mary had a thousand questions; but her aunt was adamant she would not answer them until they reached the park. With some effort on Mary's part, they spoke of other things as they walked up Gracechurch Street, and into the maze of streets beyond; and it was only when they were seated on a small bench in an enclosed green space beneath some very fine trees that Mrs Gardiner was ready to explain.

'I must tell you that I have been in correspondence with Lizzy since you first arrived to stay with us.'

Mary kicked at the gravel of the path with the toe of her boot.

'About me?'

'Yes. She was concerned when she heard you'd left Longbourn so suddenly. It was not what you had planned. She thought perhaps something had happened there to upset you.'

Mrs Gardiner paused expectantly, but Mary stared fixedly at two pigeons contending for a crust of stale bread. She could not bear to discuss with anyone, even her aunt, what had driven her to leave her old home.

'Anyway,' went on Mrs Gardiner, seeing that Mary was not to be drawn out. 'She wanted to know how you did, and I was happy to tell her I thought you were settling down very well.'

'That was kind of her.'

'Indeed. But her letters were so frequent that I began to wonder whether there was something more to them than merely solicitude. It struck me there was perhaps the faintest hint of guilt about them. As if she thought she had done you some wrong and wished to be assured you were not suffering for it.'

Mary leapt up from the bench, alarming the pigeons. They flew off in a flutter of wings, leaving the crust on the ground.

'These are not matters I find easy to discuss.'

'I have no wish to pry,' replied Mrs Gardiner mildly. 'Come, do sit down. I shan't press you to say more.'

Mary seemed not to have heard her. Preoccupied, she walked over to the patch of ground the pigeons had abandoned.

'It is true Lizzy once caused me a great deal of pain. It was some time ago, before our father died. It affected me very deeply, but I did not imagine she had thought much of it since.'

'I think we can safely say that she does think of it,' replied Mrs Gardiner. 'Indeed, it explains a great deal.'

Again, she indicated the empty place beside her; this time Mary sat down.

'Lizzy often asked me if there was anything she could do to make your situation with us any easier. When she posed the question for the third time I told her the truth – that you were in need of outfits suitable for London, and that I suspected you would not accept them from our hands. I'm sure you won't be surprised to hear she has generously offered to pay for them herself.'

'I cannot take her money.'

'Then let me attempt to protect you from your own good intentions,' urged Mrs Gardiner softly. 'Lizzy is rich enough not to notice ten times the amount she intends to give you. And it would please her very much to think she had been the means of making you happy.'

'So I am to be embarrassed in order to make Lizzy feel better?' cried Mary, angry now.

'As I do not know what occurred between you, it is difficult for me to say. But unless she has done you some unforgiveable wrong, I cannot agree it is shameful to accept a gift from a sister who, for whatever reason, wishes to make you happy.'

Mrs Gardiner opened her bag and took out a letter.

'She has written you a little note, which I am to give you, to make her case directly.'

She passed the letter to Mary, who pulled out her spectacles and opened it.

My dear Mary,

The fact you are reading this is proof that you have done exactly as I predicted and have refused my present. It is entirely to your credit that your delicacy makes it hard to accept; but I hope you will change your mind. It would please me very much if you would allow me to be generous to you. I should like to make some small amends for a moment when I know I was unkind. I think we both know what I mean. I don't flatter myself that this gift excuses my behaviour, but I hope you will consider it as an apology – and indulge me accordingly.

E

Mary held the letter in her hands, not knowing what to think. It touched her very deeply to know Lizzy was aware of the pain Mary had suffered that night at Netherfield, and acknowledged the part she had played in inflicting it. It moved her even more to discover Lizzy regretted her actions, even to the extent of seeking a kind of forgiveness from her. But for all that, she was still not sure it obliged her to accept Lizzy's money. She looked sombre as she folded the letter and took off her spectacles. Her aunt looked at her expectantly.

'I understand that Lizzy means well,' Mary began. 'But it is a hard thing to accept charity, even from a sister. Not only because it reminds me of my own dependence, but also because of what it implies about how I am perceived. Does everyone think I look so very dowdy? Is my appearance so odd, so very much in need of improvement, that it is considered a subject for discussion throughout the whole family?'

Her voice shook a little. She was afraid she might exasperate her aunt, but Mrs Gardiner did not seem angry.

'As you clearly wish to hear the truth rather than some easy platitudes, I shall answer as honestly as I can. It is pitching it a little high to say you look odd; but nothing in the way you carry yourself suggests you set much store by your own value. I am very far from suggesting a woman is to be judged solely by how she dresses. There are some amongst us who pay no attention at all to what they wear and do so with a cheerful nonchalance. But that is not the case with you. Your appearance does not suggest a blithe indifference but an acute awareness of your choices. You dress as you do because you do not believe you deserve anything better; and in doing so, you communicate that low opinion of yourself to everyone who sees you. If you were to embrace a few improvements, I believe it would signify something more than merely a desire to look a little smarter. I think it would suggest a willingness to allow yourself the self-respect you deserve, and which you have been reluctant for so long to grant yourself.'

Mrs Gardiner did not seem to expect a reply, and Mary did not offer one. After a while, her aunt resumed the conversation in her usual cheerful tone.

'I think I've said quite enough for now. But I have one small task to perform before we leave.'

She pulled her bag towards her once more and withdrew from it a muslin-wrapped bundle, which she undid to reveal several large pieces of stale bread. With some gusto, she threw them towards the grass, watching with pleasure as a crowd of pigeons descended from the trees and eagerly pecked away at them.

'I always bring them something when I come,' she remarked, brushing the crumbs from her dress. 'I like to think they know me. Well – shall we go home? I shan't press you any further about the clothes. If your conscience is too tender to accept Lizzy's gift, let us leave it alone. But please think a little about what I've said before you decide.'

She held out her arm, and Mary took it. They walked back to Gracechurch Street, both very thoughtful but saying little on the way.

CHAPTER FIFTY-ONE

When they arrived back at the house, Mary went straight to her bedroom. She lay on her bed thinking until it was almost time to go down for dinner, when she roused herself and made her way to the wardrobe. Wrapped in tissue paper at the back was the gold and cream dress. She took it out and draped it on the back of a chair, where it shone palely in the gathering dusk. She lit two candles and placed them by the large mirror, then stood in front of it, staring at her reflection, examining her hair and her figure. She held the dress up before her, and even in the darkening room, she could see how it flattered her. Suddenly inspired, she struggled out of her faded brown printed cotton, and threw the gold gown over her head. She could not manage the ties at the back without help, so she left them undone. She threw back her shoulders, as she had seen Lizzy do, straightened her back and held her head up high. She forced her features into a different expression, less abject, more assured. She could hardly believe the improvement it made – for an instant, she was a different person altogether.

Mary sat down at the dressing table, her mind racing. She had been struck very forcibly by her aunt's words about self-respect, especially as they resembled so closely those used by Charlotte Lucas at Longbourn. 'It is my situation I dislike, not myself.' Mary knew the same could not be said of her. She had been told so often she was a failure that she had come to believe it. A woman with her disadvantages did not deserve to wear handsome clothes. Nor was she entitled to enjoy the other pleasures that made life worth living – love and affection chief amongst them. From these too she was excluded, and nothing, she had told herself, would change this, or make the slightest difference to her future.

This was how, for as long as she could remember, she had been accustomed to think; but Mrs Gardiner's cool reasoning had somehow robbed this familiar dark vision of much of its power. For the first time in years, Mary found herself questioning why she had so willingly resigned herself to such a miserable fate. Where was it written that her destiny was fixed? Why should she not, by her own efforts, seek to change it?

She shivered, and knew her tremor indicated something more than the chill of the room. It was shock too – it was the shock of understanding that the gloomy certainties which had sustained her for so long were loosening their grip upon her. She pulled the gaping dress around her to prevent it slipping off her shoulders and put her head in her hands, trying to think. Suddenly, the line which Mr Collins had transcribed for her burst into her mind.

'*Our happiness depends on ourselves.*'

The saying was familiar enough. She had read it many times and had even copied it into her book of extracts. But as it ran through her head, she realised that she had never really absorbed its meaning. It had made no impact on the way she thought of herself. In that respect, her mother's ideas still loomed larger than those of Aristotle. She had been unable to free herself from Mrs Bennet's conviction that happiness arose from drawing the winning tickets in the lottery of life, especially those of a pretty face and a graceful figure.

Then she arrived at Gracechurch Street and everything changed. There she saw what true happiness looked like; and, for the first time in her life, understood what it felt like to be wrapped in its embrace. At Pemberley, she had been an observer, watching the contentment of others from the margins, but in the Gardiners' home, she was included, invited in and immersed in their kindness. For a while, she had allowed herself simply to bask in such an unfamiliar pleasure; but it had not been long before her enquiring mind awoke, and she began to look around Gracechurch Street with a questioning eye, asking how the Gardiners had achieved their happy state. It was only now that she finally grasped how it was done; as she saw, with a flash of comprehension, that Aristotle had a far better idea of how happiness was to be achieved than Mrs Bennet.

The happy contentment which defined life at Gracechurch Street was not the product of beauty, wealth or luck. It was true the Gardiners enjoyed some marks of good fortune – a comfortable income and good health chief amongst them – but none of them was outstandingly handsome, and they possessed no broad acres or rolling parklands. In fact, thought Mary, it might be argued that many of the same advantages from which they benefited had been equally bestowed upon Longbourn – but without producing a comparably happy state. No, she decided, her ideas solidifying in her mind – the difference was that the Gardiners worked hard at the business of happiness, exerting themselves tirelessly to coax it into being. They did not consider happiness a matter of chance or destiny. Instead they did everything in their power to cultivate it, prizing generosity over petulance, preferring kindness to umbrage, and and always encouraging laughter rather than complaint. The result was the happiest home Mary had ever known. If anyone might be said to have made their own happiness, she concluded, it was her uncle and aunt.

She sat up straight, alert and thoughtful. If her uncle and aunt could do it, why should she not follow their example? She might begin by adopting some of the habits of mind that served them so well. None of the Gardiners were ashamed of themselves. Perhaps she could persuade a little of their confidence to attach itself to her? She could try and smile more and frown less, telling herself that not everything she said was dull and awkward. It would not be easy to shift a lifetime's experience of snubs and rejections; but she was sure she was ready to try.

Excited, she walked to the window and pushed up the sash, leaning out into the darkening evening. The lights of the Gracechurch Street shops glowed yellow and the smell of coal smoke hung acrid in the air, but she did not mind. She had never expected she would grow to love London. But its sights and sounds, which had once seemed so overpowering, now seemed exhilarating and full of promise. She could not remember when she had last felt so eager, awake, and ready for something new. She took a deep breath and closed the window. The most important habit to conquer was the habit of misery itself. Nothing was so inimical to happiness as the settled conviction it was not for her. It was a conviction that ran very deep in her; but she knew she must fight to rise above it.

As she passed the mirror, she caught sight of herself, her dress hanging loose at her shoulders, her shawl wrapped untidily around her, her face a little flushed from the night air. She cut a dishevelled figure, she thought, picking up a fold of the glittering gold dress and running it gently through her hands. The delicate silk felt pleasurable to her touch. If she was to open herself up to the possibility of happiness, where better to start than with the purchase of some new clothes? She would write to Lizzy tomorrow, signifying her readiness to accept her kind offer. She would make sure it was a cheerful letter. She would begin as she meant to go on.

CHAPTER FIFTY-TWO

When their carriage pulled up outside a magnificent stuccoed building with a tall, pillared entrance, Mary was convinced the coachman must have mistaken the address.

'Can this be right? It looks more like a palace than a shop.'

Mrs Gardiner gathered together her cloak and gloves, eager to begin.

'That is exactly what you are supposed to think. But I promise you, it is a shop – although a very grand one. Mr Gardiner always says there is nowhere in the world quite like Harding and Howell, and I do not argue with him. If we cannot find what we want here, it is simply not to be had.'

As an established Londoner of some three weeks, Mary imagined that in her walks around Cheapside, she had already encountered the most lavish displays of goods the capital had to offer; but, as she followed her aunt through the shop's great doors, she realised she could not have been more wrong. She had never seen anything like Harding and Howell. In both size and magnificence, it was incomparable. Room after room opened out before her, each with its own distinct offering of beautiful things. Mahogany counters shone in the light that poured in from high windows. At some, gentlemen stood examining cravats; at others, ladies looked closely at stockings.

'We did very well to come so early,' said Mrs Gardiner as they strode past a display of hats. 'If you arrive after eleven, the queues are intolerable.'

When they arrived in the fabric hall, the sight was even more splendid. Every wall was lined with wide shelves reaching up to the ceiling. Upon them, bolts of every kind of cloth were stacked: cottons, poplins, muslins, and lawns. Long swathes of silk hung from tall poles, showing off their colours and patterns to glorious advantage. On a table in the centre of the room were spread out the most beautiful paisley shawls Mary had ever seen. This shimmering palace of fabrics could not be more different from the dark little haberdashers at Meryton.

'It is magnificent, is it not?' whispered Mrs Gardiner as they sat down at one of the broad counters. They were attended to by a very superior assistant, whose immaculate clothes made Mary painfully conscious of the shortcomings of her own. She thought she saw his eyes flicker over her unremarkable outfit; but once reassured by the amount Mrs Gardiner intended to spend, his manner was quickly all consideration and attentiveness.

They began with muslins. Mary could not believe how many were laid before her, all miracles of lightness and delicacy. At first the sheer extent of the choice seemed to make it impossible to decide, for there was always something more to see; but gradually, she found her eye and began to discover what she liked. With growing confidence, she decided first upon a pale spotted pink and then a rich glowing cream. The cottons proved more difficult, for they came in so many colours and patterns; each fresh example seemed as alluring as the one before. Eventually, she fixed upon a yellow and white stripe and a lavender decorated with cream leaves; though, for her final choice, she could not decide between a design of green and gold or one of blue and grey.

As she turned over the samples, Mary could not quite credit how much she found herself enjoying an occupation she would not long ago have dismissed as frivolous. How was this to be explained? Part of it, she thought, was simple. She had closed her ears to her usual scruples and allowed herself to enjoy the physical pleasure of handling such beautiful things, admiring the texture and feel of them.

But she knew she would never have dared attempt it if her mother or Lydia had been there to witness it. They would have laughed at her change of heart. Mrs Bennet would have been scornful, and Lydia could never have resisted the opportunity it offered for a good tease. In London, however, there was no one to judge her. Here, she thought, she might alter everything about herself if she wished to; and if that meant finding satisfaction in handsome cottons, then so be it. Soon she was so absorbed once more in comparing the different patterns that, until he was almost upon them, she did not notice a young man making his way towards their counter, his hand raised in greeting. Mrs Gardiner sprang up, delighted to see him.

'Mr Hayward! Whatever are you doing here?'

'Nothing very particular, I'm afraid,' the young man replied, with a polite bow. 'I left home with the definite intention of buying myself some gloves, but so far, I've done nothing but saunter about.'

Mrs Gardiner laughed.

'Men have so little sense of urgency when it comes to the

business of buying. We, on the other hand, have set ourselves diligently to the task and have already acquired a very respectable number of purchases.'

'You have begun as you mean to go on, then?'

'Indeed we have.' Mrs Gardiner turned to Mary, who looked up a little uncertainly, but did her best to produce a welcoming smile.

'Mr Hayward, may I introduce my niece Miss Mary Bennet? When not leading me astray amongst the muslins, she is staying with us at Gracechurch Street. Mary, this is Mr Thomas Hayward, the son of a cousin of mine, a good friend of all us Gardiners, and a frequent guest in our house.'

Mr Hayward was tall and broad-shouldered, with a shock of dark hair. He was not particularly handsome, but his expression was so affable and amused that by the time this fact was noticed, it was too late for it matter.

'I am proud to be both distant relative and close friend,' he declared, 'for one might be said to have led to the other. Are you up from the country, Miss Bennet?'

Mary made herself speak up clearly, determined to allow no hint of a blush or a mumble.

'Yes, sir, I am quite new to town.'

'And how are you enjoying it?'

'I was a little overwhelmed at first, but the better I get to know it, the more I like it.'

'Exactly the right answer! I am a great advocate for London and hate to hear it criticised. After all, where else could we find ourselves in such a building as this? Where the best that commerce and industry can afford is offered to us, all under one roof?'

His enthusiasm was so open and infectious, his expression so encouraging, that Mary found it easy to reply.

'Yes, sir, I must admit I have never been anywhere like it. They have cottons and silks in every colour of the rainbow, including some so extraordinary I would not know what to call them.'

'Perhaps we should set ourselves to supplying that deficiency,' mused Mr Hayward. 'It is very inconvenient not to be able to ask for exactly what one wants. What do you think of "coromandel" for that fiery shade between red and orange hanging over there? Or "jonquil" for the rather queasy tone of yellow to your left?'

'Now, Tom,' said Mrs Gardiner severely, 'you are not to inflict your whimsy on poor Miss Bennet before she has had a chance to know you. She will not know what to think.'

Unabashed, Mr Hayward drew up a chair and seated himself at the counter beside them.

'You are quite right,' he replied, with a good-natured air which suggested this was not the first time Mrs Gardiner had scolded him in this way. 'I promise to conduct myself hereafter in a manner that will neither surprise nor entertain. I shall be exactly as dull as politeness requires.'

'I am sure there is some happy medium between the two,' observed Mrs Gardiner.

'Then I shall certainly endeavour to find it.' He smiled at her aunt, and Mary saw immediately how fond they were of each other.

'So, Miss Bennet,' he went on, in a more formal voice, 'you are in the very best place to find materials of every kind. The quality here is excellent. May I be allowed to see what you have chosen?'

'Really, sir?' asked Mary, puzzled. 'Do you honestly wish to see what I have been looking at?'

'Indeed, I do,' insisted Mr Hayward. 'I'm reckoned an excellent judge of cottons and muslins. Though not silks. Silks are not my province at all.'

Mary glanced at him to see if he was making game of her; but obediently, she passed him the book of samples she had been examining.

'We cannot decide,' she said, 'between the blue and the green.'

It felt very strange to be discussing such matters with a man she had barely met; but Mr Hayward was not disconcerted. He looked at both swatches closely and felt them between his fingers.

'You should take the green. It will wear better.'

'Now you are teasing me, sir.'

He closed the book, as if all was now decided.

'Well, perhaps a little. But you really should choose the green, on grounds of beauty if not of utility. It is a very handsome pattern. I think it would suit you.'

Mary felt herself begin to blush and looked down once more at the swatches.

'How did you come to know so much about cottons, sir?' she asked. 'Are you in the trade yourself?'

'Oh, no,' he said, laughing a little. 'But I had a very good apprenticeship. With four sisters, all older than me, it was impossible I should not learn something about the intricacies of dress. I grew up surrounded by hems and flounces!'

'An excellent qualification,' remarked her aunt, 'but is it enough for us to take his advice?'

Mary hesitated. She was not sure she wished to be so easily

influenced by a man who was quite unlike anyone she had encountered before.

'I see I may have confused matters by giving my opinion too decisively,' said Mr Hayward soothingly. 'Please let me make amends. May I offer you some tea? There is a refreshment room here with an admirable view of the Park. Miss Bennet can reflect on the contesting virtues of her cottons over a toasted tea cake.'

'In the circumstances,' said Mrs Gardiner, 'I think that is the very least you can do.'

CHAPTER FIFTY-THREE

Mary and her aunt made their excuses to the shop-man, who promised to keep the samples in readi-ness for them until they returned; and, together with Mr Hayward, they made their way through a series of colonnaded rooms until they arrived at a salon, whose tall windows overlooked the trees and lawns of St James's. Once they were settled, with tea and cakes laid out before them, Mrs Gardiner turned to Mr Hayward with an enquiring look.

'So, Tom, are you writing anything just now? It's a while since I've had the pleasure of reading something of yours. Is there a work "on the stocks", as I believe you writers say?'

Mary put down her cup, suddenly alert and interested.

'Are you an author, sir?'

'Indeed he is,' replied Mrs Gardiner. 'He has written sev-eral extremely interesting pieces.'

'Your aunt is very kind,' said Mr Hayward, laying down his slice of fruitcake, 'but I fear "author" is a title I don't really deserve. It suggests far too much. I have contributed a few art-icles to magazines – but as a reviewer of the work of others, rather than producing something original of my own.'

'But that is not to be dismissed,' ventured Mary. 'The work of the critic is essential to the formation of correct taste. And it must be a wonderful thing to support yourself by your pen.'

'Yes, Miss Bennet, I'm sure it is. But I cannot lay claim to such distinction. I am a lawyer, ma'am.'

He poured himself another cup of tea and returned to his fruitcake.

'And a very good one,' added Mrs Gardiner. 'He has finished eating his dinners at the Temple and is now a barrister.'

'Quite a junior one, I am afraid.'

'But not for long, I am sure,' said Mrs Gardiner indulgently. 'We have great hopes for you, Tom.'

'Do you write about legal matters, then?' asked Mary. 'Constitutional questions, perhaps?'

'No, I do not. The law is my profession, but my passion is poetry.'

Mary could hardly believe what she heard. To meet a man who wrote for magazines was surprising enough, but to discover the subject of his pen was poetry was doubly astounding. She was not sure how she imagined such a person might look and sound, but Mr Hayward, with his frank, open manner, dark curly hair, and healthy appetite was not what she would have expected.

'Poetry, sir?'

'Poetry, ma'am. Do you care for it yourself?'

'I cannot say I do. I used to read Young's "Night Thoughts" quite often, but I haven't looked at it for many years.'

'If that gloomy verse was your sole experience of the poetic art, I'm not surprised you gave it up. Have you really read nothing more recent?'

'I'm afraid not, or if I have, I do not remember it.'

For the first time since Mary had met him, Mr Hayward was now wholly serious – serious enough to put down his second piece of cake and throw his napkin onto the table.

'Really, Miss Bennet, this is a sad thing to hear. You cannot remain in this unenlightened state – you must allow me to introduce you to some newer works! If my favourites don't affect you as they do me – don't strike you speechless with admiration – then I promise never to mention them again.'

'Let us not begin upon poetry now,' said Mrs Gardiner, looking warily at Mr Hayward. 'Once we start, we shall never stop. And we still have shopping to do.'

Mr Hayward looked sheepish. 'Yes,' he admitted, 'I tend to bore on the subject if not checked.'

'Oh, no, sir,' said Mary earnestly, 'it is very exciting to hear someone speak with such conviction about things of the mind.'

Mr Hayward's gratified smile encouraged her to go on.

'My ignorance of modern poetry is a great weakness in my reading, and one I should very much like to remedy,' she said hastily, as if to get out what she wished to say before her courage failed her. 'If you were kind enough to make any recommendations, you can be sure I would apply my mind to them very assiduously.'

'I'd be honoured to do so,' said Mr Hayward. 'Although I think, once you begin upon them, you'll see that your mind will take you only so far in appreciating them. They must be read with the heart as well as the head.'

He looked at her steadily. It was Mary who turned away first. Then the waiter arrived at the table to ask if they required anything more; he clearly wished them to take their leave, and Mrs Gardiner began to prepare herself to go.

'It appears we have outstayed our welcome and must be off,' she said. 'We shall return to our silks and cottons, but you and Tom may continue your conversation at our next dinner.

Mr Hayward is one of our regulars, so he will have every opportunity to persuade you to share his enthusiasms when he is next at Gracechurch Street.'

Mr Hayward stood up and bowed again.

'I very much hope so. I shall endeavour to make a poetry lover of you yet, Miss Bennet. And I urge the green and gold stripe upon you, I promise you will not regret it.'

Mary said her farewells and followed her aunt away from the table. When they reached the door, she could not resist glancing back. Mr Hayward was occupied in paying the waiter while an impatient couple quickly claimed possession of their vacated chairs. She turned away hurriedly. She would have been deeply embarrassed if had he seen her looking. She was glad when her aunt took her arm and they began to make their way back to the fabric hall.

'Tom Hayward is a great favourite of mine,' Mrs Gardiner confided as they passed a great display of gentlemen's handkerchiefs. 'He is one of the best-natured men I know – excepting Mr Gardiner, of course. I have known him since he was a boy and cannot recall him saying an unkind word.'

'He was in an excellent humour today,' replied Mary. 'It seemed as though he found everything around him amusing.'

'Yes,' admitted her aunt. 'If Tom has a fault, it is that he is inclined to be whimsical. He gives in too easily to flights of fancy, sometimes to entertain others and sometimes, I think, merely to please himself. I have mentioned it to him before – you will have observed I did so today – but I'm afraid he doesn't attend.'

Suddenly Mrs Gardiner came to a halt, struck by the appearance of a pair of gloves that, from a distance, seemed to be exactly what she had been looking for. But on closer inspection, they revealed themselves to be the wrong shade of yellow, and they walked on, Mrs Gardiner returning once more to the subject of Mr Hayward.

'Tom is naturally of a very lively disposition,' she went on, 'and does love to exercise his wit. It would be a great mistake, however, to imagine that because he is inclined to be jocular, he is incapable of serious feeling. Underneath his light-hearted manner, there is a very thoughtful young man, as steady and sensible as anyone I know.'

'As a lawyer, I should have thought those were essential qualities, if he hoped to rise in his profession.'

'Indeed; and I understand he is very highly regarded at the Inns of Court. Mr Gardiner says that in his professional capacity, Tom is always exacting and precise, quite unlike the easygoing character he chooses to adopt when amongst his friends.'

They had arrived at the counter once more. Chairs were pulled up for them; the shopman retrieved the book of samples they had been studying and placed it with a flourish before them; but Mrs Gardiner was as yet reluctant to relinquish the interesting subject of Mr Hayward and return to the cottons.

'It is a strange thing, Mary, but in my experience, most men like to think of themselves as serious beings. They cultivate a sense of dignity and enjoy being considered grave and severe. But it is quite the opposite with Tom. He prefers to hide his seriousness away. It appears now and then, of course, but he does not care to broadcast it.'

'Perhaps,' suggested Mary, 'spending so much time with lawyers has exhausted his appetite for sobriety. Maybe he fears becoming as pompous as they are if he does not cultivate a livelier turn of mind?'

'I suppose that is possible,' agreed Mrs Gardiner. 'And he comes from quite a numerous family, so he will have been obliged to speak up and tell a joke or two in order to be heard!'

'You mentioned he is a relative of yours?'

'His mother is a cousin of mine, somewhat older than myself. She married Tom's father, as his second wife. They lived happily until his death two years ago. I have not seen her since then, but we still write to each other.'

Mrs Gardiner opened the book of samples, as if to begin upon the cottons once more, but now it was Mary who seemed reluctant to abandon the interesting topic of Mr Hayward.

'So are the sisters Mr Hayward mentioned the daughters of your cousin, or his first wife?'

'They are my cousin's daughters. All of them are married now. Her husband had a son by his first marriage, and he inherited the family estate. As the younger boy, Tom always knew he would have to make his own way in the world. And, to his credit, he has done so with admirable determination and very good grace.'

Mary was silent for a moment, absorbing all she had heard.

'And what about the poetry?' she asked. 'Where does that passion come from?'

'Lord!' exclaimed Mrs Gardiner. 'I really cannot say. That's too deep a question for me to answer. You'll have to ask him yourself.'

She looked at the great clock on the wall.

'And on that note, I think we must leave Tom alone and return to our shopping. Have you made a decision yet?'

Mary glanced quickly at the samples and closed the book, much to the relief of the shopman, who had approached with a questioning air.

'I believe Mr Hayward may have been right about the green,' she said. 'I do believe we should take it.'

Once Mary's dresses were ordered and being made up, Mrs Gardiner turned her mind to Mary's spectacles, carrying her to see Mr Dolland the oculist. There Mary's eyes were examined again and her glasses studied closely.

'The lenses are of excellent workmanship for a country practice,' observed Mr Dolland. 'But I think we may provide you with something a little more tasteful in the way of a frame.'

'They were made for me by a very talented young man,' Mary replied in a low voice. 'I believe he is now studying at one of the hospitals here in London.'

'Where no doubt he will do very well, if this is an example of his capabilities. Now, ma'am, may I beg you to look in this direction?'

Mary peered through pair after pair of spectacles. Once the consultation was over, she chose two handsome examples with delicate silver frames, which Mr Dolland urged upon her.

'Much more suitable to a young face, I feel. Do you want to keep the old ones? I can dispose of them if you wish.'

Mr Dolland held out the glasses on a clean white cloth. Next to the new ones they seemed heavy and perhaps a little clumsy; but Mary's heart contracted a little as she looked at them.

'I should like to keep them, if you please.'

He handed the old spectacles to his assistant, who wrapped them carefully in cotton wool.

Once back in Gracechurch Street, Mary carried the little package to her room and gently unpacked it. She held the spectacles in her hands, thinking of everything that had happened since the day in the Longbourn drawing room when John Sparrow had shyly declared his intention to grind the lenses himself. That world was gone now, its inhabitants scattered and dispersed. It could never be recovered. What was done was done. She raised the spectacles to her lips and kissed them gently before folding them up in the cotton wool. Then she opened her dressing-table drawer and placed them carefully at the very back, next to the little Greek dictionary.

As for Mr Hayward, she did not allow herself to think of him at all. It was only after she had blown out her candle and fallen asleep that he sprang unbidden into her mind. There was nothing she could do to prevent him appearing in her dreams, gazing at her quizzically while holding a book of poetry in one hand and carrying a length of the green and gold cotton in the other.

CHAPTER FIFTY-FOUR

On the night of the Gardiners' first dinner, Mary found herself in the unfamiliar situation of having a choice of new clothes to wear. It did not take her long to decide upon the gown made up from the pale cream muslin she had bought at Harding and Howell, which had turned out just as simple and elegant as she had hoped, with not a flounce or a lace trimming to be seen. Mrs Gardiner's maid put up Mary's hair into a smooth chignon with only the smallest curl attempted at the sides; she refused all other ornaments. As she stood before the mirror, examining the result of her efforts, Mrs Gardiner appeared at her door.

'Ah, that is a great improvement! The colour gives you a little warmth, which helps your complexion. The style looks well on you. Indeed, the whole effect is very pleasing.'

To a beautiful woman accustomed to extravagant compliments, this would not have seemed like much; but its sincerity delighted Mary. She stared at her reflection one last time and decided that she too was satisfied with what she saw. She would not embarrass the Gardiners; dressed as she was, she could take her place amongst their party with as much assurance as anyone else. She was nervous; but the knowledge she would not look an oddity at her first London dinner gave her the courage she needed to face it bravely, and even with a little excited anticipation.

There were twenty guests at the table, and Mary was relieved to find them talkative and lively. They were all city people who knew each other too well to stand on ceremony; and soon the conversation flowed freely, with steadily increasing volume. Once a gathering of this kind would have made Mary painfully aware of her own isolation; but she had been relieved to find herself seated next to Mr Hayward, who soon put her at ease. He introduced her to her neighbours, made sure her wineglass was never empty, and helped her to the oyster patties with which the dinner began. In a low voice, he explained who everyone was, discreetly indicating the wealthy banker, the powerful alderman, the cultivated tea importer, and the wife of London's largest greengrocer. His manner was so genial and his conversation so entertaining that she soon forgot to be self-conscious. When she looked around and took in the splendid dining room, illuminated by more candles than she had ever seen in one place, whose light sparkled against the gilt mirrors and gold picture frames, she did not retreat into herself, calculating how soon it would all be over; but instead gave herself up to enjoying the spectacle, never thinking for a moment that she did not belong there.

When she and Mr Hayward had exhausted the topic of their fellow guests, it was an easy step to begin discussing themselves; and, as the main course was brought in, Mary asked him how he had come to choose the law as his profession. But before he could begin to answer, a fine shoulder of veal was passed in their direction; and it was not until he was satisfied that she had as much of the dish as she wanted that he was ready to reply.

'It is often said we younger sons have only three careers to choose from – the church, the army, or the law. And as I thought myself entirely unsuited to the first two, it was inevitable I should end up in the third.'

'Really, Mr Hayward?' A servant filled her glass with wine. Perhaps it was that which gave her the boldness to continue. 'You do not strike me as the kind of man who decides upon his life's occupation merely because it is – well, I shall not say the lesser of three evils, as that would be disrespectful to the clergy, but I think you know what I mean.'

Mr Hayward looked amused.

'Yes, I cannot deny it. There were many other considerations that propelled me towards the law. As you may have noticed, I enjoy the sound of my own voice, an essential qualification for a barrister.'

'So I have been told,' persisted Mary, 'but I cannot believe that eloquence is the only quality a lawyer requires. It must also demand a good understanding and a great deal of study, the getting of quantities of facts by heart.'

'You speak as if you imagine those things beyond me!'

'Why no, sir. Our acquaintance has been as yet too brief for me to make such a judgement. Shall you have some cheese? I can hand it to you if you wish?'

'Really, Miss Bennet, I am most dreadfully affronted! You seem to suggest I'm incapable of applying myself to weighty subjects. I cannot think of taking any Stilton until I have been allowed to defend my character as a most diligently dull student of the law!'

'You will excuse me if I try some.' Mary took a very small piece of cheese and placed it carefully on one of Mrs Gardiner's best Wedgwood plates.

'I did not mean to imply you were incapable of serious study. On the contrary, I do not imagine you could have achieved your current place in your profession without it. You must have worked long and hard to master its principles. And to me, that suggests you have more fondness for it than you like to admit. I think you chose the law, not because your other choices were so few, or because it allowed you to exercise your skill in argument – but because there was something in it that you enjoyed and wished to pursue.'

Mr Hayward, who had watched her closely as she spoke, now laughed once more.

'A hit,' he exclaimed, 'a palpable hit! You have clearly missed your own vocation, Miss Bennet. You would be a most formidable addition to the Bar!'

He reached for the cheese and cut himself a piece.

'You are quite right, however,' he continued. 'I went into the law because a part of my mind finds it deeply satisfying. I enjoy its precision and exactness, its attempts to comprehend every eventuality, to provide for every possible occurrence – and to do so with as much cool, calm, one might say, indifferent rationality as possible. The language of the law – which so many find dull and arid – is fascinating to me.'

'I knew you could not devote yourself to a profession in which you had no real interest,' declared Mary, triumphant. 'It took a little effort for you to confess it, but I was certain it was the case.'

'I'm not sure a taste for the dustier recesses of the law is a thing one would want generally known,' said Mr Hayward ruefully, 'but as it seems to have raised me in your estimation, I am prepared to admit it.'

Mary felt her face grow warm. She was not sure whether the cause was Mr Hayward's amused gaze, or her uncle's wine, of which she had drunk more than usual. The noise around the table suggested she was not the only guest who might have done so. There was a cheer as the servants came in, carrying three large trifles and a great number of spoons.

'And yet, you have no such inhibitions about declaring your love for poetry.'

'No, that is a pursuit of which I have never been ashamed.'

'May I ask where your passion comes from?' Mary could not quite believe she was asking more questions, but she could not stop. 'Has it always been so marked a taste for you?'

'I cannot remember when I did not care for it,' replied Mr Hayward simply. 'I have loved it since I was a boy.'

'And do you write verse as well as read it? I imagine the two impulses are often found in company.'

'Indeed, they go together as well as this excellent trifle and this jug of cream. Will you take a little?'

Mary shook her head; it was impossible she should ever eat another mouthful. Even Mr Hayward seemed defeated and pushed away his plate.

'Yes, I tried to write,' he said. 'I tried very hard. Like many another foolish young man, I believed that because I loved poetry so sincerely, I must be able to write it too. But I was wrong. I could not do it.'

'That must have been a great sadness to you.'

'At the time, I thought it was the end of the world.' He smiled in recollection of his youthful grief. 'Now I'm thankful I understood my limitations so early. If I don't have the genius to create a thing of beauty myself, at least I have the judgement to appreciate the art of others. It is better to accept what I can do than to yearn hopelessly after what I cannot. "Know thyself", as the Greeks tell us.'

Mary murmured a phrase, quite low, almost to herself.

'Really, Miss Bennet, that sounded very like Greek,' remarked Mr Hayward. 'Could it have been? It isn't a language with which young ladies are usually familiar.'

'Oh!' cried Mary, embarrassed at having revealed knowledge she was not expected to possess. 'I really know very little, only the alphabet, some grammar, and a few quotes from the great philosophers. I was taught it – by a friend of the family.'

'You are full of surprises,' replied Mr Hayward. 'I look forward to learning that you also draw in the Chinese style or have lately prepared your own translation of Goethe.'

Mary was suddenly wary. Was he mocking her? She could not bear it if he was. Mr Hayward caught her anxious expression.

'I see I have upset you. Please understand that was not my intention.'

He appeared genuinely distressed as he sought to make amends.

'My words were ill-chosen. I will always attempt a witty remark, even when I had far better not. But I did not mean to tease you. A cultivated mind is a wonderful thing in a woman and should be everywhere encouraged, not despised. If I gave the impression I thought otherwise, I am sorry, and ask your forgiveness.'

It was impossible to doubt either his candour or his concern, and Mary felt relief flood through her. She could not recall when she had enjoyed anyone's company so much, and it would have been painful for the evening to end on an uncomfortable note. For there could be no doubt now that the dinner was coming to a conclusion. The plates had been cleared and the crumbs were being swept from the cloth. For the first time she could remember, Mary did not welcome the prospect of its being over; she had no desire to hurry away.

'You are very kind. But the offence, such as it is, is not all on your side. I too have a case to answer, for I prodded and poked you about so many things – poetry and the law – and you bore it all with the utmost patience.'

'Well,' replied Mr Hayward, his cheerfulness restored, 'if we are both equally at fault, can I suggest a plan of restitution? You shall recommend a book for me to read that you believe will improve me in some way, and I will do the same for you. The terms are these: the work must be read in its entirety – no skipping – and a full account of the sensations it produced is to be given by the reader to the recommender before a period of not more than fourteen days has expired. What do you say?'

Mary was delighted. There was nothing she would enjoy more.

'I am pleased to accept your terms and will do all I can to discharge my obligations as required.'

The noise at the other end of the table had now increased to such an extent that ordinary conversation was no longer possible, for one of Mr Gardiner's friends had announced his intention to favour the party with a song. Knowing that a gesture must take the place of words, silently Mr Hayward raised his glass to toast their agreement; and Mary, shyly, lifted hers.

CHAPTER FIFTY-FIVE

Mary was quick to decide upon her choice of book. In Mr Gardiner's library, she found the volumes of Mrs Macaulay's *History of England*, which had so enthralled her when she first discovered them at Longbourn. She could not help but notice, as she opened them, that they did not look as though they had been much read; but then Mr Gardiner, unlike her father, had a business to run, and perhaps preferred less demanding fare in his leisure hours. He certainly raised no objection when she asked if she might borrow them. She took them away to her room, looking forward to the moment when she should present them to Mr Hayward.

A few days later, she and Mrs Gardiner were sitting in the drawing room when his name was announced. The children, who were supposed to be reading, leapt up with excitement, for Mr Hayward was known to carry peppermints with him on his visits, and once, on an occasion that was never to be forgotten, had presented each of them with an entire candied orange. Mary was almost as excited as the young Gardiners, as their mother could not help but observe.

'You look very expectant,' she remarked. 'Are you hoping Tom might have sweets for you as well?'

'Oh, no, it is something far better than that. Mr Hayward

and I have set ourselves a little task. He is to read a book of my choosing; and I am to read one of his.'

Mrs Gardiner frowned. 'Poor Tom, I suspect he has drawn the worst of the deal. I hope you are not planning to give him anything too indigestible?'

'Only Mrs Macaulay's history,' replied Mary airily. 'And just two volumes, so he has nothing to fear.'

As Mr Hayward strode into the room, still innocent of what awaited him, he was assailed on all sides by the children begging to know what he had brought them. Ah, he said, it was really too bad – he had intended to bring lemon drops – but had forgot them – he had meant to pick up some pralines – but they had slipped his mind – had thought to buy sherbets – but had been distracted. He could only hope they would forgive him. Then, just as they began to think they were really to be disappointed, he pulled from his pocket a very large bag of sugarplums, which sent them happily away to the corner of the room, where they consumed their booty in silent satisfaction.

'You spoil them, Tom.'

Mr Hayward shrugged good-naturedly and sat down upon one of Mrs Gardiner's pale sofas.

'I am come to learn what fate Miss Bennet has in store for me. You will have heard about the task we have set each other?'

'Yes, I understand you are contracted to it and that there is no escape for you now.'

Mary leapt up eagerly.

'I wondered if we might begin with my choice,' she said. 'I have it waiting for you upstairs.'

Mr Hayward said he would be delighted; and Mary rushed

to her room to bring down Mrs Macaulay. When she placed it on the table in front of him, Mr Hayward's face fell.

'Come, Miss Bennet, what is this? Two volumes? We agreed on one book, singular, as I recall.'

'Yes, you're quite right, but I hoped I might persuade you to read the chapters on the Civil War. I long to hear your opinion on what she has to say about it. And I'm afraid half the story is in one volume, and half in the other.'

Mr Hayward picked up the two volumes, and held them in his hands, as if weighing up whether to accept them or not.

'I'm not sure that doesn't amount to a breach of our agreement.'

'But surely,' Mary protested, 'it's true to the spirit of what we intended, even if not to the letter of the law.'

'I think you'll find it is the letter of the thing that counts, as far as the law is concerned,' observed Mr Hayward dryly. He replaced the books carefully on the table, rose from the sofa, and walked to the long window, staring out into the street with a very severe expression. 'I must consider my position, Miss Bennet, if you will grant me a moment.'

Mary knew he was teasing, but was too excited to indulge him any further.

'Please say you'll read it.'

'Indeed, I believe you must,' interjected Mrs Gardiner, 'if you aren't to show yourself up as a man of feeble spirit and no powers of concentration.'

'Very well,' declared Mr Hayward. 'I throw myself upon the mercy of this honourable court. I undertake to read the chapters up to and including the restoration of Charles II – but nothing further.'

He held out his hand to Mary – and after a moment's hesitation, she shook it.

It was ten days before Mr Hayward returned, bringing with him the two volumes of Mrs Macaulay, a notebook full of jottings, and peppermints for the children. Mr Gardiner had agreed they might have use of his library, and for the rest of the afternoon, Mary and Mr Hayward were closeted there, discussing what he'd read.

At first, Mrs Gardiner called in upon them now and then, to offer them tea and see how Mr Hayward was bearing up; but each time she did so, she found them either deep in discussion of the role of church and state, or arguing animatedly about the guilt of Charles I or the virtues of Oliver Cromwell. Having satisfied herself that Mr Hayward was in no need of rescuing, and indeed seemed to be enjoying himself quite as much as Mary, she decided to leave them alone. They did not emerge until Mr Gardiner appeared at the library door to tell them it would shortly be time for dinner, and that he assumed Tom would join them?

When they sat down at the table, Mary felt as invigorated as if she had just finished a long and very breezy country walk.

'So, Tom,' said Mr Gardiner as he carved the beef at the head of the table. 'You appear to have survived your encounter with Mrs Macaulay.'

'I don't think he found her anywhere near as tedious as he expected,' declared Mary, glancing at Mr Hayward with a triumphant air. 'He certainly entered into a very lively discussion of her work.'

'You must never forget,' remarked Mrs Gardiner, 'that Tom

is trained to argue – it might be said that debate is his calling, so we should expect him to be good at it.'

Mr Hayward put down his knife and fork. 'I cannot let that pass, ma'am. This was a purely private encounter, nothing in the professional line at all. I argued with Miss Bennet purely for the love of it.'

He smiled at her over the dish of peas and carrots that was making its way down the table; and Mary felt happiness flood through her as she placed a spoonful of each on her plate. She hoped her pleasure was not as apparent to the others as it was to herself.

'It was an excellent recommendation,' continued Mr Hayward, 'because it reminded me not only that Mrs Macaulay is singularly well informed, but that she marshals her facts with admirable skill.'

'I suppose that counts as praise,' remarked Mr Gardiner, 'if not of the most effusive kind.'

Mr Hayward attacked his beef, and declined to reply.

'You have obviously been much improved by it,' observed Mrs Gardiner. 'I cannot wait to hear what task you intend to offer Mary.'

Everyone turned in her direction; but this time Mary did not look away as she might once have done.

'I hope I'll be able to rise to your challenge with as much enthusiasm as you have to mine.'

'Well said,' cried Mr Gardiner. 'That's the spirit!'

'I've already chosen the work,' said Mr Hayward, 'and it is of a rather different nature to Mrs Macaulay. It speaks less to the intellect than to the emotions.'

'I see. And shall I enjoy it, do you think?'

'I will deliver it to you later this week, so you won't have to wait too long to find out.'

As they ate their lemon posset, Mary did all she could to persuade Mr Hayward to divulge the title of his choice, but he would not be drawn; and by the time coffee was served, she had resigned herself to its remaining a surprise. She very much hoped it might turn out not to be poetry, but she thought it very probable that it would.

The next day, a package arrived for her. As she carried it to her room, it did not feel heavy enough to be a novel, let alone something more scholarly. Her heart sank – there seemed little doubt it must be verse. She pulled out the small volume and opened it. '*Lyrical Ballads* by W. Wordsworth.' It was a name she recognised, but she had never read anything of his. She frowned slightly as she turned the pages. Between them, she found a note.

My dear Miss Bennet,

I have no doubt your worst suspicions are confirmed now that you hold my choice of book in your hands. I urge you, however, not to give in to first impressions, but to persevere, with the same energy with which I tackled Mrs Macaulay. Mr Wordsworth is in my opinion the greatest poet now living in England. He very much deserves your <u>unprejudiced</u> attention, which I beg you will extend to him. I should not presume to suggest which poem you should read first or with most care; any of them will well repay the time spent in their company. Some do not give up their meaning easily, but if you approach them with an open, generous mind, I think you cannot fail to be affected by them. Remember what I said – that this is writing for the

heart, not the head. That may be unfamiliar or even at first
unwelcome to you, but I do not doubt you have it within
you to appreciate it. Time will prove if I am right.
    Tho. Hayward

Mary held the book in her hands, struck by the directness
of Mr Hayward's words. She thought of him saying them in
person, his grey eyes fixed upon her – for she was aware now
that his eyes were grey – and imagined the playful tone in
which he would have spoken. But this would not do – this
was no way to think. She picked up her shawl, and wrapped
it tightly around her. She did not look forward to the task
before her. She thought it was unlikely she should enjoy Mr
Wordsworth's poems, but it was her duty to read them with
the open, generous spirit which Mr Hayward had urged upon
her. She would do her best to satisfy his request, and would
begin tomorrow.

CHAPTER FIFTY-SIX

Mary spent most of the next few days alone in Mr Gardiner's library, studying the *Lyrical Ballads*. At teatime one afternoon, when her aunt came searching for her, she was so deeply immersed in her reading that, when Mrs Gardiner gently touched her shoulder, she sprang up in surprise.

'I'm so sorry, Mary,' exclaimed her aunt. 'I didn't mean to alarm you. You must be lost to the world in that book.' She looked over at the title. 'It is poetry, then, just as you feared. How are you finding it?'

'Some of the poems are quite simple to grasp and easy to enjoy; but others puzzle me. I have read them over and over, but I still don't know what to think of them.'

'That must be a new sensation for you, I imagine?' asked Mrs Gardiner, noting Mary's preoccupied air. There was no point in asking her to take a view on young George's attempt at copying out the alphabet; her mind was elsewhere. 'I should warn you, a confession of that nature will be irresistible to Tom. He will explain them to you, at great length, from now until dinner time, unless you keep him in check.'

Mary smiled politely and went back to the little book. She was not sure that explanation, in the usual sense, would be of much help to her. She had begun to suspect that the more opaque poems were not susceptible to analysis at all, or at least not of the rational kind she knew best. They seemed to ask something very different from their reader. She was not sure yet exactly what it was, but she would do all she could to discover it. She was determined to have something intelligent to say to Mr Hayward when he came to discuss them.

He arrived on a sunny Saturday morning, freed from his office and eager to talk of something other than the law. Mrs Gardiner was occupied with the children in the nursery upstairs, and Mr Gardiner was occupied with writing letters in his library, so he and Mary had the drawing room to themselves. Mr Hayward looked around, as if something was not quite to his liking, before boldly lifting one of the several card tables scattered about the room and placing it in front of the high windows. When he had satisfied himself that it was now in the perfect position to take best advantage of the sharp morning light, he drew up two chairs at either side. From the sideboard, Mary fetched the jug of lemon water she had arranged to be there for their use; and soon they were both seated comfortably at the table, each with a copy of the *Lyrical Ballads* in their hands.

'This reminds me a little of preparing for my examinations,' remarked Mr Hayward. 'So, where shall we start? How did you like the *Ballads*?'

'I began rather slowly,' said Mary. 'I did not realise before that poetry requires a special concentration all of its own. I had to learn how to read them properly before I could begin to think of enjoying them.'

'Yes, a poem demands a particular kind of effort, if it is to be appreciated. But I cannot believe you did not persevere?'

'I did – and I was rewarded, for there were many poems

that pleased me. The simpler ones – those about humble people.'

She opened the book and began to turn the pages.

'I very much liked "We are Seven". No one could fail to be moved by it, if they had any feeling heart.'

She found the place and began to read.

> 'Their graves are green, they may be seen,'
> The little Maid replied,
> 'Twelve steps or more from my mother's door,
> And they are side by side.
> My stockings there I often knit,
> My kerchief there I hem;
> And there upon the ground I sit,
> And sing a song to them.'

She looked up, her eyes bright. 'It is very affecting, is it not? But there were others which, as you hinted to me, did not give up their secrets so easily. I had to read them again and again before I began to understand their meaning.'

She reached for her glass and filled it with lemon water from the jug. Her hand trembled very slightly as she did so. She knew once she began to describe what had happened – the great discovery she had made – she would find it hard to stop.

'But, oh, Mr Hayward – when you finally understand – when a poem speaks to you at last, as one did to me last night – it is wonderful, is it not?'

She longed to describe to him how it happened – the flash of insight that had come upon her unawares as she lay reading in bed – the excitement she had felt in grasping what the poet intended – the way she had hugged herself with the sheer pleasure of seeing it at last – but this was too much to be said, even to Mr Hayward.

'So poetry has touched you, then?' he replied, with a playful smile. 'It has broken through that rational reserve?'

'It is unfair to mock me, sir. And very ungenerous too.'

'Yes, I am wrong to do so,' he admitted, his expression gradually becoming more serious. 'In truth, I am delighted for you. You have experienced a sensation I know I could not live without, and I am exceedingly happy for you. Will you tell me which poem it was that affected you so strongly?'

She turned to a page marked with a piece of paper.

'It is this one.'

She reached across the table and handed the book silently to him.

'"Tintern Abbey".' He looked up and their eyes met. 'How extraordinary that this should be your favourite. It is mine too. I like it best of all Mr Wordsworth's works.'

In the distance, she heard the muffled rumble of the City streets. Upstairs, the children ran around in the nursery, their footsteps loud on the wooden floors. The drawing room, in contrast, seemed remarkably still. In the silence, she was suddenly very aware of Mr Hayward's presence, of his hands holding the book, the whiteness of his cuffs against his dark coat.

'I am very pleased,' he said softly, 'that we think as one about this poem – that it moves you as much as it does me. But I am not surprised. I think you have it within you to feel very deeply when you will allow yourself to do so.'

Mary was at a loss to know what to say. From the street, she heard the cry of a woman selling cherries from her barrow.

'Round and sound, five pence a pound.'

Her voice was pure, clear, and very loud. Mr Hayward started up and seemed to recollect himself. He handed the book back to Mary, drew his own copy from his pocket, and turned its pages until he found 'Tintern Abbey'.

'Before we talk more about the poem itself,' he said in a more even tone, 'I should be interested to know what happened to make you appreciate its power?'

Mary considered his question. In the past, her instinct would have been to say nothing, to reveal as little as possible of her private self. But now, with a new courage, she resolved to be candid.

'I suppose it is my habit to dissect and analyse what I read,' she began. 'Indeed, it is how I make sense of things in general. But with 'Tintern Abbey', it did not work. No matter how hard I tried, I could not get to the heart of it. Something always eluded me.'

She shifted in her chair. Perhaps the bodice of her new dress was a little tight? Suddenly she felt very warm; but she continued.

'Then it occurred to me that I was coming at it in quite the wrong way. I was trying to think it into submission. I began to fear I might be about to destroy the very thing I wanted to understand. It struck me that a poem was perhaps too fragile an object to bear the weight of too much rational examination.'

She ran her fingers across the smooth cotton of her dress, playing with the pleats as she spoke.

'I must say, I was not entirely pleased with that idea. It was very unsettling. If I could not call upon my intellect to help me make sense of things, what else was there for me to rely upon?'

'So what did you do?'

'I made the hardest possible choice for someone like myself. I left it alone. I stopped examining and underlining. I made no more notes in the margins. I allowed myself to do nothing more than read and quietly reflect upon it. And then a few days later – when I least expected it – I made the leap. That is the only way I can explain it.'

'Ah yes!' cried Mr Hayward. 'The leap! I know exactly what you mean! It is the moment when we enter fully into the poet's imagination. When we truly understand what it is he means.'

'Yes,' replied Mary quietly. 'That is what happened. It was a very surprising sensation for me, unlike anything I have experienced before.'

'You should be very pleased with yourself,' declared Mr Hayward. 'Many people never make such a connection. I long to know which parts of it particularly affected you. Tell me exactly what you felt when you read it.'

Mary took another glass of water and tried to compose herself. She wanted to make no mistakes. She opened her book at the marked page, and began.

'At first, the poem seems both very beautiful and very simple. The poet sits beneath a tree at the top of a high valley, gazing down to the river below.'

'"O sylvan Wye,"' murmured Mr Hayward, '"thou wanderer through the woods."'

Mary noticed he did not consult his book; he knew the poem by heart.

'Mr Wordsworth describes the landscape with great brilliance. We feel ourselves plunged into the heart of "the wild secluded scene".'

Mr Hayward did not hurry her, so she took a deep breath and continued.

'All this is excellently done. But just as we think we have the measure of what the poet wants to say, we realise he has something far more extraordinary to convey to us.'

She turned the pages of her book, her excitement growing.

'We begin to understand that the landscape he has conjured up so brilliantly is not merely a view to be admired. It is far more than that. It is nothing less than the means by which we may connect ourselves to a higher truth. If we will only allow ourselves to surrender to its beauty, it will transform us – for then we will leave behind "the weary weight of all this unintelligible world" – and become what we are meant to be – "a living soul".'

She was speaking faster, exuberant with the thrill of understanding.

'That is it, is it not? That is what Mr Wordsworth means to show us. How through nature we become one with the world – how we become "a living soul"!'

'Yes, yes,' declared Mr Hayward, as animated now as Mary. 'You have it, Miss Bennet, you have it indeed!'

He sat back in his chair, much affected. 'I'm sorry I interrupted you, but really, I could not resist.'

He stood up abruptly and went to the window, where he stood looking into the street. Mary sat quite still, hugely elated and a little shocked. Neither of them spoke until Mr Hayward returned to the table and took his seat again.

'I told you a while ago, Miss Bennet, that you were full of surprises. But I did not expect you to astonish me again so quickly.'

She allowed herself to bask in his praise for a moment,

aware of the admiration with which he regarded her; and this emboldened her to make a final disclose.

'You asked me to tell you what I felt when I read the poem, sir. I hope I may confess the truth to you without seeming foolish – but, oh, Mr Hayward – it made me long to become a living soul myself.'

She was not sure how he would respond to such an intimate declaration. She very much hoped he would not be playful or satiric, for she did not think she could bear that; but when he spoke, she saw with gratitude it was with all the seriousness she had hoped for.

'That is the power of poetry,' he said simply. 'It allows us to imagine ourselves anew, if we will permit it to do so. It reveals to us the hidden wishes of our hearts.'

From the street, the sound of the cherry seller's barrow could be heard once more as she pushed it over the cobbles, making her way back to Cheapside. She did not call out this time; had she sold all her wares, wondered Mary, or was she simply too tired to cry them again? It was a melancholy thought, and it darkened her mood.

'Yes, it shows us those things,' she replied. 'But what if we cannot act upon them? What if it inspires in us longings we can never achieve?'

'I am not sure what you mean,' said Mr Hayward.

'There is nothing I should like more than to experience what Mr Wordsworth describes,' cried Mary. 'But I cannot think it will ever happen for me. I have altogether the wrong sort of character for that.'

'Why should you think that?'

'Mr Wordsworth says elsewhere that nothing of value is to

be gained from books. For him, our affections are the only real guide worth following.'

She felt tears begin to well up in her eyes.

'And I'm not sure I have any. Or none strong enough for me to follow with confidence. Perhaps they are too weak – too frozen – to help me find my way.'

Mr Hayward gazed at her with such concern that for a moment Mary thought he was about to take her hand. But if that was his intention, he mastered it, and instead pulled the jug of lemon water towards him and filled both their glasses.

'I fear you are creating a difficulty where none need exist,' he said, pushing the drink towards her. 'Perhaps I may cite myself as proof of my argument?'

He crossed his arms, and looked at her across the table, both serious and fond at the same time.

'My passion for poetry is so strong that I know there are some – and I must include your aunt and uncle amongst them – who find it very amusing and just a little odd. But it has not diminished my appetite for other, very different authors. I do not think my love for Mr Wordsworth requires me to give up my appreciation for – well, let us say my respect – for Mrs Macaulay. There is room for both in my life. The same is true for you, I believe.'

Mary closed *Lyrical Ballads* and placed it gently on the table.

'It seems to me,' he went on, 'that, in the real world, it is impossible to be guided solely by either the impulses of feeling or by rational calculation. Neither is likely to make us happy. In my own view, we have need of them both. Wisdom, I suppose, lies in knowing when to call upon one and when on the other.'

'I think you will always find that easier to achieve than I do,' answered Mary. 'You are accustomed to expressing your feelings. You have exercised them with poetry until they are robust and familiar to you. Mine, I often think, are feeble, frozen and largely unknown to me.'

Finally Mr Hayward smiled at her.

'No one who has spoken with the passion you have shown so freely this afternoon can possibly be a stranger to strong emotions.'

Mary was suddenly mortified by the candour with which she had spoken.

'I have said far too much,' she cried. 'I am so sorry – I was carried away. I cannot believe I have been so forward!'

'That is not how I regard it at all,' said Mr Hayward, soothingly. 'I beg you not to think of it in that way. You have nothing with which to reproach yourself. Our conversation has been invigorating and very illuminating. I should very much like to read other poems with you. May I be allowed to suggest a few more?'

His expression was so inviting and so sincere that her embarrassment evaporated, and she knew there was nothing she would enjoy more.

'Yes,' she replied simply. 'I would like that very much.'

'I intend to do all I can to help you become a woman of feeling,' said Mr Hayward lightly. 'I shall unlock the sentiment buried beneath all that good sense. See if I do not.'

Mary blushed; but more from surprise than delicacy. She was shocked to realise that she was not at all offended, and that indeed, she rather hoped he would do so.

After he had gone, she could not settle. She felt excited, invigorated, alive. Not knowing what else to do with herself, she walked to the Gardiners' piano, lifted the lid, and for the first time in long while, began to play.

Upstairs in the nursery, Mrs Gardiner heard the music as it echoed round the house and was puzzled at first to think who could be playing. It was carried off with so much spirit and vigour that she did not think it could be Mary at the keyboard. When she realised it must be her, she stood leaning on the door, wondering what had provoked such a change in attitude, as the children danced about behind her.

CHAPTER FIFTY-SEVEN

Mrs Gardiner made several cautious attempts to discover how Mary and Mr Hayward had spent their afternoon together; but her niece deflected every mild enquiry and batted away every innocent question. Mary had barely allowed herself to dwell upon how pleasurable it had been, as she was not sure what she should conclude from Mr Hayward's manner. Did his behaviour suggest that he enjoyed her company as much as she did his? It seemed probable, even likely; but beyond that she would not go. She told herself she would not think about him too often; and for at least a few minutes a day, she was successful in this endeavour. For the rest of the time, however, he was very much in her mind. So it was that she was thinking of him one morning, while around her the children ate their breakfast and the Gardiners drank their coffee. When the post was brought in, Mary took no notice, for there was never anything for her. It was only when her uncle held up a letter, with every appearance of surprise, that she paid attention.

'Here is a note from that quizzical young man Tom Hayward. He asks a favour of me. You will never guess, my dear, in a hundred years, what it is.'

'I'm sure I shall not,' his wife agreed, spreading jam on the bread of her youngest daughter. 'I hope you will tell me.'

'He asks if I would be kind enough to bring Mary early

one morning to Westminster Bridge, where he says he will meet us.' He turned to Mary, incredulous. 'He writes that he wishes to show you the City as the sun comes up and read us some lines about it.'

Mary could not quite believe it; nor, it seemed, could Mr Gardiner.

'What can he mean by it?' he asked his wife. 'For such a respectable lawyer, he has some very strange ideas.'

'I'm sure he imagines it as a treat,' she replied, 'an opportunity to see something remarkable. What do you think, Mary? Should you like to go?'

'It must be a very extraordinary sight,' said Mary, trying to keep the eagerness out of her voice. 'I should very much like to see it, if it won't inconvenience Mr Gardiner.'

Her uncle shrugged.

'Of course I will take you if you wish it. But it's a very odd errand – and a very early one too. Tom will owe me a very decent bottle of claret in recompense.'

'Does that mean we are to go?' asked Mary eagerly.

'I believe it does,' replied Mr Gardiner. 'There are times when I am astonished by my own magnanimity,' he declared, as his wife offered him the last rasher of bacon.

It was still dark when, a few days later, Mary and her uncle made their way in a slow carriage through the early morning streets. Far from being deserted, the pavements were already filling up. Country people carried baskets of fresh fruits and vegetables; apprentices passed them with the tools of their trade wrapped in their aprons. In a side street, Mary thought she saw a dairymaid leading a cow.

'I had no idea, sir, that the City was so busy at this time!'

'London starts work early. No one makes money by lying too long in bed.'

When they arrived on the southern side of the bridge, Mr Hayward was there waiting for them. He thanked Mr Gardiner profusely for his kindness and hoped neither he nor Mary would be disappointed by their outing.

'Do I understand,' asked Mr Gardiner cautiously, 'that you mean to read a poem?'

'Yes, sir. But I shall do so very quietly, without drawing undue attention to us. And it is very short.'

Somewhat relieved, Mr Gardiner put his hands into his pockets, and walked a few steps away. Mary stared across the river at the City landscape spread out before them. The rising sun had just begun to appear above the roofs, touching everything with a thin rime of gold.

'It is wonderful, Mr Hayward. I wish I had the words to describe it.'

'I suggest we allow Mr Wordsworth to say what we cannot,' he said in a low voice. 'Now, what I ask of you, Miss Bennet, is not to think too much about what you feel as I read, but instead, to allow the sensations to wash over you.'

He drew a book from his pocket and began in a quiet, ordinary tone, without flourishes or affectation.

> 'Earth has not anything to show more fair;
> Dull would he be of soul who could pass by
> A sight so touching in its majesty; ...'

As he went on, Mary gave herself up to the rhythm and beauty of the words, and began to see the City through Wordsworth's eyes.

'Ships, towers, domes, theatres, and temples lie
Open unto the fields, and to the sky;
All bright and glittering in the smokeless air.'

She leaned on a parapet, staring at the view, the dark water below her, the church spires glinting beyond. It was like nothing she had ever seen before.

'Ne'er saw I, never felt, a calm so deep.
The river glideth at his own sweet will.
Dear God! The very houses seem asleep,
And all that mighty heart is lying still!'

Mr Hayward closed his book and stood staring for a moment into the dawn-flecked cityscape. When the sun finally cleared the rooftops, he turned to look at her.

'This is sensation, is it not!' he declared. 'Do not tell me your feelings are not aroused by it – that it has not stimulated your mind to awe and admiration!'

'Oh, but is has, truly it has,' Mary replied. 'I am amazed. Speechless!'

They both took one last long look at the view. Mr Hayward sighed and put the book back in his pocket.

'It is one of the most remarkable experiences I know,' he said, as they walked back to the carriage, where Mr Gardiner stood talking quietly to the coachman. 'I saw it first when I was little more than a lad, just up from Hampshire.'

An image of him as a lanky, excited boy flashed in Mary's mind's eye. It was not hard to imagine him standing on the bridge, declaiming Wordsworth silently to himself in the early dawn light. She looked at him from the corner of her eye, taking in his animated, intelligent expression. They were nearly at the carriage now; but before they reached it, he stopped and bent his head to her ear.

'I hope that encourages you to accept that your capacity to feel is as strong as anyone's,' he said quietly. 'You need not fear that you are, in any way, "dull of soul". That is not you at all.'

He held the door open for her, and soon they were all inside, heading back to Gracechurch Street. Mr Hayward was invited back for breakfast – he readily accepted – then no more was said. Mr Gardiner closed his eyes, Mr Hayward sat preoccupied, seemingly lost in thought, and Mary stared silently from the carriage window at the streets as they passed. She felt quite unlike herself, both very close to the world outside, and at the same time, distantly remote from it, as though she was regarding it from the wrong end of a telescope. It was not until they were back in the breakfast room, being served with everything hungry people could possibly require, that she began to return to her usual state of mind.

Mrs Gardiner sat at the table, watching them eat. 'Was it as remarkable as you expected it to be?' she asked Mary. 'Was it worth getting up so early?'

'Oh, indeed it was,' exclaimed Mary. 'It was a wonderful thing to see! To know that we stood where Mr Wordsworth stood, looked at the very scene that had inspired his words! What is it like, Mr Hayward, to do the same in the Lakes? It must be very splendid to stand in that wild landscape, reading his poems in its midst.'

'I am sure it is,' replied Mr Hayward, 'but I'm afraid I would not know. I am sorry to say I have never been there – though I have often promised myself the pleasure of a visit.'

'But that is so sad,' exclaimed Mary. 'The Lakes interest you so much, it seems very unfair you should not have seen them.'

'I have no one to blame for that but myself,' replied Mr Hayward. 'I have allowed my work to keep me here in London, with the result that I have yet to set foot in the countryside I most wish to visit.'

'I too long to see the Lakes,' said Mrs Gardiner. 'We once planned a trip there – indeed, we actually set out – but at the last moment, Mr Gardiner's business obliged us to cut short our time, and we got no further than Derbyshire.'

There was a brief silence while everyone considered how much they regretted never having beheld the grandeur of the northern hills, crags, and lakes. Then Mr Gardiner reached across the table and gently took his wife's hand.

'I have always been sorry that you did not get your wish, and I think the time has come to put that right. The days are beginning to lengthen – what do you say to an expedition to the Lakes as soon as it is possible for us to leave? I am not too much occupied with business just now, so I do believe it might be done. And fortune favours the brave, they say.'

Mrs Gardiner rose from her chair, hurried round the table, and kissed her husband on both cheeks.

'If you really think it can be managed, there's nothing I should like better.'

Delighted at the success of his suggestion – he could not imagine why he had not thought of it before – Mr Gardiner now wanted nothing more than to see everyone around him as happy as he was himself.

'Mary, you will accompany us, of course. And, Tom, if the law can spare you for a short while, I hope you will come too?'

Mr Hayward said he would be honoured to join them, if it

could be arranged; and soon, he and Mr Gardiner were deep in conversation, discussing dates, itineraries, and the best way of making the journey.

'What an unexpected treat!' exclaimed Mrs Gardiner. 'I cannot quite believe we are to go at last. I wonder if Jane would be happy to take the children for a short while – it would not be much to their liking, to travel so far and find nothing but mountains at the end of it! But you seem very quiet, Mary. Don't you want to come?'

'More than anything. But you have already been so kind to me. I must ask – are you certain you want me with you?'

'Really,' said her aunt, giving her a little embrace, 'how should we manage without you? You can keep us entertained on the long road north – you're sure to be able to point out all manner of curious rocks and historical ruins.'

Mrs Gardiner reached out and took the last roll left on the plate.

'And Tom will be able to show us all the scenes that inspired the poetry of the place. Between the pair of you, we shall be excellently supplied with information. It will be hardly worthwhile buying a guidebook.'

CHAPTER FIFTY-EIGHT

Mr Hayward and Mary were much in each other's company over the next few weeks. He was often at Gracechurch Street, sometimes calling briefly to pay his respects and drink a glass of Mr Gardiner's wine, sometimes dining with the family on terms of such familiarity that he seemed to belong there as much as Mary herself.

At first, Mary had wondered whether, after their conversation about 'Tintern Abbey,' she would feel self-conscious and a little uneasy in his presence. She had talked to him with more freedom and honesty than to any man she knew, revealing aspects of herself she had confessed to no one else. When they had spoken together, it seemed the most natural thing in the world to be so open – but now, part of her blushed to think of it, as if she'd shown him her petticoat. And she wondered, when he came to reflect upon it, if he would come to regret his own candour?

It was soon apparent that none of her fears were justified. There was no breach in their cheerful relations. On the contrary, their intimacy deepened as they became more familiar with each other, as they chatted together on the sofa, or sat alongside each other at dinner, talking and laughing. At first Mary congratulated herself on having found so good a friend and strove not to imagine anything more. She told herself she was grateful to have found a like-minded confidant, with whom she shared so many interests, and whose conversation was more interesting to her than that of any other man she had known. But as time went on, Mary gradually understood that her affection for Mr Hayward went beyond that of friendship. She waited for his visits with keen anticipation and felt a little rush of pleasure when she heard his name announced. When he smiled at her in a particular way all his own, when he commented approvingly on something she said, when he told a story that made her laugh – and above all, when his hand once grazed her own as he handed her a book – then she knew without a doubt that these were feelings of an altogether different kind.

She kept this new knowledge strictly to herself. Mrs Gardiner was not blind to their liking for each other, and did not object to it, for she loved them both and thought them admirably suited to one another; but when she attempted to gauge Mary's feelings in the matter, Mary would not be drawn out. She merely replied that she was always pleased to see Mr Hayward, which was indeed the truth; the rest she kept resolutely to herself.

She feared that if she confessed her liking, it might somehow imply she thought it was returned; and this seemed in every way presumptious. But there were times, however, when even she was inclined to think she caught a glimpse of something warmer in his behaviour, a look, a gesture, or a remark that suggested emotions on his part which went beyond those of friendship. But she could not be sure – and a small voice from deep within her sometimes whispered it was impossible a man like Mr Hayward should take a serious interest in a woman like herself. It spoke lower than it once did, but it cautioned her to say nothing at present. So she did not share her hopeful feelings with her aunt, but kept them all to herself, to be enjoyed in private until such time as she was convinced it was safe enough to declare them.

Spring was well advanced when Mr Gardiner announced one evening that he had arranged a great surprise for them all.

'I thought our journey to the Lakes was excitement enough,' replied Mrs Gardiner.

'This is more by way of a local excursion. Does anyone want to guess what it might be?'

The children ran about, shouting louder with each suggestion – a visit to the lions at the Tower, a trip to feed the queen's zebras at Buckingham House. When Mr Hayward arrived, he wondered if it might be a climb to the top of the Monument – a prospect greeted by the younger Gardiners with markedly less enthusiasm – or perhaps an afternoon's indulgence at Mr Birch's pastry shop, which was far more favourably received.

'None of you have it, I'm afraid,' said Mr Gardiner, 'so I will tell you. The Vauxhall Gardens open next week for the season, and I have tickets for all of us to attend. We shall see the fountains, hear a little music and enjoy a good supper. You children may have as many pastries as you can eat without being sick, and if you're very lucky, I shall take you to see the tightrope walkers before we go home.'

This exceeded the children's wildest expectations, and their joy was noisily unconfined. When were they to go? Tomorrow? The next day? They had heard there was a dog that juggled – stood on his hind legs – should they see him too? Amidst the clamour, Mr Hayward was obliged to raise his voice when he tried, for the second time, to make himself heard.

'Were you ever in Vauxhall, Miss Bennet?'

Mary admitted she had never been.

'There's nowhere else like it. It's London in a nutshell – loud and glittering, a little rough around the edges, crowded and gaudy. I like it very much.'

'I understand you can see every kind of spectacle there.'

'Everything you have ever thought of, and much you have not. There's a vast great pavilion in the Chinese style – elegant covered walks to stroll along – comedies and plays to watch, dancing if you chose to join in – even its own romantic ruins, built to look as though they've always been there – lots to drink and lots to eat – it has everything a Londoner's heart could possibly desire.'

'And dancing dogs,' added George.

'Dancing horses too,' agreed Mr Hayward. 'And I saw a pig there once who could tell the time. Really, Miss Bennet, how can you resist?'

'You cannot think of yourself as a Londoner until you've seen it,' declared Mr Gardiner, at which the children began to argue about which of them most longed to go, and who should enjoy it more than anyone else – it was not until their father rapped the table sharply with a spoon and pretended to look fierce that order was at length restored.

A few days later, Mary and her aunt were once more to be found shopping at Harding and Howell. Mrs Gardiner had decided that it was impossible to venture to Vauxhall without equipping themselves with new hats, and now they sat before a large tray of ribbons, examining them closely. They had decided upon their hats with relative ease; it was the dressing of them that proved more difficult. Mary was weighing in her mind the relative virtues of green and pink trimmings, thinking how much she would value Mr Hayward's advice on such a weighty matter, when she heard a voice from the next counter that could not be mistaken.

'I'm afraid none of these is at all satisfactory. Is this all you have to show me?'

A tall female figure sat with its back to her, rigid with displeasure.

'It is *most* disappointing.'

The shopman, disinclined to help further, gathered up his samples, clearly hoping his next customer would prove easier to please. The woman rose to leave, much affronted. Mary looked quickly down at her ribbons, desperate not to catch her eye. She had no desire to be recognised by Caroline Bingley, especially not when she was so cross. Who could guess what she might say to relieve her frustrations if a likely victim presented herself? Mary averted her face until the imperious rustle of a silk dress told her it was safe to look up. When she did so, Mrs Gardiner was coolly watching her departure.

'I do believe that was Miss Bingley who has just made such a flouncing, ill-natured exit.'

'Yes, I'm afraid so. She is not at her best when she considers herself thwarted.'

'I was about to observe it is surprising she did not have the courtesy to let you know she was in London. But I suppose that is quite in character for her. She and her sister came to visit us when Jane was staying in Gracechurch Street, and her manner was most superior. She is a most disobliging person.'

'It is true she has a talent for unpleasantness,' Mary

replied. 'It is very painful to find oneself on the receiving end of it.'

'Then we should be pleased she has not deigned to notice us, as now we shan't be required to spend any time in her company. I am sure that is a great relief to us both. Now, how are you coming along with those ribbons?'

Impatient with her own indecision, Mary quickly chose the green over the pink, but whether because Mr Hayward had once expressed a preference for that colour, or simply because it was closer to hand than the pink, she found it impossible to say.

CHAPTER FIFTY-NINE

Although the children had begun to think it would never happen, the night of the Vauxhall excursion came around at last. When they finally set out, the little Gardiners could barely contain themselves. Even the journey there excited them, for it involved a rare trip across Westminster Bridge to the city's southern side. This was a treat in itself, and there was much cheering and hallooing as the carriage made its way over the Thames. Shortly afterwards, they were dropped off at the tall iron gates which marked the entrance to the gardens and were quickly absorbed into the large crowd of well-dressed visitors, who milled around, waiting to be joined by tardy friends and family. It was some time before they caught sight of Mr Hayward, deftly making his way towards them through the knots of people, looking like a man with every expectation of enjoying himself. Once they had shaken hands, kissed cheeks, rumpled the children's hair – in short, had done everything necessary to signal their readiness to embrace all that the gardens had to offer, – they headed to the great turnstile, where upon presenting their tickets they were admitted to the cool green park within.

Once inside, they found themselves walking on gravel paths through avenues of high trees, towards a spacious, elegant square, lined on each side by four stately colonnades. In the centre, on a little plinth, strung all about with tiny lights, an orchestra played. At one side of the small stage stood a statue of Handel, above which a single lamp was hung, so that it appeared to illuminate his genius. Around them strolled other visitors, families, friends, couples, all in their best clothes and determined to appear as smart and as at their ease as possible. It was clearly not done to look too impressed by the surroundings – only a bumpkin would gape and stare – but Mary had never seen anything like it and was not afraid to express her wonder.

'Oh, it is so beautifully done – the effect of the trees and the vistas they produce is truly lovely – and the sound of the music in the open air is wonderful!'

It was a fine evening, still warm and light enough to explore the woodland walks, where their little company marvelled at the music that accompanied them wherever they went – 'there are musicians stationed all around us so that there is always something pleasing to hear,' explained Mr Gardiner, who, as an old stalwart of the gardens, considered it his duty to supply such information to those less familiar with their pleasures. He led them towards the Rotunda, a huge circular building with an elaborately painted interior. 'It can seat two thousand persons,' he declared proudly. His wife added in an aside to Mary that it was intended to provide patrons with somewhere to shelter from the rain; but Mr Gardiner seemed to feel this detracted from its dignity, and looked faintly affronted.

'I suppose that may be said of anywhere with a roof that does not leak; but this splendid place has a far greater claim to fame – it has been the scene of many extraordinary performances by the most notable artists. It was here, my dear, that we saw the incomparable Anna Maria Leary sing – do you recall it?'

'Indeed I do,' replied Mrs Gardiner. '"The Siren of Vauxhall". What a talent she was.'

There were, however, no concerts to be heard that night. Instead they watched a display of horsemanship, extremely well done, and a remarkable acrobatic exhibition on a tightrope, which thrilled all who watched it; but, in the opinion of the children, neither could compete with what followed. This was the performance they had dreamed of, featuring a trio of dancing dogs, two of whom stood on their hind legs while the third caught oranges in his mouth, which was worth the price of admission on its own.

By the time Mr Gardiner had walked them round the gushing fountains, it was almost time for dinner, and they began to make its way to the supper boxes where it would be served. Mr and Mrs Gardiner walked in front, shepherding their children before them, and Mary followed behind with Mr Hayward. To entertain them on their walk, Mr Hayward, who was in high spirits, set himself the task of inventing imaginary characters for the visitors whom they passed on the crowded path.

'There,' he whispered, nodding discreetly towards an overdressed gentleman whose finery looked shabbier with every step that drew him closer to them, 'is Lord So-and-So, an unlucky gambler living off his expectations at very much the *wrong* end of Brook Street with a single blackguardly manservant. He's here tonight looking for some wealthy widow, who'll fall gratefully into his arms and provide him with the income he knows he deserves.'

Mary felt a little guilty as she laughed. 'Really, Mr Hayward, for shame! I'm sure he is a most respectable person.'

'Not with that hat and waistcoat. Both suggest a man capable of the most desperate acts. Very unlike the large family making so much noise to our left, who, I suggest, are exactly what they seem to be. Up from the country, Somerset by their accents, on their yearly jaunt to town, where they are fleeced mercilessly at every turn, but greet every new outrage with the greatest good humour. I believe they're relations of Squire Allworthy. Don't they remind you of him?'

'I'm afraid I don't know the Allworthys, sir. Are they acquaintances of yours?'

'Only through Mr Fielding's great book. Have you not read *Tom Jones*, Miss Bennet?'

'I'm afraid not,' Mary said, a little ashamed to be so exposed. 'I'm not well acquainted with fiction, as I believe I have told you.'

'Yes, but not to know Fielding when you know so much else! Your reading is like a two-legged stool, well-supplied in some respects and completely deficient in others. I see we must add some novels to our reading scheme.'

Her discomfort at having the gaps in her knowledge shown up was instantly expunged by pleasure at his suggestion he would be keen to rectify it. Soon she felt bold enough to join in his little game, drawing his attention to a group of elegantly dressed females, sauntering along the opposite path, arm in arm, laughing and joking as they went.

'And what story do you imagine for those ladies, Mr Hayward?'

Mr Hayward looked towards the smart little group, only to have his gaze coolly returned by one of their number, unblinking and direct.

'I'm not sure they are ladies, or at least not of the kind you would be expected to know.' He lowered his voice to explain. 'They are women of the town, I'm afraid. The more discreet of the sisterhood are allowed to walk in the gardens, providing they behave respectably.'

Mary glanced quickly back at the women, who strolled onwards, unhurried and unashamed.

'Lord, sir, I can certainly say I have seen something of the world tonight! I should never have known them if you had not explained. They look like women of the highest fashion.'

'Yes, they are very much at the upper end of their trade. Evelina meets a similar group of ladies in Miss Burney's book, do you remember?'

'I must disappoint you once again. I've tried to read Miss Burney's books, but I'm afraid I could never finish them.'

'I'm surprised you should not like her, for in many respects, she is exactly the author for you – a sharp mind, a keen idea of right and wrong, a great curiosity about how people behave. Now I come to think of it, she rather reminds me of you.'

'You make her seem so severe that I'm not sure that is much to my credit.'

'Not at all. She has a delightful wit, which is the most pleasing aspect of her work.'

'Now I know you're making game of me. I can't imagine why you think I merit such a description.'

'No, you would not see it,' replied Mr Hayward, 'but I do. And as you aren't accustomed to acknowledging your most attractive qualities, I consider it my duty to remind you of them from time to time.'

With that, he smiled and they walked on together. Mary said nothing – but inwardly, she exulted. He had paid her a compliment – how could that not make her happy? She arrived at the supper box reserved by Mr Gardiner with the greatest readiness to be pleased – and it did not disappoint. It was a spacious booth, for their use alone, set into an arcade which faced onto the central square of the gardens. As such, it offered an unrivalled opportunity to indulge in one of the favourite activities of the place – watching the other visitors, as they promenaded about, arm in arm, desiring nothing so much as to see and be seen. When this spectacle paled, there was the box itself to admire, decorated with several handsome painted murals.

'They are painted to designs made by Mr Hogarth,' Mr Gardiner observed, leaning to look more closely at the design behind them. 'This one is *The Milkmaid's Garland*, I believe. It must be older than me and has suffered from the ravages of time and stupidity – people *will* touch them, often with greasy fingers – but you must admit they are still very fine.'

Mr Gardiner had prudently tipped the head waiter handsomely enough to ensure their supper should not fall victim to the gardens' famously meagre way with portions; and, as a result, the plates of ham served to them were thick and juicy, their chickens large and golden, and the blackcurrant tart that followed handsomely topped with cream. In short, thanks to Mr Gardiner's carefully bestowed largesse, their supper was everything they could have wished it to be; and everyone was full and happy as the plates were cleared away. Darkness had fallen properly now, and Mr Gardiner took out his watch and turned to his wife.

'If I'm not mistaken, we are about to witness a very remarkable event.'

A clock struck nine, a loud whistle blew – and at that precise moment, every light in the gardens was instantly illuminated. Small tapers hanging in the trees, large lamps by the paths, each one lit up at the exact same moment. Gasps of astonishment, and a ripple of applause greeted the success of the undertaking, which impressed even the most sophisticated visitors.

'They do it every night,' said Mr Gardiner, highly satisfied at seeing a difficult thing well done. 'Apparently, it has never been known to fail.'

Mr Hayward was explaining to Mary how the trick was achieved – by means of cotton wool fuses and very accurate time-keeping. She was listening with the greatest attention, when, looking up to sip her coffee, she noticed a young man hurrying eagerly towards their table. When he reached them, he called out to Mr Hayward with friendly familiarity.

'Tom, I thought it was you! I spotted you from afar – have been calling your name this ten minutes or so – I was obliged to run away from my companions to seek you out.'

Mr Hayward rose, smiled in recognition, and shook the hand of the young man, who looked expectantly at the party around the table.

'May I introduce you all to my friend Mr William Ryder? We studied the law together some years ago. Mr Ryder, may I present Mr and Mrs Gardiner, various small Gardiners, and Miss Bennet.'

As Mr Hayward named everyone at the table, Mr Ryder bowed to each of them, even the children, which made them giggle behind their hands. At this, he bowed to them once more, accompanying his flourish with an exaggerated wink, which, as he had intended, provoked even more delighted laughter. Unperturbed, he turned to the rest of the table, addressing them with the greatest good humour.

'I beg your pardon for interrupting you. I hope you will

forgive me for trespassing on your privacy, but your little circle looked so inviting, I could not resist approaching you.'

'We are always glad to meet a friend of Mr Hayward's,' replied Mr Gardiner. 'Will you join us for some wine? We shan't be staying a great deal longer. The lights have been lit, which means it is best for families to take their leave quite soon. But we have time to offer you a glass, if you wish it?'

Mr Ryder, it appeared, did wish it; and in a few moments, he was seated amongst them, a rapidly emptying glass before him, chatting in the liveliest manner. In the course of a quarter of an hour, his hosts learned he had been in the country for the last few months, that he usually lived in Brook Street – here Mary could not help looking towards Mr Hayward, who inclined his head gravely at this news – and that he was a great frequenter of the gardens, visiting them whenever he could. His conversation, though it did not allow much opportunity for others to interrupt its flow, had that transparent willingness to be pleased that rarely fails to recommend itself to its listeners; and it did not take long before Mr Ryder had secured an invitation to take tea at Gracechurch Street the following week. As he was preparing to take his leave, his name was called from a little way across the grass.

Mary looked up – she knew that voice. There on the path, staring towards the Gardiners' box with a look of barely concealed indignation, stood Caroline Bingley. As their eyes met, Miss Bingley allowed herself a chilly nod of recognition. Beside her stood her sister, Mrs Hurst, and her sister's husband, neither looking pleased.

'Ah, I see I am summoned,' murmured Mr Ryder.

He made his goodbyes and was quickly borne off by his friends, Miss Bingley giving a last toss of her head which left no doubt of her sentiments at having been deserted in such a way. Her gesture was no doubt intended to leave everyone at the table feeling a little affronted, but Mary could not help believing it had been particularly directed at her.

'How extraordinary to see Miss Bingley again,' Mrs Gardiner remarked as they left their box. 'It was not very well bred in her to be so standoffish, especially when you consider she has been entertained in our house. But I am more affronted than surprised.'

Mrs Gardiner looked as if she might have enlarged on this theme, but it was plain that Mr Gardiner had on many previous occasions been compelled to a listen to recitations of Miss Bingley's faults; and for all the love he bore his wife, he was not eager to hear it again.

'Your friend is certainly a prodigious talker,' he said hastily to Mr Hayward, in an attempt to change the subject. 'I imagine that must be an asset to him in his profession?'

'It might have been, if he had persevered with it,' replied Mr Hayward. 'But he did not finish his studies. I don't think Ryder was born to be a lawyer.'

'So how does he support himself?' asked Mrs Gardiner.

'He has some money of his own. And he's related to a great lady in Kent, who makes him an allowance that enables him to live as he wishes.'

'I wonder, sir,' asked Mary, suddenly seeing in her mind the pieces of a jigsaw coming together, 'is Mr Ryder's benefactress by any chance Lady Catherine de Bourgh? My sister Elizabeth is related to her by marriage, and she is well known to other friends of mine. I wonder if that is how Mr Ryder came to know Miss Bingley? If he is a favourite of Lady Catherine's, they might have met at family gatherings in Derbyshire.'

'That could perhaps be the lady's name,' replied Mr Hayward, 'although I cannot quite recollect it.'

Mary was about to ask more, when it occurred to her that even as a subject of conversation, she had no desire to introduce Lady Catherine's baleful presence into their happy circle.

Now it was dark, as Mr Gardiner had suggested, the gardens had begun to take on a character not at all suited to the presence of families. There were more young men about than Mary had noticed before, and the smart, bold-eyed ladies, whose occupation she now fully understood, paraded with unmistakeable purpose round the colonnades. It was time for the Gardiners' party to take their leave; and as they traced their way back to their carriage, through the winding paths, illuminated with thousands of tiny candles, Mary found herself again walking alongside Mr Hayward. As they were alone, she felt herself able to indulge her curiosity about his friendship with Mr Ryder.

'If you and Mr Ryder no longer share a common interest in the law, may I ask what continues to draw you together as friends?'

Mr Hayward shot her a quizzical look.

'You do ask the most extraordinary questions!'

'You told me earlier I displayed an interest in human nature, so here I am, seeking to extend my knowledge.'

He turned away to hide a smile.

'I'm not sure I shall tell you. I think you will laugh.'

'I'm sure I shall not.'

'Well, then – the truth is, it was poetry which brought us together. We read it tirelessly when we were students – anything to distract ourselves from the tedious burden of torts and case law. It was my passion, I believe, that drew him to it,' continued Mr Hayward. 'I cared for poetry with an even greater intensity then than I do now, if you can imagine such a thing. But I sometimes wonder if I did Ryder much service in encouraging him to share my dedication. I am not persuaded it was entirely good for him.'

Mary drew her coat around her. The night was growing damp. She picked her way carefully along the path, avoiding the wet grass.

'I'm not sure I understand. Why should it have harmed Mr Ryder to be introduced to something he came to love?'

'For a nature like mine, which is, I suppose, essentially settled and steady, poetry was like a great, noisy thunderbolt,' replied Mr Hayward. 'It woke me up, alerted me to feelings I did not know I had, or certainly had not the words to describe. I don't doubt I'm better for what it has taught me. I'd be a far duller creature without it.'

You could never be dull, thought Mary fondly; *I have never met anyone who less merited that description.*

'But I think poetry had a very different impact upon Will,' Mr Hayward continued. 'He was already of a lively and volatile disposition. He needed no further encouragement to give way to his feelings. He has never put a check upon himself, never stood back and tried to think rationally about what he wants. His heart has always ruled his head. I fear the poetry we read together only encouraged this tendency, with results that have not been wholly beneficial to him.'

They walked a few more paces in silence before Mary spoke.

'That seems a heavy responsibility to lay solely at the feet of poetry. Perhaps if Mr Ryder had been obliged to follow an occupation, had been compelled to apply himself to some useful purpose, he would have learned different habits.'

'I have often thought so,' agreed Mr Hayward. 'The comfortable situation he enjoys has not perhaps been the best friend to him. The world has largely delivered to him anything he desires, with very little effort required on his part to achieve it. He is used to obtaining what he wants merely by asking for it – although I must admit, the asking is always done in the most charming way imaginable, so that it seems a pleasure to indulge him if you can.'

They were nearing the limits of the gardens now, and Mary could see in the darkness a queue of visitors making their way through the gate into the streets beyond, where lines of carriages stood waiting. Suddenly, Mr Hayward stopped and stood still.

'I confess I am ashamed to hear myself talking about a friend in such an unmanly, ungenerous way. I do not know what can have provoked me to say such things. In my defence, I can only say that I speak to you with a freedom I would not extend to anyone else. It is very easy – perhaps too easy – to tell you what is in my heart. I hope you will not blame me for it.'

'I could never do that, Mr Hayward.'

'And I am giving you a very partial picture of Ryder. His impulses are generous and there is no malice in him.'

'I am glad to hear it,' she replied, thinking nothing at all of Mr Ryder and only of his friend. As they stood amongst the shadows of the darkening trees, she longed to reach out and take his hand. For a heartbeat, she thought he was about to do what she could not – but at that moment, her aunt came hurrying back towards them, declaring that Mr Gardiner had found their carriage, and would Mr Hayward like a ride back across the river?

CHAPTER SIXTY

A few days later, Mr Ryder presented himself at Grace-church Street to drink his promised cup of tea. Mary had not imagined that he would act upon his invitation so promptly; but here he was, sitting on Mrs Gardiner's sofa, sipping her best china tea. He was as tall as Mr Hayward, but fair-haired where his friend was dark, with a bright-eyed, agile face, and an air of expansive good nature that made him somehow appear to take up a great deal of space in the neatly decorated room. He was completely at his ease, complimenting Mrs Gardiner on the excellence of her taste, and the advantages of a window looking straight onto the street, where every variety of human experience was to be seen passing by.

'Not quite every variety, I hope. This is one of the better parts of the city.'

'Yes, ma'am, but who can say what range of emotions may be concealed behind the severe expressions of even our most respectable citizens? The shopkeeper may feel as deeply as the poet, even if his features do not reveal it.'

Mrs Gardiner agreed a little reluctantly this might indeed be so and promised to attend more closely to the physiognomies of her neighbours in future. Mary poured out more tea.

'Mr Hayward tells me that you share his passion for poetry, sir?'

'Yes, we learned to love it together while we pored over our law books. I sometimes think it was the only thing that prevented me doing away with myself!'

'Really, Mr Ryder!' exclaimed Mrs Gardiner.

'Well, perhaps I exaggerate a little.'

'Did you find the law so very uncongenial?' asked Mary.

'I'm afraid so. A temperament such as mine isn't suited to the tedium of it.'

'I understand your circumstances do not require you to practise some profession,' said Mrs Gardiner.

'I'm very glad to say they do not. I am lucky enough to be master of my own time; and when I see how hard Tom works, I fully appreciate my good fortune. Now, Miss Bennet, I think it is time for me to discover something about you. Hayward says you are a great reader of serious books. Please tell me which are your favourites and why.'

He put down his cup, folded his arms and waited. Mary had not expected to be interrogated and grew a little flustered under his scrutiny.

'As to my favourites – well, it is hard to say – I shall always hold Mrs Macaulay in high esteem. Mr Hume too of course. The histories and some of the philosophical works. And I have just begun upon something new, Mr Godwin's *Political Justice*. I thought it would be good to read a work written so recently, that speaks to our times.'

'Are you are a radical, then, Miss Bennet? That is a *most* dangerous and revolutionary book, I believe.'

Mary turned away, refusing to rise to his teasing manner, and sought diversion amongst the tea things.

'That is its reputation, but it is in fact a very sober, thoughtful work,' she said, pouring hot water into the teapot. 'It contains some very interesting ideas about how relations between men and women might be improved, if a more rational scheme of behaviour was adopted by society in general.'

Mr Ryder's air of playful condescension had irked her; but she hoped she had not sounded too pompous in reply. Mr Ryder, however, did not seem in the least put out.

'I'm afraid Mr Godwin's book is far too long for me,' he replied, holding out his cup for more tea. 'I only do well with short works. And I have very little time for philosophies based purely on reason, especially when they attempt to reform relations between the sexes. In affairs between men and women, the only thing that should guide us is the heart.'

'I believe that makes you as great an enemy to polite society as Mr Godwin,' declared Mrs Gardiner. 'If there are to be no rules except what we feel at the time, the result will be nothing but anarchy.'

'Yes, that is a point of view,' said Mr Ryder genially, nevertheless implying it was not one he shared himself. 'But there are many others who would welcome such a change – who would embrace it, as ushering in a long-overdue freedom. I am myself in favour of sweeping away the tired old rules that constrain the natural expressions of our souls – and of replacing them with liberty to follow one's inclinations, as and when one wishes.'

'I think you will find, Mr Ryder,' interrupted Mrs Gardiner, 'that the liberty in such a situation tends to be enjoyed by the man, while the consequences are borne – quite literally, in many cases – by the woman. Now, unless we change the subject, I shall have to declare my modesty affronted and ring the bell. Let us talk of something else.'

With an amused glance at Mary, which she once again refused to return, Mr Ryder readily agreed, apologising if he had offended, and declaring himself happy to speak of something else. Mary could not but admire the charm with which he managed the transition – for soon they were safely immersed in conversations of a kind far more proper for the tea table. From these, Mary and her aunt learned that Mr Ryder was indeed a connection of Lady Catherine de Bourgh's, and that it was at Rosings, her house in Kent, that he had first become acquainted with Miss Bingley. He understood now that she and Miss Bennet were related by marriage. Mary did not like to imagine the relish with which she was sure Caroline Bingley had recounted to him the details of the less creditable events in the Bennet family's recent history. But then, she told herself, if Mr Ryder was such an advocate for following one's passions, perhaps Lydia's elopement would not strike him as so very wrong?

The visit went on agreeably enough to the moment when it was appropriate for Mr Ryder to take his leave; he understood perfectly when this moment was reached and departed just before it would have been necessary to hint to him that it was time to go. Mrs Gardiner lay back in her chair and threw her feet onto the sofa opposite her, uttering a great sigh of relief.

'Heaven preserve me from wild young men with dangerous ideas!'

'Do you really think him wild or dangerous?' asked Mary. 'I agree his ideas about men and women were somewhat unorthodox, but beyond that, he did not seem disagreeable. And Mr Hayward says he has a good heart.'

'His being agreeable and his having a good heart, which I do not deny he may possess, makes him more not less of a risk to impressionable young women. And of course, he is very good-looking, if you don't mind a broader type of build.'

'I cannot say I took much notice of his looks.'

'If that is so, then I'm glad to hear it. But I think he noticed yours.'

Mary put down her cup, genuinely surprised.

'My looks? What do you mean? There is never anything to notice about me.'

'If that was once the case, it is not so now. You are nicely turned out, all spick and span, and you smile a great deal more than you used to. Some might say there is a positive bloom about you.'

Mary was both pleased and embarrassed, and not wishing her aunt to see either emotion, she looked determinedly down at her shoes.

'I don't know what to say.'

'I hope you'll accept it as a compliment, which was what I intended. But' – Mrs Gardiner leaned forward, her expression serious – 'do, I beg you, be a little wary of Mr Ryder. An unworldly girl like you can be very appealing to young man who fancies himself beyond the rules that govern the rest of us. There may be no harm in him. But do keep a little distance. Especially as there is someone of infinitely more value so close at hand.'

Mary had resolved some time ago that she would not allow herself to blush again; it seemed such a sign of weakness. But she felt herself redden under her aunt's mild smile. A few seconds of silence ensued, while Mrs Gardiner waited to see if

Mary would speak; but when she saw Mary would not do so, she continued briskly on, as though nothing had happened.

'Well, that is the end of my little sermon. But it is said in fondness, you know.'

CHAPTER SIXTY-ONE

For a week, neither Mr Hayward nor Mr Ryder appeared at Gracechurch Street. Mr Hayward was occupied with a particularly onerous piece of business, and let it be known that he must sacrifice the company of his friends until it was completed; while Mr Ryder, on the other hand, was simply out and about, engaged with the small obligations and more numerous pleasures with which he filled his days. Once, to her surprise, Mary met him on one of her regular walks in the City. She had decided to spend the morning exploring St Paul's Cathedral, and was standing outside it, staring upward at its soaring dome, when she heard his voice beside her.

'Miss Bennet! How delightful to find you here! You are clearly a lover of beautiful buildings, as I am myself.'

He joined her and looked up eagerly into the sharp blue sky where a few white clouds were scudding along in the unseasonably cold wind. Mary was obliged to hold on to her hat, and hope that the many pins she had pushed into her hair that morning would keep it in place, for a while at least.

'It is a noble sight, is it not?' he enthused. 'And one of which I am particularly fond. When I discovered that none of my friends had visited it – imagine that, Miss Bennet, if you can – I was appalled. Nothing would do but that we rectify such a sad omission with all possible haste. So, we leapt into a carriage and here we are. They will be out presently, and I'm sure you'll be delighted to see them, especially as they are already so well known to you.'

Mary's heart sank. It did not take long before her forebodings were realised. Two ladies, also paying close attention to the security of their hats, came striding down the steps that led out of the cathedral; and Mary found herself once again the reluctant recipient of Miss Bingley's and Mrs Hurst's brittle greetings.

'What a pity we could not join you when we saw you at Vauxhall,' began Miss Bingley smoothly. 'We had another engagement that evening, so it was impossible. And I fear we had already exhausted the limited enjoyments the gardens have to offer. But your little party looked entirely satisfied.'

'I've often observed,' agreed Mrs Hurst, 'that it is City people who feel most comfortable at Vauxhall. You all looked very at home there.'

'Yes,' replied Mary, refusing to rise to their jibes, 'we enjoyed it very much.'

'I would have expected nothing else,' said Miss Bingley. She turned to Mr Ryder, who had been surveying the cathedral's great pillared frontage, touching his sleeve lightly with her gloved hand.

'When Mr Hurst joins us, I think it is time for us to go.'

'I don't believe we are in any hurry,' Mr Ryder remarked. 'Besides, I am very keen to hear Miss Bennet's thoughts upon this building. Come, do tell us what impressions St Paul's has awoken in you.'

Mary considered. Whatever comment she made would provoke a sneer from Miss Bingley. She supposed she could say nothing at all, or confine herself to the blandest possible observations, hoping to not to excite that lady's contempt; but to her surprise, she felt herself disinclined to be cowed. She would say what she thought, and Miss Bingley could make of it what she liked.

'It is undoubtedly magnificent,' she began, 'and no one who sees it could fail to be impressed. But I can't help but feel there's something a little cold about it. It's a building more to be admired than loved. I prefer Westminster Abbey. The abbey is a jumble, grown up over the ages, a positive hotchpotch of styles – but I confess I was moved by it in a way I have not been here, much as I wished to be.'

'How unfortunate for poor St Paul's,' murmured Caroline Bingley, 'that it has failed to win your approval. I myself found it remarkably fine. But then I do not pretend to be an expert in such things.'

She looked sideways at Mr Ryder; but he seemed not to have heard her, and it was Mary, and not Miss Bingley, to whom he spoke.

'Yes, I can see that its classical lines would not please everyone. But I'm surprised to find *you* such an advocate for the abbey's gothic charms. I should have thought the severity of St Paul's would be much more to your taste.'

'Once that would have been true. But it really makes no sense to confine one's liking to what one already knows. I'm trying my best to appreciate anything that's pleasing and interesting, wherever it is to be found.'

'How very fascinating,' declared Miss Bingley. 'I hope you will be sure to communicate to all your friends the results of your reflections.'

'I could not agree more,' enthused Mr Ryder, ignoring Miss Bingley once more. 'We should always acknowledge our appreciation honestly, even when it is inspired by the most unexpected objects.'

The wind whipped across the cathedral steps and blew the ribbons securing Miss Bingley's hat in all directions, increasing her mounting impatience.

'Really, where *is* Mr Hurst? I had no idea he was so interested in church architecture. He must have found a verger to buy him a pot of beer. Come, sister, we must go and find him or we shall never get on. Good day to you, Miss Bennet.'

She gave Mary a curt nod of dismissal, and strode away, Mrs Hurst hurrying along in her wake.

'It would seem I must leave you,' exclaimed Mr Ryder, as he hastened after them. 'But I hope to have the pleasure of your company again very soon.'

Mary watched them as they hurried back towards St Paul's, Miss Bingley's irritation obvious in her every angry step. Mary hoped Mr Hurst had indeed found himself some beer to drink. It might enable him to bear the full force of his sister-in-law's displeasure, which was sure to be soon vented upon him.

As she walked briskly back to Gracechurch Street, Mary found herself thinking about Mr Ryder and his charm. She understood now what Mrs Gardiner had meant when she warned her against it a few days before. There was something very powerful about a man who paid one such particular attention. It was impossible not to thaw a little when asked, with every appearance of sincerity, to venture an opinion or offer up a thought. She laughed inwardly at this idea – would such an invitation flatter any woman, or was it only bookish females like herself who would be gratified by it? She supposed a man like Mr Ryder knew only too well how to please and could tailor his manner to suit a variety of dispositions.

But, making her way down Cheapside, Mary concluded that last thought was ungenerous. It suggested calculation in Mr Ryder's manner; and the more she considered it, the more Mary was certain that was not the case. She knew she had little experience of the world, but she did not see in him the deliberate flattery of the practised seducer. No. He was agreeable, not in pursuit of some dark purpose, but simply because that was who he was. His charm was not a weapon to be deployed, but an inescapable element of his character. He liked people to be happy, and it came easily to him to understand how they might be made so. And if that resulted in their looking upon him with indulgence and affection – well, that could hardly be reckoned his fault.

Mary could see exactly how such a thing might happen – how quickly one might fall under his spell – and congratulated herself on her immunity to any such risk. Mr Ryder could never be thought of while Mr Hayward was by. He was Mr Ryder's superior in every possible way. Miss Bingley, she thought, was welcome to him. For, even in the course of a single meeting, it had been evident that Miss Bingley regarded Mr Ryder as very much her own particular property. Whether this arose from her appreciation of his handsome person and pleasing manner or resulted from the general knowledge of his being extremely well provided for, Mary could not say. But it was impossible to ignore the avidity with which Caroline Bingley pursued him, much as she had once done Mr Darcy, finding a thousand occasions to flatter, tease, and cajole him into considering her as a possible wife. Mary supposed Caroline Bingley stood as good a chance of success as anyone. She was elegant, in a glittering, unyielding style, handsome, and clever. She was also very disagreeable, but Mary had often observed men did not seem to feel this to be as grave a disability as might have been expected, provided it was accompanied by a pretty face and a decent dowry.

Yet, for all Miss Bingley's efforts, it did not look as if she had as yet successfully secured her quarry. Mr Ryder treated her with the same good humour he bestowed upon everyone else. He was unfailingly charming, willing to act as escort, guide, or guest. He smiled obligingly at her milder remarks and seemed not to notice her more astringent asides. But he showed no evidence of any warmer feelings. He did not seem interested in *her* opinion of St Paul's, Mary observed. She knew it was an ungenerous thought – but before she dismissed it, she felt a new emotion run through her – a powerful sense of triumph. Today she had been preferred over her enemy, and it pleased her. It was not she who had been snubbed and ignored, but the scheming Miss Bingley. This was not an admirable response, and she suspected none of the great thinkers she had studied would have approved – except, perhaps, Machiavelli, who would have entirely understood why, as she made her way through the now familiar London streets, she carried her head a little higher than usual, a look of amusement lighting up her face.

CHAPTER SIXTY-TWO

Mr Hayward called at Gracechurch Street the following evening. The case that had consumed so much of his time had finally concluded to his advantage, and his mood was jaunty.

'The details are tedious, and I will not bore you with them – but suffice to say I'm pleased with both the result and myself, as I feel my client could not have had one without the other.'

'I trust you made him properly aware of his double good fortune?' asked Mr Gardiner, who had strolled into the drawing room to offer both his congratulations, and a glass of wine.

'I'm afraid I did. A barrister in search of briefs cannot afford to be modest. Someone must sing his praises, even if it is only himself.'

As they raised their glasses to toast his success, Mary studied Mr Hayward with covert approval. He was so quick, so witty, so clever, she thought, so much more estimable in every way than Mr Ryder. There really could be no comparison.

'You have been much missed, Tom,' announced Mrs Gardiner, 'but you must not think we have been solitary in your absence. Your friend Mr Ryder has been on hand to entertain us.'

'Well, that is his particular gift – and his days are far more his own than mine – he has nothing to pursue but his own pleasure. Which brings me quite neatly to the object of my visit. Ryder intends to give a small dinner, and has asked me to discover if the three of you might be persuaded to come? He won't embarrass you with an invitation if it would be unwelcome.'

Mrs Gardiner put down her glass, her expression a little wary.

'Do we know who else will be there?'

'I think it will be quite a select affair. To be honest, his apartments, while they are handsome, are not very large.'

'I imagine the Hursts and Miss Bingley will be amongst the other guests?'

'It is not very fair to put Tom to such a question,' ventured her husband. 'He can hardly answer for Ryder's guests.'

'I think it quite likely that they will be asked,' admitted Mr Hayward. 'Do you have any objection to them?'

'I cannot say I find Miss Bingley much to my taste,' Mrs Gardiner replied.

'I'm sure we should not be obliged to spend any more time with her than politeness requires,' observed Mr Gardiner soothingly. 'Come, Mary, what do you say? Shall we oblige Mr Ryder with our presence?'

Mary could see her aunt would have been relieved if Mary had said she preferred not to attend, but she was reluctant to refuse. She was more experienced now in the arts of sociable dining, and had come to enjoy her place at the Gardiners' table, listening happily to the lively conversations and sometimes contributing to them herself. It would be exciting to attend a dinner somewhere other than Gracechurch Street. Why should Miss Bingley's presence deny her that pleasure?

'It seems rather hard that Mr Ryder should be refused

because we don't find all his acquaintances agreeable. I am quite prepared to brave Miss Bingley's presence if everyone else is prepared to do so with me.'

'Very well, I bow to your wishes,' replied Mrs Gardiner. 'If you can face an evening in Miss Bingley's company, I'm sure I can do the same.'

'I think you may tell Mr Ryder that if he sends in his invitation, we will be pleased to accept,' said Mr Gardiner, opening another bottle of the hock.

Mr Hayward lifted up his glass as invited, to have it refilled.

'I'm very pleased to hear it; but I'm sorry to hear that any friends of Ryder's should be so unmannerly that courage is required to endure their company!'

'Ah, Tom,' declared Mrs Gardiner, 'if all of us were perfect, what would we have to talk about? Mr Gardiner and myself are immune to any darts the lady may choose to send in our direction. And as Mary has declared herself equal to the challenge, I'm sure we will all do very well. Though you must promise, Mary, to come and find me if her teasing becomes unbearable. She will be no match for us both, I can assure you of that.'

CHAPTER SIXTY-THREE

When Mary and the Gardiners arrived at Mr Ryder's apartments for dinner, Mary was amused to discover it was situated at very much the right end of Brook Street. There was no danger of his having to endure as a neighbour the fortune-hunting gambler Mr Hayward had so gleefully conjured up at Vauxhall. Mary was not surprised. Although he liked to declare himself indifferent to the strictest moral conventions, she thought Mr Ryder unlikely to disobey the rules of fashion. He was sure to prefer a small dwelling at the best address to a mansion elsewhere; and as they were ushered into his rooms, she saw she had been right.

Mr Ryder met them as they entered, exclaiming how pleased he was to see them, and showing them every possible attention. The drawing room was not large, but it was gracefully proportioned, with tall first-floor windows and lofty ceilings. Its furnishings were tasteful but not showy, creating an impression of comfort which pleased Mary very much. Through a pair of open double doors, she glimpsed the shine of a well-polished dining table and the dull shimmer of two fine silver candelabra. Mr Ryder ushered them towards the warmest part of the room, where a small knot of people were congregated. It was there they discovered Mr Hayward, already engaged in a lively exchange with two equally animated companions; but on seeing Mary and the Gardiners arrive, he hastened over to greet them.

'I cannot say I know many of the guests, but would be pleased to introduce you to these gentlemen, fellow lawyers of my acquaintance. We are discussing the competing merits of the verse of Lord Byron and Mr Wordsworth.'

'I suppose we need not ask whose part you take, Tom?' said Mr Gardiner mildly.

'No, indeed, sir,' observed one of the eager young men. 'Tom has been defending his hero with the greatest possible stoutness.'

'Are all you legal men such great lovers of literature, then?' asked Mr Gardiner. 'I had not imagined that to be so.'

'We think of little else,' declared the second young man. 'We must have something to distract us from our work. It is either poetry or the bottle, I'm afraid.'

Mary laughed; and Mr Hayward was about to reply, when a great bustle at the door silenced them all. Into the room walked Caroline Bingley, tall, stately, head held high. Her gown was a deep red silk, throwing her white shoulders into stark relief. Garnets shone in her dark hair and at her throat. Mary thought she had never seen anyone look as smart or as terrifying. Mr Ryder stood at her side, leading her in, almost insignificant beside her.

Mr and Mrs Hurst followed in Miss Bingley's wake, quite eclipsed by her chilly hauteur. She unbent a little, as Mr Ryder introduced her to some of the other guests. To those she considered her equals, she condescended sufficiently to be almost gracious; but she did not waste much time on cultivating the good opinions of those who did not matter. Instead, with her most engaging smile, she took Mr Ryder's arm and bore him off, halting before a large portrait which hung above the chimney piece. Mary, who had not been able to turn her gaze away from Miss Bingley's glittering progress, recognised the portrait's subject as Mr Ryder's relation, Lady Catherine de Bourgh. As the room was not large and Miss Bingley's voice was high and clear, it was impossible to ignore what was said, unless one was conversing with someone else; and as Mary stood somewhat apart from the others, she was able to hear everything that passed.

'My dear Mr Ryder, I am so glad you took my advice. Lady Catherine looks magnificent there.'

'She does look very imposing – quite her natural state, one might say.'

'The air of dignity about her is only to be expected for a woman of her rank and position.'

Mr Ryder seemed unable to find a reply to this, but Miss Bingley did not seem to mind.

'I should be very happy,' she went on, in a confiding tone, 'to offer any other small suggestions for the arrangement of your rooms. My taste is generally accounted excellent, and nothing would please me more than to put it at your disposal.'

Mr Ryder thanked her for her offer; and promised that if the occasion should arise when he was in need of such assistance, he would not hesitate to call upon her.

This was enough to please Miss Bingley, who was emboldened to ask if she might take a look at the dinner table, before the guests sat down, 'just to cast my eye across it?'

Mary had not understood that Miss Bingley and Mr Ryder were on such intimate terms. Nor it seemed, had Mr Ryder, who appeared somewhat nonplussed by Miss Bingley's familiarity. But he followed her obediently as she headed to the dining room. When they returned, a short time later, Mary was careful not to catch Miss Bingley's eye; but it was impossible not to notice the look of satisfaction on her face as she swept past her, which Mary was sure did not bode well for someone amongst their number.

It did not take long to discover that it was she herself who was Miss Bingley's victim. When the guests were called to the table, Mary was disappointed to find herself situated far away from all her friends. As he led her to her chair, Mr Ryder, clearly bemused by her placement, explained that Mary had originally been seated closer to himself and Mr Hayward, but that Miss Bingley had insisted she would be happiest alongside Mr Hurst.

'She said you did not often have the chance to talk to him,' he murmured as he pulled out her chair, 'and that you'd be delighted to do so now. Of course, I was pleased to oblige.'

As she sat down, Mary looked around the quickly filling table. At the other end, too far away for them to speak, sat Mr Hayward, who looked at Mary quizzically, puzzled by her exile. Between him and Mr Ryder sat Miss Bingley. When she saw Mary look at her, she returned her gaze with a cool, contented smile, before turning to address Mr Ryder, her hand, Mary noticed, frequently touching his sleeve.

At first, Mary's disappointment was acute. The promise of lively conversation had been the principal reason she had wished to come, and there was little chance of that, situated amongst a circle of unremarkable talkers. On one side of her was the husband of a married pair up from Mr Ryder's native place in Kent, civil enough, but with none of the bantering wit she had come to enjoy. On the other was Mr Hurst, who as yet had done no more than nod grimly in her direction before pouring himself a large glass of wine. She was about to abandon all hope when she noticed Miss Bingley once again look in her direction, too well bred openly to display her victory, but too delighted to hide it entirely. Suddenly, Mary felt a flicker of anger. Why should this scheming, vengeful woman enjoy the satisfaction of watching her sit mute, while she basked in the company of her two irrepressibly talkative neighbours? Why should she give Miss Bingley that pleasure?

She turned to Mr Hurst with a new determination. There must be some subject in which he was interested? Whatever it was, she would make it her business to discover it. This was partly for her own sake – Mary was resolved that when Miss Bingley next turned to look at her, she would see her, not awkwardly silent, but deep in conversation – but also from pity for Mr Hurst. It was true his manners did little to recommend him; he was gruff, almost speechless, and drank with a steady application that Mary found alarming. But her sympathies were always roused by those who seemed lonely and disregarded. She remembered how painful it had been to sit at her father's table, longing for someone to be kind to her. She recalled too, how at Longbourn, a simple willingness to listen and take notice had transformed even Mr Collins into a far more congenial being. *All any of us want is a little attention*, she thought, as she turned towards Mr Hurst with a civil, enquiring expression, and set herself to work.

Mr Hurst seemed to have lost the habit of talking for its own sake, and there were many false starts before Mary eventually hit upon the one subject which animated him. When the first course was served, she knew nothing at all about horse racing. But by the time the dessert was cleared, her knowledge had expanded a hundredfold. She learned not only the different qualities of horse required to succeed on the flat or over the jumps, but also exactly what was to be looked for when assessing a yearling, why Newmarket was always to be preferred as a racecourse to York; and she had made a promise never to wager any significant amount on a likely prospect without first taking Mr Hurst's advice. She could not pretend the experience was as pleasurable as it would have been if she had remained in the place which Mr Ryder had intended for her; but she acquitted herself well, even though, as Mr Hurst might have said, the going had been rough at times. By showing a little spirit, she had avoided the misery of staring silently at her plate for the course of the dinner; and had also been able to show a little indulgence to a man not used to receiving such consideration. As the ladies rose to take coffee next door, leaving the gentlemen to their port and brandy, she was pleased with herself; and certainly, Mr Hurst bade her farewell with every appearance of regret.

CHAPTER SIXTY-FOUR

When Mary entered the drawing room, she headed straight for her aunt, in whom she longed to confide the story of her dinner-table exertions, and the underhand manoeuvres that had made them necessary; but her progress was interrupted by Miss Bingley, who, much to Mary's surprise, took her arm much as she had done Mr Ryder's, and led her in the opposite direction. She stopped at the fireplace and sat down upon one of two sofas which faced each other before it. Reluctantly, Mary took a place opposite her.

'I hope you will excuse me leading you away,' said Miss Bingley, 'but I can't let this evening pass without having had the chance to talk to you properly, a privilege I have not enjoyed for some time.'

'Yes, it was a great pity we were sat at such a distance from each other,' replied Mary. 'If only we had been nearer, we could have conversed as often as we wished.'

'Ah, the mysteries of placement, who can understand them?' Caroline Bingley's smile dismissed the subject as she gestured expansively at the room around them. 'Tell me, what do you think of Mr Ryder's apartments? They are very elegant, are they not?'

'They are certainly very well arranged.'

'Much of the furniture comes from Rosings. Lady Cather-

ine graciously presented it to Mr Ryder when he moved here
to Brook Street.' Miss Bingley's glance moved caressingly
from the small table beside her to an inlaid sideboard standing
upon slender legs. 'She is very fond of him, you know.'

'That is very fortunate for Mr Ryder.'

'When I was last in her company, Lady Catherine told me
she had made your acquaintance when she visited Longbourn.'

The room suddenly felt uncomfortably hot. The idea of
Miss Bingley and Lady Catherine engaged in conversation
about her could only be upsetting; but Mary knew it would be
fatal to display any weakness. She took a single steady breath,
imperceptible to anyone but herself, and replied as calmly as
possible.

'We met when I was staying with Mr and Mrs Collins. She
paid us a visit one afternoon.'

'So I heard. Lady Catherine confessed herself astonished at
the great difference between you and your sister. She said you
were nowhere near as handsome as Elizabeth – but nor were
you so provoking.'

'That was very candid of her.'

'She is well known for her frankness,' observed Miss Bingley, turning to Lady Catherine's portrait, as if she expected it
to confirm what she was about to say. 'In fact, she was
extremely interested in you. She thought you had great
potential – as a governess.'

Mary was horrified. It appalled her to discover that Miss
Bingley was privy to the details of that shameful conversation.
To give herself some occupation while she considered what to
say, Mary reached into a Chinese bowl placed on the table
beside her and drew out a few sprigs of dried lavender, clasping them in her hand.

'But unfortunately,' continued Miss Bingley, 'it seems you left before Lady Catherine could conclude the arrangements. She was most disappointed. She thought it an excellent opportunity for you.'

'I was very grateful for Lady Catherine's concern,' Mary replied, 'but as I explained to her, I don't think I'm suited to becoming a governess. It isn't the kind of life I should choose for myself.'

'You surprise me. It would have made excellent use of all those accomplishments you have worked so hard to acquire. Well, if it isn't to be the schoolroom, you must intend marriage, I suppose.'

'I did not say so. Those are your words, not mine.'

'But as you have declined to join the ranks of one of the few occupations open to respectable females, it is hard to see what other destiny you have in mind. Unless you positively hope to end up as a spinster?'

A memory sprang unbidden into Mary's mind, of her piano teacher, poor, harassed Miss Allen, hurrying up the drive to Longbourn in her shabby black coat, her music books heavy under her arms.

'Your silence speaks volumes,' shot back Miss Bingley. 'Let us assume then that we must all marry in the end. Even clever women like yourself. In that case, perhaps you will allow me to offer you a little advice?'

'I think you intend to do so, whether I wish it or not.'

'It seems to me,' began Miss Bingley, 'that a great deal of time is thrown away in the pursuit of attachments that can never come to anything. I refer to those where the difference in rank between the gentleman and the lady is simply too wide to be bridged. The most harmonious matches are always those where there is something like an equality of position between the parties involved.'

Suddenly, they were interrupted by the sound of loud, male voices. The gentlemen had tired of each other's company in the dining room and had come in to join the ladies. Mr Ryder was first through the door; he waved happily at Mary and then at Miss Bingley, who threw back her shoulders and smiled invitingly at him in return. There could be no doubt of her intentions towards him. Mary looked from Mr Ryder back to Miss Bingley, poised and superior in her dark red dress. She felt disinclined to be bullied as she had been so often before.

'I'm afraid your meaning is a little obscure. I assume you refer to me, but I fail to understand in what connection. As I look about this room, I see no one here but gentlemen. And as I am a gentleman's daughter, I perceive no outrageous distinctions in rank.'

'That you choose not to see them does not mean they are not there,' retorted Miss Bingley.

'I do not see why that should concern you. Unless you believe, in some way I do not appreciate, that I am an obstacle to your own matrimonial ambitions?'

'I think you know very well to what I refer.'

'Do you mean to suggest I am pursuing Mr Ryder? Or that he is pursuing me? If so, I can tell you both accusations are equally without foundation.'

This time it was Miss Bingley who looked away first. Her hand flew to her hair, which she patted thoughtlessly, before returning to the attack once more.

'Really? And yet it seems you do all you can to please him. I cannot imagine why else he would speak of you as he does.

Apparently, *you* have a cultivated mind and take an interest in the world. *You* have no false manners or artificial enthusiasms. And there is never anything shallow or affected about *you*. You must have worked very hard to have left such a favourable impression.'

No woman can be entirely unmoved to learn she has been sincerely praised by a man, especially when she is not used to hearing herself admired; and Mary felt some satisfaction at hearing Mr Ryder's words reported back to her in Miss Bingley's resentful tone. But she did not allow it to alter her reply.

'You are quite mistaken in what you imply. Mr Ryder speaks well of everyone. It is his way. You, who have made such a close study of him, must have seen this for yourself. It does not signify any particular liking for me. He does not mean anything by it.'

Miss Bingley was unconvinced.

'How, then, is your own behaviour to be understood? You always seem very happy to listen to anything he has to say. And you have certainly smartened yourself up since I saw you last. What is the reason for that, if not to improve your prospects, in one way or another?'

Mary was suddenly so angry that she did not trust herself to speak; and in those few seconds, Miss Bingley recovered much of the self-possession which had briefly deserted her.

'Confine yourself to your proper sphere, Miss Bennet. Do not trespass where you cannot hope to succeed. Do not embarrass yourself and your friends by pursuing an attachment which cannot be returned. Presumption of that kind leads only to disappointment and humiliation where matters of the heart are concerned.'

Mary had promised herself she would not allow Caroline

Bingley to provoke her, that she would not sink to exchanging insults – but she could contain herself no longer. When Mr Darcy had so obviously ignored Miss Bingley's advances in favour of Lizzy, Mary had felt some sympathy for her. She did not think her amiable, but she had been sorry for her humiliation. But now any sense of pity was utterly extinguished.

'You seem to know a great deal about rejection. Is this a lesson you have learned from extensive study? Or do you perhaps owe it to experience of a more personal nature?'

Miss Bingley flinched – she had not expected Mary to land such a blow. Her outrage was unmistakeable – Mary thought she might have struck her if such behaviour had been permitted in polite drawing rooms. But instead, Miss Bingley drew her red skirt around her, as if to protect her from further insult.

'I speak only from what I have observed. It is a truth universally acknowledged, I believe.'

With a contemptuous nod, Miss Bingley rose and strode quickly away, over to where Mr Ryder and the other gentlemen stood. Mary watched as she moved as close to Mr Ryder as she dared and began to practise upon him all the little flirtatious teases with which she had once sought to attract Mr Darcy. Even from across the room, Mary could sense the archness in Caroline Bingley's tone, could imagine the playful scolding with which Mr Ryder was charmingly rebuked, and could almost feel the repeated light touch of her fan on his arm, a gesture so suggestive of her possessive intent that Miss Bingley might as well have shouted out her intentions to the entire room.

Mary remained on the sofa, disturbed by the vehemence of the encounter. The lavender stems were still in her hands and she rubbed them together more until they released their strong, pure scent, which she breathed in deeply to calm herself. She could not believe what had just happened. It was scarcely to be credited that Miss Bingley should consider her, of all people, a rival for Mr Ryder's attentions; and it was even more to be wondered at that she had not meekly absorbed the insults with which Miss Bingley accompanied her accusations. She had fought back – and with some asperity too. Had she been too cruel? She considered the question seriously for a moment, before recalling the numerous petty humiliations to which Miss Bingley had subjected her, the many small indignities she had suffered at that lady's hands. No, she did not think so. She tucked the lavender sprigs into the sash of her dress, rose from the sofa quite calmly, and went to find her aunt and uncle, entirely satisfied with her conduct.

CHAPTER SIXTY-FIVE

ary discovered Mr and Mrs Gardiner seated comfortably in the quieter part of the room, in conversation with the couple from Kent. Her aunt beckoned her to sit beside them; and as soon as politeness allowed it, took her niece to one side, and, in a low whisper, asked what had occurred between herself and Miss Bingley.

'I saw you speaking to her just now,' she began, 'and I was quite concerned. I hope she was behaving herself?'

'Oh, she was much as she always is,' said Mary. 'There were a few matters she wished to discuss with me.'

'Really?' replied Mrs Gardiner. 'That seems most unlike her. She's never shown any desire to speak to us before.'

She looked at her niece questioningly. Mary was unsure how much of Miss Bingley's conversation she should reveal. Part of her was tempted to confide in her aunt, as there was no one she trusted more. But she knew any confession would result in adverse consequences. Mrs Gardiner was already wary of Mr Ryder and what she regarded as his excessively free and plausible manner. If Mary were to tell her about Miss Bingley's jealousy, that would only add to her aunt's prejudice against him, for his being admired by a woman she disliked was not calculated to improve her opinion of him. She supposed Mrs Gardiner might even discourage him from visiting Gracechurch Street; and when Mary contemplated that prospect, she was honest enough to acknowledge she did not welcome it. If Mr Ryder were no longer to call at Gracechurch Street, there was no doubt that Miss Bingley would consider that a great victory. She would tell herself that for all Mary's bluster, she had quickly capitulated to Miss Bingley's will and had obediently forbidden Mr Ryder her company. Mary's expression hardened as she imagined the pleasure this would afford Miss Bingley, and decided this was not a satisfaction she was prepared to grant her. She would say nothing to her aunt that might result in Mr Ryder's exclusion; and would instead do all she could to ensure he came just as often as before.

Mary was honest enough to admit that her reluctance to see less of Mr Ryder did not arise solely from her desire to disoblige Miss Bingley. He was a very entertaining visitor, amusing, lively, intriguing; even his frank declarations, which had so provoked her aunt, were exciting to her. She had never met anyone quite like him before, so confident in his own opinions and so untroubled by the criticisms of others. There was something refreshing in the uncomplicated sunniness of his character, which turned effortlessly away from any difficulty, gravitating instead to what was pleasurable and, of course, gratifying to himself. She hastened to remind herself that he had none of Mr Hayward's finer qualities; but it could not denied that Mr Ryder was naturally and undeniably happy, and Mary had discovered it improved her state of mind to be amongst happy people. For that reason alone, she would have been sad to see him no more at Gracechurch Street.

All these considerations confirmed her resolve to keep to herself what had passed between her and Miss Bingley; and she managed a tolerably cheerful smile as she replied.

'Oh, it was really nothing. Nothing that bears repeating anyway.'

Mrs Gardiner did not appear entirely convinced, but before she could interrogate Mary further, Mr Ryder himself appeared before them, eager to hear that supper had been to their liking. Both exclaimed that they had enjoyed it very much, although Mrs Gardiner regretted Mary had been placed so oddly.

'I was very well where I was,' answered Mary quickly. It seemed as if Mr Ryder was about to offer an explanation for her exile, and she had no wish for her aunt to hear of Miss Bingley's stratagems.

'As I was denied the pleasure of conversing with you tonight,' said Mr Ryder, 'I hope I may be allowed to make up for my loss by calling on you tomorrow.' He looked enquiringly at Mrs Gardiner. 'Might that be convenient?'

From across the room, Mary glimpsed Miss Bingley watching them closely, and decided to deflect any possibility of refusal.

'I'm sure we should very much like to see you – should we not, aunt?'

'Of course,' said Mrs Gardiner. 'We shall be glad to offer you tea, Mr Ryder. As long as there is no more talk of unregulated passions.'

'I promise to say nothing at all about passions, ma'am, regulated or otherwise.'

Mrs Gardiner watched him coolly as he walked away.

'I'm not sure why you were so keen to have that young man at the house again.'

'It seemed the polite thing to do. He invited us here, after all.'

'I suppose you are right,' replied Mrs Gardiner uncertainly. 'But he is a little too pert for my tastes.'

Her face suddenly broke into a smile. Mary turned and saw Mr Hayward was approaching them, carrying two glasses of wine, which he presented to them before settling himself on the sofa opposite.

'Ah, Tom,' declared Mrs Gardiner with a glance at Mary, '*you* are always welcome at Gracechurch Street, for breakfast, dinner, or even children's tea, if you think you have the courage to attempt it.'

'If there was bread and butter on offer, it should hold no fear for me. Especially if there was greengage jam. We never get that at my lodgings.'

'Oh, the sorrows of the single man!' lamented Mrs Gardiner. 'When you change your situation, you may demand from your wife whatever jam you wish for. That's a husband's privilege, you know.'

'One I eagerly look forward to exercising at such future time. What is your opinion, Miss Bennet? You're sure to have one, even upon jam.'

'It is raspberry for me,' Mary declared, 'or, if that's not to be had, I may console myself with strawberry. But I venture no further into the exotic.'

'I'm sorry to hear it,' he said. 'So even if we were married, I could not obtain the wish of my heart – greengage jam at breakfast.'

Mary smiled. The idea of them as husband and wife, eating greengage jam together, affected her so powerfully that, to give herself something else to think about, she plucked the bunch of lavender from her sash and began to rub the sprigs between her fingers.

'Where did you find that?' asked Mr Hayward.

'I took them from a bowl over there,' Mary replied. 'I hope that does not make me a thief.'

'Well, possession is always said to be nine-tenths of the law.' He moved towards her. 'It smells very good. May I have a piece?'

Mary held out a sprig to him. He took it and stuck it in the button hole of his jacket.

'Your friend Mr Ryder has invited himself to Gracechurch Street tomorrow,' said Mrs Gardiner. 'I suppose I could not convince you to come too?'

He looked genuinely disappointed.

'I should like that of all things, but it's impossible. I have so much business at present that I cannot get away. I am very sorry for it.'

'That's a great pity. Mr Ryder cannot really take your place. We miss you, Tom. Don't we, Mary?

'Yes,' agreed Mary quietly. 'We do indeed.'

Not long afterwards, Mr Ryder's supper reached that point, never publicly declared but always privately understood, when everyone knew it was time to go. Soon Mary stood in the hallway, waiting while her aunt and uncle made their farewells to their host. Mr Hayward appeared with her coat, which he had undertaken to retrieve for her.

'I hope Ryder is not becoming a trial to you and Mrs Gardiner,' he said as he helped her into it. 'He takes up people he likes with great enthusiasm, but he does not always know when he has outstayed his welcome. I'm sure I could suggest he lengthen the intervals between his visits somewhat.'

'Oh, I don't think that will be necessary,' replied Mary, her mind still upon thwarting Miss Bingley. 'He is really no trouble, and I should not like to hurt his feelings.'

'I see,' he replied, somewhat taken aback. 'Of course, I shan't speak to him unless you wish it.'

Mary saw instantly that he had misunderstood her meaning. She had not meant to imply that she could not bear to surrender a moment of Mr Ryder's company; but that was clearly what Mr Hayward thought he had heard. She was about to attempt to correct such an unfortunate impression, but before she could do so, she was surprised to hear her own name pronounced, quite loudly, at the bottom of the stairs. At first, she did not recognise the voice. Then she saw Mr Hurst and his wife standing at the front door below, and she realised it was he who was speaking. His wife's words were said too low to be audible, but her husband's were only too easily discerned.

'You and your sister may say what you please, but in my opinion, that Bennet girl is much improved. It was a pleasure to sit next to her.'

His wife's response could not be heard, but to Mary's increasing distress, Mr Hurst replied with even greater volume.

'Well, she didn't look plain to me. Perfectly tolerable in my opinion. You can see Ryder's interested. If I were him, I'd snap her up before some other fellow does.'

To Mary's intense relief, they heard no more, as Mr Hurst was bustled into the carriage and carried away. In the silence that followed, Mr Hayward stepped towards her, horrified.

'Miss Bennet, I must apologise. I should have called out – I should have told him he could be heard. I was too slow.'

'I'm sure he didn't mean it – he drank a lot of wine at dinner.'

'I'm very sorry you had to hear such things,' said Mr Hayward angrily. 'I should have prevented it.'

'Really, it was not your fault. Mr Hurst is not a very sensible man. Who can say what he might come out with?'

Suddenly she was very tired and could not think clearly. First, Miss Bingley, and now this. She began to feel overwhelmed.

'I think I should like to go now. If you would take me to my uncle and aunt's carriage, I'll wait for them there. And please, Mr Hayward, don't tell them what just happened.'

Tom Hayward took her arm and led her forward. Neither of them mentioned Mr Ryder as they walked out into the darkness. But Mary thought Mr Hayward had a preoccupied look, as though an idea had occurred to him that he did not much care for, and he was turning over in his mind what he should do about it. He handed her into the carriage and bid her a polite good night. She threw herself back against the seat and closed her eyes. If it was as painful as this to live a life of feeling, then perhaps cold rationality had a great deal to recommend it.

CHAPTER SIXTY-SIX

Mary was silent next morning at breakfast, and her aunt prudently did not press her to account for her distracted state. Her experience with both Jane and Elizabeth had taught her that the best action to take with unhappy young women was often to do nothing at all. So she contented herself with passing coffee in Mary's direction, making no comment when it was politely refused; and when Mary declined to accompany her and the children on an excursion to the Park, she acquiesced graciously without fuss.

Chased from the breakfast table by servants impatient to clear it, Mary wandered into the drawing room, where she picked up her book and tried to read; but she could not settle. Her mind returned again and again to the events of the previous night. Why had she not spoken to Mr Hayward when she had the chance? A few well-chosen words might have made it clear she had not meant to suggest that Mr Ryder's company was so important to her. If she could have got them out before Mr Hurst's unfortunate remarks, so much the better. Afterwards, she had been too unhappy to speak. Mr Hayward had helped her into the Gardiners' carriage in silence, his expression unreadable. Again, she had said nothing. She would not make that mistake again. When next he called, she must make sure she was alone with him for long enough to explain what had happened. But then she recalled his warning that press of business was likely to prevent his visiting for a while – what if he did not come for weeks?

She was considering the full horror of such a possibility when the doorbell rang downstairs. She started up with surprise, her open book falling to the floor. It was far too early for Mrs Gardiner to have returned – was there any chance it might be Mr Hayward? She knew this was most unlikely, that he was certain at this hour to be at his office; but her hopes sprang up regardless. Why should it not be him, he might be passing, perhaps some errand had brought him into Cheapside? None of these were likely occurences, but when it was not Tom Hayward but Mr Ryder who was announced, Mary's spirits nevertheless fell like a stone.

'Mr Ryder! We did not expect you so early. I'm afraid Mrs Gardiner is out.'

Mary did her best not to reveal the disappointment that so unreasonably welled up within her, and it appeared she had succeeded, for Mr Ryder seemed quite unaware of the degree to which his not being someone else had distressed her.

'I'm sorry to hear that. I had hoped this was the perfect moment for coffee.'

He gazed at her expectantly, but Mary was not sure she was equal to making polite conversation this morning – and especially not with Mr Ryder.

'I'm afraid the servants are still clearing the breakfast things.'

'Then surely there must be a pot of coffee quite close to hand?'

He spoke with his usual good nature, but was plainly determined not to be refused.

'It need only be a very small cup, you know. And I am quite happy to drink it lukewarm.'

Mary wavered. She could not send him away, not after such a plea. It would be easier to entertain him than to eject him, and it need only be for a very short while. She called for coffee, and soon, Mr Ryder was exactly where had wanted to be, confidently established on Mrs Gardiner's best sofa with the Chinese yellow chintz.

'I have come to see how you enjoyed the dinner last night, Miss Bennet.'

'Very much, sir. It was a most interesting evening, in every way.'

'I think you would have liked it more at our end of the table – we were very lively there.'

'Yes,' replied Mary. 'It did seem as though your conversations required rather less effort than my own.'

'I wondered why you expressed so strong a desire to sit alongside Mr Hurst. I should not have imagined you shared many interests.'

'I am not sure I did express it; but I must say that as a result, I know a great deal more about horse racing than I did last week, both the jumps and the flat.'

'Now that I recollect,' declared Mr Ryder, 'it was Miss Bingley who insisted you would be happier seated next to him. I imagined she was acting upon your wishes.'

'I'm sure she was doing what she thought best.' Mary had no desire for the breach between herself and Miss Bingley to become more widely known. 'I expect she thought it a kindness, to one of us at least.'

Mr Ryder put down his coffee cup and shot Mary a conspiratorial, confiding smile.

'I have not observed that little acts of kindness are much in Miss Bingley's line.'

Before she could help herself, Mary laughed – then immediately regretted it, and sought to compose her features into a suitably contrite and neutral expression.

'It is very wrong of you to make such an ungenerous remark.'

'The remark was mine, it is true,' murmured Mr Ryder. 'But the laugh was all your own.'

'Yes,' replied Mary, 'and now I'm rather ashamed of it.'

'Of course you are,' said Mr Ryder, surveying her with an intensity she found disconcerting. 'It does not come easily to you to be disobliging. *You* are not someone who takes pleasure in being unkind.'

Their conversation, which Mary had hoped would be light, bright and emptily social, appeared to be taking a very different direction, one she was not certain she wished to encourage.

'Really, Mr Ryder, you hardly know me at all. You cannot say what I might do or how I might behave.'

'I must contradict you, Miss Bennet. I believe I have a very good sense of who you are. And before you protest, I will tell you why I think so. First, I am influenced by the judgement of my friend. Tom has an excellent opinion of you – he always speaks of you in the highest possible terms – and there is no one whose perceptions I trust more. Secondly, I listen to what my own feelings tell me. My heart assures me that you are exactly what you seem to be, and I am happy to believe it. There is no artifice about you, Miss Bennet. Your qualities shine out. They have not been obscured or corrupted by the false polish of the world. I do not need to know you better than I do already to know that this is true.'

Mary could not bear to sit any longer trapped in the uncomfortable directness of Mr Ryder's stare. She broke away by picking up her book from the floor on which it had fallen, and placed it carefully beside her on the sofa.

'These are observations of a very personal nature,' she said.

'I realise this is not the usual language of the drawing room,' he replied. 'But you know I have no very high opinion of the petty rules to which we submit ourselves in the name of good manners or politeness.'

'Yes,' ventured Mary mildly. 'I believe you have mentioned it.'

He stood up, warming to his theme, and began to stride about the room as he spoke.

'It is my conviction, Miss Bennet, that our inability to say what we mean, to tell the truth about what we think and feel, is one of the great curses of our age. We say we honour candour and honesty, but we do not practise them. Instead, we hide behind a thousand equivocations and disguises that we like to call politeness – and remain in wilful ignorance of the truth of our affections, when knowledge of them might have changed our lives forever, had we but been aware of their existence.'

He stopped by the sideboard and placed his arm lightly upon it, striking a very elegant pose.

'That, Miss Bennet, is what I believe. And I came here today to put that belief into practice and commit the great impropriety of telling you honestly what I think of you.'

'Is that really wise, Mr Ryder? There may be occasions when, for all manner of reasons, some things are better left unsaid.'

'I cannot agree. I intend to live my life by bolder principles.' He stood silent for a moment, imagining perhaps the multitude of possibilities contained in that thought, before moving back to his place on the sofa opposite Mary.

'I gave some thought to how I might achieve this aim,' he explained in a more thoughtful tone, 'and it seemed to me that poetry was the best way to capture what I wanted to say. I did try to scribble a few lines myself – but they did not turn out as I wished. Then I thought of some verses of Mr Wordsworth's – and when I looked them out, they summed you up so well – captured your spirit so perfectly – that I knew I need look no further.'

He pulled a piece of paper from his pocket.

'May I be allowed to read them to you?'

Mary hesitated. Propriety of the kind Mr Ryder so disdained urged her to refuse. But curiosity overcame her – which poem would he quote? What did he wish to say? She did not have the strength to deny him, so she nodded, and he began.

> *'She dwelt amongst the untrodden ways*
> *Behind the springs of Dove,*
> *A maid whom there were none to praise*
> *And very few to love:*
>
> *A violet by a mossy stone*
> *Half hidden from the eye!*
> *Fair as a star, when only one*
> *Is shining in the sky.'*

He read surprisingly well, measured, sincere, and heartfelt. Mary had not expected that; and, as a result, was unprepared for the degree to which the poem moved her.

'It captures something true to you, I believe,' he said simply, folding up the paper.

'You see me as a lonely figure then?' asked Mary.

'Isolated, perhaps. "She dwelt among the untrodden ways . . ."'

Mary knew she must fight against surrendering to the emotions the poem had aroused in her. If she allowed herself to succumb, she might lose her self-possession in front of him – and that would never do.

'I was brought up in Hertfordshire, sir,' she said, brightly. 'The road to London was barely five miles away.'

'It is possible, I have heard, to feel oneself alone, even in such close proximity to town.'

'In my village,' she continued, 'it was quite untrue to say that "there were none to praise, and very few to love". There were scores of people only too eager to praise my sisters. And they had no difficulty in finding people to love, as they are all married now.'

Mr Ryder considered for a moment.

'Then I direct you to the later lines. Perhaps the attractions of your sisters kept you "half hidden from the eye". Now they are claimed, you can be seen as you deserve at last, "fair as a star, when only one is shining in the sky".'

Mary caught her breath. His words reminded her powerfully of what Mrs Hill had once said to comfort her, back in the days when she had felt so alone and unhappy that she had not known what to do with herself. Mr Ryder had surprised her; she had not imagined that he possessed such insight into the hopes and fears of others. Perhaps there was more to him than she had thought? From under lowered eyes, she looked up at him, broad-shouldered, well made, his fair hair catching the morning sun, a striking figure in his dark coat.

'You are very direct, Mr Ryder. You do not hold back.'

'As I said before, we owe to ourselves to speak the truth as our heart feels it, Miss Bennet. I think you are about to come out from underneath your own mossy stone and become visible for the first time. I should very much like to be there when you emerge, blinking a little, into the light.'

It seemed to please him that he had ruffled her composure.

'I feel I've said enough for one morning. Please keep the poem. I hope it will help you think kindly of me. Good morning to you.'

He bowed and left the room. As he went downstairs, Mary heard Mrs Gardiner and the children return, Mr Ryder exchanging a few pleasantries with them as he went away. She stuffed the piece of paper quickly into her pocket and did all she could to appear as self-possessed as possible as her aunt hurried into the room.

'What on earth can Mr Ryder be thinking, calling so early? That is a young man who follows his own inclinations far too readily for my taste.'

'I think he was merely in search of coffee and some company. He did not stay long.'

She looked out of the window, watching Mr Ryder as he strode confidently down the busy street. She did not know what to think as he disappeared from view. There could be no doubt now he had some regard for her. She could not say what form it took, or how deep it ran, but his liking could not be denied. Nor could she pretend that the encounter had not been exciting.

And yet, at the same time as she gave herself up to the

unfamiliar pleasure of knowing herself the subject of a man's admiration, she could not help asking what that admiration was worth. Was his manner perhaps rather too easy and untroubled to suggest true emotion? Could truly deep sentiments be quite so readily expressed? She did not think that he was insincere. But it occurred to her that he had rather enjoyed playing the role of the man of feeling, that part of him had been observing himself as he did so, and that he had gone off convinced he had acquitted himself pretty well.

It was just as well, she thought, that she did not harbour strong affection for him. It was impossible not to feel some warmth towards a man who was so open in his professions. But in her heart, she knew that it was not from him that she longed to hear them. She wished more than anything she had had the courage to ask him what Mr Hayward had said about her. It thrilled her to know that he had spoken well of her to his friend – but who knew what he might think now?

'Mary,' said Mrs Gardiner. 'Mary, are you listening to me at all?'

Mary looked up to find herself the object of Mrs Gardiner's enquiring glance, and realised she had been so lost in her own thoughts that she had heard nothing of what her aunt said.

'I was asking what Mr Ryder had to say about his dinner last night. Did he think it had gone well?'

'Yes,' Mary replied, 'he seemed pleased enough.'

Mrs Gardiner threw herself onto the sofa, exhaled with relief at sitting down at last, and put her feet on a little padded stool. She looked as if she was about to speak again; but Mary knew she could not bear it if she asked her anything else about Mr Ryder.

'If you'll excuse me, aunt, there's something I must fetch – I'm sorry, I will be back directly.'

As she rushed away up to her room, Mrs Gardiner sighed as she watched her go. It did not seem as though Mary's state of mind had improved at all since she took the children for their airing. If anything, she seemed even more distracted now than she had been at breakfast.

CHAPTER SIXTY-SEVEN

Mr Ryder visited Gracechurch Street again a week later, and once more laid himself out to be as winning and as personable as possible. He brought with him a pound of the very best coffee and presented it to Mrs Gardiner with a flourish, hoping it would make up for all the pots of it he had enjoyed in her house. He was gracious and charming, until even her aunt began to unbend a little, admitting he was excellent company when he chose to be. Mary did not disagree, for Mr Ryder was indeed very amusing; his stories of the grand state kept by Lady Catherine de Bourgh at Rosings always made her laugh, even when she knew it was wrong to do so – she was sure Dr Fordyce would not have approved of such ill-directed levity. So, the days passed by agreeably enough, and Mr Ryder became an ever more frequent guest. But it was his friend whom Mary longed to see – and still Mr Hayward did not appear.

He wrote to the Gardiners apologising for his absence, blaming it upon the legal case with which he was still much engaged, and declaring that he hoped to be sharing their excellent suppers as soon as he was free to do so. It was a friendly, chatty letter, and at the end of it he sent everyone his best love. Mary spent a great deal of time brooding over the precise application of that phrase, trying to decide the exact proportion of his affection which might have been addressed to her. He added that he hoped to see them all very soon – but as there was nothing more specific in the way of date or time attached to his note, it did not give Mary a great deal of comfort.

In the end, it was Mr Gardiner, one night at dinner, who put an end to all her silent conjectures. 'I ran into Tom Hayward today,' he declared, as he stood at the table, carving what promised to be an excellent leg of lamb. 'I was up near Chancery Lane, and our paths crossed. He was in a great hurry – black gown on, papers under his arm – but sends his regards to everyone. Says he misses us all very much.'

Mary picked up her napkin and, with great self-control, laid it carefully on her lap.

'I think it is most remiss of him to have left us alone for so long,' declared Mrs Gardiner. 'Surely he could have spared a few hours to call?'

Mr Gardiner began to place the carved meat onto plates and hand them round the table.

'I know you are only joking, my dear,' he said, with the merest hint of reproach in his voice. 'But that is a little unfair. Tom really has no choice. The case he is embarked upon is of the very first consequence to him, and he must devote every minute towards his prosecution of it.'

'I consider myself admonished,' replied his wife. 'But my remark was not so much a complaint, more a confession of how much I miss him. We all miss him, I believe.'

She glanced at Mary, who did not catch her eye.

'What is this case about,' she asked, 'and why is it so important to Mr Hayward?'

Mr Gardiner sat down, his carving duties over, and poured himself a glass of wine.

'I cannot tell you much about the detail of it,' he replied, 'as the law is not really my line. But I understand Tom is one of those acting for a great commercial concern – well, I suppose I may say it is the East India Company – on some question of contracts made or not made, honoured or not honoured.'

'That sounds like a very big step for him,' murmured Mrs Gardiner.

'It is indeed,' agreed her husband. 'He has already had one notable win this year. If he can bring this one off with the same success, it will be of great advantage to him.' He picked up his knife and fork, ready now to attack his lamb. 'Both reputationally and financially.'

'It could quite make his name, then?' Mary asked.

'I believe so. He told me it could produce a very material change in his circumstances.'

'I'm sure we all wish him the greatest good luck,' said Mrs Gardiner, 'but I look forward to having him back amongst us and hope we will see him soon.'

'That may be sooner than you think,' replied Mr Gardiner, 'as I took the opportunity of our meeting to quiz Tom about our trip to the Lakes.'

The original plan for their excursion had been to leave in August, and thus avoid the hottest and most uncomfortable season in the City. But, as Mr Gardiner explained, that date had begun to look increasingly uncertain, as his business affairs threatened once more to require his presence in London just at the time they should have been taking their leave of it.

'But I could not endure your being disappointed of your holiday again,' continued Mr Gardiner, looking fondly at his wife, 'so I took it upon myself to make other arrangements, to ensure that this time you should have the wish of your heart gratified, exactly as you deserve.'

Mr Gardiner had decided that the best solution was to bring their trip forward to the first week of July. If they could travel then, the whole holiday might be accomplished before his affairs became pressing. On hearing his plan, Mrs Gardiner rose from her chair, went to her husband's side and kissed him warmly on the cheek.

'How kind of you to think of all this,' she cried. 'It is the sweetest thought. But that is only two weeks away! Can it be managed in that time?'

Mr Gardiner believed it could, as he had already embarked upon some of the more pressing necessities – he had secured their rooms at inns, arranged places on coaches – had done all he could to ease matters, acting on the presumption Mrs Gardiner would be happy to go. As her aunt assured her husband that nothing would please her more, Mary's thoughts were elsewhere, concentrated on the only question which really concerned her – would Mr Hayward join them, or would he be obliged to stay behind?

'I described my plans to Tom,' continued Mr Gardiner, as if he had read her mind. 'I hoped very much he would still be able to join us, for we should all be sorry to lose his company. And he told me it was entirely possible, for his case must be done with by then.'

'Oh, I am so glad,' exclaimed Mary, overwhelmed by relief. She would see him and talk to him. They would be together for the duration of the holiday.

'He will not travel up with us, as he is not exactly sure when he will be free to leave. But we shall meet him at our inn, where I think we shall be a very comfortable little party,' said

Mr Gardiner, entirely satisfied that his plan had been so well received. He was about to serve himself a little more lamb when a thought struck him.

'Ah, Mary, I nearly forgot. Tom asked me to give this to you.'

He pulled from his pocket a small book, brand new, still in the bookseller's wrapper. Mary took it, holding it in her hand for a moment, so pleased with the gift that she was almost afraid to open it.

'What is it?' asked Mrs Gardiner, as Mary uncovered it. 'Is it more poetry?'

'No, not exactly. It is *A Guide to the Lakes*. But it is by Mr Wordsworth, so I imagine it will have something of the poetic in it.' She turned to the title page, and gently smoothed the paper under fingers. 'It contains everything in it a traveller could wish for – he recommends walks, rides, and even inns!'

'Yes,' said Mr Gardiner, 'I chose those we are to stay in from it.'

Her uncle turned to her aunt and went on to describe in some detail the characters of the inns, and the accommodation they promised; but Mary was not listening. In the middle pages of the *Guide*, she had found a single folded slip of paper – a note from Mr Hayward.

My dear Miss Bennet,
Here is something to occupy you on the journey north.
Please study it closely as I shall be sure to ask you questions about it when we meet!
I am sorry to have been such a stranger these last weeks. But when we see each other again, we shall walk in Wordsworth's footsteps, which I hope will mean as much to you as it does to me.

Please take this as notice I intend to stride up as many green mountains as may be achieved in the time we have. Perhaps we may venture a few hills together?
Tho. Hayward

Mary looked up to see if the Gardiners had noticed her reading the letter. When she saw they were deep in conversation and had not observed it, she slid the slip of paper gently back into the *Guide,* suffused with pleasure and relief. He had not forgotten her. She was still in his thoughts. As she looked around the room, she realised that she had never been so happy as she had been these last few months at Gracechurch Street. As her eye passed over the comfortable surroundings, as she took in the excitement with which her uncle and aunt were now eagerly discussing the trip they would so enjoy, Mary knew she owed a great deal of her newfound contentment to the Gardiners, and to the healing, restorative powers of their home. But she understood too that if anyone could be said to have completed that happiness, then that person was Mr Hayward. It was perhaps not surprising that she carried the *Guide to the Lakes* to bed with her that night and placed it under her pillow, touching it now and then to assure herself it was still there.

CHAPTER SIXTY-EIGHT

Gracechurch Street was soon turned upside down as everything was readied for the journey. Once her own things were packed, Mary quickly understood she was more of a hindrance than a help in managing what remained to be done. Nothing is more irritating to a harassed housewife than the plaintive insistence of a useless person that they must be allotted a task; and not wishing to add to her aunt's already lengthy list of responsibilities, Mary slipped quietly out of doors.

She had not gone far along her accustomed walk when a familiar figure turned into the street some way in front of her. It was impossible to mistake Mr Ryder's saunter, the stroll of a man with no one to please but himself. When he saw her, his smile was so broad and unfeigned that she could not help returning it.

'Miss Bennet! How extraordinary! I was just on my way to call upon you.'

'Then I'm afraid I must disappoint you. The house – and my poor aunt – are both in turmoil. I think the prospect of entertaining anyone this morning might be more than either she or the servants can bear.'

His concern was immediate – he hoped everyone was well, that nothing untoward or unfortunate had happened? Mary hastened to explain that the reverse was true, that the upheaval was the result of their plans for a holiday. She described their trip to the Lakes to him, explaining the reasons that had led to its being brought forward, and the excitement they felt at the prospect of going.

'I confess I am very jealous,' declared Mr Ryder. 'Will Tom be one of the party?'

'Yes, as such an old friend of the family, it was impossible he should not be included.'

'Then he is very lucky to have that privilege. I envy you all, Miss Bennet – I can think of nothing more exciting than to see for yourselves the place which has inspired one of the great geniuses of our age!'

His eyes shone with such passion that Mary could not decide whether his enthusiasm was charming or ridiculous, before concluding it was a little of both. Then, in the blink of an eye, his seriousness vanished, and he was playful again.

'Tell me, Miss Bennet, are you very fond of ices?'

'To be honest, I have only tasted them a few times – once at my sister's house in Derbyshire – and they were certainly very fine.'

'In that case, I have a suggestion to make. Not far from here is Angell's – an excellent confectioner who makes some of the very best ices in London. Every flavour you could possibly imagine. I should very much like to buy you one.'

He saw her hesitate.

'I promise you it is a most respectable place, quite suitable for ladies. If I had one, I would take my maiden aunt there.'

Mary knew she should probably refuse; but the day promised little else in the way of enjoyment. With the house in such disorder, she should not be able to read and would only be in everyone's way. Mr Ryder pressed home his advantage.

'If, when you see it, you don't like the look of it, I shall escort you home immediately. But behold, Miss Bennet, the sky is blue, the sun is out. Let us enjoy it while we can!'

His cheerfulness was infectious, his smile so engaging that Mary found herself agreeing. She set a whole host of conditions – she would have one ice only – she should stay for half an hour, no more – he must bring her back to Gracechurch Street whenever she asked – but nevertheless, twenty minutes later, she found herself in Angell's shop, eating a bergamot ice with every appearance of enjoyment.

Their conversation was far easier and more entertaining than Mary had expected. As she felt no need to impress Mr Ryder, she was not nervous in his presence; and as she believed herself indifferent to his charm, she was not afraid to enjoy it a little. Inevitably, they found themselves discussing what they had read, what they were reading, and what they intended to read, with Mr Ryder repeating his earlier assertion that longer works were not for him.

'I think the brevity of poetry is one of its principal attractions,' he declared, finishing his peach ice and laying down the spoon. 'The reader is not obliged to contemplate that huge block of pages which, however many of them one turns, never seems to diminish. With a few notable exceptions which need not be returned to – I shall not be picking up *Paradise Lost* again in a hurry – poems tend to be short, and are thus perfectly suited to a flighty mind such as my own.'

Mary looked up from her ice, which was just as good as Mr Ryder had promised it would be.

'If you truly love poetry as much as you say,' she replied, 'then you do yourself a disservice; for in my experience, it requires far greater application than many philosophical books. Without concentration, there is no entering into it at all.'

'Ah, Miss Bennet,' he exclaimed, 'I have no objection to embracing anything in *depth* – that holds no terrors for me – no, it is *length* that defeats me!' He folded his napkin, laid it on the table and folded his arms. 'I have no powers of application, you see. I am a sad case.'

'Only because you are determined to consider yourself one.' Mary finished her ice, searching for one last spoonful from the depths of the little glass cup in which it had been served. 'I'm sure you have the discipline within yourself to do anything you want, if you are prepared to exert it.'

Mr Ryder looked thoughtful. 'Perhaps. I am not so sure. You are probably right that I could do it. It is rather a question of whether I wish to.'

'If that is the case, then you are sadly condemned to stay as you are,' observed Mary a little tartly, 'for where there is no willingness to make an effort, there is usually little likelihood of success.'

Mr Ryder raised his hand and called for tea.

'I can see you don't approve,' he said. 'But in my defence, I must explain this is not simply laziness on my part. I believe I am perfectly capable of exertion in pursuit of those things I love. But I cannot share that attitude which deliberately seeks fulfilment in what is dull and tedious, which embraces what is dry and lifeless as a kind of virtue in itself.'

'It is always easier to concentrate upon what pleases us,' said Mary. 'It requires very little discipline to turn our minds to what we know we enjoy.'

'You say that as if attending to what we like was a failing,' declared Mr Ryder. 'I see it very differently. I am determined not to waste my energy on anything that does not either move or please me; I won't crush my spirit by weighing it down with boredom and obligation.'

'You are fortunate to find yourself in circumstances which permit you to make such a choice.'

'I don't deny it,' he agreed, 'and I very much intend to make the best of my good luck.'

A waiter took away the dirty glasses and swept their table clean.

'I sense that I have not convinced you of the justice of my argument.'

'Not entirely, Mr Ryder.'

'Then before we leave, I wonder if I might be permitted to tell you a story, which I hope explains a little why I feel as I do?'

Mary agreed to stay a little longer. While she could not approve of Mr Ryder's principles, she enjoyed the way he talked about them. When he smiled at her, she was suddenly aware, both of the fineness of his profile and the embarrassment of having noticed it. This, she supposed, was exactly the situation Mrs Gardiner had warned her against. She must ensure she did not allow herself to be captivated by his charm. She did not believe herself in danger, but it was as well to take care.

Mr Ryder, oblivious to this little inward struggle, settled himself comfortably at his side of the table and began to speak in a tone of far greater seriousness than was usual with him.

'My father,' he began, 'inherited a small estate in Sussex, but it was not of much interest to him. He was a scholarly man, and he devoted all his time to the study of every kind of curious insect. His particular passion was a certain variety of winged beetle – I cannot now recall its Latin name, but it occupied most of his waking hours. He was forever engaged in catching examples of it, killing and displaying them. It seemed a dogged sort of passion, but he was utterly absorbed by it. He rarely emerged from his study and we children hardly saw him. Then he died, quite suddenly, as I recall. I was fifteen years old.'

The tea arrived; and Mary poured it out. When she had finished, Mr Ryder continued.

'On the day he was buried, when everyone else was drinking wine in the drawing room and looking sad, I wandered into his library. There I found three of our servants, all dressed in black as I was, carrying away every one of the drawers which contained his beetles – there must have been twenty or thirty of them, each with row after row of insects, pinned out to show the patterns on their wings. The men were very respectful as they took them off. I don't know where they went. I've never seen them since. I imagine my mother wanted them gone.'

He took a sip of his tea.

'After they'd finished, I sat for a while in that gloomy room, looking at the spaces where the drawers had been. Then I opened the doors that led onto the terrace and ran through them towards the garden. The sun was so dazzling, I was blinded by it for a moment. The day was bright and hot. I stood amongst the trees and flowers and breathed in the fresh green air. I felt the warmth on my back. I smelt the scent of the grass that had just been cut. And I looked back at the dark room I'd just left, and I thought what a sad waste my father's life had been. All those hours of tedious study – all that effort – and to what end? All gone in a moment.'

'I am very sorry to hear it,' said Mary quietly.

'I was sorry too,' continued Mr Ryder, 'but not for very long. I walked round the garden again – I took off my black coat – I threw myself down on the grass and looked up at the sky – and I thought that in that moment I understood more about the point of human existence than my father had learned in a lifetime of study. Years of hard work had never delivered him the sublime pleasure I was enjoying at that very instant. I had opened myself to the pure sensations of the world, where he had spent a lifetime denying them.'

The waiter returned, and Mr Ryder asked for the bill. Upon its being presented, he paid it absently, with a tip large enough to send the man away very satisfied; then he took up his story again.

'The experience made a very powerful impression upon me; and when I was old enough to make my own decisions about how I should live, I promised myself I would not be deceived as my father had been. Life is too short, Miss Bennet, not to pursue those things which we know will please and fulfil us. And for me, that means indulging our senses as much as exercising our minds. We are often told that sensual pleasures do not last – but I saw for myself that is equally true for the products of hard work. Everything turns to dust in the end. In a philosophical sense, the servants are always waiting to take away our insect collections and dispose of them who knows where. We may as well experience some joy before they arrive.'

Mary was not sure at first how to respond. She understood Mr Ryder had confided something of great importance about himself to her and she could not help but be flattered by his trust. But much as she wished to respect the sincerity of his story, she could not agree with the conclusions he had drawn from it.

'I understand your argument,' she said. 'But some might say what you describe is merely a justification for selfishness. Sometimes we are obliged to do things we do not enjoy for the benefit of the people around us.'

'I have heard it said,' replied Mr Ryder, 'that there is pleasure to be found, even in sacrifice, when it is undertaken willingly. It is only when it is turned into a duty that it becomes tedious.'

Mary was unconvinced; but she contented herself with a vague, dissenting smile and waited a moment before she continued.

'It is very sad to think of your father's collections broken up and taken away.'

'Yes,' he replied, 'I was very affected by it.'

'I see that for you they seemed the very image of futility,' Mary continued. 'But can you be certain your father did not derive a great deal of pleasure from assembling them? They may have been his chosen form of enjoyment. We know so little of what others truly feel.'

'He did not give the impression they brought him much joy,' said Ryder. 'If they did, then I can only say it is not the kind of pleasure I wish for myself – no, I want something far more exhilarating. And as for not knowing what others truly feel – I have said before, Miss Bennet, that not speaking the truth about our emotions is one of the great miseries of our age. We would all be happier if we were more honest with

each other – I believe that most fervently and attempt to practise it whenever I can. Indeed, I intend to do so now.'

Before she knew quite what was happening, Mr Ryder
reached out and took her gloved hand, holding it firmly
between his own.

'Our conversation has made me very happy, Miss Bennet.'

'Perhaps because you did most of the talking.'

'You will be missed when you leave for the Lakes. London
will seem quite empty without you.'

'I'm sure you won't want for company, sir. You always
seem to have people about you.'

'Perhaps; but *your* loss will always be felt.'

Mary pulled her hand away. Mr Ryder relinquished it, not
in the least disconcerted. Excusing herself with a polite
farewell – she must go back and help Mrs Gardiner – she
would not wait for him to accompany her – he need not take
the trouble – she hurried off, as quickly as she could. It was
only when she had walked for some minutes down the street
that she allowed herself to look over her shoulder. She was
not entirely displeased to see him standing outside the shop,
still watching her, before he too turned and went away.

PART FOUR

CHAPTER SIXTY-NINE

The journey from Gracechurch Street, to the the Bingleys' house, where the Gardiners' little party was to break their journey, was achieved without difficulty or incident. Mary grew steadily more silent as they neared their destination. In the days immediately before their departure, her mind had been so crowded with visions of the Lakes and what they should do and see there, that she had given no proper thought to the days they were to spend with the Bingleys. It was only when they were on the road that she began to reflect upon what their stay might be like. She did her utmost not to surrender to the apprehension that had begun to scratch away at her confidence. Really, what had she to fear? Caroline Bingley would not be there to tease her. She would have the Gardiners near at hand, their kindness still to be relied upon. Mr Bingley was always cheerful and good natured; and it would be pleasant to see Jane's beautiful face again. As the coach ploughed on northwards, she allowed herself to think of meeting her sister and her brother-in-law again with something like pleasure. But they were not the only relations into whose company she would be plunged on arrival: her mother would be there too.

When they pulled up at last outside the Bingleys' house, Jane was waiting there to meet them. The little Gardiners clambered stiffly out of the coach, and were soon running about, laughing and shouting after their long confinement. It was some minutes before they were finally recaptured and led happily away, with promises of hot toast and a basket of young kittens to admire. The older people followed more soberly but no less gratefully towards the prospect of tea and a seat that did not jolt them about. Mr Bingley presided over all the arrangements with his usual affability; and in less than half an hour, everyone was happy.

Once enough had been eaten and drunk for conversation to be more general, Mr Gardiner observed that Mrs Bennet was not yet to be seen; he hoped his sister's nerves were not troubling her again? Mr Bingley smiled into his tea while Jane replied evenly that, no, her mother was not seriously indisposed; she was merely conserving her strength for dinner and looked forward to meeting everyone a little later. There was a short silence while this news was absorbed; at the end of it, both men appeared to conclude they had now paid their debt to politeness. They rose together and left to inspect a plantation of new trees, on whose state Mr Bingley wanted very much to hear Mr Gardiner's opinion.

Once they had gone, Jane cast a mild, assessing eye in Mary's direction.

'I must say, Mary, you look very smart in that dress. I don't think I have seen it before.'

Mary had almost forgotten that she had acquired a wardrobe of new clothes since she had last seen her sister. It was a strange thing; now that she was so much better dressed, she rarely gave much thought to her looks at all. She no longer stared at her reflection, looking for new reasons to disparage herself. Indeed, she rarely looked in the mirror at all, but this was not because she despised what she saw there. It was rather because she was broadly satisfied with herself; or, as content with her appearance as she suspected was the case with most women who will never be beauties. Freed from a regimen of criticism and complaint, Mary had found her own level; and she was not unhappy to be there. Jane's unfeigned praise pleased her; and she returned her sister's smile.

'I'm glad you like it. Mrs Gardiner persuaded me to buy it.'

'That was very wise of her,' replied Jane. 'It is exactly right for you.'

'In my opinion, Mary has really bloomed in the last few months,' observed Mrs Gardiner proudly. 'I only hope her improvement will be appreciated by *everyone* who sees it. And what of you, Jane,' she continued. 'How are you going on?'

Jane looked up, a little self-conscious but very proud.

'Well, I have reason to believe – that is I think – I am pretty much certain that I'm expecting a child.'

She smiled shyly at her aunt and Mary as if she had told them the greatest news they could ever wish to hear. Mrs Gardiner jumped up and kissed her lightly.

'My dear, I'm so very happy for you – and for Mr Bingley too – what a wonderful thing for you both!'

Once Mary would have searched for an aphorism or an extract from one of her favourite writers to do justice to the announcement. Now she understood that was not what Jane wanted to hear. Instead she found the courage to say simply what she felt.

'I am delighted for you, Jane. No child could hope for a better mother. I wish you both joy, truly I do.'

Jane blushed, suddenly overcome.

'It's all I've ever really wanted, a happy home, a loving

husband, and a baby. I'm not sure why I've been so fortunate, but I hope, Mary, that one day something similar will
happen for you.'

Mary's heart was too full for a reply. She could not
remember when Jane had spoken to her with such affection.

'Yes, indeed,' said Mrs Gardiner with feeling. 'I hope so
too. There is no more lasting satisfaction than knowing you
have chosen the right partner in life.'

Later, upstairs in her bedroom, Mary dressed for dinner
with as much care as if she was about to meet a roomful of
critical strangers. As Jane's maid put the finishing touches to
her hair, Mary attempted to steady her nerves. It had been
arranged as she now preferred it, with no attempt at a curl;
and she had chosen an equally plain dress, a pale yellow, with
a dull gold stripe. Once the servant left the room Mary sat
before the mirror for some time, turning this way and that,
trying to imagine what her mother would say. She told herself
she was foolish, after so many years to expect anything in the
way of encouragement from that quarter; but for all her determination not to do so, she still yearned for her mother's
approval. A kind word, an assenting nod would be enough.
Even the absence of a frown would suffice. She picked up her
shawl. The moment could not be postponed. She looked at
her hair one last time and made her way downstairs.

When Mary entered the drawing room, she found herself
alone. Why was she always the first? She thought ruefully of
Caroline Bingley's arrival at Mr Ryder's supper party, and the
stir her carefully timed entrance had created. She knew she
would never possess the confidence to be late; anxious, uncertain guests like herself were doomed always to be early, to

provide a waiting audience of admirers for those too assured or too fashionable to pay any heed to the time.

To keep herself in countenance, she walked round the room, admiring the beautiful objects her sister had arranged so tastefully: the elegant china, the delicate glass. She ran her hand over an embroidered chair cushion – she had no doubt Jane had sewn it herself – and inspected the painting of her sister which hung over the fireplace, presiding over the room with her characteristic remote and gentle gaze. She was so absorbed, that the sound of the drawing room door closing quite startled her.

'Well, Mary,' observed Mrs Bennet evenly, as she made her way towards the sofa. 'Here you are at last.'

She held her cheek out to be kissed. As Mary bent towards her, she saw that her mother had not changed at all. A few grey hairs perhaps, but nothing more. Touches of black on the neck of her dress and round her sleeves were all that remained of her mourning clothes. She no longer looked like a widow.

'I'm very glad to see you, Mama. I trust you are in good health?'

'Dr Gower who attends us here says I am very well. But I'm afraid he does not *fully* appreciate how I suffer.'

She plumped one of Jane's embroidered cushions and settled herself comfortably.

'But Jane and Mr Bingley seem very attentive?'

'Jane is an angel, of course. And Mr Bingley does what he can. But neither of them has the first idea how to run a household properly – Mr Bennet always said they would be taken advantage of by everyone, their natures are so trusting – and

I'm afraid he was right. I've offered to take things in hand –
but they won't have it. My advice is ignored, as always.'

'Perhaps they're afraid you might exert yourself too much.
I'm sure they have your interests at heart.'

'Perhaps.' Mrs Bennet's expression suggested there was
much that might be said on this subject if she chose to do so.
Instead she merely pursed her lips. 'Now, let me look at you
properly.'

It was the moment Mary had dreaded. Knowing there was
no escape, that she was about to be judged as she had been so
many times before, she did her best to breathe evenly and not
to drop her eyes. It seemed an age before Mrs Bennet spoke.

'Mrs Gardiner wrote to say you were much improved. I
see she was right.'

Mary allowed herself a small smile. Her mother, still
examining her, did not return it.

'That dress shows off your figure and the colour suits you.
It's good to see you stand up straight at last, and not hang
your head. I should like to see your hair curled, but it is
better done than it was. Altogether, there is a bloom about
you that was not there before.'

'Thank you, Mama.'

'You will never be a great beauty like Jane' – Mrs Bennett
glanced reverently at the portrait above the fireplace – 'but if
you go on as you are, you may become quite passable.'

Mary was almost angry with herself at the strength of the
emotions her mother's words provoked. She knew that to
those accustomed to more generous compliments they would
seem like very little, but to her, they were praise indeed. To
be accounted merely passable was a great improvement upon
being dismissed as plain; and it meant all the more because

Mary knew it must be true. Her mother did not care for her enough to take the trouble to dissemble.

'I suppose it is all my sister Gardiner's doing,' complained Mrs Bennet. 'Why you paid attention to her when you would not listen to me, I really do not know. No one can say I did not try. It is very provoking, to be sure.'

Mrs Bennet grumbled on until Mr and Mrs Bingley arrived, when the conversation turned naturally enough to Jane's situation. Mary was not sorry to sit and listen. She had escaped the full force of Mrs Bennet's disdain and felt almost jubilant when finally they went in to dinner.

Mary's cheerfulness sustained her over the next few days, enabling her to bear Mrs Bennet's querulousness with good grace. She did not allow herself to be provoked by any remarks relating to London suitors, the importance of looking her best at any and every moment when such an exalted being might appear – 'a woman like you cannot afford to take chances, Mary, you must *always* be prepared' – and the absolute, irrevocable necessity of *never, under any circumstances at all* wearing her spectacles in a man's presence until they were safely married.

Nevertheless, Mary thought it could not be a moment too soon until they were safely on their way; and her wishes were soon gratified. The next afternoon, as she sat with the children on the drawing room carpet, amidst a litter of puzzles and card games, Mr Gardiner strolled into the room, brandishing a letter. He announced it came from Mr Hayward, who had left London and was now travelling towards the Lakes, where he would meet them.

'He is in the very best of spirits,' said her uncle, as he handed the letter to his wife. 'It seems all that hard work was worthwhile – he has won the legal case that has caused him so much time and trouble!'

Mrs Gardiner was delighted; the children, who were very fond of Mr Hayward on account of his great generosity in the matter of sweets, cheered loudly, and Mr Gardiner, who looked upon Tom Hayward with an almost fatherly concern, beamed with pride. Mary's heart leapt at the news. It touched her very deeply to think that Mr Hayward had achieved this mark of success, which he had so hoped for.

'Will he wear his wig when he next comes to visit?' asked Edward, the elder Gardiner son, who had once been allowed to put it on, and yearned to do so again.

'He will be far too grand for that now,' declared Mr Gardiner, leaning down to place a piece of jigsaw puzzle in place. 'Next time you see him, he will be the perfect picture of a grave and steady lawyer.' The children looked crestfallen. This did not sound to them like an improvement in Mr Hayward's character. 'Unless of course,' their father continued, 'there is no one around to see. Then I imagine you might be allowed to try it on, as long as you have been exceedingly well behaved.'

He turned back to Mary and his wife.

'Tom says he is making excellent progress on the road. He warns us, that if he arrives at the inn first, he will have no qualms at all about claiming the best room for his own, and that we shall be obliged to shift for ourselves as best we can.' He took a last look at the letter and put it in his pocket. 'I think he is joking; but with him, you can never be sure. So, my dears, if you don't want to bed down with the chickens, we must rise with the sun tomorrow and crack on.'

When dawn arrived, the travellers were up and ready to go. The children, who were to remain with the Bingleys, had been kissed and hugged and wished loving goodbyes; their hosts had been heartily thanked; and by six o'clock, they were on their way. They had not been in the carriage long before Mrs Gardiner fell asleep, her head leaning on her husband's shoulder. When he swiftly followed her example, Mary pulled from her bag her copy of Wordsworth's *Guide to the Lakes*, followed by her spectacles. These she put on boldly regardless of the offence they might give to any potential suitor happening to pass by. The idea amused her, and she was smiling as she opened the little book. She had already read it so often that it was very familiar to her; but the scenes it described never failed to excite her, especially now it would not be long before she should find herself amongst them. She opened the first page and began to read.

'In preparing this manual, it was the Author's principal wish to furnish a Guide, or Companion for the Minds of Persons of taste, and feeling for Landscape.'

Taste, feeling, landscape. Mary lay back against her seat. Surely no words could more powerfully conjure Mr Hayward into her mind? Yes, she thought, he will approach the wild northern country with the right spirit, eager to be amazed by the awesome or silenced by the sublime. Mr Wordsworth could not wish for a more willing disciple. But what of herself? Was she capable of giving way to a similar intensity of experience? Sleep began to steal over her. But before she abandoned herself to it, she understood that if she was ever properly to allow her feelings free rein, the Lakes were surely the place to do it.

CHAPTER SEVENTY

The anticipation of the party increased steadily with every mile they advanced further north. They almost cheered at the sight of the first proper hills, distantly visible in the morning mist; by the time they left Kendal, and the landscape grew wilder, the knowledge that their destination could not be far away excited them even more. They chatted expectantly along the Bowness road until they caught sight of the great lake at Windermere; then they were quiet, for it was a sight magnificent enough to silence anyone. Huge, bright, shimmering in the fresh July sunlight, it seemed to Mary that she had never seen anything so beautiful. A few islands of thick green trees threw the blue of the water into striking contrast, while rough grey mountains tumbled down to the shore. Mr Gardiner signalled to the coachman to stop and the three of them climbed out into the road. There was nothing to be heard but birdsong and the sound of their shoes crunching on small stones as they walked to the lake's edge. No one spoke. Mary was so moved, she thought she might laugh or cry. In the presence of such a vision, she felt herself both magnified and diminished. Her small human concerns seemed of no account when set against such severe, indifferent splendour; at the same time, there was a kind of joy in allowing its grandeur to overwhelm her, to abandon herself to something she did not fully comprehend.

'Well, my dear,' said Mr Gardiner to his wife, 'I should not have missed that for the world. It's a fine sight, is it not, Mary?'

Her mind was so concentrated upon the view that she did not hear him. When he spoke again, Mary could not help wishing him far, far away. This was unfair, for her uncle was the kindest of men; but his mild words struck entirely the wrong note in this wild place. Mary was glad when he took his wife's arm, and they walked slowly back to the carriage, talking in low, contented voices, speculating on the likelihood of there being anything tolerable to eat at supper tonight. Mary did not follow them but stayed at the shore, staring up to where the mountains met the sky.

If only Mr Hayward were there. He would have understood what she felt. She stood still, listening to the birds in the clear air until Mrs Gardiner called her to come back to the carriage, or they should go away and leave her and she'd be obliged to make her own way to the inn.

When they finally arrived, their lodgings were everything they had hoped for, neat, clean, and, to Mr Gardiner's relief, offering the very real prospect of a good dinner that evening. Mr Hayward had indeed arrived before them – the innkeeper believed he was out walking the fells – but he had not carried out his threat to take the best bed in the place, for everyone was soon placed in admirably comfortable accommodation.

Mary's room was simple and pleasing, with a window that offered a tantalizing glimpse of the lake. It was only the smallest sliver of blue, but it was enough to excite her to desire to see more. She rushed downstairs to find her aunt and uncle, already settled with a large pot of tea placed before them. Neither were willing to be prised away from their resting-place to explore their surroundings; but on being applied to, the inn-keeper assured them there was nothing to fear from allowing Mary to walk alone nearby if she wished it. The fields behind the inn were quite safe and commanded a wonderful view of the lake. The young lady would come to no harm there.

Before Mr and Mrs Gardiner had time to reconsider their permission, Mary was gone. She quickly found the path that led up the gentle hill under which the inn was situated. She strode firmly towards the top, where she soon found exactly what she wished – a clear, unhindered view of the water spread out before her, and a suitable rock on which to sit and admire it. The breeze, which had been slight below, blew more strongly here and threatened to unmoor her hat. She tied it tighter beneath her chin, clasped her hands round her knees and gazed into the distance, doing all she could to immerse herself in the feel of the place.

So successful was she in achieving this that it was not until he was almost upon her that she saw Mr Hayward striding in her direction. He had on a large loose coat of a kind she had never seen him wear in London; and having nothing to tie his hat to his head as she had done, he carried it in his hand. He appeared both very tall and very happy. His hair blew in the wind, and his face was a little brown from the sunshine. Mary thought she had never before seen him look so striking.

'Miss Bennet! You have arrived at last!'

'Look, Mr Hayward! Isn't it extraordinary? Isn't it the most remarkable, wonderful thing?'

He sat down bedside her on the great rock and looked from sky to lake to mountains and back again.

'I have never seen anything like it.'

'No,' exclaimed Mary, 'I worried that we might be disappointed once we were here, that it was impossible for any place to be as' – she gestured again towards the view – 'well, as tremendous as this is. But it is everything I imagined it would be.'

'Yes,' he replied. '"Tremendous" is exactly the word. And on the high hills, it's even better. From some of them, I'm told you can see the sea.'

'The sea? How I should love to see that! Can ladies make the climb?'

'If they are as determined as you and own a stout pair of shoes, I don't see why not. Shall we go down?'

He held out his arm. Mary took it and they walked slowly back towards the inn. On the way, Mr Hayward maintained he heard a lark, but Mary believed it was a thrush. As they strolled down the path, they disputed the identity of every bird that flew before them or raised its voice in song; but when they were nearly at their destination, Mr Hayward confessed that the only bird he could honestly recognise with any confidence was a London pigeon. Mary laughed out loud.

'For one who loves the poetry of nature with such a passion, you know surprisingly little about it.'

'Yes, it's true that until now I've worshipped it from a distance. But seeing it here for myself – well, I think I finally feel its power.'

He looked solemnly up at the hills.

'I think you feel it too?'

'I do indeed,' she replied, her tone as grave as his.

Then he turned back to her and she saw his mood had changed. Now he was excited, smiling with pleasure.

'Then let us explore it together, Mary! We will let it work its magic upon us until we are both under its spell!'

He grinned down at her, his hair whipped by the wind.

'Yes,' she cried. 'Let us do that! There's nothing I would like more.'

It was not until they were inside the inn, sharing tea with the Gardiners, that Mary realised Mr Hayward had called her by her first name. He had not done so before. Her hand shook a little as she reached out for her cup, but she did not think it was generally observed.

CHAPTER SEVENTY-ONE

The sun was shining the next morning, and it was deemed perfect weather for drawing. Everyone except Mr Gardiner had equipped themselves with sketch-books, and they went out early, stationing themselves at the places recommended by Wordsworth's *Guide* as offering the most pleasing opportunities for their pencils. Mr Gardiner preferred a morning's fishing; and soon Mary began to think he had made the right choice. No matter how hard she tried, her drawings remained obstinately unlike the landscape around them. Everything she did to improve matters only made things worse, and after an hour or so, she closed her book. Moments later, Mr Hayward came and sat beside her; he was equally gloomy.

'I hope your efforts have met with more success than mine.'

'May I see what you have done?'

'I don't think so. Afterwards, it would be impossible for you to think of me ever again as a man of feeling.'

'Are all men of feeling gifted artists, then?'

'I have always supposed so. I used to tell myself it was want of a proper subject that explained my poor hand with a pencil. But now I see the truth of it – I have no talent at all.'

Mary laughed.

'I cannot draw either. I have tried to improve, but, as these poor daubs show, without much success.'

'We are in a sad way then,' replied Mr Hayward. 'If our failures become generally known, we must expect to find ourselves the objects of universal scorn.'

'Yes, indeed,' agreed Mary. 'No one returns from the Lakes without an album of sketches to pass around their friends. If ours are too poor to be shown, what are we to do?'

'We might say they were lost on the Keswick road.'

'Stolen by thieves.'

'Eaten by sheep!'

Their laughter made Mrs Gardiner look up. The sight of them, so easy and agreeable together, made her smile. She could not remember when she had seen her niece so happy. Mary had even forgotten she was wearing her glasses; and when she finally took them off and put them into her bag, still chatting away, it only confirmed Mrs Gardiner's sense of how natural and comfortable they were with one another.

In the late afternoon, they took a boat onto the lake. In the fine quiet weather, nothing was to be heard but the voices of their boatmen, naming the crags and peaks that towered over the water. When they arrived at the middle, the rowers pulled in their oars and the boat bobbed silently in the breeze. A fish jumped, and Mr Gardiner asked the men what kind of sport was to be had here, whether the catch was worth eating or not. Mary trailed her hand in the water. She had no desire to think, to say or to do anything – instead, all she wished was to give herself up to the pleasure of the moment. She was lost within herself when Mr Hayward turned to her and spoke so that only she should hear.

'I may not be able to capture any of this beauty on paper,' he said, 'but it still moves me very much when I see it.'

'Yes,' she replied simply. 'I'm surprised by how happy it makes me, just to look at it.'

'I'm glad. I like to see you happy.'

Her heart leapt, but before she could reply, Mr Gardiner had asked his opinion on the merits of salmon over trout, or perch over pike, and Mr Hayward was irresistibly drawn into the conversation with the boatmen. But a moment later, he caught her eye with the most affectionate glance; and she did not hesitate to smile confidently back.

Later that night, Mary sat at the tiny window in her bedroom, watching the lake in the dark. She should have been asleep some time ago, exhausted by the fresh air and sunshine they had enjoyed all day, but she could not settle. A great thought was pressing in upon her, demanding to be acknowledged; for a while, she resisted, reluctant to confess it even to herself. But when a shaft of moonlight suddenly broke through the clouds and rewarded her with a sight of the water, shimmering in the cold white light, she could hold back no longer and at last permitted it to take concrete form. She loved Mr Hayward. What she felt for him was more than friendship, more than admiration, more than just pleasure in his company. It was love. She felt a sense of release in allowing herself to say it in her mind. There could be no real doubt of it – she loved him.

She opened the window and breathed in the cool night air. Admitting her feelings for Mr Hayward, even to herself, was a bold enough step. But now she had begun upon this extraordinary train of thought, she could not stop. She believed it was not impossible – was perhaps even probable – that her affections were returned. She thought he might love her too.

The more she considered it, the more she felt it to be true. He had always distinguished her by his notice, seeking her out and sitting beside her, talking to her, laughing with her, reading to her. And since they had arrived at the Lakes, his affection for her had been even more openly expressed, in a thousand small and delightful ways. And then there was the moment when he called her by her name. She hugged her knees and rocked gently back and forth in the moonlit room, remembering how that had felt. She shivered and was suddenly aware of how cold she had become. She hurried to her narrow bed, wrapped herself in the inn's stiff sheets and gave herself up to the excitement of thinking about him.

In every way, she told herself, they were admirably matched. When she considered the similarity of their temperaments – the interests they shared – the pleasures they took in each other's company – it was impossible to deny that they were, in the cant phrase, 'made for each other'. Even Charlotte Collins would have been obliged to concede it. Mary smiled to herself in the darkness as she imagined Charlotte noting with approval everything they had in common, assuring Mary that they possessed all the qualifications necessary to embark upon a sensible marriage of the most rational kind.

But Mary knew that if she were to marry Mr Hayward, their partnership would never be one of companionship alone. There would be far more to it than that. Mary did not like to admit to herself the attraction she felt when in his presence, the desire that came upon her with increasing frequency to take his hand, or to stroke his hair. These sensations seemed to have grown more frequent since their arrival in the Lakes. It was as if the usual rules of behaviour were all but suspended in these wild landscapes. Once Mary would have told herself to suppress such unruly emotions; but in this unsettling country, she found she had no wish to do so. On the contrary, she allowed herself to hope that her honesty in acknowledging her feelings would only increase the likelihood of their being gratified.

It might have been imagined that acknowledging sentiments of such intensity would have kept Mary awake all night, tossing and turning as she considered what they meant. But the excitement she felt produced not uncertainty, but happy expectation; and very soon she was asleep.

CHAPTER SEVENTY-TWO

In the days that followed, Mary and Mr Hayward walked with the Gardiners on the less demanding fells, strolling about the green shores of the lake, riding on the little local ponies, who carried them without complaint over the tough marshy grass of the valley paths. The more they were together, the tighter the bond between them seemed to become, strengthened with every conversation, every shared smile, every small gesture. Mary began to think Mr Hayward must intend to declare himself – for what else could all his attention and fondness imply, if not a desire to be married?

It is very common for people who have just discovered themselves to be in love to imagine none but themselves can see their deepest feelings writ plain on their faces; and Mary was no exception to this rule. She was confident her happiness was apparent to her alone; but it was hardly to be expected that her aunt would not notice. Mrs Gardiner had watched approvingly as her niece and Mr Hayward grew ever closer. She and her husband could imagine no better outcome than that Mary should be united to their friend; and their pleasure in the likely coming together of the two young people was unaffected and sincere.

Until now, Mrs Gardiner had been extremely circumspect in expressing any opinion about Mary's situation. But now she began to feel matters were sufficiently advanced to allow some comment upon it. She gently encouraged Mary to look favourably upon Mr Hayward, reminding her of his good nature, so essential in a companion, his kindness, his lively intelligence and his solid prospects in the law, which were so much enhanced by his recent success. With a host of such delicate brushstrokes, Mrs Gardiner contrived to paint a picture of Tom Hayward as the very model of a suitable husband for her niece.

Mary liked nothing better than to hear Mr Hayward praised and was not afraid to let Mrs Gardiner see the pleasure she took in hearing him admired. She said little in reply; but secretly, she was delighted by Mrs Gardiner's words. They suggested her aunt also thought it likely Mr Hayward would propose to her; and that thrilled her with a pleasurable apprehension she had never felt before.

Mr Hayward was in equally good spirits, pleased with every new hill and valley, talkative, amusing, always ready to please. As a result, their little group soon took on an exceptionally cheerful character, tinged with the expectation that even greater happiness might be anticipated, if matters turned out in the way everyone seemed to hope that they would. They were all in an excellent humour, disposed to try anything that might add to their pleasure; so that when, one night at dinner, Mr Hayward mentioned that he had a new excursion to propose, he was heard with the keenest attention.

'I have been thinking about Miss Bennet's desire to view the sea from the top of one of the great hills around us,' he began, 'and the more I read, the more I am convinced she is right to want to attempt it. The prospects are said to be quite breathtaking, unlike anything else the Lakes afford.'

He brushed the crumbs on the table cloth to one side with

his napkin, produced his copy of the *Guide to the Lakes*, and laid it carefully before him.

'Mr Wordsworth says there are only a few places which offer such a view, and it appears we are lucky enough to be near one. It seems to me this is too good an opportunity to be ignored – and that perhaps we might think of walking up it.'

He handed the *Guide* to the Gardiners, opened at the appropriate pages.

'As you can see, it involves a climb up one of the hills – its name is Scafell – and promises the most extraordinary sights from the top.'

'But, Tom,' cried Mrs Gardiner, looking up with horror from the little book, 'it says here Scafell is one of the highest peaks in England! Mr Wordsworth calls it a mountain!'

'He does,' admitted Mr Hayward. 'But if you read a little further, you'll see that it is not as demanding a walk as its height suggests. The path ascends very gradually. And if the weather is kind, the view from the summit is the finest you can imagine – on a brilliant day, you can see all the way to Scotland!'

'That must be magnificent,' declared Mary.

'And it would not be necessary to go all the way to the top to see it. Look, Mr Wordsworth prints a letter here from a friend who has walked it, and says the views are just as spectacular from a much lower ridge. That I think we might reasonably try to reach.'

Mrs Gardiner, still doubtful, handed the book to Mary, who fell upon it with all the enthusiasm her aunt lacked.

'Yes,' she said, 'even from the lower height, it is possible to see the Solway Firth. We should be in the very midst of one of Mr Wordsworth's poems!'

She shut the book and turned to Mr Hayward. 'How could we go home without having seen such a sight?'

Mrs Gardiner, however, was unmoved. 'I suppose it may be done by gentlemen, but I cannot believe it is suitable for ladies.'

Mr Hayward took up the *Guide* again.

'I have it on the best authority that, although he does not name her, the writer of the letter describing the climb was none other than Mr Wordsworth's sister. She went up with a woman friend and their female servant and they made it to the very top, far farther than we should go, without coming to any harm.'

'But,' protested Mrs Gardiner, 'they may be experienced walkers, regular mountain goats.' She turned to her husband. 'Do you think we should attempt it?'

'It is a tempting prospect. The chance to see something so remarkable is not to be easily given up.' Mr Gardiner picked up the wine bottle and poured the remains of the claret into their glasses. 'But I appreciate your concerns. Before we decide anything, we shall take proper advice. In the morning, we will discuss it with the innkeeper and hear his opinion.'

Later, as Mary brushed out her hair by the light of a single candle, she felt nothing but pleasurable anticipation for what was to come. She did not doubt Mr Hayward would have his way, and they should soon find themselves on a majestic peak with a distant view of the sparkling sea. She went to sleep quickly and although a few hours later, she was woken by the rumble of a coach as it pulled into the courtyard and the irritable complaints of the servants called out to attend it, the noise did not really disturb her. She was soon asleep once more, quite indifferent to the bustle of the late arrivals and the fretful impatience with which they found their way to their beds.

CHAPTER SEVENTY-THREE

The Scafell trip was the principal subject of conversation amongst them all the next morning. Mrs Gardiner was not at all certain she should go – she did not think she could bear the heights – she supposed Mary might attempt it, but only if a pair of good boots could be procured for her – and a guide, they must take a knowledgeable guide. So intense was their interest in the walk and the practicalities attached to it, that when the innkeeper approached their table, Mary thought it must be to discuss the excursion. In fact, he brought a letter for Mr Hayward. It appeared one of the guests who arrived so late last night had asked for him by name, and on discovering he was here, had sat down and written it there and then.

Mr Hayward took the note and read it with such surprise that Mrs Gardiner asked him if contained bad news.

'No, nothing of that kind – but it is very unexpected. Let me read it to you.'

My dear Tom,

I daresay you will be as astonished to receive this letter as I am to be writing it. I have been occupied for a few weeks now with some family business in Kent. When it was resolved, I headed for London, wanting nothing so much as good company, preferably your own, only to find you were

gone. I then remembered what Miss Bennet told me, that
you had travelled North with the worthy Gardiners. When I
recalled the excitement with which she talked about it, I
decided <u>that very minute</u> to join you. There was nothing to
keep me in town, and I have long wished to see for myself
the country which inspired that poetic genius we both
revere. So, to cut my story short, I at once <u>took off</u>. I
guessed you would be following that great man's <u>Guide</u>, so
I directed myself to all the inns he recommends. I drew a
blank at the first two, but at the third, I was rewarded! I
understand my sudden arrival must be a surprise – I only
hope it will be a pleasant one. And I am sure you will be
delighted to hear that I do not come alone. Miss Bingley
and Mr and Mrs Hurst have happily consented to be my
guests on this jaunt. I'm sure you will think this as great an
advantage as I do myself, and that we may find ourselves to
be a very companionable little party.
   Wm Ryder

'Well, Tom,' declared Mrs Gardiner, 'your friend is clearly
a most enterprising young man.'

'I'm not sure what to say,' he replied. 'I can only apologise
for his inviting himself to join us in this way. I can't imagine
what provoked him to do so.'

'I'm sure there's no harm done,' said Mr Gardiner. 'I suppose we may see as much or as little of them as we wish.
And perhaps the presence of new people will stop us becoming too set in our ways.'

He smiled encouragingly around the table; but met with
little enthusiasm in return. Mr Hayward's expression did not
suggest that he welcomed any additions to their number, and

Mrs Gardiner, who had no love for either the Hursts or Caroline Bingley, looked equally severe. Mary was troubled by Mr Ryder's having mentioned her name. Was his arrival in some way her fault? If she had not described their trip to him with such excitement, perhaps the idea of following them would never have occurred to him.

'I am very sorry if I spoke about our plans to Mr Ryder with too much eagerness. I assure you, I gave him no reason to believe he should join us.'

Mrs Gardiner instantly declared that it was nonsense even to think of such a thing. Her husband patted Mary's arm and told her she fretted far too much; Mr Hayward, however, did not speak, but picked up the letter and studied it closely, as if attempting to extract some hidden meaning from it. No more was said on the subject and, shortly after, Mr Gardiner and Mr Hayward excused themselves, and went in search of the innkeeper, to find out his opinion about the Scafell walk. Once they were gone, Mrs Gardiner reached for the last of the toast.

'This is really very good. I am only glad we have so much walking to look forward to, or my figure would never survive.'

She spread her butter more thickly than she was used to do at home and began to eat, with every appearance of enjoyment.

'You don't seem very happy at the prospect of our unexpected visitors.'

'We have been so happy and comfortable together,' said Mary, 'that I find it hard to imagine our enjoyment will be improved by additions. I confess it requires more good nature than I possess to think kindly of Miss Bingley. And the Hursts have little more to recommend them.'

Mrs Gardiner put down what remained of her roll and poured herself more tea.

'I wonder – is it only the presence of the two wicked sisters that disturbs you? Or does Mr Ryder's arrival have a similar effect?'

For a moment, all that could be heard was the clatter of plates as the inn servants cleared the other tables.

'Mr Ryder? I'm not sure I understand. Why should he disturb me?'

'I think he likes you. And the obvious, undisguised liking of a handsome man is a very unsettling experience.'

Mary tried to protest, but her aunt held up her hand.

'It provokes all manner of emotions, especially when that man is being pursued by another woman. The knowledge that she wants something we could have with ease, if we chose to exert ourselves to obtain it, cannot help but make that object seem more valuable. And the more she shows she wants him, the more desirable he becomes.'

Mrs Gardiner examined the pots of jam left on the table, took a teaspoonful and placed it delicately on the last of her toast.

'I'm afraid it does not reflect very well on our sex, but there it is.'

'You speak very plainly.'

'Sometimes I think we are obliged to do so. It was clear to me in London – and to you as well, I imagine – that Miss Bingley had set her cap at Mr Ryder. Her coming here confirms it. I don't imagine she has travelled some hundreds of miles on bad roads for the pleasure of *our* company.'

'I agree that is unlikely,' admitted Mary.

'She is determined to have him if she can. And I think she sees clearly who stands in her way.'

'If you mean what I think you do, both you and Miss Bingley are quite wrong. I consider Mr Ryder as a friend, nothing more.'

'When he is absent, I'm sure that is true. But you may find it harder to preserve that indifference when constantly in his company. He is a man of considerable charm. He is lively, with a very winning manner. And I imagine he is capable of speaking very persuasively about matters of the heart – unlike others, who, for all their talk of sensation and emotion, struggle to say what they really feel, or indeed, to act upon it.'

Mary took a discarded piece of bread, and began to roll it on the tablecloth.

'I am not sure I understand,' she ventured. 'I think you know that I – well, that I have grown to think very highly of Mr Hayward. I very much hoped – I have allowed myself to imagine – that my fondness might be returned.'

Mary could not meet her aunt's eye as she said her most secret thought out loud.

'But now you seem to suggest that he may not speak – that he may not have the courage or the conviction to do so. Have I misunderstood his feelings, then? Am I wrong to believe he has some liking for me?'

When she looked up from the table, she seemed so desperate, so anxious that Mrs Gardiner reached over the table and took Mary's hand.

'That isn't what I meant at all,' she said, her voice gentle now. 'It is my honest opinion that Tom cares for you – very much indeed. I have observed a thousand little evidences that suggest it. But I have known him for very many years now, long enough to know that beneath the playful, confident surface he presents to the world, there is hidden a much more diffident young man. He is not at all as certain of himself as he likes to suggest. There is a delicacy about him – a lack of presumption, if you like – that causes him to hold back where others have no such reservations.'

She withdrew her hand; and noticing she had left a smudge of jam on Mary's fingers, attempted to dab it off with her napkin.

'I truly did not mean to imply that Tom does not feel real affection for you; but I suspect he may be slower and more cautious to act upon it than those with more impetuous natures. I wished only to warn you that those who speak with the greatest freedom about their emotions are not always those who feel most deeply. I should not like to see Tom fall at the last hurdle – as Mr Hurst might have it – because others are more fluent and more persuasive in making their case.'

Mary drew back, shocked.

'You cannot really think I would behave like that!'

'No,' replied Mrs Gardiner, 'I don't believe you would ever intend to do so. But we are told that hope deferred makes the heart sick. And in such a situation, the appeal of a man like Mr Ryder might be very dangerous. I would not say any of this if I thought he might suit you,' she continued, 'but I believe you will only ever be happy with a man whose affections are as strong and steady and unalterable as your own. And sometimes men of that character act more slowly than their rivals.'

Before Mary could reply, a servant appeared at their table,

and asked permission to clear their plates. Neither she nor her aunt spoke again until it was done, when Mrs Gardiner rose from the table, and came to sit next to her niece.

'As usual, you have borne my lecturing with the greatest patience,' she said, 'and I will not tease you with my opinions again. But I do beg you, do think about what I have said. The man who declares his affections most readily is not necessarily the man who feels them most profoundly.'

Mary was about to exclaim that her aunt's warnings were quite misplaced, that she was quite immune to Mr Ryder's powers, but before she could do so, Mr Gardiner and Mr Hayward returned to the table.

'All is decided,' announced Mr Gardiner triumphantly. 'The innkeeper assures us that the walk to the lower ridge of Scafell is quite manageable in fine weather; and he can provide a guide, a steady, sober man who knows the path well and will take no foolish risks.'

'He says it will take the better part of a morning to get there,' said Mr Hayward, 'so if we leave the inn promptly, and the weather is kind to us, we might catch sight of the sea by midday.'

He looked expectantly at Mary; but she was distracted, her mind still turning upon Mrs Gardiner's words.

'Imagine it, Miss Bennet – we should see for ourselves what Mr Wordsworth saw, stand exactly where he stood!'

'I should like that very much,' she replied, rallying her spirits. 'But would it not be correct to say where *she* stood – for you told us it was Mr Wordsworth's sister who made the ascent described in the *Guide*?'

'You are quite right,' said Mr Hayward, relieved that Mary appeared to have recovered her enthusiasm for the trip. 'I am very happy to tread in the footsteps of a lady, especially one as intrepid as Miss Wordsworth.'

Mr Gardiner laughed.

'It sounds as though enthusiasm alone will be enough to carry you two up the hill. The rest of us may be obliged to make use of a stick.'

'And a pair of proper boots,' added Mrs Gardiner. 'I cannot think of your going without them.'

CHAPTER SEVENTY-FOUR

The Gracechurch Street party spent the rest of the day walking on mild and undemanding hills, rehearsing, as Mr Hayward had it, for their grand excursion. As they marched down green paths and strolled along the banks of fast-flowing becks, Mary applied herself to studying Mr Hayward's behaviour, attempting, in the most disinterested way, to gauge the warmth of his feelings for her. She did all she could to be sceptical; but everything about his bearing suggested the strongest attachment – his conversation, his smiles, his many considerate attentions. When he presented her with a sprig of honeysuckle to wear in her hat, she thought the matter settled. Gradually, the uncertainties raised in her mind by Mrs Gardiner's words ebbed away. Mary did not think her hopes would be deferred, or not for very much longer; she had every reason to believe Mr Hayward would declare himself before they went back to London.

The walkers took best advantage of the fine weather to be out for most of the day; so it was not until they came down to dinner that they finally found themselves in the company of Mr Ryder and his companions. When they entered the inn's public room, Mr Ryder, who had clearly been waiting for them there, rushed to greet them. He first approached Mrs Gardiner, to beg forgiveness for his presumption.

'Madam, I must apologise for intruding upon you in this

way – but really, there was no help for it. The prospect of seeing you all here – in this illustrious place – was too strong to be resisted. My only hope is that we might add to your pleasure – or at least not materially diminish it.'

'I am sure that would be impossible,' she replied evenly. Pleased, Mr Ryder turned his brilliant smile on Mary.

'I cannot imagine, Miss Bennet, that when we last met in Cheapside, you expected to see me again so quickly. But once you had put the idea of the Lakes into my head, I could not dislodge it. So here we are; and from what I have seen so far on our journey, it has all been worth it.'

He was so eager to please, that it required real effort to resist his enthusiasm.

'And, Tom, what about you? I must ask your indulgence too.' He seized Mr Hayward's hand, and shook it robustly. 'I hear you have won a famous victory in the courts – that you carry all before you in legal world – I cannot say I am surprised – I expected no less – but I am very glad of it and offer my heartiest congratulations.'

Mr Hayward thanked him, a little self-conscious at the exuberance of his friend's praise. 'But really, Will,' he continued, 'what are you about? Three hundred miles is a long way to come on a whim, especially on roads such as those hereabouts.'

'I should not call it a whim,' declared Mr Ryder, 'for that makes it seem like a foolish indulgence. No – I should prefer to think of it as inspired decisiveness. The idea occurred – I acted upon it – and my wish was instantly gratified.'

'Do you always pursue what you want with such vigour?' asked Mary.

'Invariably,' replied Mr Ryder.

'Will believes anything is to be had by asking for it,' laughed Mr Hayward.

'Nothing ventured, Tom, nothing gained. I'm sure you have heard that said before.'

'Indeed I have, mostly by you.'

Mary watched the two young men talking with the easy facetiousness of an old friendship, until Mr Ryder announced that he had taken the liberty of ordering dinner for them all. He had bespoke the best dishes the inn had to offer – a good joint of beef and cheesecakes to follow – and very much hoped that would please. When he saw that it did, he shepherded them to a small private room, where a long table was set with a clean white cloth, behind which sat, rather stiffly, the other members of Mr Ryder's party, looking a little less delighted with their situation than their affable host.

'You will remember Mr and Mrs Hurst, I trust,' declared Mr Ryder, as they entered the room. 'And Miss Bingley, of course?'

Mary was apprehensive as the necessary formalities were exchanged. She and Miss Bingley had parted on very bad terms after Mr Ryder's supper; and she could not be sure how much resentment that lady would now choose to display. Mary hoped there would be no open snub, for then her aunt would notice, and explanations would be required. Miss Bingley looked as she always did, perfectly dressed and as imposing as ever. Her eyes swept over Mary with her usual assessing air, as though she had not yet resolved exactly how to treat her; then, having made up her mind, she favoured her with a cool nod.

So that was how it would be, thought Mary. A pretence of politeness, but no outward breach. That was a relief.

'I hope your journey northwards was not too trying,' she began, intending to convey her own willingness to make no reference to what had passed between them. 'It is a long way to come; but the beauties of the country make it more than worthwhile.'

'It was no trouble to me,' replied Miss Bingley. 'I have long wished to see the place that gave birth to such magnificent verse. A few inconveniences along the way are a small price to pay.'

'Do you read poetry, then? I did not know you cared for it.'

'It is a passion I share only with my friends.'

Miss Bingley looked over Mary's head and stared about the room as if hoping to discover some more interesting person with whom to converse. Briefly, she caught Mr Ryder's eye, favouring him with a charming smile which vanished when she turned back to Mary.

'As soon as Ryder mentioned this trip, I told him he could not be allowed to go alone. My desire to see the Lakes was quite as strong as his own and *must* be gratified. He straight-away declared he should not think of leaving without me – and Mr and Mrs Hurst, of course.'

'That must have been very pleasing.'

'Yes, but I was not surprised. Mr Ryder has often said he never enjoys an excursion if I am not amongst the party.'

'Well,' replied Mary evenly, 'I hope you will both find much to please you here. We have already seen many very fine views. And the boat trip upon the lake at Grasmere is not to be missed. I can't remember when I saw something quite so lovely.'

'It sounds perfect for people with mild, comfortable tastes. But I hope to see something rather more exciting. I have no wish to confine myself to the usual sights.'

'I think you will find', said Mary, determined not to rise to Miss Bingley's provocations, 'that even the more familiar prospects have much to recommend them. I have yet to see anything I haven't admired. Everything has delighted me.'

'I'm sure it has,' murmured Miss Bingley, making no effort to disguise her desire to bring their conversation, such as it was, to an immediate end. 'Anyway – unless you have any suggestions of the wilder, untamed variety to offer – you know the sort of thing – I think I will go and see if anything in that line has yet occurred to Mr Ryder.'

Before Mary could reply, Miss Bingley drifted away to the other side of the room, stationing herself as close to Mr Ryder as propriety would allow. Once she was gone, Mr Hayward appeared at Mary's side.

'It is neither polite nor generous of me to say so, but I'm afraid I don't care much for Miss Bingley.'

'She is not very agreeable,' admitted Mary. 'At least she has never been so to me.'

'She affects a very superior air. I shouldn't be surprised if she ordered me to bring her another glass of wine or fetch her cloak. I don't think she considers me worth the effort of good manners.'

'To win her good opinion,' Mary mused, 'you would need to be in possession of at least ten thousand pounds a year. She would not look at you without it.'

A servant entered, bearing several bottles, which he placed one by one on the sideboard. The room, which was small, now began to feel crowded. Mary and Mr Hayward were obliged to move into a corner to carry on their conversation, which he seemed keen to continue.

'And what about you, Miss Bennet?' he asked. 'Do you feel

the same? Do you think marital happiness depends on a healthy deposit in the bank?'

'Lizzy used to say it was only when she first caught sight of Pemberley that she realised how much she loved Mr Darcy.'

She had hoped to make him smile; but his face fell and Mary saw she had misjudged his mood.

'She meant it as a joke, of course. If you saw them together, you'd understand the impossibility of thinking otherwise. His wealth – his elevated situation – well, it is a long story, but neither had anything to do with the love she felt for him.'

Mr Hayward did not appear convinced.

'I imagine there are few women with sufficient strength of character to be entirely indifferent to the promise of a great house and a vast income.'

'And few men either,' retorted Mary, a little vexed now to hear her sex disparaged, even by Mr Hayward. 'I have not observed any reluctance amongst male suitors to carry off an heiress if they can.'

Mr Hayward's severe expression melted and he laughed.

'No, you have me there. Men certainly cannot claim the high ground in these matters. But I must admit to some envy, for those amongst us who are so startlingly well provided for. I am afraid I shall never be such a catch as Mr Darcy and the famous grounds of Pemberley.'

'There may indeed be some women for whom that would be a consideration,' said Mary quietly. 'But I promise you, Mr Hayward, not all of us think in such a way.'

She looked at him expectantly and thought he seemed about to speak – when suddenly the dining room door was pushed open, and the innkeeper strode through, carrying the beef under a tremendous covered dish. Two maids followed behind, bearing plates of vegetables and a large jug of gravy. As everyone made their way to the table to begin upon their supper, Mary knew there was no chance now of hearing Mr Hayward's response to her words.

CHAPTER SEVENTY-FIVE

Mr Ryder took his duties as host of the little dinner with great seriousness, and exerted himself tirelessly to thaw the remaining reserve of the Gracechurch Street party. He listened to Mr Gardiner's fishing stories with every appearance of interest, begged Mrs Gardiner to tell him more about the butterflies she had seen on her last walk, and encouraged Mary to recount the pleasures of their recent outing on the lake. When she had finished, he raised his glass to her.

'Well done, Miss Bennet! You describe it brilliantly. I see it perfectly through your eyes – it is as if I was there myself.'

From across the table, Mrs Gardiner caught Mary's eye; but Mary refused to respond.

'I did not catch quite everything you said, Miss Bennet,' said Mr Hurst. 'I missed the part about the islands. Could I beg you to repeat it, please?'

'Perhaps on another occasion,' replied Miss Bingley smoothly.

'Do you have any sketches or drawings you made on the lake?' asked Mr Ryder.

'I'm afraid my talent doesn't lie that way,' confessed Mary. 'I am no great hand with a pencil.'

'What a shame,' said Miss Bingley. 'I should have longed to see them otherwise.'

Ryder indicated to the servants that the plates could now be cleared, and more wine brought in.

'I must say,' he declared, 'your stories have properly whetted my appetite. Do you have another adventure planned? Or must we consult Mr Wordsworth's *Guide*?'

'As a matter of fact,' replied Mr Gardiner, 'there is an excursion we have been considering. It promises amazing sights but requires a great deal of stamina on the part of the walkers. Tom, why don't you say more?'

Everyone fell silent as Mr Hayward described the Scafell climb, outlining the drama of the ascent, the wild beauty of the landscape to be passed through and the majestic prospects to be enjoyed once they had reached the ridge. When he began upon the view of the sea with which they would be rewarded if their climb was successful, Mr Ryder declared he had heard enough – his mind was made up – if it was left to him, they should set out tomorrow, or the next day at the very latest. Mr Hayward, who was used to his friend's enthusiasms, waited until his excitement had diminished a little before commenting mildly that it was not a trip to be undertaken lightly, for although the path itself was not too steep, it was long and strenuous, and said to be rocky.

'But,' he continued, 'the landlord here has recommended a trustworthy guide. He assures us, that if his advice is followed in all things, there is no reason why it should not be attempted.'

'Then surely everything is settled?' cried Mr Ryder. 'Why did we come here, if not to experience adventures such as this? If we are too faint-hearted to try it, we had far better have remained at home. Come, Tom, when do we set out?'

'Not before we have made proper preparations,' replied

Mr Hayward firmly. 'Yes, we are here to experience adventures – but not to fall victim to them. I have walked a little on the fells nearby and have seen how harsh and difficult they can be.'

'Mr Hayward would rather we confined ourselves to smooth lakes and the calmest of views,' murmured Miss Bingley. 'I am with Mr Ryder. I'm sure I long to stand on top of a mountain.'

'You misunderstand me,' replied Mr Hayward severely. 'I am keen for anyone who wishes it to walk up the fell; but no one should attempt it who does not appreciate the risks, or who will not take trouble to prepare for them.'

'Ah,' exclaimed Mr Ryder, 'there speaks the cautious lawyer! My dear Tom, we are a long way from Chancery Lane, thank God! Let us not bring its dusty, tedious habits to the very place we have come to escape them. Come, what would Wordsworth say? He would urge you on, as I do.'

Mr Hayward said no more; and Mary saw he was stung by his friend's suggestion that he was dull and unenterprising. Once the dinner was over, and everyone had begun to disperse, he approached Mary, clearly uneasy at the turn of events.

'When it was just ourselves, I was not so concerned. But now we are to be a larger party, I am less certain we should attempt it. Will Ryder is my friend, and he is good-hearted and generous to a fault. But he does not consider consequences, especially if they stand in the way of the excitement of the moment. And his manner is so persuasive, he makes those who do not share his enthusiasms feel foolish for not following his example.'

'Yes,' said Mary, 'I can see he is impulsive.'

She sensed from Mr Hayward's preoccupied air that he was actively considering whether the climb should be abandoned. In most circumstances, she would have entirely endorsed his judgement. But on this occasion, she was not so sure. If the excursion was given up, she would lose the opportunity it offered to spend time alone in his company. That was enough to prejudice her in its favour. But she was also aware of an excitement that had begun to grip her as she had listened to talk of the ascent. Perhaps it was the influence of the landscape around them, so harsh and yet so beautiful, that had encouraged her to imagine abandoning her habitual prudence and throwing herself headlong into the unknown. Perhaps it was the fault of Mr Wordsworth – she had spent so long seeing the world through his eyes that now she truly longed to experience for herself the sensations he described with such passion. She only knew she very much wanted to walk up the fell and behold for herself the view laid out beneath her. It would be dreadful to be denied it now. But she did not think she could explain any of this to Mr Hayward, at least not in the cramped dining room of an inn, with servants carrying dirty dishes passing them on all sides. Instead she was circumspect.

'I understand the need for caution,' she began, 'and you are right to insist on our being properly prepared. But if that can be achieved, then I wonder if we should not simply take the chance. Perhaps those of us naturally inclined to prudence might benefit from being shaken up a little.'

Her reply was clearly not what Mr Hayward had expected; but before he could ask her to say more, they were joined by Mr Ryder.

'Well, Miss Bennet, what do you say to this stride up the hill?'

'It is more than a hill,' retorted Mr Hayward. 'Not quite a mountain, as I told Miss Bingley. But something in between.'

'Well, whatever it is – mountain, fell or molehill – shall we climb it or not? Come, Miss Bennet, tell me your thoughts.'

'I think Mr Hayward is right to warn us of the challenges we might face,' she said, choosing her words carefully. 'And it is of the first importance that we take every possible care. But I confess I should like to try it. The sight of the sea in the distance must be something not easily forgotten.'

Mr Ryder clapped his friend on the shoulder.

'There, even the thoughtful Miss Bennet finds you too timid! And I would trust her judgement implicitly – no one's more so.'

He looked at her admiringly. Mr Hayward, meanwhile, seemed disconcerted. It was plain that, for all her private misgivings, he had not expected Mary to take his friend's part. Mr Ryder went triumphantly on, oblivious to his friend's silence.

'When we reach the ridge,' he declared, 'as I am fully determined we shall, I intend to stand beside you, Miss Bennet, at the exact moment when you catch your first glimpse of the sea. I should not miss it for anything.' And then, without waiting for an answer, he turned to Mr Hayward and addressed him in a very different tone.

'Tom, I wonder if I might beg the favour of a quiet word with you later tonight? There are some family matters on which I should like to ask your advice. Legal questions, you know. Perhaps we might take a glass together when everyone has gone to bed? The landlord has some decent claret hidden away which might make amends for my talking business at such an hour and in such a place.'

Sometime later, when Mary followed the others upstairs, she looked over her shoulder to see the two men settle themselves in a secluded corner. The landlord brought out their bottle himself and placed it before them. In her tiny room, once she had undressed and brushed out her hair, she lay on her bed for a while, but sleep would not come. She hardly knew what she was doing as she put on her wrap and crept down the corridor to the top of the stairs. From there, quite hidden from the sight of those in the public room, she looked down on Mr Hayward and Mr Ryder, who had made short work of the good wine. Mr Ryder was speaking with great animation, while his friend listened intently, every now and again interrupting with what appeared to be a question. He looked sombre. Mary watched them for a while, before the ridiculousness of her position drove her back to her bedroom, faintly disturbed, for reasons she could not explain.

CHAPTER SEVENTY-SIX

When the mountain guide arrived at the inn, he made an excellent first impression, his calm, sober demeanour pleasing everyone gathered to meet him. He spoke quietly, but with authority, explaining that he had taken many ladies and gentlemen up the fell without incident, and that he would be pleased to do the same for them. However, it was essential that they understood his terms. The walk was not dangerous, but it was long, and could not be hurried; a whole day must be allowed for it. His son would accompany them, bringing provisions to sustain them on the way. And most importantly, it must be clearly understood that his instructions were to be attended to in all matters concerning the climb; for he knew the country, and they did not.

It was immediately agreed he should be hired at once, and the excursion was fixed to take place a few days hence. Now the trip was definitely to happen, the excitement of the little party was palpable. When the guide left them, Mr Ryder exclaimed that no better man could possibly have been found to take them, and Mr Gardiner agreed, declaring that in the hands of such an honest fellow, they could not go far wrong. Mr Ryder repeated his impatience to behold for himself the grandeur of the high crags, while Miss Bingley assured him of her willingness to bear any discomfort to be with him when he did so. Even the Hursts let it be known they were agreeable to 'giving it a try.' Only Mr Hayward, it seemed, had nothing to say. When the little group dispersed, he made his way alone into the little garden at the front of the inn; and after a few minutes, when everyone else had gone about their separate pursuits, Mary followed him.

'You are very quiet,' she said, as she came upon him, leaning on a stone wall and staring into the distant valley. 'Do you still have reservations about the climb?'

He stared out into the landscape, with a preoccupied air.

'I am not entirely happy about it, for all the reasons I gave you earlier.'

'But now we have an excellent guide, which must relieve your mind somewhat. And if Mr Ryder's impetuousness still makes you uneasy, Mr Gardiner's presence will balance him out – he would never be swayed into attempting something unsafe.'

'You are quite right of course,' he replied, finally turning to face her. 'To be frank, Miss Bennet, the excursion is not my principal concern at present. My thoughts are elsewhere this morning.'

Mary was surprised to see how low-spirited he appeared. For the first time since they had met, his usual liveliness seemed quite extinguished. His obvious unhappiness touched her deeply. She longed to take his hand, and beg him to confide in her; but instead she merely moved a single step nearer to him and spoke in manner she hoped would convey the depth of her sympathy.

'Is there anything I can do to help you?'

'I'm afraid not. This is a matter I must resolve for myself. But thank you.' He attempted a smile, with only partial success, wished her a polite good morning, and strode back towards the inn. Mary did not follow him, but took his place leaning on the wall and looking at the hills. Something had happened. She began to feel uneasy. She plucked a blade of grass from the stone wall and wove it between her fingers. Perhaps it was nothing. She did not move for some time, but stood there, reflecting, until the cloud came up, when she threw the grass onto the ground and went back into the inn.

Mary did not see Mr Hayward again that morning. She supposed he had gone out walking alone. The inn was quiet, most of the guests occupied elsewhere. Miss Bingley and her sister had strolled down to the lake. Mrs Gardiner had insisted her husband lay down his fishing rod and accompany her to Keswick. Left to her own devices, Mary fetched a book she hoped would occupy her thoughts sufficiently to prevent them returning again and again to Mr Hayward and his unaccountable change of mood. She stationed herself on a window seat, where light streamed in from the brilliant sunshine which had burned away the clouds. She found a cushion for her back, drew up her knees and began to read.

It was here Mr Ryder found her when he marched into the inn, fresh from a stiff walk, calling loudly for a cold drink. Once he had drunk it – downing it in a single swift gesture – he noticed Mary, tucked up in her retreat. He put down his glass and, with no greeting besides pulling up a chair next to her, peered at the book in her hands.

'*Evelina*. A very suitable book for a young lady on her holidays.'

Mary swung her legs off the seat and attempted to compose herself into a more suitable attitude.

'Really, Mr Ryder, you came upon me quite unawares!'

'I did not want to disturb you. You looked quite at your ease,' he replied, not in the least discomfited. 'A little like a Dutch painting, with that old window behind you. Are you fond of Miss Burney's work?'

Mary straightened her collar, very aware of his gaze.

'Not especially. I have begun her many times and have yet to reach the end of a single one of her books.' She slid a slip of paper between the novel's pages to mark her place. 'But I persevere. I am determined to enjoy her if I can.'

'That is a remark only you could have made!' exclaimed Mr Ryder. 'You realise Miss Burney's novels are designed to entertain? They are not a task to be endured, but a pleasure to be enjoyed. If you do not like them, why do you continue with them?'

'I feel it is a failing in me not to like them as other people do. I hoped I might teach myself to appreciate them.'

'That is not how pleasure works,' replied Mr Ryder gently. 'It cannot be forced into being. It arises freely from our inclinations, which are not to be dragooned into following the tastes of others.'

He took the book from her hand and laid it on the seat.

'It is really quite easy, once you get into the habit of it. Come, let me show you how it is done. It is the most beautiful day outside. I suggest we take full advantage of it and walk about a little. Just in the fields below the inn. Down to the stile and no further.'

He held out his hand in invitation. Mary's first instinct was to refuse; but outside the sun shone and the birds sang. Try as she would, she did not think she and Miss Burney would ever get on; and as Mr Ryder had, as she considered it, given her permission to dislike her book, she thought she might just as well leave *Evelina* alone. She knew she would like nothing better than to walk in the fresh sweet air; and closing her ears to the voice that told her to say no, she jumped up and went to fetch her hat.

CHAPTER SEVENTY-SEVEN

Mary enjoyed their walk together. It was pleasant to feel the sun on her face; and Mr Ryder did all he could to entertain her, describing novels he had failed to finish with such an amusing air that Mary thought she would never again blame herself for not completing a book she had begun upon, but would abandon it without the smallest twinge of guilt. It was true that he teased her once or twice, but even his playful comments suggested appreciation on his part; and on several occasions, he told her, with no equivocation at all, how very pleased he was to find himself in her company. It was impossible not to be affected by such open admiration, and by the time they were on their way back up the hill to the inn, Mary was talking to him with real animation, smiling every now and then with genuine pleasure. Indeed, she was laughing at some remark of his when they rounded a bend in the path and came upon Mr Hayward, making his way down.

Mary thought she glimpsed a look of surprise when he first caught sight of them, and perhaps of something else – sadness? displeasure? regret? – but whatever it was lasted for such a short time that afterwards she could not be sure. If Mr Hayward had been distressed to meet her in Mr Ryder's company, he did everything in his power not to show it.

'Tom!' exclaimed Mr Ryder, unconscious of any embarrassment, greeting his friend with his usual exuberance. 'How magnificent is this? The air is so pure I could drink it! I persuaded Miss Bennet to come out and share it with me – it is far too invigorating to experience it alone!'

'It seems to have done you good, Miss Bennet,' replied Mr Hayward gravely. 'You look very blooming in the sunshine.'

Mary thought he looked as unhappy as he had done that morning and her own gaiety ebbed away as she wondered once more what could have wrought such a change in him. She had often heard the phrase 'my heart went out to him' – but she had never felt the truth of it so powerfully before.

'It has been a very pleasurable little walk,' she said, hoping he would notice her attempt to convey that it had been of very short duration. 'But twenty minutes is long enough for me on such a warm day. We are heading back in search of tea. Mr Ryder feels sure we shall find some. I hope you will come too?'

He was silent for a moment as if considering the idea.

'You surely cannot refuse such a charming invitation?' asked Mr Ryder. 'I know I could not. Do come – there might even be cake!' So Mr Hayward agreed to join them, and they walked slowly back up the hill together. On the way, they talked of travel, its pleasures and miseries, its importance in opening the eyes and broadening the mind. There was scarcely a gap in the conversation as they went on, but it was Mr Ryder who did most of the talking. Mr Hayward spoke now and again, but it seemed that this afternoon he had little to say. Even when they reached the inn and sat down to tea at a little round table, placed for them in front of the bay window, he remained preoccupied and remote. Mary had never seen him so withdrawn. Mr Ryder, however, chattered happily on;

and when he elicited only an occasional response from his friend, he turned increasingly to Mary, regaling her with accounts of places he had already seen, before moving on to list others he had yet to explore. No gentleman, he declared, could consider himself properly educated until he had seen for himself the classical ruins of Greece; but even so, nowhere fired his imagination as much as Italy.

'Of all the countries in the world, that is the one I most long to visit.'

'I understand that desire,' said Mary. 'Anyone who has read Mr Gibbon must wish to see Rome.'

'Yes,' replied Mr Ryder, 'it must be an extraordinary thing to walk where the Caesars trod before you. But I should like to attempt the entire Grand Tour – to Florence, Assisi and Venice – anywhere, in short, where there is beauty, art and sunshine to be had.'

Mary turned to see what Mr Hayward thought, and found him looking at them both, as if trying find an answer to a puzzle or a conundrum, a solution which somehow eluded him.

'Should you like to see Italy, Mr Hayward?' she ventured, a little tentatively.

For a moment, he did not answer.

'Tom!' cried Mr Ryder, 'Miss Bennet asks you – do you fancy a jaunt to Italy?'

'Excuse me, I apologise. I was not attending.' He gathered his thoughts. 'I do not think it would be easy to arrange, with the state of Europe as it is.'

'A perfect Hayward answer,' laughed Ryder, 'in which pragmatism triumphs over passion! But I refuse to be put off. One day I shall stand on a terrace looking out at the sea, a glass of wine in my hand, toasting the setting sun.'

Mr Hayward, it appeared, had nothing to add to this; and soon, pleading letters to write, he took his leave and went away to his room.

'Well,' declared Mr Ryder, as he watched his friend depart, 'Tom was hardly in the best of spirits. I wonder what can have upset him?'

Mary did not know; but she feared that meeting her with Mr Ryder had not improved his mood. She wished she had not gone out walking with him; she wished even more that they had not happened upon Mr Hayward as they returned and that they had not been laughing when they turned that corner.

Mr Hayward did not appear for dinner, sending a note to Mrs Gardiner attributing his absence to headache, and expressing his hope that he would be restored to them the next day. Lying in bed later that night, Mary was restless as she tried to make sense of what had been a most confusing and distressing day. She turned over in her mind every possibility that might explain Mr Hayward's unhappiness but could find no explanation that satisfied her. If something untoward had happened to his family, surely he should have said so? If there had been some setback in his profession, would he not have confided in Mr Gardiner? In her heart, she knew neither of these explanations answered. Could it possibly be something to do with her? His behaviour towards her had been very strange all day, most unlike his usual easy intimacy. He had hardly spoken to her; and indeed, had been very little in her company, choosing to walk alone and not to dine. Could it be that he was avoiding her?

This was so appalling an idea that it chilled her to the heart, but once it had occurred to her, she could not let it alone, and spent several unhappy hours worrying away at it. It was almost dawn before she finally fell asleep, exhausted, puzzled and anxious.

After so disturbed a night, it was no surprise that she awoke late and was one of the last to come down for breakfast. There was no one at the table but Mr Ryder and Miss Bingley, who held a book of poetry in her hand. Mr Ryder looked pleased to see Mary; Miss Bingley did not.

'Good morning, Miss Bennet,' said Mr Ryder. 'You have arrived at exactly the right moment. Miss Bingley has been asking my opinion about the poems in this little volume. I'm sure we should both like to hear your thoughts on them.'

Miss Bingley looked up from her porridge, her glance as sharp as a knife.

'Oh, no, I shouldn't like to trouble her. I'm sure Miss Bennet has far *loftier* things to consider than a few lines of verse.'

She raised her chin, as if she had issued a challenge, which, in a manner of speaking, Mary supposed that she had. But Mary did not choose to cross swords with Miss Bingley this morning.

'In the matter of poetry,' she answered, bland as the milk she poured into her coffee, 'I think advice is not usually much to the point. Where verse is concerned, our own taste is usually the best and safest guide.'

Miss Bingley, who quickly saw there was to be no contest, returned her attention ostentatiously to her poetry book. Mary crumbled her breakfast roll and dipped the pieces absently in her coffee, continuing the debate she had had with herself for much of the night, her mind so engaged with the subject that when the subject of her reflections himself arrived at their table, she was taken completely by surprise. His coat was damp and under his hat, his hair glistened with droplets from the mist that was just about to be burned off by the morning sun.

'Good lord, Tom,' cried Mr Ryder, 'have you been out already?'

'I have. Nothing clears one's thoughts so much as a brisk walk.'

'Was your mind clouded, then?' asked Mary. 'Was there some decision you were obliged to make?'

He took off his hat, shook off his coat, sat down, and helped himself to coffee.

'Yes. Something of considerable importance. It has troubled me a great deal. But I have come to a conclusion and am resolved to act upon it.'

'That must be a satisfaction to you, at least.'

'No, exactly the contrary I'm afraid. I believe I have done the right thing, but I cannot pretend it makes me happy.'

Mary hesitated. It was impossible not to see that beneath his carefully maintained composure, he was very miserable.

'We are told there is comfort in the knowledge that one has acted properly. Perhaps you may come to feel it later.'

'Perhaps. But I doubt it.'

'I do not wish to intrude – but is there any advice I can offer?'

He smiled at her, and his expression – in which regret now seemed uppermost – pierced her to the heart.

'Perhaps to talk freely about what concerns you might ease your mind?'

He stared at his plate, and several moments passed before he raised his eyes to hers once more.

'You are very kind. But this is a matter I must deal with myself. I do not have the better of it yet. But I will.'

All this while, at the other side of the table, Miss Bingley had sought valiantly to persuade Mr Ryder to accompany her to some discreet corner, where they might discuss her book of poems in greater privacy. But he had refused to be drawn; and now, her efforts exhausted, she snapped shut the little volume and looked about her the table impatiently.

'Well, what a sorry picture we present. It is eleven o'clock, and as yet we have no plans for the day. What are your thoughts, gentlemen?'

It had probably not occurred to her that Mr Ryder would suggest a ride into Keswick to look at the livestock market, or that Mr Hayward would, without any real enthusiasm, agree to accompany him. But it was so, and in a few minutes, Mary and Miss Bingley were left alone at the table, a situation neither of them could wish prolonged. Miss Bingley was the first to rise, leaving to seek out her sister and Mr Hurst. Mary followed not long after, and spent her day with the Gardiners, watching her uncle fish. Disregarding Mr Ryder's advice, she took *Evelina* with her, hoping it would distract her from the even more anxious state of mind into which her conversation with Mr Hayward had plunged her. But it was hardly a fair contest. Even the best author could not compete with the anxious questions that ran through her mind, hour after hour, about Mr Hayward, his unhappy state and her own possible connection to it.

CHAPTER SEVENTY-EIGHT

The night before the climb up Scafell was due to take place, Mrs Gardiner decided she would not attempt it. The ascent was sure to be long and tedious; the guide had said the path was stony, and she did not think her ankles strong enough to bear it. Mary was straightaway afraid that, at this last minute, she too would be prevented from going; but her aunt did not forbid her. She did, however, insist on her wearing a pair of thick-soled boots she had bought for her in Keswick; and arranged for one of the maids at the inn to take up the hem on her least good dress. Mary knew that in her heart, Mrs Gardiner would have preferred it if they had remained together at the inn; she often dropped hints about how comfortable they should be while the others were away, how they might have tea together and read their books.

However, Mary was not to be persuaded. She told her aunt she was determined to see for herself the noble sights which the walk promised to deliver. But she would have divulged to no one the other reason why she would not be deterred from making the climb. There could be no doubt now that Mr Hayward's manner towards her had changed. He was never less than polite and gave no hint of any anger or resentment towards her. He was affable enough – but he was not the same. He no longer sought her out, as he had been accustomed to do, choosing the chair nearest her own, standing next to her at every opportunity. They rarely spoke in private now and laughed together even less. He no longer glanced up to catch her eye across the table when something was said he knew would amuse her. Slowly but surely, he had pulled away from her. Even when he was near her, he was distant.

When she was alone, Mary ran again and again over every possible explanation for his behaviour. None satisfied her. She knew him to be neither cruel nor deceitful. She did not believe him capable of acting unkindly without some cause. If she herself had played some part in his change of heart, she could not imagine what it was. Perhaps she simply imagined that he cared for her? While she had longed for him to declare himself, perhaps the truth had been that her feelings were stronger than his – and now he was attempting to divest himself, with as much tact as possible, from a situation that had become embarrassing to him. Tears pricked her eyes as she considered this. She supposed it was possible. But when she thought of how happy they had been together on their first arrival in the Lakes, how fond and comfortable they were with each other in the boat on Grasmere, how they had laughed about their dismal sketches, how she had teased him about his inability to tell one bird from another – she could not convince herself she had been wrong to think his affection for her was genuine.

When she reached the point where there were no more possibilities to interrogate, she did not know what to do. Staring at night into the black Westmoreland dark, open-eyed when she should have been sleeping, brought no relief. Finally, she decided she would torture herself no more. No. She would act like a rational being and simply ask him why he was behaving in this way.

She knew this was an audacious decision. It presumed on the nature of their acquaintance, which, although she could barely imagine now what life had been like before she met him, had not in fact been of very long duration. Nor was it usual for ladies to question gentlemen about the state of their affections. But she was resolved to do it anyway. Knowledge, she told herself, was always to be preferred to ignorance, even if what was revealed might be painful to hear.

It was impossible, however, to open such a conversation at the inn. The danger of being overheard or interrupted was too great. On Scafell, though, there would be a real chance of speaking to Mr Hayward alone with no one to eavesdrop except the rabbits and hawks, and they were too low in the grass or high in the sky to be bothersome. She could not say with any conviction what it was she hoped to discover. She was at a loss. All she knew was that whatever had provoked Mr Hayward's withdrawal, it did not look as if it had made him happy; for when she found ways to study him unobserved, which she very often did, he looked as troubled and preoccupied as she felt herself.

On the day of the trip, the morning dawned bright and clear. Soon everything was ready, provisions packed, boots put on, the *Guide* slipped into pockets. Mrs Gardiner waved the walkers off, the little party squeezed tightly into the inn's hired coach. They bumped off down the rutted roads, thankful that it was not long before they arrived at Seathwaite, where they met the guide and began their climb.

The path rose up behind a small row of cottages, then levelled off into a steady incline. The ground was uneven, the grass yellow and tussocky, hiding pools of dark water which seemed designed for no other purpose than to soak the feet of the unwary walker. Mary was soon very grateful for the stout boots Mrs Gardiner had bought her. The country was open and the sky was a sharp, bright blue with a few tiny white clouds scattered distantly upon it. At first, they walked to the joyful accompaniment of larks singing ecstatically as they rose upwards in the clear air; but as they made their way higher and higher, they left the larks behind, and soon nothing was to be heard but the harsher cries of buzzards wheeling overhead. Mary walked alone, preferring her own company to that of anyone else. Mr Hayward strode on, a little ahead of her, equally silent, equally alone. So now they were both unhappy, Mary thought, frowning as she watched him. And for what reason? What had soured the pleasure they had taken in one another? What had provoked such an inexplicable change of heart? With every step she took, she grew more determined to discover what had happened.

The guide and his son, a fine boy of twelve or thirteen, led the way, setting a steady pace. Mr Gardiner walked alongside them, questioning them intently, as was his way, about the country and the game to be found in it. Behind them followed Mr Ryder, his excitement visible in his every eager gesture. Now and again, he turned back to Mary, keen to share his enthusiasm.

'Could anything be better than this, Miss Bennet? Such skies! Such air!'

His pleasure was so infectious that, even in her dark mood, Mary found it impossible not to smile back, provoking an affronted glare from Caroline Bingley. She had stationed herself at Mr Ryder's side, trotting next to him, Mary thought, exactly like an officious little terrier. She should not have been surprised if the lady had growled at her and bared her teeth.

So distracted was she by Miss Bingley's hostility that Mr Hayward's voice, low, steady, and very near to her, took her completely by surprise, as he fell into step beside her.

'You seem to be managing very well,' he said. 'It looks as though you are more than equal to the demands of the climb.'

Her heart beat faster to hear him speak to her in something approaching his old, familiar tone. But she was determined to keep her countenance. If she was to find the courage to question him, she must not lose her nerve.

'Yes,' she replied, with an evenness she did not feel, 'so far at least. But this is the easiest part. I'm sure there is worse to come.'

They spoke in pleasantries, quite unlike the usual bantering style of their conversation. This was painful to Mary, as it confirmed very strikingly the cooling of their relations. But she refused to allow her distress to deflect her from her purpose. If she could keep Mr Hayward talking, the opportunity would surely present itself for her to ask him what she was to understand by his behaviour.

'Mr and Mrs Hurst do not appear to share your stamina.'

Mary turned to look at the couple, labouring with some effort further down the path.

'I'm sorry for them. It is clearly harder than they expected.'

'I offered her my arm when we forded the stream, but she brushed me away.'

'She obviously possesses in full all the gentle charm of her sister.'

She saw a smile steal briefly across his face, but it was quickly extinguished. It was as though he was doing all he could to resist the pull of their old ease and friendliness. She would speak. She must know the cause of it.

'Mr Hayward—'

She swallowed hard, determined to begin. But before she could do so, she heard footsteps behind her.

'Excuse me, Tom,' exclaimed Mr Ryder, 'but I have something for Miss Bennet.' He opened his hand to show a pale yellow flower, a little crushed but still recognisable as a primrose.

'Our guide says it is one of the very last of the season. There were two flowers. I gave one to Miss Bingley, but this is for you.'

'Thank you, Mr Ryder.'

'You could press it and use it as a bookmark. It might cheer up those pages of Miss Burney that you find so dreary.'

With that, he strode back to his place near the head of their little procession.

'Poor primroses,' said Mary, gazing at the crumpled bloom. 'What a sad end for such pretty things.' She looked up at Mr Hayward. 'You know, I kept the honeysuckle you gave me. It is in a glass in my room. It still smells very sweet.'

He seemed not to hear her, absorbed in watching his friend amble back to Miss Bingley.

'Ryder certainly knows how to make a gesture. He will always find a way to draw attention to himself.'

'That seems somewhat harsh. I think he meant it sincerely.'

'I'm sure of it.'

Mary, taken aback by the bleakness of his tone, did not reply.

'He seems to know your tastes in reading pretty well.'

'I had *Evelina* with me the other morning. He remarked upon it.'

Mr Hayward looked as though he was about to say more; but seemed to think better of it. He stood for a moment, considering; and then declared abruptly that he must ask the guide to stop soon as he did not think the Hursts could go much further.

As Mary stood watching him walk away, it struck her quite suddenly that Mr Hayward was jealous – jealous of his friend. It was such an extraordinary idea that it took a moment for her to absorb it. At first it seemed preposterous, presumptuous even – who was she, after all, to imagine two men could feel strongly enough about her to arouse such a sensation? From a deep place in her mind, to which she had attempted to banish such dark thoughts, an old familiar whisper resurfaced to insist that only the beautiful inspired such strong emotions – a woman like her was incapable of doing so. But she could think of no other way to account for Mr Hayward's behaviour over the last few days. His discomfort had been very marked when he had seen her in Mr Ryder's company. His silent withdrawal when he met them walking from the inn – his obvious ill humour just now, so unlike his usual open, frank disposition – what else could it imply but displeasure with what he regarded as his friend's overtures to her?

She pulled her jacket closer to her as a strong breeze whipped around her, blowing down from the higher ground. She had remained rooted to the spot for too long. She must go on, or she would lose sight of the others – even the Hursts were in front of her now.

As Mary struggled upwards, her thoughts were so disturbed, her feelings so turbulent, that she barely noticed the path. She supposed there was one sense in which she might be encouraged by her discovery. If Mr Hayward was indeed jealous, it suggested that his feelings for her were not entirely obliterated. If he was truly indifferent, why would he care? But the more she considered it, the more she was surprised to find that this reasoning, however logically sound, brought her neither relief nor gratitude. Instead what she felt was a swelling indignation. What right did Mr Hayward have to behave in this way? What possible reason did he have to be jealous?

She took several deep breaths, willing herself to be calm as she picked her way carefully through the rough grass. There were large stones everywhere, strewn randomly on the ground; it would be dangerous to trip over one. All her concentration was required to avoid them, and gradually she felt more in control of herself. Very well then, if that was the accusation, she would examine the evidence. Then she would know if there was truly a case to be answered.

She was compelled to admit that Mr Ryder's conduct did suggest some fondness on his part. His calling so regularly at Gracechurch Street implied it, as did his seeking her out so often for conversation. Indeed, the manner in which in he spoke to her might be said to confirm it – a teasing familiarity which even she understood suggested interest. Mrs Gardiner had noticed it, had warned her twice to be wary of Mr Ryder's charm; if she had observed it, why should not Mr Hayward have done the same?

Mary's immediate inclination was to run ahead, find Mr Hayward as quickly as she could, and, throwing discretion to the wind, try to convince him she felt nothing for his friend, that his apprehensions were entirely baseless. But something in her baulked at the idea of it. She had done nothing wrong. She had not invited his friend's attentions, and she had certainly not returned them.

If they made Mr Hayward uneasy, why had he not spoken to her and asked if Ryder's interest was returned? She would have been happy to assure him it was not. But he had not done so. Instead he had turned his face away from her, leaving her confused and unhappy, ignorant of the cause of his retreat. And yet, she was to be the one who sought to make amends? She was meekly to apologise for an offence she had not committed? Well, she should not do it. If anyone was required to justify their conduct, it should be him.

Anger was an unfamiliar emotion for Mary. In the past, she had not felt entitled to give way to anything so assertive. She had always assumed the blame for any fault, any difficulty, must be hers. Apology had become her habitual response to any form of challenge. But she no longer felt so abject. Her anger had galvanised her, had awoken her pride. Mr Hayward had done everything possible to suggest he had strong feelings for her, given every indication that encouraged her belief that he cared for her – but nevertheless, he had made no declaration. Much as she wished for it, he had not spoken. Yet he had not hesitated to show his displeasure when Mr Ryder displayed an interest in her. Perhaps he should decide what his true feelings were towards her and express them with honesty and consistency. Then – and not before – he might have some justification for what she was now convinced was, without question, jealousy on his part.

CHAPTER SEVENTY-NINE

Mary forced a few escaping strands of hair back into her hat and pushed it down upon her head. The way was harder, but she did not falter. The sun was hot and her legs ached, but she pushed onward and upwards. Her temper drove her forward and seemed to supply her with reserves of stamina, but for all her angry energy, she was glad when the guide chose to stop for refreshments and a short rest. Catching up with the others at last, she was relieved to sit down upon one of the rugs the guide had spread out for them; and when his son passed amongst them, offering around flasks of weak tea and small beer, that were as cold as they were welcome, Mary drank as eagerly as everyone else.

'We have made good time this morning,' observed their guide, 'and we're not far from our destination now. If you look in that direction – yes, ma'am, follow where I point, you cannot mistake it – that is Ashridge, that great grey shelf over there. But the walk gets harder from here, a stiffer climb than we've had so far. If any of you don't feel up to it, this is the time to turn back. My boy will take you down, he knows the way as well as I do myself.'

No one was much surprised when, after a huddled consultation, the exhausted Hursts volunteered that they had indeed had enough and wished to return. But Mr Gardiner's

announcement that he intended to join them was most unexpected. The gentlemen tried their best to persuade him not to
give up – their object was almost in sight – would he not be
sorry to miss it? – but he was adamant.

'I fear I must sacrifice my pride to my aching legs. It pains
me to admit it, but this is a climb for those younger and more
agile than myself. If I go back now, there is some prospect of
my taking a rod out on the lake, an occupation much better
suited to a middle-aged man like myself.'

He held up his hand to silence any further protestations.

'If the young ladies are prepared to continue without me –
if they are happy to rely upon our estimable guide, and of
course the two young men here – then I am decided. I'm sorry
to miss the view. But for an angler who won't see forty again,
on this occasion there can be no doubt that the fish have it.'

So only four of the original party followed the guide further up the twisting path, treading more slowly, yet determined
to reach their goal. Sometimes, when the route allowed it, they
walked alongside each other; more often, they marched in
single file, saying little. Everyone was hot and tired. Mary saw
that Mr Hayward had from somewhere acquired a stick, and
every so often, beat at the grass with it, or tossed it from hand
to hand, gestures that seemed to sum up his restless, uneasy
state. Mary steeled herself against the sympathy that leapt
immediately into her mind. The remedy lay in his own hands.
If he would only speak, all might be resolved. She thought of
the slip of paper Mr Collins had given her, with the line of
Aristotle written upon it. *Our happiness depends on ourselves*, it had said; but how, she asked herself, was that to be
achieved when there was so little candour in the world, such

fear of confessing what one really felt? It pained her to admit it, but perhaps Mr Ryder was right after all?

Her mind was so absorbed with these thoughts, that when the guide called out to them all, she started up, jolted back into reality.

'Ladies and gentlemen, we're very nearly at our destination.' He gestured towards a plateau, a little way ahead. 'Ashridge is not ten minutes' walk, if we step out bravely.'

In no time at all, they were there. As they stood, hands shading their eyes against the sunlight, triumphant on the little patch of ground they had laboured so mightily to reach, they fell silent, absorbing the full glory of their reward. It seemed as though the whole world was unfolded before them, hill after hill undulating away to the distant horizon, one succeeding another, punctuated by the occasional silver flash of a lake. The guide pointed out the principal sights in one direction – there was Keswick, there was Borrowdale and Bassenthwaite – before turning to show what lay in another – the mountains of Skiddaw, Helvellyn, and Saddleback. Finally, with the aplomb of a magician revealing his best trick, he gestured towards a line of blue water on the horizon.

'And that, ladies and gentlemen, is the Solway Firth. Beyond lies Scotland.'

Mary felt herself rooted to the spot; she could not draw her eyes away.

'So finally we "behold the distant sea", just as we had hoped we would.'

Mr Hayward had come to stand beside her. She did not turn to look at him but continued to stare, entranced, into the landscape.

'Yes,' she replied, 'it is indeed magnificent.'

'As magnificent as you expected it to be?'

'I have never seen anything more beautiful.'

'It is just as I pictured it – but somehow more so. Nature, it seems, far exceeds the power of my imagination in creating something so lovely.'

He moved a little closer to her.

'I'm very glad,' he continued softly, 'that we were able to see it together.'

She did not know what to say. She could not subdue the anger that surged through her, and the warmth of his words, after so much coldness, only fanned the flames of her discontent. What did he mean by speaking so tenderly to her now, when he had done all he could to push her away with politeness? How was she to understand his behaviour?

Part of her was bitterly hurt and wounded; but at the same time, his nearness – the unsettling fact of his proximity – stirred her very deeply. His obvious unhappiness cut her to the quick. It took all her powers of self-control not to speak, to explain that nothing was as he thought – that all might be made well again if he wished it. Her heart told her this was the moment to do it. *Speak now! If you wish to take control of your destiny – if you truly wish to make your own happiness – speak now! This is your opportunity, there may never be another. Tell him what you feel – if he cannot do it, show him you can!*

She very nearly did so – she came so close that the words were half-formed in her mind – but pride rose up within her – alongside fear and shame and resentment – and her courage failed her. Instead, she replied with a coolness intended to signal a detachment she was very far from feeling.

'Yes, we can congratulate ourselves on a remarkable achievement.'

There was a false indifference in her voice which grated even on her own ears; but she would not relent, would not soften.

'We have not spoken much to each other this morning.'

'Nor yesterday, or the day before.'

'It is true I have been somewhat distracted.'

'I have noticed that.'

She stood very still, upright, rigid. This was his opportunity to do what she had failed to do – to speak, explain, to redeem himself in her eyes. She clenched her fists tight with expectation. Another few seconds passed. Nothing. He had no more courage than she did herself. She would wait no longer for words of explanation that were plainly not to be said.

'Well,' she said, with a false brittle brightness, 'I find so much walking has made me hungry. I think I shall go and find out what the guide has brought for us to eat.'

She could not mistake his surprise as she turned on her heel and left; his face fell, but she did not weaken and did not look back.

CHAPTER EIGHTY

The guide had lain a clean cloth on a flat rock, and spread upon it a loaf of bread, cheese, and a few apples. Caroline Bingley was reaching for some fruit when she saw Mary approaching. She offered no welcoming smile, but Mr Ryder leapt up to greet her.

'If there's anything better than eating in the open air, I should like to know what it is. May I help you to something, Miss Bennet?'

Mary took some cheese and an apple. She did not wish to spar with Miss Bingley, so politely took her leave and looked for a place to eat alone. She soon found a patch of dry grass, with an accommodating rock to lean upon. She sat gratefully against it, took off her hat and shook her head, as if trying to throw off the weight of her disappointment. Tiredness washed over her. She had no more energy to reflect on Mr Hayward. For as long as she could remember, it had seemed as if she was a player in a game whose rules she did not understand, in which all the dice were weighted against her. She had done her best to learn what she was supposed to do, but somehow she always stumbled.

As she looked into the distant hills, she realised how she longed to be free of it all, to leave behind the posturing and falsity, the niceties and stratagems. Again, Mr Ryder's words echoed in her mind. Why could not relations between men and women be stripped of misunderstanding? Why could they not be as natural and honest and simple as breathing? She hugged her knees and closed her eyes, feeling the sun on her neck; her mind wandered and in a few seconds she was asleep.

She did not know what it was that woke her, but when she opened her eyes, she was astonished to see Mr Ryder himself sitting not too far away from her, a blade of grass in his mouth, staring silently at the horizon. She started up, alarmed.

'Lord, sir, I must have fallen asleep! I hope it was not for long?'

'Not more than five minutes,' he replied. 'Or perhaps ten.'

She sat up, reached for her hat, and began to rise; but he held out his hand to stop her. 'I don't think there's any need to hurry. Everyone is occupied. Tom and the guide are discussing the landscape, and Miss Bingley is resting. Wait a moment and look at the view with me.'

His quiet self-possession was soothing, and Mary could not find the spirit to protest. Together, they watched the shadows cast by the clouds race across the green sides of the hills beyond them. In the far distance, it was hard to tell where the grey sea ended, and the blue sky began. It was difficult to imagine anywhere more beautiful.

'I feel even I could write poetry here,' murmured Mr Ryder. 'It would be impossible *not* to do so. This place could make poets of us all.'

'That sky would be enough to persuade anyone to pick up a pen.'

'Even you, Miss Bennet? Can we expect some verses from you? "On Climbing Scafell", perhaps?

'I hardly think my talents lie that way.' She saw a patch of daisies in the grass next to her, picked one, then another; and set to making a chain from them. He watched her indulgently.

'Excuse me if I say I doubt that. I'm sure you could do anything to which you truly set your mind.'

'You are very kind, Mr Ryder, but quite wrong, I'm afraid. I might be capable of setting a few lines down on paper. Any of us can do that. True poetic talent, however, is a rare thing. I know I do not possess it.'

'That is what Tom says,' observed Mr Ryder. 'He has often told me – usually after reading something I have written – that the desire to write poetry has no connection at all with the ability to do so. And that if you have no feeling for it, you had far better leave it alone.'

'Yes, that sounds very like him,' said Mary softly.

'Well, if I am never to read any words of yours upon the countryside around us,' continued Mr Ryder, 'perhaps you can simply tell me how it affects you. What do you think when you look at it?'

She gazed into the shimmering blue distance as if trying to fix it in her mind's eye.

'The first impression is of beauty. The colours, the light, the airiness. But the more you look, the more you understand it is the scale of what lies before us that is most startling. It is so large, so grand and so majestic; and we are so small and insignificant in comparison.'

'Those are my thoughts exactly!' he cried. 'It is magnificent – but it is also severe. It is quite indifferent to us. And we are irrelevant to it. All our petty concerns and worries, the silly little rules by which we live, all mean nothing in its presence.'

'Looking at such a view, I understand why you might think that.'

'I do think it, Miss Bennet. This landscape gives us a proper sense of perspective. It shows us our smallness in the great scheme of things. As these mountains understand it, in the blink of an eye we, and everything we have created will be gone.'

'That's a gloomy thought, sir.'

'On the contrary, I find it very exciting. To me, it has but one message: do what you will and follow your heart, for we are all a very long time dead.'

He plucked the grass from his mouth, threw it away and leaned a little closer to her.

'Our lives are so brief and yet we spend so much of them obeying rules we did not make. The spirit of this place can't help but make me imagine what it would be like to be truly free. To speak and behave not as we thought was proper, but as we really wished to do, if we were honest enough to confess it.'

She was a little shocked to hear her own recent thoughts refracted so clearly back to her.

'If she were here, Mrs Gardiner would tell you this is nothing but libertine's talk, a justification for every kind of licentiousness.'

'Can you honestly tell me – and I beg you to be truthful now – that you have not felt something of what I describe? An impatience with the way things are ordered – particularly amongst men and women?'

Mary added the last daisy to the chain and placed it carefully in her lap.

'I cannot imagine why you should think that.'

'I catch a glimpse of it every now and then in your expression before you cover it up in that way you have.'

Her self-possession faltered.

'You embarrass me, sir.'

'Only because I have seen something in you that I suspect you don't often admit, even to yourself.'

'You go too far.'

'Then I shall stop. I don't wish to distress you. I will only say it seems plain to me that you long for happiness and freedom. But I'm afraid the first is only to be had by embracing the second, and it takes a great deal of courage to do that. Especially for a woman.'

He rose, brushing the dust from his coat.

'For you, I think it would be a risk worth taking. You weren't made to live a dull, ordinary, little life. You deserve more than that.'

'If I were fortunate enough to be with a man I loved, a little life would be neither dull nor ordinary.'

Mr Ryder smiled.

'It is when you make remarks of that kind that I admire you the most.'

He took his leave, as calmly as if they had been discussing idle pleasantries over the tea table, and ambled away to find the others. Mary did not follow him but sat for a while alone. She stared into the hills as if seeking advice or reassurance there; but they had none to offer, and presently she too rose and went to join the rest of the party.

CHAPTER EIGHTY-ONE

When she arrived amongst them, only Mr Hayward greeted her, his expression guarded, almost reproachful. Everyone else was staring intently into the sky.

'We are looking at the clouds,' he explained. 'Will thinks he can see objects in them – ships, horses and so on.'

'They are there for those with the imagination to see them,' declared Mr Ryder. 'Come, exercise your genius and tell me what you see.'

'It is far too fanciful an occupation for Miss Bennet,' replied Miss Bingley. 'I beg you, do not feel obliged to join us in such a frivolous activity.'

Mary ignored her and looked up towards the sky.

'I see – shapes like the tops of trees, clustered together, a huge forest in the air.'

'Celestial woodlands,' murmured Mr Ryder, looking first at the sky and then at Mary. 'I should like to walk amongst them.'

'I cannot see it myself,' said Mr Hayward. 'I see only clouds.'

'It works if you surrender yourself to the conceit, Tom,' urged Mr Ryder. 'I'm sure you'll see something extraordinary if you try.'

'I think them pleasing enough as they are. When I see

something naturally beautiful, I have no need to turn it into
something it is not.'

Mr Ryder shrugged.

'Very well, I cannot compel you to be playful.' He shaded
his eyes and looked once more into the sky. 'I think I see a ship
of the line in full sail in the outline of that cloud – can you see
it too?'

Miss Bingley hurried to his side and immediately cried yes,
she had it now, she could make out every detail, every rope of
the rigging and billow of the sails. Her eagerness to please was
so fervent that Mary felt ashamed for her and moved away.
She found herself next to Mr Hayward once more, and their
eyes met; but neither of them seemed to know how to begin a
conversation. Both were relieved when the guide approached
them, his hat in his hand.

'I see you're looking at the weather. You're right to take
notice. There's a change coming. We should think about going
down.'

The others wrenched their gaze away from the skies, and
turned to him, astonished.

'Go down?' asked Miss Bingley. 'But we have only just got
here.'

'Yes, miss, I know. But nevertheless, that's what we must
do. And quickly, if you please.'

'But the sky is so blue,' protested Mr Ryder. 'And these
clouds above us – they don't seem very threatening.'

'No, sir, not those,' replied the guide, patient but determined. 'But look this way. On the horizon, over the sea. That's
where the rain is brewing up.'

Mary could see nothing but the hazy blue line where the
sky met the water.

'I believe there is something there,' said Mr Hayward, concentrating hard. 'I can see a smudge of vapour or cloud, out in the distance.'

'That's it, sir,' said the guide. 'It's a rainstorm brewing. It's on its way. It might pass over quickly, or it might pelt down. Whichever it is, we don't want to be caught in it up here.'

'It seems very hard to credit,' persisted Mr Ryder, 'when we're basking in sunshine and the air is as clear as a bell.'

'Yes, it's fine now, but it won't stay that way. That's not how the weather works on these fells. It comes out of nowhere, and it moves very fast.' The guide looked away from Mr Ryder to Mr Hayward. 'Come, gentlemen, we should go back now.'

'That seems good advice to me,' said Mr Hayward. 'Our guide knows these hills. We should do as he says.'

But Mr Ryder was not to be persuaded. 'Really, Tom, look around you! Do you honestly believe we are about to be inundated?'

'In matters of such importance,' replied Mr Hayward steadily, determined not to be provoked, 'I prefer to rely on expert knowledge rather than my instincts, which are unlikely to be either accurate or dependable. I suggest we all do the same.'

'As usual we are obliged to be cautious and prudent,' cried Mr Ryder. 'It seems a pity to deny ourselves the pleasure we have just begun to enjoy, after so long a climb.'

'I'm not sure what pleasure is to be had in finding ourselves soaked through,' replied Mr Hayward dryly.

'Even if it does rain,' Mr Ryder went on, 'who is to say we should run away from it? A rainstorm in so wild a situation is likely to be a great natural phenomenon – perhaps we should stay and witness it for ourselves?'

He gestured to Mary.

'Miss Bennet, I'm sure you have your copy of the *Guide* with you. May I see it, please?'

Mary produced the little book and passed it to him.

'If I can't persuade you, Tom, perhaps you'll take more notice of your hero. Ah, here is the passage. Mr Wordsworth tells us no traveller should grudge the price of a little inconvenience to witness "the sight or sound of a storm coming on or clearing away". He says it is an incomparable experience.'

'I very much doubt he intended it to be enjoyed at the top of a great hill such as this one,' remonstrated Mr Hayward. 'Or that he intended ladies to be put to the inconvenience and misery it will doubtless involve.'

'I should not mind it,' declared Miss Bingley. 'A little rain would be nothing to me. I will gladly stay, Mr Ryder, in order to see something so remarkable.'

'You must see how foolish this is,' Mr Hayward replied, his exasperation growing ever more apparent. 'You surely understand the dangers that attend it. I beg you to reconsider. This is not a poem, to be enjoyed in the warmth of your study – this is real, this is life.'

'There lies the difference between us,' retorted Mr Ryder, equally passionate. 'You want to keep the spirit of one away from the experience of the other. I, on the other hand, long to bring them together.'

When he saw his arguments had made no impression at all upon his friend, Mr Hayward turned to Mary.

'Miss Bennet, I appeal to you – yours is a rational mind – surely you appreciate the folly of all this?'

When he looked at her so directly, so urgent and imploring, Mary's first instinct was to support him. Every sensible impulse told her he was right, that she owed him her agree-ment. But then she was suddenly angry once more, and the strength of her feelings put an end to all considered judge-ment. He would not explain the reasons for his withdrawal from her – but imagined he could still call upon her when he required endorsement for his views. Then she was of service to him – then she could be depended upon to be the voice of dull-ness and restraint. Well, she should do so no more. She was tired of passing judgement, of urging others more lively than herself back to the narrow path of duty. She would not agree with Mr Hayward, even though every fibre of her understand-ing told her to do so. For once, her heart would rule her head. She would throw off her usual restraint, and surrender to the thrill of the unknown and the unpredictable. She should not be herself at all.

'I think I should like to see the amazing sight Mr Words-worth describes. It seems a great pity to have come so far and to leave, just as something extraordinary is about to happen.'

'That is exactly how I see it,' exclaimed Mr Ryder. 'We shall embrace whatever nature is pleased to exhibit to us.'

Mr Hayward looked at Mary as though he could not believe what she had said; but she was determined not to falter.

'We will never have the chance to see anything like this again,' she continued. 'Perhaps we could stay just long enough to see the storm come towards us and begin our descent before it arrives. Then we might outwalk the worst of it, with-out having missed the remarkable scenes Mr Wordsworth describes.'

Mr Ryder thought this was an excellent plan, and went to inform their guide, who had absented himself from their circle once their disagreements began to grow lively. Miss Bingley hurried along in his wake, pausing only to direct towards Mary a glance which was both imperious and disdainful. Then Mary and Mr Hayward were left alone.

'Mary,' he said, speaking so low that she struggled to hear him. 'What are you doing? You cannot outwalk a storm! You must know that!'

'I am not sure what I know or do not know. I find it hard to say any more what is true and what is false.'

'I don't understand you.'

'I am tired of trying to make sense of things – to understand behaviours that seem to have no rational cause. I have given up on thinking for a while. All I want to do just now is to feel.'

'This is not like you at all.'

'I should very much hope not. I'm tired of my old character, and am resolved to try on a new one. Perhaps that will bring me more in the way of happiness and satisfaction.'

'I'm sorry to hear it. I was very fond of the old Mary.'

He stepped towards her; but she moved away.

'I shall be sure and tell her that. I think she often wondered what your true feelings were, so she will no doubt be pleased to know.'

He did not reply, but stood silent, his whole person a picture of distress. He took off his hat and ran his fingers angrily through his hair; but still he said nothing. The only sound to be heard was that of the guide arguing with Mr Ryder, clearly incredulous at what he had proposed.

'It seems I must leave you,' said Mr Hayward stiffly. 'I must explain to our guide why, when we hired him for his experience and promised to be guided by it, we have decided, on the flimsiest and most ridiculous grounds, to ignore his advice.'

Mary watched him join the two men and do his best to placate the angry, disbelieving guide. She saw him wave Mr Ryder away, watched as he spoke quietly to the guide, put his hand in his pocket, drew out what was plainly cash and passed it to the aggrieved man, talking all the while until the guide grew calmer. Mary swallowed hard. She hoped she had not been as foolish as her intellect now whispered to her that she had.

CHAPTER EIGHTY-TWO

The storm was not long in making itself felt. The vapour on the distant horizon coalesced into clouds, great columns of grey that blotted out the sun and shadowed the hilltops as they raced across the sky. The peaks before them were first lit up and then plunged into darkness, their green hillsides a shifting patchwork of colour. A curtain of dark rain shimmered in the distance, a rumble of thunder echoed in the far off valleys. At first, Mary was elated. Mr Wordsworth had been right, she thought. This was indeed a thing worth seeing. She stood transfixed by the boiling landscape, when Mr Ryder joined her, just as delighted by the prospect before them.

'Isn't this superb? The mighty power of Nature in action! This is why we came here!'

He turned to face her, his expression exuberant – and without warning, something of his passion leapt into her own heart. Suddenly, she was conscious of nothing but the most acute sensations – fear and joy mixed together, a sense of awe and wonderment that took her breath away. She did not know what it was or how to describe it – but as she stared into the drama unfolding in front of her, she felt both great and small at the same time, connected to the world in a way she had never been before, yet also marvellously and uniquely herself. She closed her eyes, and let the feeling pass over her, giving herself up to it, until she thought there was nothing to her but sensation.

It was perhaps a minute before the extreme intensity of her emotion began to diminish. She breathed out, opened her eyes, and was still again. Before she came to the Lakes, she had read a great deal about the sublime – sights so extraordinary they could not be adequately described, only experienced. She had never expected to feel for herself such a consummation. Her spirit was surely too stolid, too unremarkable to achieve anything of that kind. Now she knew that was not so, and a wave of gratitude swept over her.

Then the rain hit them. It was quite unlike the gentle showers Mary knew from Hertfordshire. It poured down in a great deluge, soaking her hat, drenching her clothes, and jolting her out of her trance. It fell with such force that it pricked her eyes. She stood dazed, until she saw Mr Hayward walking towards her, the guide following in his wake.

'Miss Bennet, we must leave now. This is no longer a subject for discussion. Miss Bingley, come with us. Quickly, if you please. Either you walk down in our company, Will, or you must make your way alone. We shall wait no longer.'

His tone forbade any contradiction. Mary, shaken now, tried to wipe the rain from her face and readied herself to depart. Miss Bingley too obeyed, with neither a sharp aside nor a withering look; and even Mr Ryder tore himself away from the view and followed.

For the first twenty minutes, they walked as fast as the path allowed, making their way down from the ridge to the more open country below. It had been hard climbing up, but, as Mary soon discovered, it was no easier to descend. The rain drove puddles into the saturated ground, and it required all her concentration to pick her way through the stones that littered the route, their surfaces slippery in the mud.

Their guide constantly urged them to make haste, insisting they must move faster if they were not to be drowned before they reached the bottom. But soon even he could see that the ladies, in their soaked skirts and sodden hats, needed a moment to catch their breath, before hurrying on as best they could.

'We might find some shelter over there,' he shouted, pointing towards an untidy group of large boulders a short way off the path. 'If we settle in the lee of these rocks for a while, we might avoid the worst of it.'

They hurried as best they could towards the stones, and were soon huddled against them, Mr Hayward shepherding Mary and Miss Bingley into the space which offered the most protection. The guide pulled the hood of his coat over his head, his attitude one of resentful dejection. Only Mr Ryder's spirits seemed unaffected by their situation.

'I shall walk back to the path for a moment and look into the valley. The storm must be at the height of its vigour now. I should like to glimpse it if I can.'

'Is that wise?' asked Miss Bingley. 'You will be drenched.'

'I can hardly get any wetter than I am already,' said Mr Ryder lightly. 'As there is no part of me not thoroughly soaked, I may as well take advantage of the fact.'

Miss Bingley smiled weakly as he strode away, but Mr Hayward said nothing. He had spoken no more than was absolutely required since they had begun their descent. Mary could see that he was very angry. As she considered their exposed and bedraggled state, as she imagined the difficulties that must await them as they attempted to get down, she could not deny his frustration was justified. His assessment of their situation had been correct; but he had not been listened to. And she had been one of those who had spoken against him.

'We stayed too long on the ridge,' she ventured quietly. 'I see that now. We should have left earlier.'

'You say that as though this is our fault,' replied Miss Bingley. 'But how were we to know what would happen? We have been unlucky but cannot reproach ourselves for it.'

She looked defiantly at Mr Hayward, who met her eye steadily.

'I'm afraid I disagree,' he said sharply. 'We were offered very clear advice but chose to disregard it.'

'It sounds as though you blame Mr Ryder, sir.'

'Everyone who agreed to ignore our guide bears some responsibility for our situation. And I do not exempt myself from criticism. I should have argued harder for us to leave, demanded we go when it was right to do so.'

Mary's earlier elation had been washed away by the rain. As she watched rivulets of water running swiftly through a little gully between the stones, she felt both mortified and ashamed. She stole a glance at Mr Hayward, who stood alone, looking into the rain. Despite all that had passed between them, she could not bear that he should think ill of her. The anger and indignation she felt earlier had ebbed away, replaced by a dull ache of sadness and regret. It was painful enough to think that she might have lost his affection; but to imagine that she had also forfeited his respect was almost too much to bear. When they were back at the inn, she must find a way to explain her behaviour on the ridge, to try and make him understand how provoked and wounded she had been by his own hurtful actions and beg him to account for them if he could. This time, she told herself, she would not be deflected, but would find out the truth of how things really stood between them.

It was half an hour before the sky started to lighten and the rain began to fall with slightly less intensity. All the walkers were now soaked through. Mary's coat and dress clung to her, cold, wet and heavy. Her hat dripped; her boots leaked. When the guide announced that he thought the worst was over, she was not much relieved. She knew they must walk down in this miserable condition and dreaded the prospect. But she stood up bravely, resolved to put one foot in front of the other for as long as she was capable of making the effort.

They walked in a gloomy silent procession, the guide in front, leading them towards the least demanding route. Mr Ryder followed behind, accompanied by Miss Bingley. She had seized the opportunity presented by the perilous conditions to attach herself firmly to his arm and clearly did not intend to relinquish it until they were on steady ground once more. Mr Ryder did not seem to mind; he had achieved one of the great wishes of his heart and was satisfied. He had contemplated the natural world in all its majesty and, at least until another great wish suggested itself, was content. He smiled encouragingly at Mary every now and then, but Miss Bingley's grip was tenacious, and he did not try too hard to escape from it.

Mary kept a little apart from Mr Hayward. She did not feel able to begin her explanations in such circumstances and did not see how she could say anything else until she had done so. With every step, she grew more exhausted and unhappy, until the discomfort she felt in both mind and body were pretty equally matched. Then she missed her footing – her boot slid in the mud – and she fell slowly but irrevocably onto her knees.

She caught her breath, from shock and surprise. But before she could give way to tears, she felt Mr Hayward take her hand. He raised her up firmly but gently and brushed the worse of the dirt from her dress.

'Are you hurt? Have you any pain?'

'No, I don't think so. A little bump on my knee, nothing worse.'

'Can you move it?'

She tried, succeeded, and nodded mutely. He took her arm and tucked it carefully within his own.

'No protests, please. This is the best way to get you safely down.'

She was about to speak, but thought if she did, she would never stop. It was enough simply to accept his help, to allow him to guide her through the pitfalls along the path – 'careful here' – 'step a little higher now' – 'watch for that sharp stone' – as they made their slow way down.

They had been walking for some time when she thought she heard shouting from further down the hill. The guide heard it too, and rushed forward, hollering a reply.

'I think that must be help,' said Mr Hayward, 'or at least I hope it is.'

Mary sighed with relief. The calls grew louder as their deliverers came nearer and nearer; but the drizzle was still so thick and so low that it was another ten minutes before their rescuers actually appeared out of the mist. The innkeeper was at the front of the little band, followed closely by an anxious

Mr Gardiner, with two servants each leading a stout little pony on a rein.

'Mary! Thank God!'

Mr Gardiner hurried towards her with such transparent concern that even in her wet and sorry state, Mary could not help but raise a weak smile.

'Oh, uncle, it is very good to see you!'

'I cannot tell you how pleased I am to see you unhurt – you are unhurt, I presume?'

'I twisted my knee at little, but it doesn't amount to anything. Mr Hayward helped me down. He has been so kind.'

Mr Gardiner clasped Mr Hayward's hand.

'Well done, Tom, well done. I'd have expected nothing less from you.'

Mr Gardiner turned back to Mary.

'Your poor aunt has been beside herself since the rain came on so strongly. She would not rest until we set out to find you.'

He chattered away, aghast at the mud, exclaiming at their wet clothes, before seating Mary carefully upon one of the little ponies, while Miss Bingley was mounted upon the other. The inkeeper offered Mr Ryder and Mr Hayward what Mary supposed was brandy from a small flask; but she was quite satisfied with the sweet cold tea he provided for the ladies. Even Mr Ryder seemed ready to be delivered from the storm, clearly looking forward to the more down-to-earth pleasures of a dry coat and a roaring fire. Mary was not quite sure exactly when Mr Hayward had melted away from her side. He did not bid her goodbye. She watched him, deep in conversation with her uncle, no doubt explaining to him the circumstances that had brought about their plight, although Mary doubted he would tell him the whole story. It was impossible to imagine him placing the blame upon others; it was not in his character to behave so meanly.

Their arrival at the inn threw the household into uproar. Water was heated up for baths; dirty clothes bundled away for washing, beds warmed, and fires lit. Mrs Gardiner wrung her hands, desperately anxious lest Mary should catch cold from her soaking. Even Miss Bingley was swept up in the ferociousness of her concern, compelled to submit to her insistence that both young women take themselves immediately to bed and stay there for as long as they could be made to do so.

In truth, Mary did not need a great deal of persuasion. She was exhausted and fell gratefully into the sheets. Her only regret was that she had not had a chance to talk to Mr Hayward before she was hurried upstairs. Her last thought, before sleep overwhelmed her, was that tomorrow she should seek him out in some private place and attempt the conversation she had failed to have on the fell. Tomorrow, she thought, as she fell asleep, tomorrow she would speak to him come what may.

CHAPTER EIGHTY-THREE

When Mary woke, she could tell by the position of the sunlight on the bedroom wall that it was long past her usual time of rising. She washed, dressed briskly and rushed downstairs, where she found only her aunt and Mr Ryder still at the breakfast table. Mrs Gardiner sprang up and looked keenly into Mary's face, her hand reaching out swiftly to touch her brow.

'Thank God, there's no fever! And you look very well rested.'

'Yes, thank you, I feel entirely myself.'

'I'm very relieved. And you'll be pleased to hear that Miss Bingley has also suffered no ill effects.'

'She is absent only because she is taking her breakfast in bed,' said Mr Ryder. 'All in all, I think we may count our excursion a success. A great natural event seen at close quarters, and all of us alive to tell the tale!'

'I am not yet ready to find your misadventure a joke, Mr Ryder,' replied Mrs Gardiner severely. 'I should not like to be in a such a state of anxiety again as I was yesterday afternoon.'

Mr Ryder apologised, begging Mrs Gardiner's pardon; but he smiled at Mary from under his penitent brow. She busied herself with the tea things, declining to meet his eye. She was not to be distracted from the only object of import-

ance that morning – that of seeking out Mr Hayward and
speaking to him with all the honesty and frankness of which
she was capable.

'Are the other gentlemen already out?' she asked. 'They
must have left very early.'

'Mr Gardiner is certainly gone,' replied her aunt. 'Once he
knew you were quite well, he took himself to the lake with
his rod. Mr and Mrs Hurst have gone to Grasmere village.
I have not yet seen Mr Hayward.'

'Tom often takes a walk before breakfast,' said Mr Ryder.
'No doubt he will appear at any moment, demanding strong
coffee.'

Again, he tried to catch Mary's eye, and again she applied
herself to her tea. She thought she would stay close to the
inn for the rest of the morning, waiting for Mr Hayward to
return. She was so absorbed in thinking what she should say
to him that she hardly noticed as the innkeeper approached
their table. He handed Mrs Gardiner a letter which she read
and passed wordlessly to Mary.

My dear Mrs Gardiner,

*It is with much regret that I must tell you I have been
summoned back to London to attend to some urgent
business. I'm sure you will understand nothing but the most
pressing obligation would have persuaded me to leave in so
hurried a manner. It is extremely distressing to me to be
obliged to go without saying a proper goodbye, which
seems small recompense for your prodigious kindness in
having me with you over the last few weeks.*

*I intend, once my business is concluded, to take this
opportunity to visit my mother in Hampshire and stay there*

for a while. I hope at some later date to see you once again in Gracechurch Street; but until then, I hope I can presume on your generosity to bid farewell on my behalf to Mr Gardiner, Mr Ryder, and the rest of our party, assuring them that only the need to catch the Keswick fly prevents me writing to each in person.

I beg to be remembered to Miss Bennet.

Yours in haste,

Tho. Hayward

CHAPTER EIGHTY-FOUR

The spirits of the holiday party never properly recovered from Mr Hayward's sudden departure. His absence was keenly felt. He was much lamented by the Gardiners, although Mrs Gardiner took care not to be overly extravagant in her regrets. She was too astute not to perceive that some breach or misunderstanding had occurred between him and her niece, and did not doubt it was that which had led to Mr Hayward's leaving them; but she had no wish to add to Mary's obvious unhappiness, and therefore gave no direct hint of her suspicions. Mr Ryder seemed oblivious of such a possibility, although whether that was by design or innocence was impossible to say. His manner was as easy and as open as ever, with nothing to suggest he thought of his friend with anything other than sympathy for his situation, and slight incredulity at his bearing it so well.

'Tom has always been of a very conscientious turn of mind,' he declared as they sat round the inn's dinner table a few nights later. 'He is a prodigious worker. It is not in his character to leave anything undone, or to throw off a responsibility he believes is his.'

'I am glad to hear it,' observed Mr Gardiner firmly. 'Such an attitude is essential in business, and I imagine it is the same in the professions. There are times when the demands

of one's occupation must take precedence over private pleasures.'

'As I have cause to know,' murmured Mrs Gardiner.

'Come, my dear,' her husband replied. 'You understand
how it is. Sometimes a man has no choice but to attend to
such matters, however much he may wish it was not so.'

'It must be very unpleasant to be at everyone's beck and
call,' said Miss Bingley smoothly. 'Of all the many aggrava-
tions involved in pursuing a trade, the knowledge that one is
not one's own master must be the most trying.'

She favoured the table with a brilliant, unapologetic smile,
while everyone around it silently absorbed the sting of her
remark. Mr Gardiner frowned. Mrs Gardiner was clearly
taken aback at such a very obvious snub. But Mary was outraged. She had learned to ignore Miss Bingley's jibes when
they were directed towards her; but she could not bear to
hear them aimed at those she loved.

'I imagine you must have seen many such occasions yourself at first hand,' she remarked, with a bland calmness quite
equal to that of Miss Bingley. 'As your own father was deeply
engaged in business, he must often have been called upon to
subordinate his wishes to the requirements of his trade.'

It was a moment before Miss Bingley collected herself sufficiently to reply. 'I cannot recall examples of that kind,' she
said, looking a little agitated as she applied herself to butter-
ing her bread. 'My father had been long removed from any
such necessities by the time I was old enough to know about
them.' She quickly recovered her usual assurance; but Mary
knew too that in so publicly reminding her of her origins she
had only intensified the lady's hatred for her, that her remark
would not be forgotten, and that she should eventually pay

for it some way she could not yet imagine, but she did not care. She was glad she had spoken.

When dinner was over and the others left the table, Mary remained, brooding once more over the question of Mr Hayward's departure. She had thought of nothing else since he left; and had quickly arrived at conclusions identical to those of her aunt. She was convinced that she herself was the reason he was gone. She knew he had been bitterly disappointed by her refusal to take his part during the argument on Scafell; and she was painfully aware her ill-judged support for Mr Ryder on the ridge had both shocked and hurt him. But had that really been enough to drive him away?

She did not know what to think. She could not persuade herself he was entirely indifferent to her. His leaving as he had, rushing away at dawn with no polite goodbyes or apologetic farewells, was not the act of a man who did not care; on the contrary, it suggested passions strongly and deeply felt. She supposed he might have been driven by the jealousy she thought she had detected; but how was that to be reconciled with the marked tenderness and consideration he had shown to her on their descent down the fell? The careful concern he had displayed for her then did not suggest either resentment or dislike. He could not have been more kind, more solicitous for her safety – but at this, she felt herself about to cry, and did not allow herself to think any more of his steadying arm, linked so firmly with her own. Why had he simply not opened his heart to her then and there, explaining the truth of what he felt? If he had spoken, she would not have hesitated to have given him the answer she still believed would have pleased him; but instead he had left with nothing explained, abandoning her to make what little sense she could of his behaviour.

What could he have meant by it? She thought of nothing else, but as day followed day, she was no closer to arriving at a conclusion, no matter how many hours she spent considering it.

She did everything in her power to hide her mounting unhappiness from those around her. She refused to be drawn by Miss Bingley's frequent speculations on the probable reasons for Mr Hayward's departure, greeting them with an expression of studied indifference that revealed nothing of her inner misery. She declined Mr Ryder's frequent invitations to take the air with him, knowing she would be utterly unable to match his air of cheerful unconcern. It made no sense, Mary told herself, to blame Mr Ryder for what had happened – he had never disguised the principles by which he lived. She could hardly complain when he acted upon them, as he had done on Scafell. It had been her choice to decide whether to follow his example or not; and now she must deal with the consequences of her judgement. But when she watched him go about his business, his natural affability untouched by any sense of guilt or regret, she could not entirely suppress her resentment. He had followed his inclinations and had paid no price at all for doing so – while she was left mired in misery and regret. So, no, she would not walk down the hill with him, or even take a short stroll round the inn. Instead, she wrapped herself in politeness and found a thousand civil ways of refusing him.

It was much harder to disguise what she felt in the presence of her uncle and aunt. Mary knew they were concerned about her. She had several times come upon them deep in discussions which they broke off as soon as she arrived, the subject of which was only too plain to them all. Only once did her aunt attempt to broach it directly, asking Mary if she did not think

Tom's leaving them so suddenly had been most out of character? But when Mary showed herself disinclined to speak on a subject which was so painful to her, her aunt did not press her. Mary was grateful for Mrs Gardiner's discretion; and on more than one occasion, she was tempted to confide everything to her. But for all her aunt's kindness, Mary knew it would do no good. The only conversation which could relieve her distress was one between herself and Mr Hayward; but that could only happen if they returned to London. So when Mr Gardiner finally suggested it was perhaps time for them to go home, Mary was obliged to conceal her eagerness to do so, lest it seem she was ungrateful for having been brought on holiday at all.

She was not the only one to feel their stay at the Lakes had come to an end; everyone agreed it was time to leave and soon all was in readiness for their departure. Mr Ryder's party was the first to go. Miss Bingley was coolly civil as she climbed into the carriage, clearly hoping she would not be forced into Miss Bennet's unwelcome company again. In contrast, Mr Ryder was keen to ensure they would meet again soon once back in London.

'I very much hope to see you in town, Miss Bennet. Perhaps we could make up a party and return to Vauxhall? I should be very happy to arrange it, if you say the word.'

'It is very kind of you, but I don't intend to go abroad too much when we return. I think I shall stay close at home for a while.'

'Then perhaps I may come and visit you there? We could read a little poetry together.'

'Of course, if that would please you.'

It was not the most enthusiastic invitation; but Mr Ryder

was satisfied. He sprang into the carriage, the driver cracked his whip, and as Mary watched them disappear, it occurred to her she had been right to have found their unexpected arrival in the Lakes unsettling. They had brought nothing with them but trouble.

PART FIVE

CHAPTER EIGHTY-FIVE

It took two days to get to the Bingleys' house and retrieve the children and another two to reach London. During these long hours, Mary thought of little else but Mr Hayward. She missed him more than she could say – and could not quite believe the situation in which she found herself. Time and time again she rehearsed the circumstances which had divided them, trying to find an explanation for what had happened; but nothing satisfied her. To have returned home – for thus she now considered her uncle and aunt's house – with matters so dreadfully unresolved was agony. She did not think she could bear the pain of unknowing; but what was she to do? She was powerless; even if she wished to, she could not act. It was impossible for her to call upon him; he was not in London, but even if he had been in town, it would have been unthinkable. Respectable young women did not visit the houses of single young men uninvited. Nor could she write. She supposed she might ask Mrs Gardiner for his family's address in Hampshire; but knew her aunt would, in all probability, refuse to give it to her. She could not begin a correspondence with him – every rule of custom and delicacy forbade it. There was nothing to be done but wait to see what he would do – the world offered her no other choice.

Once back at Gracechurch Street, she tried to make the long days bearable. She took out her books and tried to study;

but concentration eluded her, and she put them away. She read stories with the little Gardiners, and heard the lessons of the older children. She sat patiently next to the piano as the girls practised their scales and arpeggios, encouraging them gently as they stumbled through a few simple airs. She did not play herself; she had not the spirit for it.

She attempted to help Mrs Gardiner in her household tasks, volunteering to inspect the linen cupboards; but in her distraction, she confused the good sheets with those needing repair and the whole business of sorting and assessing had to be done again. She volunteered to wash the best china, the cups and saucers too fine to be entrusted to servants; but a wet plate slid out of her inattentive hands and broke into pieces on the floor. She looked so distraught that her aunt did not have the heart to scold her; but Mrs Gardiner did not think her household valuables would survive much more of her niece's assistance and urged her to put on her coat and go out for a walk.

Obediently, Mary did so; but the lively City streets no longer excited her as they once had. The shop windows that had once entranced her seemed familiar, even tawdry. The roads were dirty, the pavement crowded. Everyone was in a hurry; she was jostled and pushed. The one sight she longed to see was that of Mr Hayward, in the long brown coat he had worn on the fells, on his way to call at Gracechurch Street – but no matter how fervently she hoped for it, there was no sign of him.

Mary had been back in London over a week when she returned back home one afternoon, dusty and discouraged from yet another dutiful expedition. As she walked into the hall, she saw one of the servants disappearing towards the cloakroom with a gentleman's coat draped over his arm. She did not stop to ask who the visitor was, but raced up the stairs to the drawing room. Her heart was in her mouth as she reached the door, but when she opened it, it was not Mr Hayward who rose, delighted, eager to greet her. It was his friend Mr Ryder.

'My dear Miss Bennet! How very pleased I am to see you! I have come to pay my respects. I would have come sooner, but I have been down in Kent. Yet more family business to attend to – although I hope all that is finished now.'

'Mr Ryder! I thought – I imagined – I'm sorry, I was not expecting you.'

'I hope I have not come upon you at an inconvenient time, as so often seems to be my fate?'

Mary recovered her composure enough to invite him to sit down. She called for tea; and by the time it arrived, she felt tolerably in command of herself.

'I hope your time in Kent went off well, sir. I have never been there. Is it a beautiful place?'

'It is pleasant enough. Fields and orchards and sheep. You know the sort of thing. Not to be compared to the beauty of the Lakes, of course.'

He began to talk fondly of the great grey mountains and bright blue skies they had so recently enjoyed, and she slowly felt herself more at ease. He did not seem to require much in reply except an occasional smile of reminiscence or assent. The conversation went on well enough with only the occasional question from her, which she found suited her mood admirably.

'Should you like to return there?' she ventured politely. 'To a different part of the Lakes, perhaps?'

'To tell the truth, Miss Bennet, the next time I travel, I am resolved to go abroad – to Italy, if I can. If the Westmoreland fells had such an effect upon us, imagine the impact of the Alps!'

'I am not sure I have much appetite for mountains any more. Our walk down Scafell in the storm seems to have cured me of any desire to climb another.'

Mr Ryder laughed politely. It was plain he did not consider their saturated, struggling descent worthy of further remark.

'And what of you, Miss Bennet? How have you been occupying yourself since our return? What are you reading at present?'

'I am ashamed to say I have nothing particular about me at the moment. I seem to have lost the application a serious book requires.'

'That sounds most unlike you. But I have the perfect solution. What you require is a review – they are the very thing for a distracted mind. You can read what you like and ignore the rest, picking through its articles as if you're looking for the ripest pear in the bowl. Let me bring you one. Which do you prefer, the *Edinburgh* or the *Quarterly*?'

'Mr Hayward used to give me the *Edinburgh* sometimes. But he said its judgements were not entirely to be trusted.'

'That's because its reviewers have not always been kind to his adored Wordsworth. You know how loyal he is, once he has found something to love.'

Mary looked away, putting the lid back on the sugar bowl.

'Have you seen him since we returned to London?'

'I have not,' he replied. 'I imagine he is still with his family. It will come as no surprise to you to hear that he is a very dutiful son.'

Mr Ryder had nothing more to say about his friend's whereabouts, nor could he be prevailed upon to suggest when he might be seen amongst them again; and, perhaps feeling this subject had been thoroughly exhausted, announced shortly afterwards that he was obliged to take his leave.

'I have an appointment with my bankers. It is nothing but business and more business for me lately, which has made even this short interlude feel like a snatched pleasure – as though I've been let off my lessons, as it were.'

He downed the last of his tea and stood up, entirely at his ease in Mrs Gardiner's drawing room.

'I shall bring you copies of both the *Edinburgh* and *Quarterly* reviews – you can decide for yourself which you like best. It will be an excellent excuse for me to call again.'

A few days later, he returned, bearing the promised copies of the magazines. Of course, it was necessary to offer him tea, during which he declared his intention of returning again to hear what Mary made of them. Soon he was almost as regular a presence in the Gracechurch Street drawing room as his friend had once been.

'You must have a great deal of time to call your own,' observed Mrs Gardiner one afternoon a week later, when Mr Ryder was once more to be found in her drawing room, drinking her tea and eating her cakes. 'Of course we are always glad to see you – what should we do with our currant tarts otherwise? – but you seem somewhat solitary at present. What of Miss Bingley? I have not seen her for a while.'

'She is visiting her brother, but returns shortly, I think.'

'And is there any news of Mr Hayward? We've heard nothing from him since we left the Lakes.'

Mr Ryder flicked a few crumbs from his waistcoat.

'No, not a line. But I expect we will hear from him soon. It isn't like Tom to stay silent for long.'

Mary placed her hands in her lap, hoping to convey the impression of a serenity she did not feel. Mr Ryder's company had only made her miss his friend more. His visits sharpened her loss, magnifying her sense of abandonment. The better she came to know Mr Ryder, the more she longed for Mr Hayward.

It was not that Mr Ryder's company was distasteful. She was used to him now. She knew how to appreciate his better qualities; and his less admirable traits no longer disturbed her as they had once done.

Even his self-absorption no longer bothered her; after a while, there was something restful in it. His reluctance to make moral judgements came to seem equally soothing. It gave him an easy tolerance of the shortcomings of others – and also of himself. He preferred things to be agreeable rather than not, but, Mary suspected, did not in truth feel anything particularly strongly. He craved sensation, but she doubted he was a man subject to profound and lasting passions. Those would involve rather too much trouble. His feelings were like jam spread thinly on bread and butter – sweet, all-encompassing and readily available, but not penetrating very deeply.

The contrast with Mr Hayward could not have been more stark. His affection, she supposed, would be like a long-simmered beef stock – a great while in the making, but strong and rich and unmistakeably flavoured. It amused her when she thought how ridiculous a simile this was. Yet even as she smiled inwardly to herself, she felt a sharp pang of regret. She missed his passionate enthusiasms which sat so unexpectedly with his otherwise steady temper. She missed his sharp mind and ready wit. She missed the warmth of his smile, the look of amusement in his glance as he caught her eye across the dinner table. She had hoped that as the days passed into weeks, she would have begun to miss him less, but this had not been so. If anything, the opposite was true.

'Have you written to Mr Hayward, sir? Perhaps he needs a little encouragement to begin upon a correspondence?'

'I am not a greater writer of letters, I'm afraid. No, in Tom's case, there's nothing to be done but wait. He is determined to try our patience, but we are equal to it. He will write when he is ready to do so, and not a minute before.'

Mary nodded at Mr Ryder's words with every appearance of taking them to heart; but each day she looked for a letter from Mr Hayward; and each day she was disappointed. When the post arrived, she sorted through it with as much appearance of unconcern as she could muster; and when she found nothing there for her, put it back on the tray with an equally unconvincing display of indifference. She did this for nearly three weeks; yet every morning, she hoped against hope that today would be the day his letter finally appeared.

So one morning, when her aunt approached her as she sat at the piano with her niece, ready to begin their practice, the first thing Mary noticed was the envelope she held in her hand.

'I have some most unexpected news,' announced Mrs Gardiner. 'We are to have a visitor, it seems. Your mother is coming, Mary. She expects to arrive next week.'

CHAPTER EIGHTY-SIX

Mrs Bennet's trip to London was not, as she explained at length to anyone unwise enough to ask about it, undertaken in pursuit of pleasure. Left to herself, she should not have risked it, for the journey was tedious and the inns unsatisfactory. But her doctor insisted upon it.

'Dr Gower would hear no contradiction. "Your well-being depends upon it, ma'am." That was what he said – and the orders of a medical man are never to be ignored, so here I am.'

'No, indeed,' replied Mrs Gardiner, as she, Mary, and Mrs Bennet sat in a rather formal circle, drinking their morning coffee. 'You were very wise to come. And who is it you are to see?'

'His name is Dr Simmons,' said Mrs Bennet, respectfully, 'and he takes a particular interest in ladies who suffer with their nerves. He charges a guinea a visit, but what is money where one's health is concerned?'

She is still very handsome for her age, thought Mary, covertly watching her mother from under lowered eyes, *and as proud of her appearance as ever*. As if to confirm the truth of Mary's observation, Mrs Bennet glanced quickly at her reflection in one of her sister-in-law's pier glasses, made a minute adjustment to her hair, and another to her cap, before

turning away with the satisfaction of having found everything as much to her liking as usual.

'You look very well, Mama,' ventured Mary. 'Have your
nerves been troubling you? I should not have guessed it from
your appearance.'

'I would not expect you to understand. You have no
notion of what I suffer.'

'And how long will the treatment last?' interrupted Mrs
Gardiner.

'Usually a week is sufficient, although with a particularly
difficult case, it may take up to ten days. I only hope Jane
can spare me for so long.'

'I'm sure she must have been very reluctant to see you go.
Especially in her condition.'

'Oh, she was beside herself. But Mr Bingley was all consideration, urging me to think of myself. He insisted I was
not to hurry back until I had been properly attended to. *He*
has sympathy for my state, even if *others* do not.'

Mary decided to ignore her mother's pointed glare and
reached out instead for one of the little cakes that sat so
invitingly amongst the coffee things. Before she could take
one, Mrs Bennet removed them to the other end of the table.

'I don't think so, Mary. Sugar is most injurious to com-
plexions such as yours.'

With a sigh, Mary understood that her mother had been
provoked by her remark about her nerves; and that she must
expect to suffer for it until Mrs Bennet felt herself revenged.
And just as Mary had expected, when Mrs Gardiner left the
room to see to her children, her mother settled down to the
pleasure of delivering a few more disobliging observations.

'I cannot say your holiday has been of much benefit to you.' She moved a little nearer, to examine her daughter more closely. 'You don't look anywhere near as well as you did when you set out. You are quite pale. Washed out, even.'

'I'm sorry you think so, Mama.'

'A little rouge might not go amiss. But judging from her own complexion, Mrs Gardiner has none about her.'

'I do not know, I have not asked her.'

'Well, as everything of hers is always to be preferred by you to anything of mine, I shall not offer you any of my own. Were there any young men to be met with in the Lakes?'

'There were two gentlemen in our party, Mama. As I believe I wrote to tell you.'

'Did you? I cannot recall. But neither of them showed you any particular attention?'

'I did not go to the Lakes in search of a suitor,' replied Mary, as evenly as she could, 'but to see for myself the beauties of the landscape. And with that, I was very well satisfied.'

Boldly, she reached across to the plate of cakes and took one; but her defiance was not equal to actually consuming it in the face of her mother's frank disapproval, and she set it, untasted, on the edge of her coffee cup.

'Were you indeed? Well, I suppose we must hope your luck will change now you are back in town.'

Mrs Bennet leaned over and rang the bell.

'The girl can come up now and do the dusting. This furniture is a disgrace.' She ran her finger across the top of a little side table and looked askance at the results. 'I suppose you remember what I told you about your spectacles? Did you wear them at the Lakes? If so, you have only yourself to blame for coming home in the same situation in which you left. But my advice is never heeded.'

Mrs Bennet's visits to Dr Simmons met all her expectations, as he took a most gratifying interest in her complaints, without prescribing anything unpleasant to cure them. Her only regret was that the consultations were over so quickly. They occupied no more than a few hours every other morning, leaving her with a great deal of time on her hands; which required Mary and Mrs Gardiner to give up their other occupations to entertain her. With Mrs Gardiner, Mrs Bennet found many engaging topics to discuss, from the inadequacy of the children's breakfasts, to the unaccountable negligence of the head parlour maid; but her conversations with her daughter followed a much narrower path. Her interests remained pretty much what they had always been, and she had nothing to say to Mary on any subject other than her looks and her marriage prospects.

On both these questions, Mary refused to be drawn. She was particularly determined that no mention of Mr Hayward's name should reach her mother's ears. She did not think she could bear the interrogation she knew would follow if any hint of her feelings for him were to escape her. Mary was sure Mrs Gardiner could be trusted with the secret; her relations with her sister-in-law were not such as encouraged the exchange of private intimacies. If anything, Mary was more afraid of betraying it herself, revealing it by some unguarded expression forced out of her by her mother's questioning. To avoid such an accident, Mary did all she could to reduce the hours she was obliged to sit with Mrs Bennet; and in pursuit of fresh air and a little relief from her mother's presence, she spent more and more time on her walks around the City. As she retraced her old routes, she slowly recovered the enjoyment she had once found in them, and usually came back happier than she had set out; but as she left the house one morning, the weather was against her. The skies were low and grey and threatened rain; and she got only as far as St Paul's before the showers began. She took shelter in the great doorway for a while; eventually, she had no choice but to pull up her collar and make her way back to Gracechurch Street.

When she arrived back at the house, she was surprised to hear her mother's laughter drifting down to the hall from the drawing room. Perhaps the great Dr Simmons was paying a house call? But when she entered, there was Mrs Bennet, sitting delightedly on the sofa, gazing with every appearance of approval at the smart, manly figure of Mr Ryder. Her aunt, from the other side of the room, caught Mary's eye and made the tiniest shrug; but Mrs Bennet did not see it. She was far too fascinated by Mr Ryder to notice anything occurring beyond the space occupied by his captivating person.

'Miss Bennet,' he exclaimed, jumping up to greet her, 'I am so glad you have come back. I should have been very sorry to leave without the pleasure of seeing you.'

'I was out walking—' began Mary, before her mother interrupted her.

'Your hair is damp, my dear,' she cried, with a brilliant smile Mary did not recall seeing directed at her before. 'I'm sure you will want to attend to it before you join us.'

'May I request that you do not,' said Mr Ryder eagerly. 'It is charming exactly as it is. Very natural and becoming.'

Mrs Bennet was somewhat taken aback to hear so

unmistakeable a compliment addressed to Mary; but she quickly recovered herself.

'All my girls were brought up to be as natural as possible, sir. I do hate to see anything false in a young woman.'

'I cannot speak to the virtues of your other daughters,' declared Mr Ryder smoothly, 'not having had the pleasure of meeting them; but I can say that with *this* Miss Bennet, you have succeeded admirably. There is no artifice in her at all.'

He smiled knowingly at Mary, his expression conveying with amusement that he understood the part he was expected to play in the conversation, and would not scruple to indulge himself in doing so.

'I might add,' he continued, 'that having been introduced to Mrs Bennet, it is only too apparent from whom her daughter has inherited her delightful manner.'

'Really, Mr Ryder!' exclaimed Mrs Gardiner. 'That is a little too much, even for you!'

'I am never afraid to offer praise where praise is due,' he murmured.

Mrs Bennet, not at all disconcerted, moved a little forward on the sofa.

'I should very much like to hear about your trip to the Lakes, sir. I have always longed to see them, have not been lucky enough to do so. My desires are not much attended to, but as long as everyone else is happy, I do not mind it.'

Mary touched her hair, feeling the raindrops wet on her hand. Mr Ryder launched obligingly into a lively account of their trip, occasionally appealing to Mary or Mrs Gardiner to confirm some detail. He did not, Mary noticed, mention the Scafell climb, for which she was very grateful. She obediently added an aside now and then; but she had no desire to

establish in Mrs Bennet's mind a picture of herself and Mr
Ryder as inseparable fellow travellers or indeed, good friends.
She knew her mother would already be thinking of him as a
potential suitor, and she did not wish to offer her any further
encouragement.

When Mr Ryder eventually took his leave, Mrs Bennet
could barely contain her excitement.

'What an extremely interesting young man! Such manners, such presence, such consideration. It is long time since
I have met with anyone quite so charming!'

'Yes, Mama, he can be very agreeable.'

'Agreeable? Is that the best you can say about him? What
are his circumstances? Who are his people?'

'His family resides in Kent. I believe he is quite comfortably situated,' replied Mary. 'His income is such that he is
not to be obliged to follow any profession.'

She did not mention his connection to Lady Catherine.
She knew this would only sharpen her mother's appetite to
push her into Mr Ryder's arms.

'Then he is a most eligible young man. I assume he has no
existing ties? He is not promised elsewhere?'

'I believe not,' admitted Mary, 'although another lady has
shown herself ready to oblige him, if he could be persuaded
to ask her.'

There was a moment's silence as Mrs Bennet absorbed the
implications of this knowledge.

'I am not sure I quite believe my ears.' She leaned forward, fixing her daughter with a disbelieving stare. 'Here is a
young man with every advantage – rich, obliging, very good-
looking – a man who is interested in you – very interested,
from what I have just seen. And yet you talk about another

woman pursuing him with no more concern than if he had been a pound of butter.'

She sat back in her seat, exasperated by such wilful stupidity.

'I think of Mr Ryder as a friend,' replied Mary uncertainly. 'A good friend, but no more than that.'

'A single young woman cannot have a man as a friend!' exclaimed Mrs Bennet. 'He is either a suitor or he is nothing! And there is no doubt in my mind that, whatever you may say, Mr Ryder was here very much in the character of a suitor.'

Mary rose up from her chair and walked quickly to the window. She did not want her mother to see how her words had affected her. In her heart, she knew they were true – but she had not wished to acknowledge that fact, even to herself.

'I have not considered him in that light.'

'Then it is time you did, before it is too late.' With this final disbelieving exclamation, Mrs Bennet turned her infuriated attentions to Mrs Gardiner.

'I am amazed, sister, amazed that I have been told nothing about this young man. And then, just as I learn of his existence, I discover that there is a rival for his affections – that there is a chance Mary may be cut out!'

'She cannot be "cut out" if she does not wish to marry him,' replied Mrs Gardiner. 'And I have not heard anything from Mary that suggests that is what she wants.'

'Of course it is what she wants, even if she does not know it yet. Marriage is what every woman wants, and, while she was in your care, it was *your* duty to persuade her of that.'

'I am not sure interference on my part would be either helpful or desirable,' retorted Mrs Gardiner, who had made up her mind not to be provoked and, not without difficulty, continued to keep her temper. 'In my experience, these matters are best left to the young people to decide.'

Mrs Bennet waved a dismissive hand.

'How can they possibly do so, when they are neither old enough nor experienced enough to know their own minds? It is up to us to show them what is for the best, and make them act on it if we can.'

'Then I'm afraid we must disagree,' declared Mrs Gardiner icily. 'Their affections are not to be forced or coerced. They must find their own way. All we can do is prevent the very worst from happening – to keep our daughters away from blackguardly men and instil in them enough sense to resist their blandishments.'

The words 'elopement', 'disastrous' and 'Lydia' hovered in the air, but Mrs Gardiner thought better than to utter them; and Mrs Bennet was too distracted to perceive any personal application in what had been said, which, if she had, would have required her to leave her brother's house that very evening, if not before.

'You are entirely mistaken,' declared Mrs Bennet. 'The cleverest girl is sometimes utterly blind to where her true interest lies; look at Lizzy, if you like. Having safely married four daughters, I think I may be allowed some experience in these matters.'

Mrs Gardiner thought it prudent to say no more, but Mrs Bennet was not to be silenced. 'And what have you been doing in all of this to advance your cause? No, miss – don't speak – I can see – nothing at all!'

She shook her head, unable to believe a daughter of hers could be so indifferent to her own best interests.

'Even you, Mary, must surely see,' her mother continued, 'that if Mr Ryder has made no offer to this other lady – who appears to have a better grasp of her position than you – it must be because he likes you.'

'He may not wish to marry either of us, Mama. Have you thought of that?'

'Don't be ridiculous Mary. A single man in possession of a good fortune *must* be in search of a wife.'

'As I say, I consider us as friends only. I have no reason to believe he thinks of me in any other way.'

Mary knew this was disingenuous; but her mother's eagerness frightened her.

'Nonsense,' retorted Mrs Bennet. 'He looks at you with real admiration. I suppose you are not used to it, and don't recognise it when you see it, but I assure you, it is so.' She turned towards Mrs Gardiner. 'Even you must agree with me on this point. It is impossible to deny he admires her, is it not sister?'

Mary could see her aunt had no wish to encourage Mrs Bennet, but could not bring herself to lie.

'Yes, Mr Ryder is very fond of Mary. He sees qualities in her that others have not appreciated – even those closest to her – and that is greatly to his credit.'

'In that case, I am all the more amazed you haven't done more to advance matters. But fortunately, I am here now and will have everything settled before I go back to Jane.'

CHAPTER EIGHTY-SEVEN

It did not take Mrs Bennet long to discover that Mr Ryder was a distant relation of Lady Catherine de Bourgh – Mary supposed she had extracted the information from Mr Gardiner – and this drove her to even more determined efforts to secure him for daughter. When he appeared at Gracechurch Street, which he did increasingly often, he was plied with coffee, tea, and every kind of cake. At Mrs Bennet's insistence he was invited to dinner and served Mr Gardiner's best claret. He was coddled and flattered and treated to every kind of delicacy until Mary thought he might burst. He did not seem to mind it, and remained his usual easy, cheerful self; but after one particularly trying afternoon, when she thought she might curl up and die from shame, Mary summoned up her courage and complained.

'I do beg you, Mama, to leave Mr Ryder alone. It is very unseemly to encourage him as you do.'

'Don't be ridiculous,' exclaimed her mother. 'We are only making him welcome. Inviting him into the family circle, you might say.'

'It isn't fair. It raises his hopes. It makes him feel as though he has some special claim on us – on me.'

'Yes, that is the general idea. How else will we get him to make you an offer?'

Once an idea had taken root in Mrs Bennet's mind, it was

almost impossible to dislodge it. Mary knew she could throw herself endlessly against her mother's iron will, without making the slightest dent in her convictions; nevertheless, she persevered.

'But I do not think I want to marry him.'

Mrs Bennet did not look up from her sewing, as if this was not an idea to be seriously entertained.

'Don't be silly. You won't do any better, I can promise you that. You were prepared to take on Mr Collins before that sharp little hussy Charlotte Lucas plucked him out of our grasp – and Mr Ryder is a great deal better-looking, richer, and infinitely more agreeable than Mr Collins. If you throw this opportunity away, who else do you think will have you?'

His friend, cried Mary to herself, *I would willingly, joyfully take his friend*. But Mr Hayward had not written. Perhaps he would never write. It was possible that she would never see him again. Grief suddenly overwhelmed her. She could not control herself; and fled out of the drawing room, into the hall, where she passed a shocked Mrs Gardiner, and up the stairs to her bedroom where she covered her face with a pillow so that no one should hear. There she cried and cried until she could cry no more.

It was half an hour before she mastered her feelings. She lay, dry-eyed, for a little time before she rose up and smoothed down her dress. Then she washed her face, combed her hair, and pinched her cheeks to give herself a little colour. When satisfied she was presentable, she made her way down towards the drawing room.

Before she could enter, she heard her aunt and her mother arguing within, their voices tight and angry. She stood, rooted to the spot, her hand grasping the bannister, unable to move, although she knew she should.

'I really do implore you to leave matters alone for a while,' urged Mrs Gardiner. 'I know you mean well; but when I see the unhappy state she's reduced to, I fear any further interference risks doing more harm than good.'

'I'm sure I don't know what you mean by "interference". It is the second time you have used the word. I cannot see it applies in a mother's case.'

'She is not a child any more,' exclaimed Mrs Gardiner, 'but a thoughtful young woman. A flighty girl might need to be cajoled into doing the right thing, but Mary is far too steady to require coercion. She is quite capable of making her own choice.'

'I was not aware that there was a choice to make. It is this young man or nothing. And that, as we both know, amounts to no choice at all.'

Her aunt did not reply immediately. When she did speak, her voice was more conciliating.

'I believe there is another gentleman for whom Mary has a preference, a very decent, respectable man, a good friend of our family. He accompanied us to the Lakes and while we were there, it seemed that a real affection was growing between him and Mary. I had great hopes for it.'

'Indeed? May I ask then, where he is? I have been in Gracechurch Street for ten days now and have not been introduced to him.'

'No,' admitted Mrs Gardiner. 'His absence is most unusual. Something went wrong in the Lakes, a misunderstanding or a quarrel of some kind. It is that, I believe, which is the cause of Mary's unhappiness.'

Sensing victory, Mrs Bennet rose up to deliver her verdict.

'Well, if the gentleman is not here, I think that tells us all we need to know about the strength of his affection. Mr Ryder, on the other hand, is both present and interested. There is such a thing, Sister, as a bird in the hand.'

Mary had heard enough. She dreaded meeting her mother on the stairs, as she emerged from the drawing room, and tried to think of somewhere to hide; but she feared that wherever she went in the house, Mrs Bennet would seek her out, and continue to hector her there. She had no choice but to put on her outdoor things and venture out into the City again. When she was halfway down Gracechurch Street, she stopped for a moment, quite overcome. The London air was smokier than usual, and the coal dust stung her eyes. That must be why she felt tears on her cheeks once more. She brushed them away angrily and walked on, with no clear sense of either direction or purpose.

CHAPTER EIGHTY-EIGHT

The next morning, promptly at eleven o'clock, Mr Ryder rang the bell. Mary was alone; her mother had gone to see Dr Simmons, and her aunt had taken the children for their morning walk. Mr Ryder looked pleased to discover this. He appeared smarter than ever, in a coat Mary had not seen before, his hair neatly brushed. He strolled into the drawing room with the greatest ease and, when invited to sit down, took up his position in what had become his accustomed chair.

'I have brought you some fresh magazines. Both the *Edinburgh* and the *Quarterly* have new editions out. I thought you would like them.'

Mary was so relieved to discuss a subject other than matrimony that she leapt upon the prospect of a rational conversation. Encouraged, Mr Ryder exerted himself to be as sensible and discriminating as he could. At the end of a lively hour, in which their discussions ranged over subjects as varied as the history of the Ottoman Empire, a new translation of Dante, and the surprising advances made in the science of cooking ranges, both felt they had acquitted themselves creditably.

'It is a while since I have had the pleasure of speaking to you alone,' Mr Ryder observed, closing the *Edinburgh Review* very decidedly, as if to indicate that their discussion would move into new territories. 'I must say I have missed it.'

'Yes, my mother has been very much with us.'

She hesitated; then decided she would speak candidly.

'I'm sorry if her manner was a little trying – if her matchmaking intentions were so very obvious. It is her way, I'm afraid. But I'm very sorry if you were at all embarrassed.'

Mr Ryder laughed.

'Really, Miss Bennet, I am not a man who is much troubled by embarrassment. You must have observed that for yourself.'

'Indeed,' she replied, 'it is not a quality I've often noticed in you.'

'But,' he continued, 'your mother's hints did have the effect of concentrating my thoughts.' He paused, then looked into her eyes with the greatest earnestness.

'I think you must have been aware, both when we were in the Lakes, and back here in London, how very much I relish your company – how very much, in fact, I admire you.'

Mary put down her copy of the *Review* carefully on the table, attempting to avoid his gaze. She very much hoped he was not about to say what she feared.

'My preference for you must have been quite plain. So I imagine it will come as no surprise when I say I have developed the greatest affection for you.'

He looked at her encouragingly, a little self-conscious now, but not unpleased with himself.

'I have allowed myself to believe,' he added smoothly, 'that my liking may perhaps be returned.'

He sat back a little, still looking at her intently, waiting for her answer.

'Your liking, sir, I do return. We have become very good friends.'

'But perhaps a little more than that? You seem to enjoy my visits – my company does not seem objectionable to you. And on Scafell – when we spoke alone – I felt a deeper connection between us. I believe you did too.'

Mary dropped her eyes. She had not imagined he would remember that.

'Yes, there was a moment when I was – when I took to heart the things you said.'

'You must understand,' he declared, excited now, 'that I meant it all – about living a life freely chosen – about leaving behind all the dreary constraints that prevent us from being truly happy.'

'I understand you spoke sincerely.'

'I would do everything in my power to make that life real. For both of us. I don't want the kind of existence that satisfies most men. I want something more than that. And I think you do, too.'

'You have always made it very clear that an ordinary domestic life would not be enough for you.'

He drew his chair closer to her. She could feel his breath as he spoke.

'I have a mind to go abroad – to Italy, as I said before – somewhere with a lake in front of me and mountains behind. Come with me! We could read poetry all day and drink wine every evening. We should be very happy!'

Mary could hardly believe this was happening. For most of her life, she had considered it impossible that any man should speak to her in such terms, let alone one as handsome as Mr

Ryder. She sat very still and looked around her. She supposed his words marked a great moment in their way. She should not die without hearing that someone wanted and desired her. Her world should have been turned upside down by such an experience; but in reality, everything looked just as it did the moment before he had spoken. The late summer sun poured through the drawing room windows, catching in its beams the London dust that could never be entirely eradicated, no matter how often the room was swept and the furniture polished.

The chintz on the sofa shone dully. The flowers on the sideboard were past their best and should really be changed. Everything was the same; and she herself was no more transformed than her surroundings. She could not deny that she was gratified to hear his words – or that they had provoked in her a brief thrill of – of – what? Was it relief? Was it satisfaction? But that had been all. She was not overwhelmed. She felt no transformative flood of feeling. Mr Ryder was not the man from whom she yearned to hear a heartfelt declaration of love.

'You are very honest, Mr Ryder, so I will attempt to be equally so in return. I'm very touched by the openness with which you've declared your feelings. But I fear I am not the right match for you. I like you very much – but I don't love you – and it would not be right to pretend that I do.'

Mr Ryder frowned, stood up, and walked to the window. His disappointment was evident as he stared down into the street, tinged with perhaps with the merest hint of surprise. Mary imagined he was not often frustrated in achieving his wishes. It seemed a new experience for him, and not an agreeable one.

'In time, you might feel differently.'

'I don't think so. And eventually, I fear I would bore you. I don't have your lightness and levity. In the end, you would find me dull.'

'That would never happen. Never.' He turned from the window to face her. 'I thought you had more courage.'

'I'm not really very brave, you know. And I don't think the life you describe would make me happy, at least not for long.'

He returned to his chair and sat down with a sigh and an air of reluctant resignation.

'Then there's not the slightest point in my raising the subject again?'

'I'm afraid not. I'm sorry if I've given you pain. I hope you'll believe it was not my intention.'

She reached out her hand and touched his arm. He sat, crestfallen for a few minutes, during which both were silent. Then he stood up, with a rueful smile.

'I thank you for your candour. I said before that I was not much troubled by embarrassment. I did not expect to be tested in that respect quite so quickly or so powerfully. But I hope to be able to summon up enough self-possession to call upon you again soon.'

'I hope you will. I should be sorry to lose your friendship.'

Once he had gone, she went to the window and pushed it up. The breeze that wafted in could hardly be called sweet-smelling, but at least it was cool. She let it play over her face as she considered what had just happened. It was a little while before it struck her that it was not exactly what she had first thought. When she considered what Mr Ryder had actually said, she realised that the word '*marriage*' had never crossed his lips. For a moment she was puzzled; what then had he meant? Then suddenly she understood – his offer had nothing to do with matrimony! She gasped as she remembered that in this very room he had assured Mrs Gardiner he looked forward to a day when men and women came together freely, without the necessity of banns or vows. Is that what he had intended for her? That she should become his mistress? That he would 'take her into keeping,' as Mr Wickham had attempted to do with Lydia?

It was so incredible and unlikely an idea that she almost laughed. She supposed she should be insulted; outraged even; but somehow she could not summon up any anger. If he had suggested apartments in Mayfair and an allowance of five hundred pounds a year, she would indeed have been deeply offended. But she understood that what he wanted was not a discreet liaison of the irregular kind – the usual mercenary transaction where money was exchanged for reputation – but something very different. Had he received enough encouragement to elaborate on his offer, she knew how he would have described it – as a partnership of like-minded spirits, emancipated from tired old customs, living free and independent under sunny skies amongst poets and artists in a world where only the emotions mattered. He had not wished to insult her; no doubt he genuinely thought such an arrangement preferable to marriage. What would he have done if she had accepted? Would he have been shocked at her boldness? And what would her mother say when she discovered the nature of the offer Mr Ryder had made her? There would be no more fond looks and encouraging smiles then. Or perhaps not. Perhaps Mrs Bennet might prefer to see her daughter living in Italy in an ambiguous connection with a rich man rather than embarrassingly present around the house as the unmarried sister nobody had wanted. The more she thought of it, Mary wasn't at all sure which possibility her mother would consider the most disappointing outcome.

CHAPTER EIGHTY-NINE

For all his assurances that he would soon return to Gracechurch Street, Mary had not expected to see Mr Ryder for a while. Surely even his easy temper must have been a little lowered by her refusal? But only a single day elapsed before his arrival was again announced, and this time to a drawing room in which Mary sat accompanied by her mother and aunt. When he came in, Mary saw that his bearing was quite different from his usual demeanour; he was formal, even a little grave. He did not sit down, but stood before her mother and aunt, and asked if he might be allowed to speak to Mary alone.

Mrs Bennet could not hide her excitement and leapt up eagerly from the sofa.

'Of course, just as you wish! Come, sister, let us leave the young people to themselves.'

Mrs Gardiner, however, was not to be hurried away.

'I should like to know first if that is what Mary wishes. Do you want us to go, Mary?'

Mr Ryder stared at Mary with a silent, beseeching appeal. She knew she could not refuse. It would be too cruel, too public a humiliation.

'Thank you, aunt. I am happy to speak to Mr Ryder alone.'

Delighted, her mother beckoned to Mrs Gardiner, who rose to join her without enthusiasm. Mrs Bennet bustled over to

Mary, and under a great show of embracing her, whispered loudly into her ear.

'This is the moment, Mary! He means to declare himself, I am sure of it!'

When the door closed, and Mrs Gardiner could be heard ushering Mrs Bennet away from the door and swiftly downstairs, Mr Ryder unbent a little.

'I must begin by thanking you for your kindness in seeing me at all. Not many ladies would been so generous after what I suggested yesterday. I am here, in part at least, to ask your forgiveness.'

'I have to admit, sir, that it was not until after you had gone that I understood exactly what your proposal implied. If I had grasped it at the time you made it, I might not have been so considerate in my reply.'

He had the grace to look uncomfortable.

'I am truly mortified. But I want you to understand that my intentions were not what they must have appeared. I did not have in mind something cheap and sordid. My head was full of ideals, not low, disreputable arrangements.'

'Yes, that was what I imagined. But I must tell you, Mr Ryder, that for the woman in the case, I am not sure there is as much distance between the two as you like to think. The world in general will not make the distinction that you do.'

'I am afraid you are right. The gulf between the world as we would like to it to be, and the world as it is remains as vast and unbridgeable as ever.' He attempted an apologetic smile. 'I know I do not deserve your indulgence, but I hope I might beg it anyway? May we sit down and speak like rational people for a moment?'

Mary agreed – the earnestness of his request would have

made it difficult to refuse – and settled herself once more on the sofa. Mr Ryder stationed himself opposite her. It was obvious now that he had come to do more than deliver an apology.

'I shall not, as they say, beat about the bush,' he began, 'but will go straight to it. I spent most of last night turning matters over in my mind. And I have concluded I shall do what I should have done yesterday, and make you an offer which cannot be misconstrued. I would be very honoured, Miss Bennet, if you would accept my hand in marriage.'

Mary could not conceal her surprise; and Mr Ryder looked across at her sadly.

'Your astonishment does not do me much credit, I feel. But perhaps that is no more than I deserve.'

'I'm sorry – but I am – that is, I never imagined – that *this* was what you intended.'

'And now that you know, may I ask what you think?'

'I'm afraid my answer must be the same I made to you yesterday. I am very sensible of the honour you do me by asking, and for understanding that marriage – and not what you suggested before – is the only offer I could seriously consider accepting. But I do not love you, Mr Ryder. And I cannot think it would be fair to either of us for me to accept you unless I did.'

He left his chair and moved to join her on the sofa. He began to speak in a serious, confiding tone Mary had not heard before.

'I knew you would say that. But I beg you to think again. We are good friends, are we not? And, I ask you, Miss Bennet, might not friendship be a firmer foundation for matrimony than love, which burns itself out in the end?'

Mary clasped her hands together. That was indeed what

her books had told her. Dr Fordyce had insisted upon it. She had thought herself prepared to marry Mr Collins on exactly such terms. But now, called on to apply the theory to the most momentous decision she had yet made in her life, she found she could not do it.

'Yes, we do very well as friends. But as husband and wife – I'm not sure our tempers would ever agree.'

'You think me too frivolous? Not thoughtful enough for you?'

'That would be presumptuous of me. I do not mean to give myself airs I'm sure I don't deserve. I only meant that our characters are so different, we should not find much common ground between us.'

He sat quite still, considering how to reply.

'Do you know why I wish to marry you, Miss Bennet?'

'No, Mr Ryder, I confess I am a little puzzled to understand it.'

'There are all the usual reasons, of course. I enjoy your company. I find you kind, unaffected, modest, and charming. Yes, don't look away, that is what I feel. But I must tell you, there is a more selfish dimension to my preference. I think you would improve me. You are serious where I am flighty. You work hard where I am lazy. You think deeply where I am shallow. Think what a good deed you would do in marrying me. Imagine how your influence would change me for the better. Perhaps, for those reasons, if for no other, you are obliged to accept me?'

He stood up, as composed as she had ever seen him.

'I won't ask for your final answer now. I will leave you with that thought. But I would be grateful if you would think it over and favour me with a reply as soon as you have decided?'

Mary's voice shook a little.

'Of course, sir.'

He bowed and was gone. Mary saw her hands were trembling. She had never heard him speak so sincerely before. What was she to think of it?

She had no time to consider further before her mother bustled excitedly into the room.

'Was I right? Did you make you an offer?'

'Yes, Mama. He did.'

'I knew it! I knew it! Did I not say so?' She was almost beside herself with joy. 'Imagine! I shall see you married, after all. And to such a respectable, good-looking man! Who would have thought it!?'

She leaned down and kissed Mary on both cheeks, a gesture she had never made before. When Mrs Gardiner entered the room, Mrs Bennet rushed over and took her hand, bursting with the good news she had to impart.

'Mary is to be married! To Mr Ryder! He has just this minute asked her.'

Mrs Gardiner started, taken aback.

'Really, Mary? Is this so? Are you really engaged to him?'

Mary looked from her mother to her aunt, taking in the joy of one and the astonishment of the other, steeling herself to say what had to be said.

'Not exactly. He has made me an offer, but I have not accepted. He has asked me to give him a final answer as soon as I can.'

Mrs Bennet grasped at Mrs Gardiner's arm as if to steady herself. When she had caught her breath, she lowered herself into a chair, from where she stared at Mary with appalled incomprehension.

'What can you mean? Why on earth did you not accept him? What if he thinks better of it?'

'If he were to behave so basely,' declared Mrs Gardiner, 'then he is hardly the sort of man we could wish Mary to marry.'

'You must write to him, this minute!' Mrs Bennet cried. 'Tell him it was girlish silliness – you were overcome – your head was turned – but you are delighted to say yes now – nothing would make you happier. Let me get a pen and some paper –'

'Please, Mama. I want to please you – really, I do – but I don't love him.'

'What do your feelings have to do with it? He is a decent enough man and he wants to give you a home. You would have been pleased enough to take Mr Collins on those terms.'

'You have mentioned that before. But since then – I can't explain it, exactly – I have changed.'

'Is that so? Well, if there *has* been a change, it has definitely been for the worse. You used to pride yourself on your rationality. Now, it seems, you have lost all sense of where your *real* interest lies.'

Mrs Gardiner placed her hand soothingly on Mrs Bennet's sleeve, attempting to calm her anger; but Mrs Bennet shook it off.

'Take care, Mary. You are about to make the biggest mistake of your life.'

CHAPTER NINETY

The next day was one of the most agitating and miserable Mary could remember. Mrs Bennet lost no opportunity to badger her, beginning before breakfast and following her from room to room to argue Mr Ryder's case. Finally, when her aunt saw that Mary could bear it no longer, she led her away to her bedroom, and closed the door behind them. They sat together on the bed, Mrs Gardiner holding Mary's hand.

'You should stay here for a while. You will never be able to reason clearly if you are always to be harassed and annoyed.'

Surprised, Mary pulled away from her aunt.

'Does that mean you too believe there is something for me to think about? That I should seriously consider accepting Mr Ryder?'

Mrs Gardiner did not reply but rose calmly and walked across to Mary's dressing table.

'Your hair is coming down at the back, my dear. Why don't you take it down and let me brush it a little for you? I have always found that very soothing to a troubled mind.'

Mary looked wary; but Mrs Gardiner was not to be denied.

'I will put it up again afterwards. I promise you it will do you good.'

Seeing she had no choice, Mary joined her at the dressing table and pulled out the pins in her hair. When it was released,

Mrs Gardiner began to brush it in long, sweeping strokes, speaking quietly as she did so.

'Now, do not be angry or upset at what I'm about to say. You know me well enough, I hope, to understand I would never urge you to act against what you believe to be right. But before you make up your mind to reject him, I think you must give Mr Ryder's offer the careful and sober consideration it deserves.'

'I believe I have already done so.'

'I know you have thought about little else since yesterday. But there are a few points I should like to mention to you. I want to be certain you have given them their proper weight before you make your decision.'

Mary knew that her aunt would not hector her; and her steady, rhythmic attentions to her hair had indeed brushed away some of her agitation. So she did not object when Mrs Gardiner began to speak.

'I shall be very candid with you,' her aunt began, 'as I believe you are sensible enough to benefit from a little straightforward advice. Now, we both know that your mother is often selfish and silly, and that you have had a great deal to bear from her. But, hard as it is to accept, that does not mean everything she says is always wrong. The truth is, Mr Ryder might indeed be a perfectly good husband for you. He has many worthy qualities. He is kind, cheerful, and obviously very fond of you. Yes, his fancies and passions make him now and then a little absurd – but that is a complaint known as youth, one which we all grow out of, soon enough.'

She laid down the stiff brush she had been using, and picked a softer one from the dressing table, before continuing.

'He is essentially good-natured, and, as even you must have

noticed, not ill-looking. It appears he has enough money to provide you with an easy life and a comfortable home. You would have a place of your own to live in, with all your things about you. I think you would like that. If you are lucky, you may also have children too. I think you would like that too.'

She paused for a moment and looked at Mary in the mirror.

'I will also observe that it is unlikely you would have much trouble managing him. Your mind, Mary, is superior to his, as both you – and he – must know.'

'He told me I would improve him,' murmured Mary, 'that it was my duty to marry him, because I possessed qualities he did not.'

'Did he indeed? I would not have thought him so perceptive. There, you see, he may have capacities as yet unthought of.'

'But I do not love him. You know that. And you also know to whom – to whom my affections truly incline.'

'Yes. I do.'

Mrs Gardiner picked up a pair of combs and a handful of pins and began to put up Mary's hair.

'On which note, I should tell you that I wrote to Tom's mother a week ago. I wanted to know where he was, and when he planned to return to London.'

Mary closed her eyes. Just to hear his name pronounced was enough to upset her.

'What did she say? Is he well? Did she have news of him?'

'He was with his family until last week. Then he left. He went off quite alone, saying he was not sure where he would go, only that he wished to be in a place where he could take solitary walks, should not be bothered, and might have time to collect his thoughts. Mrs Hayward did not seem to think this unusual. She supposed he was off to explore 'some new poetic landscape'.

'Then she does not know where he is?'

'Apparently not. She said he intends to come straight to London once he is done with walking, but she could not say when that might be.'

Mary imagined him striding through wet grass, a stick in his hand, a lone figure in an empty landscape.

'He has never written to me, you know. I have not heard a word from him since he left us at the inn.'

'I thought as much. But I'm sorry to hear it confirmed. It is not what I would have expected from him.'

'No. I would have thought the same until we went to the Lakes.'

'I knew something untoward occurred there, but as you did not wish to speak of it, I did not press you to do so.'

Mrs Gardiner had now secured Mary's hair into a neat chignon. It looked smooth and elegant – in contrast with the pale, worried face beneath it. Pleased with the result, her aunt smiled encouragingly into the mirror, and Mary was suddenly stricken with an overwhelming need to throw off her reticence, and confide to Mrs Gardiner everything that had happened. Perhaps, in the telling of it, she might at last discern some explanation for why it had ended as it did. What difference could it make now, anyway? She watched as her aunt put the brushes and combs back in their proper places and returned to sit once more on the bed, waiting expectantly. This time, Mary did not reject her unspoken invitation, but joined her there.

'You are quite right,' she said, 'something happened between us in the Lakes, but even now I am not sure what it was. When we first arrived – well, I have never been happier. Mr Hayward and I – we were so pleased with each other – so easy in each other's company. I believe I told you a little of what I felt. He was so attentive – he said such affectionate things – he suggested he had feelings for me – or I thought he did – that I allowed myself to believe he was truly attached to me. I even imagined – that is, I hoped – that he might finally declare himself while we were there. But then Mr Ryder and his party arrived, and everything changed.'

She shivered a little and reached for her shawl from the other side of her bed, wrapping it carefully around her shoulders so as not to disarrange her hair.

'It was not long afterwards that Mr Hayward began to pull away from me. I don't know how else to describe it. Suddenly, with no explanation. Each day he was cooler, more distant. At first, I was at a loss to understand his behaviour. But then I thought I understood. He was jealous of Mr Ryder.'

Mrs Gardiner took her hand once more but offered no comment; and Mary went on.

'I did all I could to suggest where my own preference lay; but he seemed not to see it. On the contrary – he seemed to grow ever more diffident, while Mr Ryder did not hesitate to show the strength of his feelings. I bore it as long as I could but then I grew impatient. Why could he not say what he wanted? And then on Scafell, there was – there was a misunderstanding. There were things I said that I believe confirmed Mr Hayward's suspicions, that made him think I returned Mr Ryder's admiration.'

She felt tears well up in her eyes.

'I wish I had not said them. I was foolish, angry, irrational – I displayed all the qualities I have worked so hard all my life not to indulge! What was wrong with me?'

'You were miserable and disappointed,' replied Mrs Gardiner gently. 'Emotions that all of us feel, no matter how hard we try to inoculate ourselves against them.'

'When we came down from the fell,' continued Mary, 'I was determined to put matters right. I thought I could explain to Mr Hayward that I had spoken in haste, that he had misinterpreted both my words and my actions. But before I could do so, he was gone.'

Mrs Gardiner drew a handkerchief from her pocket and handed it to Mary, who wiped her eyes.

'It is very unfair,' she cried. 'I did not invite Mr Ryder's attentions. I did nothing to encourage them.'

'I am sure you did not,' replied Mrs Gardiner. 'But if Tom convinced himself there was some feeling between you, that might explain his actions. Or if, for some reason, he believed it was his duty to stand aside, to let Mr Ryder do exactly as he has done and make you an offer – that could also account for his long silence and his strange, hurtful absence.'

'I don't understand!' cried Mary. 'If he feared I might prefer his friend, why did he not simply ask me what I felt? I should not have been afraid to answer a direct question. But he said nothing. Why did he not speak?'

'In matters such as these, my dear, even the best men can be very proud. They will bear a great deal of pain rather than humiliate themselves or act in a way they consider dishonourable. They will inflict it too, even if they do not mean to do so. They do not always appreciate what preserving their honour costs those around them.'

Mary hid her head in her hands and began to cry.

'Is there no way things can be made right between us?'

Mrs Gardiner stroked her hair gently; but her expression was sober.

'In all honesty, I do not know. I cannot say what Tom will do. I am very fond of him and think him incapable of acting wrongly to serve his own selfish interests. But I am not sure what he might sacrifice if he thought it was for the good of someone he cared for.'

'Even if that person does not wish it? Does not want the sacrifice?'

'He might feel – as your mother does – that the person in question is not the best judge of where their true interest lies.'

'But I am not a child, to have my decisions made for me!'

'No, you are not a child,' replied Mrs Gardiner gravely. 'But you are a woman, which, as you grow older, you are likely to discover puts you only slightly above the condition of an infant in the eyes of most of the world.'

She raised Mary's face towards her, very serious now.

'You have a hard choice to make, Mary, and what you have told me only serves to make it harder. I understand and I respect what you feel for Tom. But I cannot promise you that he will return and all will be well. It might happen, or it might not. And I'm afraid there is very little you can do about it. In such a situation, there is nothing a woman is allowed to do except wait – and who knows how long that wait will be, or with what outcome in the end? Meanwhile, Mr Ryder offers security, a settled life, a place in the world. I do not think he will stand about to see if his friend reappears and decides to make you an offer himself. He is a mild, easy sort of man, but I don't think even he would stomach that.'

'You seem to say,' cried Mary, 'that I am obliged to take the most important decision of my life in ignorance of what Mr Hayward feels, because convention dictates I must do nothing? What if I were to write to him and confess the true state of my feelings? Then at least I should be certain of his thoughts.'

'Every rule of polite society says you must not. A man would be shocked to get such a letter – amazed at the bold-ness of the woman who wrote it.'

'But you know him,' persisted Mary. 'Do you really imagine Mr Hayward would respond in so irrational a way?'

'I think his absence and his silence suggest we cannot know how he might behave in such a situation. But to return to Mr Ryder. If you have any interest in accepting him, you are really obliged to do so without any further delay. However, if you decide to reject him, you must do so in the understanding that if Tom does not step forward as you hope, you may be left with no husband at all. And I do not need to rehearse to you how hard the life of a single woman can be. In short, as your mother would have it, Mr Ryder is your bird in the hand. Only you can decide if you are ready to surrender him for the uncertain prospect of his friend in the bush.'

Mrs Gardiner stood up, touching Mary's cheek as she did so.

'It may seem as though all my arguments favour Mr Ryder. That is not quite what I intend. I see the strength of your feel-ings for Tom and appreciate you may decide they are too powerful to ignore. But you should understand what you stand to lose if you decide to gamble everything upon them.'

She bent down and gave her a final kiss.

'Tea is in half an hour, if you feel inclined. I should like you to join us if you can, but will quite understand if you do not.'

CHAPTER NINETY-ONE

Mary did not come down for tea, or for dinner. Her mother often spoke of going up to her, but Mrs Gardiner was adamant that Mary must be left alone; and with an ill grace, Mrs Bennet was at length persuaded that no good would come of berating her daughter any further.

Upstairs, Mary sat at her writing desk. When, so long ago, she had suggested to her mother that she might marry Mr Collins, she had known nothing of emotions such as those Mr Hayward had awakened in her. Even her brief encounter with John Sparrow had only hinted at the depth of feeling that possessed her now. It had not been so difficult to consider abandoning the idea of love when she had never truly experienced it. And had her ignorance continued, it was possible she might not have been entirely miserable. If by some chance, she had indeed become Mrs Collins, she thought she would have made the best of things, done everything in her power to make their partnership as pleasant as it could be; and would surely have made a better job of it than Charlotte Lucas. If she had known nothing else – if she had never had a hint of what real love looked like, she might have been content with the pale facsimile of happiness a pragmatic marriage offered. But now she had known Mr Hayward, it would not do. Now she had met a man she truly loved, she could not marry another.

The absence of love was in itself enough to make marriage to Mr Ryder impossible. But the more she considered it, the more Mary knew there was another powerful reason why she could not accept him. He had, as he intended, touched a nerve when he suggested it was her duty to marry him and make him a better man. Once, that would have appealed to her – once she would have embraced such an invitation with the greatest eagerness. What had all her hard work and study been for, if not to be directed to some practical application? And to what more noble purpose could they be put, than the moral and intellectual improvement of another human being? But she understood now this was no foundation on which to build a marriage. She did not wish to be her husband's instructor any more than she wished to be his pupil. What she sought was a union of equals, a coming together of like minds and sympathetic intellects.

At Longbourn, with the Collinses, she had seen how want of esteem was fatal to a marriage, how it soured good will, chilled relations between husband and wife, and snuffed out all sympathy. She had watched it freeze Charlotte Collins's feelings, even as it plunged her husband into an unhappiness he struggled either to comprehend or escape. But that was not the first time she had witnessed the corrosive effects of contempt in that house. She understood now very clearly how it had poisoned the marriage of her own parents. Mr Bennet's studied detachment, the ironic scornfulness of his teasing, the bitter amusement he took in the failings of others, especially his wife and daughters – all those cruel jibes flowed from the frustrated knowledge that he had married a woman he could never think of as his equal. Lizzy had once told her, with tears in her eyes, how their father had admitted the truth of this to her, on the day she had sought his permission to marry Mr Darcy. 'Let me not have the grief of seeing *you* unable to respect your partner in life.' It was not until this moment that Mary fully understood and felt for herself the significance of his bleak admonition.

She reached out for a pen and paper, pulled both towards her, and began to write.

The next morning, when she came down to breakfast, a letter with her name upon it sat bold and unmissable on her plate. She swallowed hard; she knew what it was. She had sent her message to Mr Ryder last night, had it carried to his apartments by a willing servant for a few shillings and a bottle of beer. She had written because she did not feel equipped for the strain of another interview and hoped that, in a carefully composed note, she stood a better chance of conveying both the strength of her regard and the finality of her refusal.

She picked up the letter and slipped it into her pocket, hoping that as she was the only person at the table, it had not been noticed. But just as she thought she was safe, her mother came into the room. She sat down quite calmly and poured herself some tea.

'Good morning, Mary. I was here a moment ago, and I saw you had a letter. May I trouble you to know who it was from? Did it come from Mr Ryder, by any chance?'

'Yes, Mama, it did.'

'I imagine it is in reply to a letter you have already sent him. Which presumably contained your answer to his proposal?'

Mary picked up the teapot with as much steadiness as she could muster. Now that she had made her decision, she must not waver under her mother's angry stare.

'I am astonished you did not show it to me before you sent it. Am I permitted to know what you told him?'

'I thanked him for the honour he did me in asking, but I explained that I could not marry him because I did not love him. I hoped we might continue to carry on as friends, if he wished to do so, and added I was sure he would have no trouble in finding very soon a lady who would be delighted to be his wife.'

Mrs Bennet sat very still. From down the hall, one of the Gardiner boys was heard calling to his brother.

'Prettily written, but then you always were a dab hand with a pen. Although I must tell you it is without doubt the most ridiculous and harmful piece of work you have ever produced.'

Mary steeled herself to keep her composure. She would not be intimidated by her mother's disdain.

'I made no secret of what I intended to write.'

'You did not attend to any of my objections.'

'I listened to what you said with the greatest attention, but I am persuaded I have done the right thing.'

'I always knew you to be a stubborn, contrary girl, but I did not think you a fool.'

Mrs Bennet poured herself a little more tea. Her hand, Mary saw, did not shake at all.

'You have thrown away your last and best chance of a comfortable settlement. I have no idea how you plan to live. I suppose you must fling yourself upon the charity of your sisters, for I cannot help you. What you intend to do with yourself for the rest of your life I can't imagine.'

She reached for a piece of bread.

'Nothing to say, miss? Well, perhaps you are right to stay

silent. You have made your bed and must lie on it. I did everything a mother could to help you – no one could have done more – but my efforts were not wanted. I shall go back to Jane immediately. Perhaps there my advice may still have some value.'

'I am sorry, Mama, if I have angered you.'

'I am beyond anger, Mary. I wash my hands of you.'

CHAPTER NINETY-TWO

Mary kept her countenance pretty well over the next few days, during which the house was turned upside down by the preparations for Mrs Bennet's hasty departure. She did not crumple when her mother climbed into her carriage, her whole person stiff with affront, refusing to make so much as a farewell nod to her disobedient daughter as she drove away. Later, Mary was still tolerably in control of herself when she finally plucked up courage to read Mr Ryder's letter. It was a gentlemanly epistle, containing neither recrimination nor offence. Only one line in it caused her a moment's pause. *'Had you taken me as I am, I have no doubt I should eventually have become the man I ought to be. For that, I am sorry.'* She bit her lip at that; but there was no point in torturing herself anew. She had made her choice, taken her gamble, and now she must live with the consequences.

It was not until life returned to its regular rhythm that she really began to suffer. While there had been crisis and urgency and drama, she had sustained herself tolerably well; but now there was nothing but the everyday and the ordinary to greet her when she woke. Her spirits plummeted. She could not work, could not settle to her books. She had no energy to read to the children. She had consigned herself to an existence whose main, whose only purpose was waiting; and that, she discovered, ate away at her until she could barely force herself to leave her room. At night she did not sleep but stared into the darkness, when doubts and fears crowded in upon her. Her mother was right. She was a stupid fool. She had lost the one man who would have made her truly happy. There was no reason to think he would appear now. And she had rejected his friend, who might have rescued her from a future she had feared for as long as she could remember. She would become that most despised of creatures, an old maid; and this was how it would feel, on and on and on, forever, until she was too old or too sad to care.

As she walked past Mary's door on her way to bed, Mrs Gardiner often heard her crying. She stood outside, wondering if she should go in; but what comfort she could offer? She asked her husband whether she should write again to Mrs Hayward or try to discover where Tom Hayward was walking; Mr Gardiner thought not. It was a very difficult business all round. When the law courts opened again in the autumn, Tom must return to his work, then perhaps Mr Gardiner might try to speak to him; but now it was best not to interfere. No good would come of it. The young people must be left to resolve it for themselves.

At first, her aunt was relieved when Mary was not to be found in tears quite so often; but soon she was not sure whether her dry-eyed misery was much to be preferred. In the absence of any other useful tasks with which to occupy her time, Mrs Gardiner encouraged Mary to take as much exercise as possible. Walking, she thought, must be good for her; or at least could do no harm; and each morning she urged Mary to take an airing, in the hope that she might return a little less miserable. Mary did not protest – what else had she to do? – and it was on one of these aimless walks that she felt someone fall into step beside her. Looking around, she was astonished to discover her new companion was none other than Caroline Bingley – the very last person likely to be found striding so confidently along such an unfashionable City street.

'Good morning, Miss Bennet. I have been looking for you. Your aunt was kind enough to suggest where I might find you, since you were not at home when I called.'

Her careful politeness gave no hint of the hostility of their previous encounters, but Mary was not deceived into thinking her appearance boded well.

'If I had known you planned to visit us, I would have ensured I was there to receive you.'

'But then I would have missed the pleasure of walking through such a very interesting district,' replied Miss Bingley sweetly. 'It is not a part of town with which I am at all familiar. It positively bustles, does it not?'

Mary's heart was racing, and she knew she must show no sign of weakness or hesitation in Miss Bingley's presence. She gathered up all her courage and smiled back at her with equal insincerity.

'Since you have found me, I am at your disposal. Should you like to come back to Gracechurch Street, where we could have some tea?'

'Well, that would be charming,' declared Miss Bingley, her tone implying that it would be nothing of the kind, 'but the children seemed in a particularly boisterous mood this morning. The ambience wasn't entirely conducive to the quiet conversation I had hoped to have with you.'

She touched the collar of her perfectly cut jacket, as if to brush away any specks of City dirt which had had the temerity to attach themselves it.

'I passed a respectable-looking pastry shop a few steps back. It appears they have private rooms upstairs for ladies. I suggest we take ourselves there instead.'

They walked in silence to the very shop where Mary had been taken by Mr Ryder in what now seemed a lifetime ago. Miss Bingley swept into its precincts, commanded the best table on the first floor, and ordered China tea, sliced lemon, and a plate of macaroons.

'It is not exactly Gunter's – one could hardly expect that, so far from the West End – but I think it will serve our purposes,' murmured Miss Bingley, dismissing the waiter and pouring out the tea herself. Mary had decided to say nothing until she had some idea of Miss Bingley's intention in bringing her there. She did not have long to wait.

'I don't think there is anything to be gained in making idle conversation, Miss Bennet, so I will come to the point directly.'

She wiped her mouth delicately with a napkin.

'I understand that Mr Ryder came to visit you not long ago. I should be grateful to know what he spoke of while he was there.'

Mary looked up, nonplussed. She had not expected such a direct approach. She was surprised to find her apprehension falling away, replaced by resentment that Miss Bingley should see fit to question her in such a manner.

'It was a private matter. It seems odd you should ask about it.'

Miss Bingley inclined her head, as if to indicate that although she had heard the displeasure in Mary's voice, she did not choose to acknowledge it.

'He mentioned to me that he saw you.'

'Then you should ask him about what was said.'

'But I am asking you.'

'I'm not sure with what aim.'

'Was there a declaration of some kind?'

At this, Mary finally awoke from the miserable lethargy which had engulfed her so long. Who was this woman to interrogate her in this way? What right did she have to demand answers from her? All the humiliation and misery of the last months suddenly turned into a kind of rage. She would not be treated like this. She had had enough and would no longer bear it.

'That is an extraordinary question. I cannot imagine why you think you have the right to ask it.'

'That was the impression Mr Ryder gave me.'

'I am amazed he felt able to discuss our conversation with one whom it did not concern. Did he volunteer this information freely? Or did you demand it of him?'

Mary was pleased to see Miss Bingley's composure waver a little.

'I saw he was upset. When I asked why, he seemed happy enough to tell me. He is not a man who hides his feelings from himself or others. He implied you had not given him reason to hope.'

'If you have had that from him, I do not see why you require anything further from me.'

'Because I wish to understand from you directly if it is true. Or whether it is just a ploy to whet his interest, to make him even more eager to have you. After all, that was a ruse that worked very well for your sister. Darcy never wanted her more than when she was clever enough to refuse him!'

Mary was really angry now but determined not to show it. Miss Bingley should not have the satisfaction of knowing she had provoked her.

'That is as ignorant as it is insulting,' she replied deliberately. 'Elizabeth would never trifle knowingly with the affections of a decent man. Nor would I.'

Miss Bingley leaned across the table, her face taut with bitterness.

'Yes, you Bennets all talk a fine game, but in practice, you're as hard-headed as the most consummate husband-hunters. You have a remarkable record of reeling in the men you want, and then looking around as if it was all an amazing accident, nothing to do with you at all, just love finding a way! I've seen it happen twice, in front of my eyes, so please don't play the innocent with me.'

'As I do not love Mr Ryder, it would make no sense for me to marry him.'

Miss Bingley laughed out loud.

'Oh, come, Miss Bennet, we are not children! When you think of the alternative, marrying a man one does not love may be the most rational decision a woman can make. Do not pretend you haven't considered it. Especially now that Ryder is to be so rich. I cannot believe you were unaffected by *that* piece of news.'

For the first time, Mary was genuinely surprised by Miss Bingley's words. To give herself something to do while she marshalled her thoughts, she took the napkin off her lap, folded it carefully, and placed it on her plate.

'I have no idea what you mean.'

'Please don't treat me as a fool.'

'I do not know what you are talking about. If you will

not enlighten me, I do not see how we can continue this conversation.'

Mary held Miss Bingley's gaze, determined not to be the one who looked away. In the end, it was Miss Bingley who flinched, accepting that she would learn no more of Mary's true intentions without disclosing what she knew.

She had had the story from Mr Ryder himself. He told her that shortly before their trip to the Lakes, he had been called to Kent, to attend Lady Catherine de Bourgh at Rosings. There he had found his relative so beside herself with fury and frustration that it had taken some time for him to understand the cause of her anger. A whole day passed before the terrible truth was revealed to him in all its horror and shame – her ladyship's daughter, Miss Anne de Bourgh, was engaged to be married – to her doctor. 'You might think such a thing impossible, Mr Ryder – it *should* be impossible – if there were any gratitude and obedience in this world, it *must* be impossible – but I regret to tell you that it is not.' The affair, it appeared, had been going on under Lady Catherine's unseeing eyes for some time – 'for years, Mr Ryder, years!' – the silent couple concealing their affections until Miss de Bourgh reached her majority. 'Think of the deceit. The flouting of my authority!' Now that she was twenty-one, however, Miss de Bourgh was free to contract a marriage with whomsoever she chose, however distressing her intentions were to her mother. 'This is how I am repaid for a lifetime's care and trouble. This is how I am defied and humiliated.'

Lady Catherine now demanded that Mr Ryder seek to achieve what her own efforts had failed to do, and bring her daughter to her senses. He doubted very much whether his endeavours would have any more success than her ladyship's;

and he was quickly proved right. His attempts to make Miss de Bourgh consider, if not her own position, then what she owed to her mother, fell on very stony ground indeed. It was quickly evident that she had no sympathy at all for a parent whom she considered had always bullied and belittled her; and that she could not wait to begin a new life at as great a distance away from her as possible. It was an additional blow to Lady Catherine to discover, so late in their dealings with each other, that her daughter's will was quite as strong as her own, and not to be deflected by either threat or inducement.

When it was certain Mr Ryder could do no good, there was nothing left for the beleaguered Lady Catherine to do but apply to her nephew for his help. Only in such pressing circumstances was she reluctantly prepared to acknowledge Mr Darcy's position as the titular head of the family. But when the Darcys arrived at Rosings, she began to regret the decision to invite them. Neither her nephew nor his wife seemed inclined to pursue the matter with the harshness she thought appropriate. Mrs Darcy she suspected of harbouring some sympathy for her daughter's situation, having come upon them more than once closeted in conversations she could not but regard as disloyal; and she did not doubt Mrs Darcy's opinions were reflected in her husband's ultimate conclusions as to the best way to proceed. Having interviewed the doctor, Mr Darcy declared himself satisfied that he was no fortune-hunter, but a respectable man with a genuine affection for Miss de Bourgh. That lady was as determined to marry him as he was to marry her; and it was therefore difficult and probably unprofitable to imagine how or even why, they should be prevented from doing so.

Miss Bingley took a sip of her tea. Mary sat in silence until she was ready to continue.

Mr Darcy, it appeared, had advised Lady Catherine to reconcile herself, with what good grace she could muster, to a union that was likely to take place, whatever she thought of it; and to do what she could to salvage some fond feelings in her daughter by not appearing vindictive. Lady Catherine paid not the slightest attention to this latter advice; but she was finally persuaded to agree to the marriage itself, once Miss de Bourgh made it clear she was quite prepared to elope with her doctor if her mother refused to countenance more usual arrangements.

Lady Catherine laid down two conditions. The marriage should take place as privately as possible, with all who knew of it agreeing to say nothing about what had transpired. And the happy couple should immediately afterwards go abroad and stay there, on as prolonged a honeymoon as was possible. When these requests were agreed to, they were married, by private licence, in the drawing room at Rosings.

'I believe,' observed Miss Bingley, 'it was your old friend Mr Collins who did the honours – he was always ready to do anything in his power to oblige her ladyship. And Mr Darcy made all the arrangements, ensuring that – for the moment at least – it has attracted no public attention nor any breath of scandal. Rather as he did for your sister Lydia, as I recall?'

Describing the misfortunes of others had quite restored Miss Bingley's self-assurance, and she poured herself more tea with all the calmness in the world. Mr Ryder, she continued, had attended the wedding, as had Mr and Mrs Darcy, although Lady Catherine had not lowered herself by doing so. She had been compelled to accept the fact of her daughter's choice, but had resolved never to forgive her for it; and while Miss de Bourgh was exchanging her vows, her mother was consulting lawyers, determined to extract via the law the revenge she had not been able to elicit by any other means. By the time the new husband and wife were on board the boat to Calais, Lady Catherine had decided exactly what was to be done. The properties bequeathed to Miss de Bourgh by the terms of her father's will could not be withheld from her, except by ingenious legal challenges, which were certain to be protracted and whose outcome must be unknown. But Lady Catherine's own money remained hers to dispose of as she wished; and she was absolutely determined it should not be bestowed upon such a wicked, ungrateful child as her daughter had revealed herself to be.

'So,' concluded Miss Bingley, 'to everyone's surprise, including his own, she made Mr Ryder her heir. Mr Darcy and his family she considered wealthy enough already; and I think she had a particular disinclination to add to the riches your sister already enjoys. There being no other near relation, Mr Ryder was the lucky man. He will not be as wealthy as Mr Darcy. But he will certainly be what is called "comfortable". Whoever marries him will be assured of a very agreeable situation.'

For a moment, Mary sat stupefied. It was some time before she spoke.

'I am surprised no word of this story has yet found its way to Gracechurch Street. But I do not see why you think it should affect my feelings for Mr Ryder. If I did not encourage his advances before I was aware of his good fortune, you cannot think I would change my mind when I was told of it.'

Miss Bingley smiled her little smile.

'I think it is entirely to Mr Ryder's credit that he did not mention it to me himself,' continued Mary. 'A more foolish man – certainly a less honourable one – might have thought it would make a difference. And with some women, it might well do so.'

'That is a strike at me, I imagine,' said Miss Bingley, 'but I do not feel it. I cannot be lectured by a Bennet on the relationship between love and money and be hurt by it. It is impossible for me to take your protestations at face value when I consider your sisters' histories, or what your mother would be likely to advise, were you to confide in her.'

Mary picked up her cup and drank what remained of her tea. She did not hurry as she stood up, plucked her coat from the hook on the wall, and began to put it on.

'You have insulted me and my family in every possible way,' she said quietly. 'There is really nothing more to be said between us.'

Now Miss Bingley rose, pushing her chair to the wall with such force that it scraped along the floor.

'Can you promise me you will not marry Mr Ryder? That your refusal was not mere strategy on your part?'

'I make no promise, I give you no undertaking. I owe you nothing at all.'

'But I *know* you don't want him – it's the friend for whom you have such a *tendresse*, isn't it, the boring lawyer? Does he know how you feel? Perhaps someone should enlighten him?'

The venom in Miss Bingley's voice was unmistakeable, but Mary was surprised to discover herself unaffected by it. With an evenness she did not think she possessed, Mary was quite calm as she tied the ribbons under her hat.

'For a long time, I was frightened of you, just as you intended me to be. But your power over me is finished now. I see you for what you are – a bitter, angry spirit, so eaten up with unhappiness that you can do nothing but make others as miserable as yourself. If I was a better woman, I should pity you. Instead I am merely grateful that you cannot touch me any more because I will not allow it.'

Mary straightened her hair and picked up her things, with as much equanimity as if she had been bidding Miss Bingley a polite farewell.

'If you wish to make trouble, you will do so, whatever I say. But I will not live in fear of it and am therefore quite prepared to tell you what you seem so desperate to know. Yes, I do love Mr Hayward. He is the only man whom I think would ever make me happy. No, I have no wish to marry Mr Ryder. That is the truth. You may do with it what you will.'

She turned and left the room, closing the door quietly after herself, and walking down the stairs, head held high. It was only when she reached the street that she trembled a little with shock. But she mastered herself; she was not ashamed of how she had conducted herself or of what she had said. She did not look up once at the great bay window of the pastry shop, behind which she knew Miss Bingley still sat, but walked steadily into Leadenhall Market, heading towards Gracechurch Street and home.

CHAPTER NINETY-THREE

Once back at the Gardiners', Mary felt at first as though a great weight had slipped from her shoulders. She had slain the dragon that was Miss Bingley by calling upon hitherto unsuspected reserves of bravery and self-possession. She had spoken her mind and told the truth, and there was relief of a kind in that. She did not allow herself to dwell on the extraordinary story of Mr Ryder's good fortune. For when she did think of it, it could not help but raise him in her estimation. His declining to mention it suggested a delicacy on his part which was wholly admirable, a desire to be accepted for himself and not for his expectations. That made her think better of him as a man; but it did not encourage her to reconsider his offer. Any doubts that had lingered about whether she had been right to refuse it had been swept away in the tea shop. The strength of her affections had been put to the test, and her bleak declaration to Miss Bingley had summed up the truth of the matter. She loved Mr Hayward and only he would make her truly happy.

This knowledge, however, was not calculated to bring her any peace. She supposed she must assume whatever affection he had once felt for her was quite obliterated – what else could explain his long-continued silence? But that did not prevent her from thinking about him at all hours of the day and night. She missed him at the dinner table, where his jokes and observations had made her laugh, and in the drawing room, where she had first heard him talk properly of poetry. Her heart contracted when the children asked where he was, and when he – and his pockets full of sweets – would return. She no longer wore the dress made from the cotton he had recommended when they first met at Harding and Howell's, but folded it up and put it away. Every knock at the door, every arrival of the post was a new occasion for pain. She did not know how she would face him when he returned to London, as she knew eventually he must. How she would conduct herself? What would she say? No matter how often she imagined it, she did not know.

As the days went by, Mary attempted to impose some discipline on her feelings, telling herself she must find ways not to dwell upon her sadness. To abandon herself to misery was to allow the Miss Bingleys of the world victory over her, and confirming the correctness of all her mother's opinions on the relations between marriage and happiness. In their different ways, Mary understood that neither of these ladies would have been disappointed to learn that she was miserable; and this spurred her into making efforts that she would not otherwise have had the energy or spirits to attempt. Thus, she forced herself to rise early, to have her hair properly dressed, and to keep herself neatly turned out. These seemed minor victories over such a profound sense of loss, but she saw them as essential battles in a campaign she could not afford to lose. If she allowed unhappiness to swallow her up, she might never escape its clutches again. So she dusted off her books, got out pen and paper, and tried to think of a new course of study to engage her mind. She played with the Gardiner children; she practised on the piano once more. And when she went out on her City walks, she pushed herself to explore beyond her usual territories, forcing herself to discover new streets, unfamiliar monuments and different districts. It was always better, she found, to do something rather than nothing; and thus, for week after week, she occupied herself.

It was on exactly such a journey that one afternoon Mary found herself in an area she did not know at all. She had gone beyond St Paul's, and was attempting to find her bearings, when she heard the sound of shouting and singing approaching along the street. She shrank into the shelter of a nearby shopfront, resolving to escape inside if the noise proved to indicate trouble; but as it drew nearer, it became clear that it was a very good-natured hullaballoo. She stole cautiously out of her refuge to see what it was, and beheld a large group of young men, cheering and huzzahing as they marched along. On the pavement, an older man stood watching them with the greatest satisfaction, beating time to their singing with his stick. He looked prosperous and respectable enough for a woman alone to speak to him; and Mary decided to risk an approach.

'Excuse me, sir, but may I ask you what is going on? Who are the marchers and what are they celebrating?'

The gentleman doffed his hat and smiled at her, seemingly pleased to be asked.

'Why, ma'am, they are medical students from Barts Hospital. They have finished their exams and they are parading in triumph, off to a grand dinner at a tavern to mark their efforts.'

He gazed at them indulgently and turned back to Mary.

'I was one of them myself more years ago than I care to admit; and I like to see the old traditions kept up.'

'They will be doctors then, sir, as you are now?'

'Yes, if they survive their time on the wards. Usually there is one amongst them who has done better than the rest and is appointed their king for the day. He is distinguished by the wearing of a crown of oak leaves – like the Caesars you know – ah, here he is now, right in the midst of them!'

He pointed at the crowd, and Mary found herself looking directly at the flushed, happy face of John Sparrow. He was a young man now rather than a great boy; but there was no mistaking his familiar features. The oak leaf crown had slipped a little and gave him a slightly tipsy look; but beneath his excitement, she could see a sharp, intelligent face. His fellows patted him on the back, cheered and joshed him; it was plain he was utterly at home in their company. *He has found his place*, thought Mary, deeply moved. *He is happy. I did not injure him so badly that he could not recover his spirit. He will become everything he wished to be, with his brass plate on the door and his carriage outside*. She turned away, for she did not wish to catch his eye and ruin the moment. She was part of his past and had no place in his joyous, noisy present.

Her face was shining as she bid the older man goodbye.

'Thank you so much, sir, for explaining it to me. I am so glad to have seen such a remarkable thing.'

He tipped his hat to her again as she left, pleased to find that he was not old enough to have lost his appreciation for the smile of a charming young woman.

Mary did not know quite why it was, but somehow her encounter with John Sparrow began to soothe her anxious mind. Seeing him so carefree and fulfilled released her from a burden which she had been carrying for so long that she did not appreciate the weight of it until it slid away. If she was not any happier, she felt steadier, more able to contemplate a future in which Mr Hayward played no part. If she must find her way forward alone, then so be it. Perhaps the life of a single woman need not be as miserable and as humiliating as was universally insisted upon. Perhaps much depended on the circumstances and the woman. After all, Mary thought, she would never be as poor and as desperate as the unfortunate Miss Allen. Her sisters' marriages had rescued her from that fate. They would always provide her with a place to live. She should never find herself hurrying up the drives of country houses to teach young ladies the piano, unable to say where she should find her next shilling. She would always have some little space that was hers; and perhaps a room of one's own was all a thinking woman really required. She could read and study. She might even attempt to write something herself. Mrs Macaulay had shown it might be done. Why should she not follow in those footsteps? It was hardly what Mrs Bennet would regard as a suitable occupation for her daughter. But then her mother had washed her hands of her. She was free now to think as she wished on such matters.

Through all this, Mrs Gardiner watched her niece, uncertain what to think. She admired Mary's strength of will. She applauded her bravery. She was relieved to see her no longer so hopelessly, desperately miserable; but for all her dry-eyed fortitude, there was something quashed and doused about her that was painful to watch. Resignation was clearly to be preferred to the alternative, but perhaps only just.

CHAPTER NINETY-FOUR

Mary was upstairs putting her books in order one quiet afternoon when she heard the bell sound, the front door open, and a visitor arrive. She had trained herself to pay little attention to such comings and goings – why should they concern her? – and continued dutifully to her task. She was so absorbed that she did not hear Mrs Gardiner come hurrying up the stairs, did not notice her at all until, breathing hard, her aunt burst through the door into her room.

'Mary, *he* is here! Tom is here – downstairs – in the drawing room.'

Mary was dumbstruck. These were the words that for so long she had longed to hear. Time and time again, during dark, sleepless nights, on silent afternoons in the airless drawing room, as she walked down dusty City streets, she had imagined them being said, had wondered how they would sound, what she would feel, how she would act. And now it had actually happened, and she sat rooted to the spot, speechless.

'Come, this won't do. He is asking for you. You *must* go down.'

Mary saw her aunt, felt her agitation and concern, heard the anxiety in her voice – but all these things somehow seemed at a great remove from her. It was if she stood quite apart from herself, watching her aunt, the room, her books, all from a distance. Then suddenly the shock passed – she understood – took a deep, shuddering breath – and was somehow herself again.

'He is really here? He has come at last?'

'Yes, yes, he has, and he wants to talk to you. Do please come down.'

Mrs Gardiner held out her hand; but Mary did not take it.

'I need a minute alone. To compose myself. Please tell him I will be there shortly. I have waited so long for him, I think he may wait a little now for me.'

Mrs Gardiner looked at her imploringly.

'Mary, I beg of you, do not give in to angry feelings yet. Give him a chance. Let him speak to you.'

'I will. But I hope he will also listen to me. And I cannot come down before I have it clear in my head exactly what I want to say.'

Mrs Gardiner hesitated; but Mary was immoveable. Once her aunt had gone, she sat staring blankly at her writing desk, before laying her head gently against its cool smooth surface. She could smell the faint scent of wood polish, and it occurred to her that it was not quite as pleasant as the recipe of which Charlotte Collins had been so proud. She closed her eyes and remained there motionless for a minute. Then she sat up, reached into a drawer, and pulled out a small black bag. Inside, she found the Greek dictionary Mr Collins had given her and withdrew from its pages the single slip of paper on which he had written a few words of Greek.

'Our happiness depends on ourselves.'

She looked at it intently, then folded it up and pushed it

down the front of her dress. Only then did she smooth down her hair and make her way downstairs.

It took a great deal of courage to walk into the drawing room. She hesitated for a moment outside the door. Then somehow she was inside, and there he was, standing at the long window, staring out into the street. A dark man in a dark jacket. Whenever she had thought of him, he had always been wearing the loose brown coat he wore on the fells. Now here he was, in City clothes. Tall, and thinner than when she last saw him. When he turned towards her, she was shocked – he looked as drawn and as unhappy as she knew she did herself.

'Miss Bennet. I cannot tell you how pleased I am to see you again.'

At the sound of his voice, her self-control nearly deserted her; but she was determined not to falter.

'Yes, sir. It has been too long, I think.'

He moved towards her and was about to reply – but Mary interrupted him.

'I did not mean that as a mere politeness. It has been nearly two months since we last saw you.'

'I know it,' he answered, his voice grave. 'I have counted every day. Every hour.'

He stopped, standing in the silent, sunlit drawing room, as if he would go no further towards her without some encouragement.

'I am here to tell you how very much I have missed you. And to discover if – as I very much hope – you may have missed me too.'

He is very brown, thought Mary, no doubt tanned by his walking. It made his eyes seem very bright in his face.

'I have come to explain, Mary, if you will allow me to do

so. And to ask your forgiveness. I know I do not deserve it. But I hope you will grant it anyway.'

When he spoke her name, she thought she must capitulate, give in to the desire rising up in her to let him talk and explain as much as he wished; but she made herself resist such a surrender. There were things she was resolved to say, and she would not be prevented from doing so, even by her own unruly feelings.

'I know it is not usual,' she said, surprised at the steadiness of her voice, 'for a woman to put herself forward in this way, but I hope on this occasion you will allow me to speak first. I have had a great deal of time to think about what I would say if this moment were to come to pass. And now that it has, I want very much to make no mistakes. Shall we sit down?'

She moved to the sofa, and arranged herself there, back straight, head held high. He took his place opposite her in the chair he had so often occupied in that room, and looked at her, serious, expectant.

'I hope you will excuse me if I begin with a personal observation.' Mary knew her words were stiff and formal; but she had chosen them carefully. She was determined not to lose her composure, and the chilly exactness of her words helped her preserve it.

'For as long as I can remember, I have tried to use my intellect to understand the world. I have been teased and laughed at for it, as it is not thought a very attractive quality in a woman; but when I was lonely and unhappy, as I was for much of my life, it served me well enough.'

She shifted in her seat. She was nervous; but she had begun and knew now she could continue.

'Then I met you, and everything changed. You introduced

me to poetry. You showed me the beauty of the natural world. You made me laugh. You gave me warmth and kindness and affection. In short, you taught me to feel, as I had never done before.'

He sat absolutely still, making no further attempt to speak.

'And I did feel, Mr Hayward. I experienced every kind of emotion in your company. It began as friendship – but soon I began to think – I allowed myself to hope – that you intended something more.'

She cast her eyes down. She wanted to continue, but was not sure she could look at him as she did so.

'That made me very happy. In fact, I don't think I have ever been happier. But then, up in the Lakes, everything went wrong. I felt I had lost your affection – but I did not know why. The sensible thing, the rational thing would have been to ask how I had offended you, and not to have given up until I had discovered the cause of your change of heart. But my emotions got the better of me. I was angry, confused, unhappy – and in the end, I said nothing. And neither did you.'

Down in the hall, Mr Gardiner's prized gilt clock began to strike the half hour. Its chime was very carrying; and Mary paused until it was done.

'I cannot say what kept you silent. I only know I quickly began to regret my own stupid failure to speak. But by then you had gone away. And I could do nothing to put right my mistake. I was told that as a woman, it was not my place to act. All I could do was wait. That is what I have been doing until this very afternoon.'

Mary looked up, and their eyes met.

'But I think I have done enough waiting now.'

She leaned forward, and the words began to spill out of her.

'For I must tell you, sir, that some weeks ago I made a promise to myself that if we ever saw one another again, I would hold back no longer, but would speak, would act, no matter what the world thought of it. If you lacked the courage to declare yourself candidly, I did not. I swore I would confess my feelings to you regardless of the consequences. I would rather tell the truth and risk humiliation than pass up the chance of happiness because I was not brave enough to say honestly what I felt.'

Now that she had come to the point, Mary's spirits almost failed her. She could not stay where she was, but rose and stood behind the sofa, grasping its chintz back tightly with both hands, willing herself to break every rule of propriety, modesty, and good behaviour and continue.

'So this is what I wish to say. I love you, Mr Hayward. I have loved you for a very long time and know I will never love anyone as much as I love you. You are the only man who could ever make me happy, and I have missed you – oh, I have missed you so very, very much.'

Then her self-possession finally deserted her – her voice broke and a sob escaped her. And before she knew it, he was beside her, had taken her in his arms and was holding her tight against him.

'Mary, my own dearest Mary – everything you say – it is exactly what I feel – I love you, Mary, so very deeply – I am so very sorry if I hurt you – I shall never do so again – all I want is to love you as you deserve – for the rest of my life, if you will allow it.'

He released her a little, just enough to look earnestly into her eyes.

'I love you even more for the courage of your words, for

your having found the bravery to say them. There is no one like you – so serious, so severe, so true – how could I *not* love you?'

He stroked her hair; she lifted up her face to smile at him, and he kissed her very tenderly. For a moment, they did not move, but stood together in a triumphant embrace, utterly content. She laid her head against his heart, certain it was where she belonged.

'Shall we be married, then?' he whispered in her ear. 'As soon as ever we can? Will you have me as your husband, Mary?'

She thought she might die of happiness. But that is a very rare event, even when the dearest wish of one's heart has been so thoroughly and unexpectedly gratified. So for all the delight that coursed through her, she was able to make a tolerably sensible reply.

'Oh, yes, Mr Hayward. I should be proud to be your wife – there is nothing I want more.'

They gazed at each other, suffused with pleasure, as if it were impossible to imagine anything as fascinating, as magical, and as entirely and utterly satisfying as themselves and their love for each other.

'You must learn to call me Tom, you know. If we are to be married, it is entirely proper!'

'Tom,' she repeated quietly. It was exciting to say it – but intimate too. When she thought what it suggested – how things would be between them now – she caught her breath. 'It feels a little strange at first. But I'm sure I shall come to it.'

'I hope so. I'm not sure I can endure being Mr Hayward any longer to a woman I have kissed.'

'Really, for shame!'

He leaned over and kissed her again, very gently, on her

cheek and on her brow, before leading her to the sofa, where they sat down together. Then his arm was round her, and she noticed for the first time the way his hair curled over his collar. She liked that very much, she thought. Eventually, she might find the courage to run her fingers through it – but not yet.

'Oh, Tom' – she felt she could say his name now – 'my heart is so full – I don't know what to say – or how to describe what I feel.'

'There is nothing you need to say. It is I, not you, who should be explaining myself.'

He removed his encircling arm and sat up, a little apart from her.

'Mary, I am so grateful – so very, very thankful – that you have returned my love. But I am not sure I deserve it. Nothing in my behaviour over the last months would suggest that I do. I can only imagine the pain I must have caused you. I don't how I could have been such a fool.'

He stood up and began to pace about the room.

'I should like to try to account for my actions, if you are prepared to listen. I can neither excuse nor justify them – I know they do not do me much credit – but I cannot leave you in ignorance as to why I acted as I did.'

'I must admit,' she replied, 'that I long to know the truth of it.'

Relieved, he returned to the sofa and took up his place beside her once more. Then he began, describing the origins of his fondness for her – how he had enjoyed her company from the very beginning – how their conversations on poetry had delighted him – how her presence had gradually become essential to him, the source of more and more of his happiness. He had looked forward to their meetings with ever-increasing pleasure – thought their tastes agreed perfectly – found himself happier in her company than in that of anyone else – and in short, soon knew himself to be very seriously attached.

'In truth, I knew I loved you,' he confessed. 'But I did not know what to do about it. I was uncertain. I worried I was not grand enough to make you an offer. That I was – well, let us say, too undistinguished for you.'

Mary was astonished. It was a moment before she found her voice.

'But why should you think such an extraordinary thing? Our circumstances – the circumstances of our families – they do not seem so dissimilar.'

'No, perhaps not. But your elder sisters – their situations are very different. Both have married very wealthy men. Powerful too, in the case of Mr Darcy. My prospects, while respectable, cannot compete with his. I knew I should never be able to offer you Pemberley, Mary. Or even what Mrs Bingley enjoys.'

'And do you seriously think I would have cared?' Mary exclaimed. 'I am *not* my sisters! I have been compared to them for as long as I can remember, but I am *not* them, and have no wish to be! My expectations are very different. And if you had only asked me, I could have willingly – readily – eagerly told you so!'

Her vehemence made Mr Hayward smile. 'If I did not understand that before, I know it now.' He reached out and stroked her hair. 'It is true I did not speak when I might have done. But I had a plan I was convinced would answer. I did not consider I had abandoned the idea of making you an offer. I imagined I had merely postponed it.'

From the remoter regions of the house, the voices of the Gardiner children were suddenly to be heard, loud, confident, excited. They must have finished their morning lessons, thought Mary. Mr Hayward paused until they had thundered past the drawing-room door, then went on.

'I had reason to believe that I stood on the brink of making a great advance in my profession. You remember those two cases over which I laboured so long and hard before we went to the Lakes? I knew if I won them, they would involve a great step up for me. I told myself I should wait and see how they turned out. If I was successful, I should be in a better position to speak to you as I wished. I thought I had all the time in the world. But then my old friend Will Ryder and his entourage arrived in our little circle.'

'Yes,' replied Mary. 'Nothing was quite the same after that.'

'I thought at first Will was entirely taken up with Miss Bingley,' continued Mr Hayward. 'She certainly made her preference for him very plain. And sometimes it appeared as if her admiration was not unwelcome. I suppose it is difficult for any man to remain entirely indifferent to such an obvious liking. But then I began to notice how he sought you out and took pains to talk to you. He told me he often called on you here. Something about you intrigued him, and I began to wonder if you did not – well, I shan't say returned his feelings, exactly – but I know he can be very winning. I did not know whether he had charmed you as he has so many others.'

'And again, I must ask – you did not think to speak to me directly?'

'I wish more than anything that I had. But I suppose I was afraid of what you might answer. I think many men lack confidence in this respect. In truth, we are not all as bold or as confident as we are supposed to be in these matters. Diffidence is far more common amongst us than is generally admitted.'

He looked a little shame-faced.

'Although I was sometimes uneasy, I did not yet feel able to act. Instead, I applied myself to my work and did all in my power to banish uncharitable ideas. My feelings for you proved far stronger than my doubts. And by the time we began our excursion to the Lakes, I was in a far happier state. I had won both my cases and had been given my promotion as a result. My expectations were considerably improved. I was sufficiently confident now to make you an offer and was fully resolved to ask you. There were a number of occasions when I nearly began upon it – I almost did so that day when we were drawing together. But before I settled on the right time and the right place to speak – out of the blue, Will Ryder and his party appeared once more in our company. I confess I did not know what to make of it.'

'I thought you blamed me for his arrival, that you imagined I had encouraged it in some way.'

'I could not rid myself of the unworthy suspicion that even if you had not actually invited him, you had hinted that his presence might not be unwelcome. It was unjust to you, I know. But I was unhappy and not thinking clearly. Then, after dinner one night at the inn, you may recall that Ryder asked to speak to me privately about his affairs. As a result of what he told me, I convinced myself I must not think about you any more.'

As he spoke, Mary discovered that on the night when she had leaned over the bannisters, obscurely troubled as she watched the two men in intense conversation, Mr Ryder had confided to his friend the entire story of what had passed at Rosings, describing Miss Anne de Bourgh's unsanctioned marriage, Lady Catherine's fury, her subsequent determination to disinherit her daughter and bestow instead her personal fortune upon his own surprised but grateful head. He had sought the advice of Mr Hayward, not just as a friend, but also as a lawyer; and had begged him to act on his behalf in managing the business involved in such a delicate transaction.

'I felt I could not refuse such an urgent request. Ryder was anxious to find someone in whom he could place absolute trust, and on whose discretion he could entirely rely. Lady Catherine had informed him that if the least hint of her situation were to leak out, she should reconsider her decision; I was sworn to the completest secrecy. Naturally, he described to me the contracts drawn up by her lawyers; and as a result, I knew exactly how very generously he would one day be provided for. It was an amount considerably in excess of my most optimistic expectations for myself, even after my victories at the Bar. And I knew Ryder thought well of you. I decided there and then that it would be dishonourable in the extreme for me to speak to you as I had intended. If you said yes – as I very much hoped you would – I would be denying you the chance to accept any proposal Ryder might make to you, which would have placed you in a situation far more advantageous than anything I could offer.'

'Oh, Tom, you could not have been more mistaken! If you had offered me the choice – I would have told you how much I cared for you, that I would always choose you over any other man, no matter what their expectations.'

'I know that now. But then I was not so sure.'

'How was I to make clear to you what I felt? I did my best to show you how I felt by all the petty hints and signals permitted to us poor females. But it seemed to me as if you did not or would not see what I was trying to tell you. I began to think I had misunderstood your feelings for me, that you only wished to push me away.'

'I told myself that I must harden my heart against my feelings for you, that although it looked cruel, I was acting in your best interests. I argued that any hurt I caused you would not last long once Ryder had made his offer. But it was one thing to tell myself I must withdraw. It was quite another to see the confusion and disappointment on your face as I tried to do so. And it was all but unbearable to watch Ryder, as I thought, step so eagerly into the breach. That day on Scafell was almost insupportable for me. It seemed he was doing his utmost to make himself agreeable to you – and that you had begun to take notice of his efforts.'

'I admit I was angry with you and he was kind and appreciative. He did not seem confused about his feelings – and I will confess there was a moment when I found that consoling.'

'I cannot blame you. But when Ryder refused to take the advice of the guide and leave before the rain arrived – when he looked to you for support and you gave it – I was so deeply wounded that I thought I could not endure it.'

'I know, I saw – and am sorry for it.'

'You need not be. I had many opportunities to make things right; I did not seize them. I was blinded by my own reticence – by a misplaced sense of pride and honour. And then I made matters even worse. I thought I had the strength to give you up if I convinced myself it was for your benefit. But after Scafell, I knew I could not actually witness what in practice that must mean. It was impossible for me to stand and watch what I thought would happen next, as Ryder recommended himself to you with ever greater success. That was why I left. I wrote that letter to Mrs Gardiner and I fled, as quickly and as desperately as I could. It was probably the most impulsive act I have ever committed – and the most stupid.'

He stood up again and began to walk round the room once more.

'As soon as I reached Hampshire, I knew I had made the most dreadful mistake. I had given up the woman I loved best in the world – and for what? For some perverse idea of honour? What was I to do? I did not know, and so I did nothing – the very worst thing of all. I was paralysed. I dreaded each day that a letter would arrive, announcing your engagement to Ryder. And when this became a torture to me, I fled again. I sought out a place where no message could find me, where I could find a little peace to put my thoughts in order and think what I must do next. I went to Herefordshire, and I walked for a week above Tintern Abbey.'

At this, Mary could not help but smile.

'You consoled yourself amongst Mr Wordworth's "steep and lofty cliffs"?'

'I am predictable, am I not? But the walk settled my mind and bolstered my courage. I understood I must come back into the world – I must return to London and discover what had happened – and here I am.'

'I could not be more glad of it,' replied Mary softly. She held out her hand, inviting him to sit again beside her. This time, it was he who leaned his head on her shoulder.

'I am so very sorry, Mary. I acted wrongly. I hope you will forgive me.'

'There were moments when both of us behaved irrationally, it is true. But I think we may safely say all is well now.'

'One last observation occurs to me, though. You said earlier I had taught you how to feel. That is very generous, but I'm not sure it is correct. I think feelings always ran very deep in you. If I did anything at all, it was merely to encourage you to reveal those feelings and not to deny them.'

'Even if that is true,' Mary replied, 'it is still no small achievement. Especially when those emotions have been buried so deep for so long.'

'Perhaps. But if I have taught you something of value, I should like you to understand what I have gained in return. From you, I have learned it is not enough simply to experience feeling. You showed me that one must find the courage to act upon it. There are times when happiness must be fought for, if we are to have any chance at all of achieving it.'

She took his hand and held it in hers.

'I am not sure I could have expressed it better myself.'

'I might add in my own defence that if I had loved you less, I might have ventured more. It was hard to be bold when I was only too aware of what I stood to lose.'

The room was warm, and they were both thrilled by their good fortune at finding themselves happier than they had ever expected to be. At that moment, there was nothing they wanted more than to sit together in loving, companionable silence. It might seem an unromantic circumstance; but in truth, there is no state that better demonstrates real firmness of affection than the ability to remain quietly comfortable together without conversation. And in such a situation of peaceful content they remained for some time, contemplating their pleasure in each other, until Mr Hayward recalled something suddenly to his mind.

'Mary! I nearly forgot! I had so much to say to you that this completely slipped my mind.'

He pulled a letter from his coat pocket, and looked at it, as if surprised at its existence.

'When I returned to London, I found a great pile of correspondence awaiting me. I sifted through it with some trepidation – I still feared coming upon the announcement of your engagement hidden amongst it all. Instead, I found this.'

He handed it to Mary. It was short and to the point.

Dear Mr Hayward,

I presume on our small acquaintance to take the liberty of writing to you. It may be a breach of good manners; but I am sure that when you have absorbed the contents of this note, you will conclude the intrusion is justified.

I believe it will interest you to know that yesterday I took tea with Miss Bennet. At the end of a conversation best described as very <u>direct</u>, she informed me that she had no wish to marry your friend and mine, Mr Ryder, as she entertained no warm feelings for him. On the contrary, she told me she felt a deep affection only for <u>you</u>, whom she described as the one man she thought could ever make her happy.

As she went on to declare that this was a truth of which she was not ashamed, and with which I might do as I pleased, I have had no hesitation in communicating it to you, to act upon as you see fit.

Caroline Bingley

Mary lay down the letter, amazed.

'Well! I knew she was a bitter, angry woman, but I never imagined she would act in such an extraordinary manner!'

'Indeed. But it had a most galvanising effect upon me. As soon as I read it, I knew my worst fears had not been realised. You were not married to Ryder. Indeed, the letter implied you had refused his offer. And although I did not deserve it, it appeared my behaviour had not destroyed your feelings for me.'

He took the letter back and folded it up.

'I read it late last night and came here first thing today. Such was its effect.'

'But what did she hope to gain by it?' asked Mary. 'I admit I do not entirely understand her motives.'

'She obviously hoped her letter would prompt me to tell you what I felt for you. And once we had declared ourselves, the field would be clear for her to press home her advantage with Ryder.'

'It was a very bold action,' replied Mary. 'Even I am surprised that she would employ stratagems of this kind.'

'I cannot find it in my heart to be too angry with her,' declared Mr Hayward, cheerfully. 'I would have come here to find you whether she had written to me or not; but I came a little quicker and with far greater expectation of success than if she had never sent it at all. We must learn to live with the knowledge that there is the tiniest sliver of our happiness we will always owe to her.'

'It's an interesting philosophical question,' Mary observed with a smile, 'whether a good deed can be truly considered good, if it is motivated by malice.'

'A nice theological point,' replied Mr Hayward. 'I'm not

sure it matters as long as it has delivered us such a very happy ending.'

'Is it very wicked of me to admit that knowing how much that would provoke Miss Bingley adds quite considerably to my pleasure?'

'It does not speak well to your morals, but your honesty does you credit.'

Then he took her in his arms again, and they found ways to express their happiness that required no further words from either of them.

CHAPTER NINETY-FIVE

The satisfaction of the Gardiners, when informed of Mary and Tom's good news, hardly requires description. That the two people, other than their children, whom they loved best in the world had decided to unite themselves with each other was as pleasing to them as can be imagined. The wedding was to take place as soon as it could be arranged, no one seeing any reason for delay. The happy couple were to be married from Gracechurch Street, although both Lizzy and Jane offered to make their houses available, declaring either would be delighted to take charge of the arrangements. Mary was touched by their generosity, and knew their good wishes were very sincerely meant; but she was pleased when Mr Hayward admitted his desire was for a London ceremony. She had spent enough of her life in her sisters' shadow; and as a new chapter opened for her, she had no wish to begin it once again as their pale satellite, made invisible by the brightness of their dazzle. This time she would be the star, with all eyes for once on her.

A further advantage of a City wedding was the improbability of Mrs Bennet's being disposed to attend it. And indeed, as was expected, she wrote to Mary explaining that the state of her nerves would not permit her to make the journey. But there was in her letter a genuine sense of satisfaction. Against all expectations, she had achieved her life's ambition – she had lived to see every Bennet sister married, even the daughter whom she was certain would never find a husband, especially after the unfortunate business of the spectacles. She did not display much interest in the gentleman himself once she was informed of his circumstances. The mere fact of the marriage was enough to gratify her and bring forth what limited congratulations it lay within her power to give. It was not much of a blessing, but Mary was content to regard it as such.

Two further letters arrived from Hertfordshire. One was from Charlotte, expressing her good wishes with a warmth more polite than heartfelt. Her two boys were well, the new baby bouncing and healthy. The house looked even neater and smarter than when Mary was there and the rose arbour flourished mightily. Mr Collins begged to be remembered to her. She concluded with an invitation to visit them at Longbourn, which both she and Mary knew would never be taken up. The second note gave Mary far more pleasure, because she knew the joy it expressed could not have been more sincerely felt. Mrs Hill wrote that she had always known Mary would one day find the happiness she deserved – had she not often told her so? – and she could not be more delighted than to learn she had been right. She begged a slice of their wedding cake as a marriage favour, which Mary would not have denied her for the world.

Even Mr Ryder was generous enough to send a short but cheerful note, the briskness of which he excused by reason of its having been written in extreme haste. He was about to leave for Italy, a trip they both knew he had long meditated, and which, due to the recent improvement in his circumstances, he now felt confident enough to undertake. He did not mention a companion; but it was soon after generally known that he had been joined on his travels by Caroline Bingley; and that the two of them were now established in a villa overlooking the sea outside Genoa, living as man and wife. There was no agreement as to whether they had actually undergone the rites that entitled them to be so described. Tom was sceptical, but Mary, considering the power of Miss Bingley's will, and influenced by her own wish to see everyone as happy as she was herself, preferred to believe that Miss Bingley had achieved her heart's desire of being married to a man of wealth and position, by whatever means she had considered necessary.

Late one afternoon, a few weeks before their wedding, Mary found herself standing alone in an empty house in a north London square, where she and Mr Hayward were to live after they were married. She strode through its rooms, spectacles perched unashamedly on her nose, notebook in her hand, measuring, thinking, planning. Now she stood in the drawing room, looking out from the large, long windows into the gardens beneath, imagining exactly how it should be arranged. There was just enough room for all their books – she should have hers situated on this wall, with a chair next to the shelves where she could read in the sun. Her piano should go here – and round the fireplace, she would have several sofas, positioned to encourage both comfort and conversation. She was determined this would be a convivial house, full of liveliness, laughter, and good talk. It should be as much as possible like Gracechurch Street, a place where friends would visit often, good dinners would be served, and no one would ever stand on ceremony. She should keep the tables well polished and she would have flowers upon them whenever they could be had. She smiled to herself as it occurred to her that for someone who had never expected to have a home of her own, her ideas about how it should be arranged were remarkably precise.

A home of her own. Her heart still beat a little faster when she thought of it. But that was nothing compared to what she felt when she considered the husband with whom she would share it. She and Tom were to be married. She had found a man she loved, who loved her in return. And here, in these rooms, in this house, they would make a life together. There were moments when she asked herself, as Lizzy had once done, if she deserved to be so happy. As she ran her finger down the window shutters, she felt one of those moments creep up upon her. A shiver passed through her when she thought of how it might never have happened. But this feeling did not last long. She had gradually discovered that the best response to glorious, unexpected happiness was not to seek explanation for its appearance but simply to embrace it and be glad. This was a new lesson, but she did not think it would take long to master. With a satisfied glance around the room, she made a final note and prepared to leave. She longed to tell Tom her thoughts for the wallpaper.

ACKNOWLEDGEMENTS

This book would never have been written without the passionate encouragement of my agent Caroline Michel. She held my hand as I made the leap from the world of fact to fiction, and her support has been unwavering throughout the journey. She has been mentor, strict task-mistress and, above all, a clear-eyed friend to me. I will always be grateful for her enthusiasm, her kindness and her extraordinary patience with an anxious new novelist.

I have also been especially fortunate with my editors. Both Sam Humphreys at Pan Macmillan and Barbara Jones at Henry Holt have been brilliant collaborators in bringing *The Other Bennet Sister* to life. I've benefitted hugely from their hard work, their incisive judgements and, above all, from their heartfelt commitment to the story. With the added assistance of Henry Holt's Ruby Rose Lee, I could not have been in better hands. I would also like to thank Stephen Rubin, who believed enough both in the idea and also in me to commission *The Other Bennet Sister* in the US.

I'm also very grateful to Rosie Wilson and Pan Macmillan's publicity team, who worked with such energy and keenness on the book's behalf in the UK; and to Sarah Fitts and Pat Eiserman at Henry Holt who were equally active and imaginative whilst publicising *The Other Bennet Sister* in the US.

My thanks also go to my copy and production editors,

Marian Reid and Pan Macmillan's Kate Tolley in the UK, and Kathleen Cook and Kenn Russell in the US. Their sharp eyes, exacting questions and mastery of detail were invaluable in the book's later stages.

I'm very conscious too of the generosity of those friends who have so kindly read and commented upon the book in all its various manifestations. It would not be the same without the insightful suggestions and observations offered by Claire Powell, Daisy Goodwin, Julie Gardner and Jane Tranter. They gave me both their time and their judgement, and, knowing the value of both, I'm both very touched and very appreciative.

Finally, I'm conscious of the huge debt I owe my husband Martin Davidson, who has read every draft, given his opinion on every twist and turn of the plot, and never for a moment wavered in his encouragement. No one could have been more lovingly supportive. 'I am not sure I deserve him, but am resolved to act as if I do', as Mary Bennet might have said.